P9-BJX-309

The Cactus Garden

Also by Robert Ward

The King of Cards
Red Baker
Cattle Annie and Little Britches
Shedding Skin

The Cactus Garden

Robert Ward

For Matt—
who always
disappears!
(But we love
you anyway)
Best
Robert Ward

POCKET BOOKS
New York London Toronto Sydney Tokyo Singapore

This book is a work of fiction. Names, characters, places and incidents are products of the author's imagination or are used fictitiously. Any resemblance to actual events or locales or persons, living or dead, is entirely coincidental.

POCKET BOOKS, a division of Simon & Schuster Inc.
1230 Avenue of the Americas, New York, NY 10020

Ward, Robert, 1943–
The cactus garden / Robert Ward.
p. cm.
ISBN: 0-671-88265-1
I. Title.
PS3573.A735C33 1995
813'.54—dc20 95-2809
CIP

First Pocket Books hardcover printing October 1995

10 9 8 7 6 5 4 3 2 1

Printed in the U.S.A.

For Larry Sullivan,
Wise and Loving Friend

ACKNOWLEDGMENTS

Many people helped me in the writing of this novel, but first and foremost was Special Agent Ralph Lochridge of the DEA. Lochridge went beyond the call of duty in every way—from setting me up with crucial interviews, showing me the border in San Diego, and teaching me how to shoot a machine gun. Thanks, amigo, you're the best.

Thanks also to Special Agent John Marcello and Special Agent Sal Leyva, both of the Los Angeles DEA.

In El Paso, I'm grateful to Travis Kuykendall, Special Agent in Charge of the El Paso District Office, Group Supervisor Jeff Atkinson, Special Agent Earl Hewitt, and Special Agent John Moring.

In San Diego, I'm indebted to Special Agent Jack Hook, who took me to the weirdest place of all.

Among my civilian friends, I'm indebted to novelist/screenwriter Mike Perry, my smart editor Jane Rosenman, and her capable assistants, Donna Lynne Ng and Matthew Futterman.

I'm also grateful for the support I've received from William Grose, Editorial Director of Pocket Books, and my agent extraordinaire, Esther Newberg.

Finally, thanks to my wife, Celeste Wesson, for her love and emotional support through three years of hard work.

The Cactus Garden

Chapter

1

Charlotte Rae Wingate sailed along in front of them, cruising over the smashed Dixie cups, old L.A. *Times*, three piles of dog shit, and one 1976 Barbie doll head, which lay smashed in the sunbaked street of Hollywood Boulevard. Charlotte Rae drove a perfectly restored candy-apple red 1965 T-Bird, and her bleached blonde head and thirty-eight-inch breasts bobbed up and down to the thunderous sound of Guns 'N' Roses. Two car-lengths behind her was a black Dodge Ram Charger. Jack Walker peered at her through his marine binoculars; C.J. Jefferson crouched forward behind the steering wheel, looking like a diver about to sail off one of the cliffs of Acapulco. Walker rubbed his jaw with his left hand and smiled.

"I love her. She's perfect. Completely self-invented," he said. "The retro car, the bottle-blonde hair, the latest greatest in silicone jobs, the pink-frosted-lipstick, Jackie Kennedy redux thing, the shitty taste in music."

"You don't dig Axl, man," Jefferson said. "I thought all you white boys dug Axl."

"Axl's an asshole with an attitude and a fag falsetto," Walker said. "They should pay Al Green to give him singing lessons."

C.J. Jefferson growled a little.

"You got the bad attitude, but I'm gonna forgive you for liking somebody in my generation."

"Still, I could see improving her mind over a bottle of wine," Walker said.

"Nah, only time you're gonna meet Charlotte Rae is when we turn the key on her," C.J. said.

Jefferson's gold tooth shone when he smiled, and Jack sighed and went back to his glasses.

"Think of it," he said, "a broad who looks like that. In any other city she'd be a star. Out here she's just one more bad actress who can't find any new hooker roles to play."

C.J. shook his head.

"Yeah, ain't it tragic. 'Course I do remember seeing her in a couple of pictures, *Die Roach Die* and *Bride of the Slime Master*. You see those beauties, maybe you get a better understanding why she's happy in the drug biz."

"Yeah, I saw the second one on USA. The honeymoon slime thing was a bitch," Walker said. "Think she ever gives any of this shit a thought?"

"Nah. That's where the metal music comes in," C.J. said.

"How's that?"

"Keep it loud enough and drop enough pills, and you can pretend you're not a flunked out actress who goes home to Buddy Wingate."

In front of them, Charlotte Rae Wingate cruised past three earnest young Hare Krishnas dressed in their orange robes, walking in lockstep down the street, ready to fill the denizens of the boulevard with ecstasy. She looked over at them, sneered a little, and then reached down to the Mexican briefcase made from a red-and-black hand-stitched blanket and aged-down buckskin. She slowed the car down as she got to Mann's Chinese Theater and stared at the giant poster of Clint Eastwood. Buddy had said they were going to meet him soon. . . . Clint . . . Clint . . . she liked the sound of it, like rocks, rhymed with flint, something solid a girl could hang on to. She waited, waited for the man with the "End of the World" sign to cross the street. He was three feet away, wore a rust-colored beard that stopped at his knees, smelled like a buffalo, had a giant rip in the side of his pants, out of which one of his hairy, scabbed legs stuck. She wished to hell he'd move . . . there was work to do. She ripped the Axl disc out of the CD player and slapped in Pearl Jam. She pumped up the volume to ten, gripped the wheel, when suddenly she felt something cold sticking into the bridge of her perfect starlet pug nose. She looked up and saw a black man, six feet three, two hundred and fifty pounds. His face was in some kind of terminal grimace, and he had a half-moon tattoo wedged into his cheek.

"Step out of the car, bitch."

"Jesus Christ, don't shoot," Charlotte Rae said.

He pulled back the hammer of the .38 Colt semiautomatic. And smiled. But he didn't look happy.

"See, I need me a T-Bird," he said. "You get out real slow and normal like, maybe I won't make your pretty white face look like an explosion in a pizza factory."

"Oh, Christ," she said. "Oh, my God. Please."

Behind her, the black van stopped at the traffic light at Highland. Walker sucked in his breath, listened intently on the speaker phones.

"Unscheduled party, C.J."

"Oh, man. Big trouble."

Walker whirled the steering wheel to the right, jammed the van into a screeching halt at the curb in front of the Hollywood Wax Museum. He leapt from the car door and saw a Charlie Chaplin mime who stood frozen at the museum door, badly pantomiming the shoe-eating scene from *The Gold Rush*. Jack blinked, watched him as he twirled his derby on the tip of his cane.

Jack looked back at Jefferson.

"He's gonna do her, C.J. I'm going in."

"Jack, wait, man."

"Trust me, partner," Jack said. Then he was on the street, running full-tilt at the big black man, who had already pulled Charlotte Rae out of her car and was sitting behind the steering wheel. As Jack raced toward him, he could see the gun's silhouette, refracting the morning sun. Very poetic.

"You gonna kiss this white world good-bye, baby," the carjacker said, smiling.

"Yo, homey," Jack yelled. "Check this."

Then he lifted off the ground, sailed through the smog-deadened air over the back of the little T-Bird, and smashed his forearm into the man's neck.

He heard the jacker groan as his head hit the windshield and a wild shot fired off into the sky. That should have been the end of it, Jack thought, but it wasn't. They were moving, the two of them . . . the car rolling to the right, fast, too goddamned fast. Jack looked down at the thief's foot, saw it lying heavily on the accelerator. As he looked back out in the street, he saw the End-of-the-World man scream and fall back on his ass, and then there was this huge red coiling dragon looming above the speeding car.

The T-Bird stopped dramatically as it smashed into the glass ticket booth at Mann's Chinese. The car thief's forehead was crushed as it smashed through the windshield. The shock of the impact flung Jack's head into the fashionably restored chrome and leather dashboard. Glass shattered like diamonds, the windshield bent and bucked grotesquely, and behind them the End-of-the-World man had a vague smile of recognition on his face. Oh, this was it, this was the Day, the Great Day he had been waiting for, the Day of Fiery Judgment, Praise the Lord. He stared amazed as the red, forty-foot Mann's Chinese dragon slumped from its perch atop the battered ticket booth and flopped on the crunched-up hood and smashed windshield of the car. Twenty feet down the street, C.J. Jefferson watched in pure disbelief, silently mouthing the single word, "Motherfucker," while on the sidewalk the little Chaplin clone stood mute, amazed, his white-gloved hand over his painted *O* of a mouth.

Inside the crushed T-Bird, Jack braced himself on the unconscious thief's bald and tattooed head, then pushed himself up and back, onto the trunk, and slid down in a heap next to the back left tire. He turned and looked at Charlotte Rae, who walked toward him, taking one halting step at a time, like a sleepwalking toddler.

"Oh, my God," she said, in a dazed monotone. "Oh, my God. . . . My God."

Jack managed a crooked smile. Rubbed his hand across his bloody forehead. He could feel interesting dents in it, holes from where his skin had met the chrome knobs on her radio. Blood dripped down his eyebrows.

"Have a nice day," he said. "You okay?"

"Yes, but you . . . Oh, my God. You saved my life. Really."

Jack nodded, looked at the wrecked car, the destroyed Hollywood landmark. The dragon's serpentine head had landed just a few feet from him, and he reached over and gave it a friendly pat.

"Nice dragon," he said. "Looks a little hungry, though."

"You . . . you saved me," she said again.

"I don't know," Jack said, looking around at the debris. "Considering how little resale value your car is gonna' have, maybe I should have let him go."

"No. You saved my life. 'Cause he was gonna pull the trigger. There was no doubt, I could see it in his eyes. Oh, God."

Charlotte Rae slumped down beside him, her arms flopping like overcooked pasta.

"Deep breaths," Jack said. "In and out. Slow and easy. You survived the mugger, now you gotta make it past the bystanders."

He looked out at the pathetic ragtag group who stood gawking. The End-of-the-World man smiled at him with toothless gums. This was a Sign, oh, yes yes yes. The three Hare Krishnas stood stiffly in their flowing saris. They sported confused looks on their well-scrubbed faces; there was something they should do here, they were sure of it. Every catastrophe was an opportunity to serve the Krishna and win a few more converts, but in this case, it was unclear to them exactly how they could turn chaos to their advantage. Next to them, two foul-smelling bums dressed in rags, smiled at the tableau as though it were Christmas come early.

Charlotte Rae swallowed hard, put her soft hand in his.

"God," she said. "Jesus, God. City of fucking Angels."

She began to cry, and Jack had to restrain himself from putting his arm around her and pulling her to his chest. Even with her standard Malibu Makeover, it was obvious she had the kind of beauty that stopped clocks.

The manager came racing from the dark theater. He was a round little Armenian man with bad skin and great owl eyes. His black hair was combed forward to a perfect point in the middle of his forehead, just like Nero. He wore a shiny blue suit, with the Mann's logo on the pocket and the pants legs two inches too short, revealing bright orange socks. His shoes were gray Hush Puppies. They had a mottled look, like old oatmeal.

"Look," he screamed. "Look what you done to my dragon."

"Fuck the dragon," Jack said.

"Fuck the dragon?" the manager said, staring down at Jack with watery eyes.

"Right," Charlotte Rae said, "and while we're at it, fuck you too."

She looked at him and began to laugh.

"You have no idea what you done. This dragon's historic landmark," the aggrieved manager said.

"Not anymore," Jack said.

The manager said nothing after that, but wandered around touching the fallen serpent, shaking his head and making small sighing sounds.

"How?" she said. "Where were you?"

"Behind you. Me and my buddy in his van. Our day off, and we were heading for the beach. Hey, there he is now."

Calvin Jefferson was jogging toward them, smiling and shaking his head.

"Son of a bitch," he said. "I knew you played ball, Jackie, but that was an All-Pro hit, you all right?"

"It only hurts when I cough up blood," Jack said. He spat a little on the street.

"Jack?" she said. "Jack who?"

"McKenna," Jack said. "You?"

"Charlotte Rae Wingate," she said, blushing a little. "Pleased to meet you . . . very pleased."

She leaned over and kissed him on the cheek, and Jack felt the spot burn a little.

"This is my friend Larry Washington," Jack said, pointing at Jefferson.

"Hello, Larry," she said. "Tell your friend Jack he has to go to the hospital. Now."

"She's right, Jackie," Jefferson said. "You're dripping blood all over Joan Crawford."

Jack looked down at the footprint to his left. It was Joan Crawford's. There was a nice little pool of his blood collecting in the big masculine. "J."

"No wire hangers," he said. "We can beat the kids just as well with plastic."

"Is he always like this?" Charlotte Rae said to Jefferson.

"'Cept when he's sleeping," Jefferson said.

"Good," Charlotte Rae said. "Now come on."

She looked at Jack with her blue eyes in a way that made him want to bleed a little more.

Jack looked back at the big guy behind the wheel. His head was jammed through the windshield. He seemed to be snoring. One of Salazar's boys, no doubt. No way this was a legit car-jack.

"I think the cops are gonna want to talk to us first," Jack said. "The good old LAPD. I hear their sirens down the block, so they should be here by tomorrow."

"Oh, God," Charlotte Rae said. "Do we have to talk to the police? They are so dumb and slow. And you're bleeding to death."

Jack stood and felt the earth whirl a little beneath his feet.

"I'm just fine," he said. "No one could be finer than me."

With that he started to topple toward her, and Jefferson had to grab him by the shoulder.

"I'm taking you to the hospital now," she said. She sounded almost motherly.

But the sirens had stopped now, and three black-suited Darth Vaderesque LAPD cops were walking toward them through the crowd.

"It's L.A.'s finest come to arrest your attacker," Jack said. He spat out a little more blood and felt weak in the arms. Maybe he had broken a rib after all, punctured a lung. It would be just his luck—get a break on a case and die coming out of the chute.

"What's going on here, miss?" a big cop with a face like a Wendy Burger said.

"They have killed my dragon, that's what's going on," the theater manager bleated.

"Now you're bleeding on Sidney Poitier," Calvin said.

"Shows I'm an equal opportunity bleeder," Jack said.

"Somebody has to pay," the manager said. "This is historic fucking dragon."

"Watch your mouth in front of this here lady, sir, or I will bash in your teeth," the cop said.

"My husband will take care of it, officer," Charlotte Rae said. "This man saved me from that creep. My husband is Buddy Wingate, and he'll want to give this man a reward."

"You mean Buddy Wingate the Furniture King, from on the TV?" the cop said. He looked impressed, and Jack felt a measure of cool contempt for him.

"That's him," Charlotte Rae said. "Now I'm taking this man to the hospital."

"There's an ambulance on the way," another cop said. "Meanwhile, somebody has to explicate all this stuff, as we got reports to make."

Charlotte Rae laughed and turned her perfect lips to Jack's ear.

"I love it when you talk to cops. They do dialogue."

Jack smelled her perfume and felt a little weaker. She put her arm around his waist, and he leaned on her. He looked over at Jefferson then, and his partner shook his head.

"Too much," he said. "Some day at the beach."

Jack managed to laugh at that too. Then he felt faint again and sat back down—right on the slain dragon's head.

Chapter 2

He could feel her eyes on him as Dr. Ravi Whani cut off his blood-soaked shirt, and he was glad he'd spent the last two weeks eating sushi and pumping up at the Agency gym. Behind her, out in the cluttered hallway, Jack saw Calvin hitting on one of the black emergency room nurses, a tall, foxy-looking woman about ten years younger than him. Not a good move, Jack thought. C.J. was already having trouble with his marriage, and things sure as hell weren't going to improve if he messed around. But there was no use saying anything about it to him; Jack had already tried that, and C.J. had told him to butt out.

"Does it hurt a lot, hero?" Charlotte Rae said, wincing a little in sympathy as the doctor wrapped the bandage tight around Jack's ribs.

"The ribs are fine, but the crushed aorta's a bitch."

"You should not laugh, sir," Dr. Whani said, his dark eyes flashing humorously. "You are so very lucky you did not puncture an organ of importance. The car driver has perhaps suffered brain damage."

"He had that before the crash," Charlotte Rae said.

Jack laughed. She was a real surprise, nothing like he had thought when they were watching her cruising through the streets. She was fast, funny in a hip actressy way, the kind of girl who could riff and keep up with the bad boys. It was better when you liked them on a case; you didn't have to act so much.

"So, Sir Galahad, where do you come from?" she said, rubbing a finger across her lips.

"Back East," Jack said. "The Big Apple. Came out in January."

"Lucky for me," she said and batted her eyes in a comical way. "You going to tell me what you do, or is it top secret?"

"Do whatever I can to pay the rent," Jack said. "Met some theater people where I was tending bar and thought I could maybe do some acting."

"Ahh, bitten by the bug," she said, shaking her head. "It's a worse addiction than drugs. Take it from a girl who knows."

"You too, huh? *Aahhhh.*" Jack groaned as the doctor wound the tape tighter.

"I am certainly sorry," the doctor said. "But you will need this for support. And please restrain all future impulses to perform heroism."

"Don't worry, I get an irresistible impulse to save someone else, I'll beep you, Doc," Jack said.

"I wouldn't let him do it anyway," Charlotte Rae said, rubbing Jack's forearm with her index finger. "He's my personal hero and I never learned to share."

She put a hand in Jack's, and he felt an electrical charge shoot through his skin.

"You out of work, then?" she said, smiling.

"Got a little tending-bar gig right now," Jack said.

"Sounds awful," she said. "You know my husband is producing a film right now. A low-budget action flick. Maybe he could find a couple days work for you. When this is done, why don't you come home with me? I know he'll be dying to talk to you."

"Oh, no," the doctor said. "My patient will sleep. No visitors. Tomorrow he will feel serious arm pains."

The doctor smiled as if he were happy about the fact and walked off toward a man who had just been wheeled in. The guy had a pearl-handled knife sticking out of his chest, but the vacant look in his eyes said it didn't look like it was hurting him much anymore. Three nurses wheeled him behind a blood-spattered curtain.

"Cheerful, isn't he?" Jack said. "Look, I appreciate it, but I don't want a handout. I can keep my bartending gig until they start throwing three-picture deals at me."

"You don't know Buddy," she said, laughing as though at some private joke. "It won't be a handout, you can count on that."

C.J. was heading toward him now, stuffing a piece of paper in his slacks pocket. The nurse's phone number, no doubt.

"How you feeling, baby?" C.J. said.

"Like you care," Jack said. "I'm drowning in my own blood and you're out in the hall hitting on the nurse."

"I figured you had you a thing happening here"—C.J. smiled—"so why shouldn't this fine-looking black man help liberate one of the uptight middle-class sisters?"

"Whoever said it was right," Charlotte Rae said, laughing. "Men are all pigs."

"Who did say it?" C.J. said.

"Everybody's said it," Jack said. "It's been said so many times now it's folk wisdom, like 'calm before a storm' and 'the bigger they are . . .' "

" '—the dumber their kids'," Charlotte Rae said. "Listen, Jack, I insist you meet Buddy. He'll want to thank you personally."

She punctuated her remark with a killer smile.

"How come I get the feeling I don't have much of a choice," Jack said, smiling back.

"You don't," she said, scraping his arm with her long red nails. "Nobody turns down Buddy and lives to tell the tale."

"Better do like she says," C.J. said. "That man is got the best commercial onna' tube. They showed 'em in the movies, I'd stand in line. Come to think of 'em, haven't I seen you in a few of them?"

Charlotte Rae pretended to blush and waved her hands like she wanted to disappear behind them.

"Yeah, I did see you," C.J. said, "and wearing next to nothing. Oh, my my my . . . look what fate has tossed our way."

He gave a wicked grin, and Charlotte Rae shook her head.

"I stand convicted. Hey, I'm an actress, okay?"

Jack flashed C.J. a look. The man was a genius of jive.

"We're shooting at a soundstage in Burbank," Charlotte Rae said. "Right on Riverside. Can you make it?"

"Only if you're gonna be in it wearing a bikini," Jack said.

"Sorry," she said. "This one is a little too low budget even for me. I'm grabbing a producer credit. But come anyway. It's a suspense-action thing. Called *The President's Cabinet*. I think you'll be amused." She opened her buckskin fringed bag and pulled out a card and an over-fat, midnight-blue, ballpoint with a little golden filigree of stars painted on it.

"Here," she said. "Shooting starts at seven, but we'll be there all day."

The doctor suddenly reappeared, carrying a little package for Jack.

"Codeine and Tylenol," he said. "Good for you. Will make this all seem like a dream."

"Maybe it already does," Jack said.

He looked at her again, and this time their eyes locked and he felt a shadow pass between them. She looked away fast, helping steady him as she and C.J. got him off the examining table and sat him in a wheelchair. C.J. pushed him toward the swinging door, and she walked alongside him, her hand lightly brushing his neck.

"Tell me you'll come," she said.

Her tone had changed suddenly; she sounded like a scared little girl, pleading and plaintive. The transformation was so sudden that it took Jack's breath away. Maybe she could act after all.

"Okay, sure. I'll stop by," he said, trying to keep his own tone light, "because I can see that you'll hound me every day for the rest of my life if I don't."

"You got that right," she said. Her voice was butter.

C.J.'s van was parked just across the street, baking in the midday heat. Suddenly, Jack felt a small panic in his stomach.

They had come from the crime scene in the ambulance, but what if she asked for a ride home?

Now she leaned down and kissed him on the cheek.

"Thanks for my life," she said. "I owe you. And I never forget a debt."

She turned and walked away; Jack blinked and saw a long, black limo waiting across the street.

"Jesus, that woman is a woman," C.J. said.

"Yeah, how 'bout that?" Jack said. His mouth felt dry, and he was suddenly conscious of himself staring after her, saw himself sitting in the wheelchair staring at her hard, tanned legs, the way her ass moved under her skirt. She got to the car, turned, and gave him a little toss of her golden hair, then slipped inside, flashing her muscular tanned thighs, and shut the door. The limo cruised off down George Burns Boulevard, and Jack gave out a little whistle. The doc was right. His ribs had already begun to send out a singing, radiating pain, but when he thought of her face, her body, he didn't mind it so much.

"Come on, kid," Jefferson said to him, wheeling him toward the sun. "Get that thing outta your mind, 'cause we gotta call the Director. We gonna have some serious explaining to do."

Chapter 3

"So what you are telling this committee, Walker, is that you had to ram the car into Mann's Chinese Theater, destroying their ticket booth, not to mention their antique dragon?"

Jack sat at the end of the long conference table next to C.J. He rubbed his hands over his temples. He felt like getting up and walking out of the briefing, out of this sterile, gray room.

His ribs were so badly bruised that he had trouble breathing, his head felt like a crushed cantaloupe, and he was sick of Assistant Director Ted Michaels staring at him in his officious way. Michaels and Jack had been at loggerheads from their very first meeting. They were, Jack sometimes thought, temperamental opposites: Jack freewheeling and improvisatory by nature; Michaels the cautious, maneuvering insider. But there was more than that between them. Michaels seemed to enjoy harassing Jack; it was almost as though he were trying to prove to the others that Jack didn't have what it took to be an agent.

"I asked you a question, Walker," Michaels said.

"I know," Jack said. "And a brilliant question it was too, Ted."

At Jack's right-hand side, C.J. Jefferson sighed heavily. This was going to get ugly. There was no doubt about it. Michaels bit his thin lower lip as he spoke.

"If you think being a wiseass is going to help your cause, you've made a serious miscalculation, Walker," he said.

"Oh, well mercy me," Jack said.

"I'm sure Jack tried to keep the car off the sidewalk, Ted."

The speaker was the other assistant director, Richard Brandau, an expert in the domestic demand for drugs. Brutally divorced four years ago, Brandau had taken refuge in food and had gradually put on a lot of weight. Formerly a linebacker at Notre Dame, Brandau had begun to look like too many old jocks in their forties—red-faced, bloated, the perfect heart-attack victim. There had been a time when his drinking had threatened his career and his health, but recently Brandau had managed to put his life back together. Jack credited his renaissance to Brandau's charming new girlfriend, Suzie Chow, a court stenographer, who kept him from his dark moods. Suzie, in her spare time a budding screenwriter, had rekindled a taste for life in Brandau, and in what little spare time he had, they frequented art openings, clubs, and restaurants. Jack was happy that the good-natured Brandau had survived his divorce; it had been touch and go for a while.

Professionally, Brandau had one of the toughest jobs in the Agency. He spent half his time trying to stop the off-loaders of drugs inside the U.S. borders, and the other trying to educate teachers, families, and the local police concerning ways to prevent drug dealers from infiltrating a neighborhood. Everyone knew that the latter job was a useless task. The poor did drugs because they felt helpless, the rich did drugs because they were bored, and both groups dealt them because they could make a lot of quick, easy money, and no amount of tough-love talks, neighborhood watches, or scare tactics was going to change a thing. But Jack respected Brandau for his Herculean effort and his seemingly endless supply of optimism—and appreciated his support in the briefings.

"Well, I'm glad you're so certain, Richard," Michaels said. "But it seems to me that Walker has continually flouted Agency policy, and acted recklessly and without regard to the possible negative publicity that the Agency would incur."

"Excuse me," Jack said, his voice rising in anger. "But the perp had a double load aimed at Miss Wingate's charming face. I didn't exactly have time to write a position paper on the case."

This got a small cough-laugh from Bob Valle, intelligence director of the West Coast DEA. Valle was a short, aggressive, blunt-faced Sicilian in his early forties. Normally, Valle was a great joke teller and general all-around bullshit artist, but lately, Jack noticed, Valle had lost his sense of humor. Jack considered Valle a friend and had tried talking to him about what was eating him but had gotten nowhere.

Now Michaels stared hard at Bob Valle.

"I don't really see what you find so funny, Bob," Michaels said. "I'm very serious about this."

"Sorry. I wasn't trying to step on your toes, Ted," Valle said, immediately backing off.

"Then, listen to what I have to say," Michaels said.

"I am listening, Ted," Valle said, "and I don't need any lectures from you. Okay?"

Jack was surprised at the hostility in Valle's tone. He hadn't seen him much since he started staking out Charlotte Rae, but judging from the controlled fury in Valle's voice, he was still very angry.

"Sorry, Bob," George Zampas said, his voice thick with sarcasm. "Just trying to move this along."

Valle nodded and grumbled, "That is exactly what I'm trying to do too."

Jack felt the tension growing exponentially in the room, but Zampas ignored Valle's bad mood.

Zampas was the director of West Coast Intelligence for the Agency. He loomed at the far end of the table, a man with a large head and a shock of curly black hair. Zampas's thirst for life was legendary. He was a great cook, ate prodigiously, drank too much ouzo, loved jazz, cars, and Cigarette speedboats. Women found him irresistible. As a result, it was rumored, his long-standing marriage to ex-actress Ronni Hart was on the rocks.

The affection between Jack and Zampas went well beyond professional affability. A friend and trainee of Jack's father, Zampas had known him since Jack was a kid. Jack had thrown his first baseballs to Zampas, been taken to Lakers games with the big Greek. In many ways, Zampas had been closer to him than his father, Dan Walker. Zampas had been easy to talk to and sympathetic when Jack's mother died.

Not that any of this did Jack much good in these meetings. Sometimes his closeness to the Director actually worked against Jack. Zampas was a warm and exactingly fair boss and had no intention of playing favorites. The truth was, he partially agreed with Michaels. Jack was a daredevil, a risk-taker, the kind of guy the Agency couldn't do without, but also the kind of agent who had to be carefully monitored. Now Zampas poured himself a glass of sparkling water and shook his head.

"This isn't a tribunal, Ted," he said. "And, Jack, just give the answers without the attitude, okay?"

"Right," Jack said.

"You know, Jack, there is one thing that worries me."

The speaker was Brandau, and Jack cocked his head.

"What's that, Richard?"

"What are the chances that this was a setup?" Brandau said.

"I've already considered that possibility, but it doesn't seem likely, for a lot of reasons. Number one of which is that C.J.

and I didn't start tailing her until five days ago. Even if she made us, say . . . on the second or third day, I doubt that Wingate could come up with anything this elaborate in such a short time."

"Yeah, and why would he bother?" C.J. said. "No, this is real . . . I'd bet my pension on it."

Michaels sighed.

"I don't think this is a setup either," he said. "That's not what worries me. It's this whole cowboy play of Jack's. I don't understand why you attacked the guy at all."

"Wait a minute, man," C.J. said, coming quickly to Jack's defense. "What was he going to do, let him blow her away?"

Michaels turned and glowered at C.J.

"He didn't know if the car-jacker was going to shoot her or not. Jack's job and yours too, C.J., was simply to perform surveillance. This play could have totally compromised Operation Cactus."

The short, pugnacious Valle shifted in his chair. Then stuck a blunt finger across the table at Michaels.

"You know, Michaels, Jack could have turned this whole thing into an opportunity, you ever think of that, goombah?"

"That's right," Jack said. "She wants me to come to Wingate's set tomorrow. I go, maybe I get inside. Find out a few things."

Michaels sighed and shook his head.

"But this wasn't designed to be an undercover operation. Not yet."

"Well, why not change the fucking design?" Valle said.

Ordinarily, Jack appreciated Valle's support, but his anger—anger that Jack was certain had nothing to do with what they were talking about—was probably doing Jack's case more harm than good.

"Look, with all due respect," Jack said. "Wingate is a careful man. You can't get him with the usual sting methods. He won't deal with the new drug dealers, which is why we've been having zero luck nailing him."

"That's true," Valle said. "That's been Wingate's strength as a dealer. He only does business with very old connections."

"That's only true up to a point," Michaels said. "We intended to try a new strategy to get him next month."

"Yeah," Jack said quickly, looking imploringly at Zampas. "But by that time, he could have done his big number. Look, all I'm saying is, let me try. Maybe the Discount King's grateful I saved his little sweetie's butt and he lets me hang out. Maybe I learn something about his next big deal. The truth is, sometimes in an investigation you get breaks, and if you don't ride with them, you lose momentum."

"You got it," Valle said.

"I think Jack's onto something too, Ted," Brandau said. He tapped his pipe ashes into the ashtray and smiled. "She'd be dead meat now, and I think we all know that this wasn't any ordinary car-jacking. The perp was probably working with Pedro Salazar's boys. They've been trying to muscle in on Wingate's action for the last six months."

"I'm aware of the history, thank you," Michaels said. "But let me remind you, the perp hasn't admitted any such connection. We aren't really sure he's part of Salazar's crew."

"Come on," Jack said. "Salazar is trying to scare the shit out of Wingate, so he can take over his business."

Valle nodded and pulled at the cuff of his new sport jacket.

"Hey, Ted, let us not forget that somebody firebombed Wingate's Studio City store just last week," he said. "We got every reason to believe it was Salazar's crew who pulled that one. It's their style. Intimidation before assassination."

Zampas cleared his throat, and all of them turned toward him.

"C.J.," he said, "what's your take on this?"

"I think Jack's right. The Salazar people have been upping the ante every week. Wingate might be getting a little nervous. I think we got the ball, and we run with it. Let Jack go in and see what he can dig up."

"I agree," Brandau said, blowing a comforting puff of cherry-blend tobacco out over the room.

"Well, I disagree," Michaels said. "I don't think this is a wise move at all. We are trying to build a picture of Wingate's whole operation. We want to know as much as we can about his couriers, his meetings . . . all of that. We build our profile first and . . ."

"And meanwhile he does another massive drug deal," Jack interrupted. "Our CIs have told us that he's got something planned with Eduardo Morales from Colombia. And we've been told it's going to happen soon. This might be a way to stop it. We've got to take the chance."

"I'll be honest, Walker," Michaels said. "One of my problems with sending you in there is that you've never run up against a guy like Buddy Wingate before."

"No. But you said that about Jose Benvenides too," Jack said.

"Precisely my point," Michaels said. "You handled him by shooting him, dead. A major player in the international drug trade; a person we badly needed to interrogate."

Jack felt an electric anger sweep over him.

"Gee, I'm sorry, Ted," he said. "When good old Jose pulled that magnum on me, I should have read Robert's Rules of Order to him."

"It should have never gotten to that point," Michaels said. "You played cowboy and blew it."

Jack pressed his palms on the desk in front of him.

"Wrong," he said. "You blew it because I had to arrest him without backup, which you failed to send in."

"That's bull," Michaels said.

"That's enough, guys," Zampas said. "It's over now. Jose Benvenides is old news. We have to decide what to do here and now."

The Director got up from his chair and stretched. He had a wrestler's build, squat and powerful.

"Here's the deal," he said. "A shipment of Colombian white heroin is coming into the country, probably from Eduardo Morales, to be delivered to Buddy Wingate's boys. Wingate will then off-load it throughout California, Arizona, and New Mexico. Bob Valle and I checked with all our field people in Mexico City just one hour before this meeting, and they haven't been able to nail down the time, the place . . . anything. If Morales pulls this off, it'll set us back five years. This new Colombian skag is purer, more deadly than anything the Asians have to offer us. It's going to mean that a couple million new people become addicted. The gangs are already trying to get into it, which is going to mean more drive-bys, more guns on the streets. Not to mention smack is back in fashion with all the young, hip Hollywood actors, directors, and producers. They do it themselves and they glamorize it in their fucking movies, and that gets another half million kids to shoot holes in their arms. To put it bluntly, this new smack connection is going to be a fucking unparalleled disaster. We've got to stop the streets from being flooded with this shit. So maybe it is a wild card to throw Jack in with Wingate this way, but maybe we have to take what breaks we get. The bottom line is, we're running out of time."

Zampas walked toward Jack now, looking him straight in the eyes.

"You go to the meeting, Jack, and you play it close to the vest, understand? Wingate acts like a buffoon, but he's one deadly son of a bitch. And from all reports the girl's no better. See if you can get next to Buddy, but don't push it."

"You got it," Jack said.

Underneath the table he kicked C.J. lightly in the shins.

"Don't get behind in your reports, Jack," Zampas said, running his big hands through his shock of curly black hair. "And keep your dick in your pants."

There was a little chuckle from everybody at the table, except Michaels, who said nothing but stared down at his case sheet as if he were trying to bore holes through it.

"All right, gentlemen," Zampas said, "if that's all our business, I've got other work to attend to."

The agents filed their notes in their briefcases and got up from the table. Jack looked at Michaels, but the assistant director's back was turned, and he was already heading out the door, his gator-skin briefcase tucked under his arm. Jack felt C.J.'s hand on the back of his neck.

"Looking good, baby. You're gonna nail this dude."

"Yeah," Jack said. "Buddy Wingate and his crew are going downtown."

"Good work, Jack," Valle said tensely. "You need anything, let me know. And I'll keep you informed."

"Thanks, Bobby," Jack said. "Hey, man, you all right?"

Valle kept walking, but Jack could hear him suck in his breath when he talked.

"Fine."

"You sure?"

Valle stopped and turned to Jack. His lips were tense.

"I said, I'm fine."

"Good," Jack said. "But if you want to talk about it, lemme know."

Valle nodded slightly, then turned and walked in the opposite direction. It was more obvious than ever that something was wrong, but Jack had too much to worry about to think about it now.

Jack hustled down the hallway and caught up with Zampas as he headed into his office.

They walked into the Director's office. Jack said hello to Jane Hawkins, Zampas's pretty young secretary. She smiled at him, but her eyes really lit up for her boss.

"Call from the FBI and from the task force and one from your wife," she said.

"Oh, good," Zampas said, in a strained voice.

Jane smiled at him with something a little deeper than sympathy, Jack thought.

They walked by her into Zampas's inner office, a large corner space with a great view of downtown Los Angeles. Jack looked out the big window and stared at the clean lines of the new Otani Hotel. Zampas looked through some letters on his desk and picked up a car brochure.

"What do you think of this?" he said.

Jack looked at some flashy color pictures of a new Lexus.

"Not bad for fifty grand," Jack said.

"Maybe I could get a deal on it," Zampas said.

"Be better if we could seize one and commandeer it for office use."

Zampas smiled and sighed.

"Yeah, you're right, Jackie. That's about the only way I'm

going to get one. I mentioned it to Ronni last night . . . not a new one, mind you, but an old one, and she went through the roof."

"Ah, who needs it?" Jack said. "The bigger the car, the bigger the asshole inside."

Zampas laughed.

"Sounds like one of your dad's lines," he said.

Jack smiled sadly. Zampas and his father had been best friends and partners for twenty years, right up until the day his father died of a heart attack, five years ago. Jack still had trouble believing the tough, roughneck Dan Walker was gone.

Now Jack turned and saw Jane Hawkins leaning in the door. She was dressed in a tight black silk skirt, and she looked at her boss in a sexual way.

Zampas walked over to her and put his big arm around her.

"Janey thinks I'm still Superman."

"That's because you are," she said.

Zampas kissed her on the top of the head in a fatherly way, but there was heat in it, all the same, Jack thought. There were rumors that they were seeing each other after hours.

Jane hugged her boss back and winked at Jack.

"Even Superman has to make it to his meeting with the FBI on time," she said.

"That's right," Zampas said. "I almost forgot. What would I do without you, Jane?"

"I don't know," she said. "Let's not find out."

She gave him a sexy smile and returned to the outer office.

"Jesus, she's terrific," Zampas said.

"Yeah, she is," Jack said lamely.

"Makes me feel younger just to see her," the Director said, and there was a smile on his face. Then he seemed to catch himself in mid-fantasy.

"Listen, Jack, I want you to forget the accident at the theater," the Director said. "You did the right thing on the street. And forget any bad vibes you heard in the meeting today. I want you inside, I want Wingate and Morales brought down, and I believe you can do it."

Jack looked at Zampas's broad slab of a face, his dark eyes. He felt the old current of affection switch on inside of him.

"But I want you to proceed with extreme caution, you understand?"

"Yeah, I hear you," Jack said.

"Wingate is bad enough. But the guys he's working with . . . Morales and his friends, are worse. They have a lot to lose if we nail them. Political careers, serious money. If they make you, you'll be lucky if they kill you."

"But they won't make me," Jack said.

"Of course they won't. There's something else too. I don't want you to antagonize Michaels anymore. He's a very political guy, has a lot of friends in Congress; we need him on our side. *Comprende?*"

"Yeah, okay," Jack said. "It just bugged me what he said about Jose Benvenides. The last thing I wanted to do was shoot the kid. He gave me no choice."

"I know that," Zampas said. "Michaels was being Michaels, so just ignore it."

"I'm trying," Jack said. "But Teddy just gives me too many fucking straight lines."

Zampas laughed in spite of himself.

"Well, I know you're gonna do a hell of a job on this case."

Zampas smacked him on the ear, and Jack turned and walked out of the room. As he left, Jack remembered Zampas, his dad, and himself going to Rams games when Jack was a kid. His old man used to get so wasted that Zampas and Jack would carry him back to their old Chevy.

Zampas's new obsession with aging bothered Jack. Jack felt that he ought to take better care of himself. Zampas was getting overweight, often looked tired. Something was bugging him, probably his home life wasn't so great, and there was this tension in the office. Jack rubbed his jaw. If anything happened to Zampas . . .

But he couldn't dwell on such things now. After all, this had been a good day. Only forty-five minutes ago he was on the carpet for crashing the car, now he was involved in the biggest undercover of his life. He thought of something his old man once said to him about careers. Some guys could go through twenty years and never have a career case. Just one small-shit case after another. Other guys waited a lifetime and got one in the twilight of their careers, when it did them little or no good. Then there were the few lucky agents who fell into cases that made them, right at the beginning. Jack had been an agent three years, and he had gotten lucky—last year, the Benvenides caper, and this time Wingate, a case that would make him a legend in the Agency or, if he blew it, set him back a decade.

It was scary and it was great. It was juice.

Down the hall C.J. was waiting, slouched against the wall.

"Hey, baby," C.J. said, pulling a toothpick out of his mouth. "No sweat in there, huh?"

"No sweat at all," Jack said.

"We gonna kill, right, kid?"

"Dead," Jack said.

He slapped five with C.J. and hoped his partner didn't feel how cold his fingers were.

Chapter 4

"Cut! No, no, no. That just don't begin to make it, Jules. Where's the intensity? Man, it's gotta look like he wants to fuck her, not kill her."

Jack and Charlotte Rae watched from the edge of the Burbank soundstage as Buddy Wingate stormed onto the set. Wingate wore a black uptown-Dallas-cowboy business suit, six-hundred-dollar Nicona boots, and sported a pinky ring with a striking likeness of Bill Clinton's face made out of diamonds, rubies, and emeralds. He was about five foot eight, but that was counting the boots, and moved in a dynamic swirl, his short arms and legs pumping furiously. He looked slightly comical, Jack thought, until you noticed the size of his wrists and hands. They were huge, and the fingers were gnarled, lumpy, as though they'd been broken a few times.

Now this ball of electricity, greed, and ambition moved toward the young writer-director, Jules Furthman, who backed toward the arc lights, his Dodgers baseball cap falling at his feet in the process.

"Now, listen up, Jules, 'cause I am gonna say this only one more time. The scene here is about love not death. I mean this here is where the president reveals to the woman he loves his terrible fucking secrets. But he don't intend to kill her. He's brought her here to share! Get what I mean, Jules?"

"Sure, Buddy. Yeah, you want to play against the text, find a subtext that'll make the scene something more than a typical fucking slasher movie. I get it and I am totally with you, believe me!"

"Good man, Jules. By the way I really dig your shoes." Jack looked at Furthman's sneakers and saw little red lights blinking on each heel.

"Very street, Jules," Wingate said. "Very South Central. Man, you keep wearing clothes like that, you'll be making movies with the bros, soon."

Furthman blushed, and Wingate slapped him on the back and turned toward Jack.

"Hello there. This must be the hero, hey, darlin?"

Charlotte Rae smiled, took Jack's hand, and pulled him out on the soundstage to meet her husband. Jack shook Wingate's hand and felt his powerful grasp.

"Good to meet you, son," Wingate said. "And, by the way, don't let my tone put you off. That's 'jest my manner . . . comes from dealing with too many assholes. Truth is, I flat out do consider you a hero. You saved my wife's butt, and I ain't about to forget it."

"Just did what I could," Jack said, playing it like Gary Cooper.

"Lemme show you round. You may recognize some of our cast."

Wingate led Jack and Charlotte Rae across the room to where two actors, a man and a woman, sat in their canvas chairs. They were chatting quietly but grew more animated as Buddy came closer.

Buddy gave a friendly little open-hand wave, as if he were an eager new kid on the block, just bopping down the street trying to make friends.

"Hi ya, guys," he said. "How's it going anyways?"

"Oh, just great," the woman said. "Marky here is trying to get me to fuck him in the trailer before the scene."

"Hey, it's a bonding thing. I'm only thinking of the work," Marky said.

Jack winced a little, but everyone else laughed nervously.

"Well, maybe you could jest give him a little head, Kaye," Buddy said. "Hell, my feeling is 'head' don't even count."

Again there was nervous laughter, and Jack suddenly realized he recognized both the man and the woman sitting in front of him. The actress was Kaye Williams. She'd been a slasher movie star in the seventies, then graduated to playing a mom on the TV series *Ronda's Gang*. Just as the show had taken off, she'd had a famous accident in a Jaguar, driving it off a curving, rain-slicked road in Los Virgines Canyon. They'd found her lying next to her dead lover, an eighteen-year-old pool boy–actor named Louie Salvado. Kaye had almost died herself, but survived and went through a series of operations—a liver transplant and a couple new hips later she was as good as new. But the boy's parents sued her for thirty million dollars and accepted an out-of-court settlement rumored to be half that. After that little episode, Kaye was finished as a TV mom. Then came a long period of depression, alcoholism, and a couple of visits to clinics not quite as nice as Betty Ford's. Jack and the rest of America had kept up with her career, by reading *People* magazine's "Where Are They Now?" issues. She'd been arrested for shoplifting a couple of times and had to be rushed to Cedars on three or four occasions due to pill overdoses. Now, after ten years of "invisibility," Kaye Williams was acting in a Buddy Wingate production.

The lead actor's story was just about as grim. His name was Marky Martin, and he'd had a hit series on TV at one time called *Meet Mr. Assistant,* in which he played a famous detective's assistant, who is the one who actually solves the crimes. Martin had a tall rubbery frame, a goofy, country-boy laugh, and had won the hearts of Americans everywhere. *TV Guide* called him the "Tube's Answer to Jimmy Stewart." Then he, too, had dropped out of sight. Jack hadn't heard of him in fifteen years. Now his country-boy face was lined with wrinkles and broken red veins, which the makeup department had tried to hide by coating with about a ton of powder and greasepaint.

"Remember, Marky," Wingate said now, "this new scene is really all about love. Yeah, you're stabbing her with your knife, but as far as you're concerned, it's really a love tap."

"No problem," Martin said. "For motivation, all I need to do is remember my third wife."

There was more anxious laughter, and Wingate led Jack and Charlotte Rae toward the door of the set and the silver Airstream trailer he had parked on the steaming macadam.

"This here ought to be a pretty good picture," Wingate said, smiling at Jack. "The setup is the president has this cabinet in the Oval Office. He tells people he wants to show them some historical treasures. But what they don't know is he's got like dismembered heads, hands, and other body parts in there."

"Sounds great," Jack said.

"A work of genius," Charlotte Rae said. "Maybe now you'll realize why I chose not to act in it."

"Well, ain't you Miss Arty," Wingate said, smiling at her. "Tell you what, this little baby works. You know why? It's a good script. Know how you can tell when a script works?"

"No," Jack said, playing the straight man. "How?"

"Well, in my estimation every good script answers a question. The question here is 'What would happen if the president of the United States was a serial killer?' With all his power, think of how easy it would be to get away with it."

"Hah," Jack said. "Well, that's one I hadn't thought about."

Charlotte Rae laughed and squeezed Jack's arm.

"No reason you should. But I'm telling you, this little director, Jules Furthman, ain't half bad. He's a fucking pain in the ass, with his Beverly Hills bullshit gang clothes and shit. . . . Other day he's telling me how he used to hang with the homeys in South Central. Right. But I gotta admit he's got chops. And Kaye is fine. The question is Marky. Man, I wonder if he can stay off the shit long enough to cut it."

"He's using drugs?" Jack said.

"Yeah, and you'd think he would know better. He already snorted a whole series and had his nose collapse. Then he went to a cut-rate plastic man and ended up with a bump in the middle of his face. Had to get it redone twice, and the asshole is still wandering off to the bathroom three, four times a day."

They came to the trailer steps.

"Why'd you hire him?" Jack said.

"'Cause they love him in the Philippines and in the third world. They still think he's Mr. Fucking Assistant over there. That's the problem with this business, you got to appeal to such lowlife motherfuckers like the gooks and slopes or you can't afford to make movies. Come on in, *amigo,* we got a heap of talking to do."

The walls of Buddy Wingate's trailer were filled with pictures of his favorite person, himself. There were pictures of Buddy in pink pants with elephants on them, playing golf with Arnold Palmer; Buddy in a blue shirt with lobsters on it, having mai-tais with Jack Lord. In that one Buddy had his hair conked up as high as Jack's, so that they both looked as though they were Venusians from a fifties' science fiction movie. And there were numerous pictures of Buddy with his idol, William Shatner. Jack looked at these the hardest, and Buddy smiled bravely through his pain.

"That's me aboard the *Enterprise*. I had a charity tennis thing last year for the Colitis Foundation—I'm a big sufferer myself—and Bill took me on deck. I got Mr. Sulu's hat on."

"My husband, the Trekkie," Charlotte Rae said, shaking her head.

"Best show ever done. Now, you can take that *Deep Space Nine* and kiss my butt. They got everybody dressed up in spandex, but they'll never replace Captain Kirk."

"Damn right," Charlotte Rae said, mocking him a little. Wingate gave her a smile that was almost sweet, and for a second Jack thought that he saw what might pass between them when Buddy wasn't doing his redneck producer act. Because Buddy was obviously enjoying it so much, Jack looked at a few more of the photos; there was one of Buddy and Charlotte Rae with Ricardo Montalban and Herve Villechaize on the set of *Fantasy Island*. The Wingates wore leis around their necks. Charlotte Rae sat in Buddy's lap, a goofy, almost happy smile on her face. She wore a grass skirt and a halter top with porpoises on it, but she didn't look silly, she looked radiant.

Buddy smiled and opened the freezer in the mini-fridge. He took out a blue bottle of chilled Skyy vodka.

"Have a taste?" he asked Jack. "This stuff is the absolute best."

"No thanks," Jack said. "A little early for me."

"Suit yourself," Buddy said, pouring himself a large glass and taking a long sip.

He smiled and looked at the wall of photos. "Ah, memories, memories," Buddy said. "Charlotte Rae was guest starring on *Fantasy* in that one."

"Yeah," Charlotte Rae said. "It'll go down in the annals of great drama, right along with *The A-Team*."

Jack laughed, but Buddy wagged a finger at her.

"Hey, don't lemme hear you talk like that, darlin'." He turned to Jack with a what-are-you-gonna-do? look on his red face.

"That is her whole problem in a nutshell. She lacks belief in herself. Now, it so happens that episode of *Fantasy* was very very innaresting. Hey, I know the show ain't no *Hawaii Five-O*, but how many of them you ever gonna see? In this one Charlotte played a woman dying of cancer, makes love to a porpoise, and finds everlasting peace. Real mystical shit."

"Yeah," Charlotte Rae said, rolling her eyes. "Deep."

Buddy waved his hand at her.

"Now, honey, you know that script gave you a chance to act up a storm. Hey, on one of the takes the whole crew broke out in spontaneous applause."

"Because you gave them fifty bucks apiece," Charlotte said.

"Untrue, completely and totally untrue. You shouldn't oughta run yourself down so, darlin'."

"You're right," she said. "Thank God I have you around to help keep up my self-esteem."

Buddy ignored the crack, grabbed Jack's arm, and pulled him eagerly along. They stopped in front of a picture of Charlotte Rae and Buddy hanging out of the cab of a semi. Both of them were dressed like truckers, with flannel shirts, dirty jeans, and scruffy work boots. Standing just below them on the ground was an actor Jack couldn't name holding a lovable-looking chimpanzee.

"Now, this was a great shoot. Charlotte played a hitchhiker who gets picked up by BJ and the Bear. Personally, I thought this one would get an Emmy nod, but no such luck. They ended up giving the Emmy to Glenn Close 'cause she played a battered dyke who shoots her husband."

"Bastards," Jack said.

Charlotte Rae laughed aloud, and Wingate gave Jack the fish-eye.

"That damned chimp was more honest 'n most people," Buddy said, pouring himself another drink. "But therein lies a sad tale. The show was real popular for a couple of years, but then folks got tired of it, so it was canceled. And the chimp couldn't find any more work. So they eventually take him back to the zoo, but he can't relate to it no more. I mean, after having people making him up and the press asking him to do his over fifty words of vocabulary, and actually being able to drink scotch and smoke a cigarette at breaks—he was partial to Larks—well, he just can't get back into the raw-vegetables-and-banana regime at the zoo, not to mention being caged up like a fucking animal, and so his trainer, Lance, comes in one day to get him up, and he finds him hanging there by his tire swing. See, he'd learned to tie knots on his show in order to get BJ out of trouble, and he ties himself a noose, and *eeeeeck*, he's finito, kaput. Can you believe that? But, you know what, I can't say I blame him. 'Cause it goes to show you one thing, he would rather die like a man than live like an ape."

"Now, that is sad," Jack said.

"Check this out in here," Buddy said. He opened the door to a small bathroom completely done in pink and black. There on the wall were pictures of Buddy Wingate with the President of the United States, Bill Clinton. "How you like that?" Buddy said.

"Business associate?" Jack said.

"My buddy from back home, son. Tell you what, I have lived in Dallas, and Nashville, been to Paris, France, but there is only one Arkansas. Jack, I will tell you this, ain't too many of us ole boys from the Razorback State who's made it national. I feel a real link with that man."

"Does he know about it?" Jack said.

Wingate looked at him and smiled. "Damn straight he does. Accepted my check, didn't he? This here is the Committee to Elect the President. Hey, we had a hell of a time, didn't we honey?"

"That we did, Buddy," Charlotte Rae said. She was trying for sarcasm, but Jack could hear the pride in her voice.

"I'll tell you what it is. People from Arkansas never forget one another," Buddy said, waving his arms theatrically. "Bill Clinton is going to call on me one of these days from the Oval Office. And when my phone rings, I shall be ready to serve."

"Don't you think he might be a little offended by *The President's Cabinet?*" Jack said.

"Not at all," Buddy said. "He'll take it for the homage it is. Ole Hillary might not like it too much though."

"The insensitive bitch," Charlotte Rae said.

Jack laughed out loud, and Buddy squinted at him.

"I know, I know, you think I'm a little nuts," Buddy said

now. "They all did, until I was invited to the goddamned inaugural."

"It was beautiful," Charlotte said.

"Bottom line is Bubba's a Razorback and he recognizes other Razorbacks. Know what I mean, Jackie?"

"Absolutely," Jack said. "Got it."

Buddy smiled and straightened his string tie in the mirror.

Jack smiled and looked at Charlotte Rae.

"Congratulations," he said.

"For what, pray tell?"

"Marrying a genius," Jack said.

Charlotte Rae laughed and put her arm around Buddy, and suddenly Jack felt a surprising jolt of irritation. It was as though she had slapped him in the face. The power of these sudden unwelcome feelings shocked him.

Wingate smiled at him now, a calculating, mocking smile. He was flaunting his power over his wife, and he wanted Jack to see it. Jack met his gaze steadily but with some effort. He tried not to let anything in his eyes, in the tilt of his head, or the shape of his mouth, reveal how much he wanted to take Charlotte Rae out of Wingate's arms.

"Buddy," Charlotte Rae said, as they shut the bathroom door. "Aren't you forgetting something?"

"Of course," Buddy said.

Suddenly, Wingate reached up and patted Jack's cheek. It was all Jack could do to hide his revulsion.

"I haven't forgotten. You saved my wife's life. We live in a world where nobody wants to help nobody, and you stepped right up and put yourself at risk. Frankly, it amazes me, and I'm grateful. Where you from, Jack?"

"Live in Hollywood now," Jack said. "Before that I grew up in Manhattan."

"Ah, now that *is* a city," Buddy said. "They got everything a boy needs to get hisself in serious trouble."

"And you should know," Charlotte Rae said.

Buddy turned toward her, and Jack saw something change in his face, a quick rage burned in his eyes. For a mini-second Jack thought Wingate was going to slap her. Charlotte Rae obviously thought so too, because even though he never moved a muscle, she winced and jumped back, as though warding off an invisible blow.

"Listen, darlin'," he said. "It would be better if you didn't editorialize on every little thing I say. All right?"

"I'm sorry, Buddy," Charlotte Rae said in a small, meek voice. She seemed to physically shrivel up, and sat down on a love seat a good five feet away from them both. Buddy smiled and sat down himself, nearly disappearing in a huge recliner chair with a Santa Fe Indian blanket draped across it. He motioned for Jack to sit down as well.

"So I understand you are bit by the acting profession."

"Yeah," Jack said. "Though it hasn't bit back much."

"That's the way it is. Cold and cruel. You got an agent?"

"Not yet," Jack said, trying to sound and look humble.

"Can't do a thing without one. Maybe we could help you along those lines. How about it, babe?"

Buddy smiled over at Charlotte Rae as if the violent vortex that had whirled like a tornado between them only seconds ago was ancient history.

"Yes, of course," she said. It was clear at once that she hadn't forgotten it. Her voice was halting, tremulous, and strangely formal. "I could introduce him to Elliot."

"Elliot Minsner," Wingate said, "he's a tough little prick, but he can do things for you."

"Hey, that would be great," Jack said. "But I don't want to put either of you out. You don't even know if I can act."

Wingate laughed at that one.

"I got a feeling about you," he said.

"Right," Jack said.

"No, I'm serious. You got the look. . . . Don't you think he's got the look, make the girls go wet in the wee-wee, Charlotte?"

"You have such a way with words, Buddy," Charlotte Rae said. She seemed to have gotten over the threat, because there was snap in her voice again.

Buddy laughed and waved his hand, as though he were dismissing her remark.

"Yeah, acting's a tough, tough business," Buddy said.

"I know," Jack said. "Some days I'm not sure about it. Don't want to end up being some kind of security guard at the studio when I'm fifty."

"I hear you," Wingate said. He leaned forward and looked intensely at Jack.

"Cold truth is though, son, that most actors don't become stars. Hell, most of 'em don't even get any work after a while. They go home to places like Palmdale, end up working at K mart, using their acting talents by talking through one of them microphones: 'Shoppers, today on the Blue Light Special, we got your jalapeno Mexican cheese and fat-free kosher baloney.' Hell, I've hired quite a few of them Mel Gibson wanna-bes at my furniture stores."

He gave out a tough little laugh then and shook his head.

"Glad I ain't never had the acting bug. Jack, lemme ask you a question. How'd you make a living in the Apple?"

"Did a little bartending," Jack said. "But mainly I ended up working as a companion to a guy named Joey Rizzo."

That stopped both Wingate and Charlotte Rae cold. They turned and looked at each other, and for a second Jack had the sensation that everything was moving in slow motion.

"As in, Joey Rizzo, from newspaper and tabloid TV fame?" Charlotte Rae said.

"One and the same," Jack said. "It's a long story. Joey had a thing about boxing. He used to come to Gleeson's Gym down on Union Square. I ended up being his trainer, and after a while our relationship got more personal."

"Well, well, now *that* is very interesting," Wingate said. "Very interesting, indeed. I hear Joey is in excellent health."

"Yeah," Jack said. "I had him working out three times a week, got him on a fat-free diet. We spent a lot of time together."

"Come on, you can say it right out. You mean you were acting as his bodyguard?" Buddy said.

" 'Companion' was how Joey liked to put it," Jack said.

"Right. Companion. Very nice word. Classy."

"Well," Jack said, "it's been great meeting you Mr. Wingate . . ."

"Buddy," Wingate said. He bounced out of the chair and blocked Jack's way to the door, but in a ball-of-the-feet friendly way.

"Where you going, son?"

"Surely, you don't have to leave, Jack," Charlotte Rae said.

"Yeah, 'fraid I do. I'm bartending over at Topper's on Las Palmas. And my shift starts soon."

"Well, wouldn't want to make you late for work," Buddy said. "But listen up a minute, will you? I might have an opening coming up, something you'd be good at. It's kind of behind the scenes, instead of acting, but there could be a real future in it."

"Really?" Jack said.

"I mean, if you are open to offers?" Buddy said.

"Depends on what they are. They got a wonderful retirement plan at Topper's. All the cheap red wine you can drink, absolutely free. And a free trip to the hospital to have your stomach pumped."

Wingate smiled and stretched his short, muscular arms above his head.

"Not sure if it's happening just yet, son, but long as we know where to reach you, I got a feeling it could work out real good."

"Sounds like fun," Jack said. He took out a business card from Topper's restaurant and handed it to Buddy. "You can usually catch me here."

"Fine," Wingate said. "You take it easy. I'll be in touch, soon. And thanks again for saving my darling here."

"My pleasure," Jack said.

Wingate threw his right arm around his wife's waist, and Jack felt like smashing him in the throat.

Instead, he managed a smile, nodded like a cowboy to the two of them, and opened the trailer door. Outside it was killer hot, but Jack gulped down the smog as if it were ambrosia. Even bad air was better than none at all.

Chapter 5

Topper's was a chrome-and-black-leather topless bar on Sunset Boulevard. The restaurant specialized in pizza, tequila, strippers, and lap dancers. It had formerly been owned and operated by a drug dealer named Topper Glasby, a three-hundred-pound, Mexican-food-loving smack freak who had hustled everything from stolen securities to rock cocaine. Two years ago he'd been popped by the DEA, and his place of business had been seized by the Agency. Eventually, the place would be forfeited to the government, sold off, and the money would be put into the super slush fund designed to build more jails. Meanwhile, the Agency continued to run it, using Topper as the front man. The waiters and bartenders, however, were all DEA agents. So far, running Topper's had been an Agency gold mine. Dealers, hustlers, and prospective buyers of every kind of dope frequented the place because the girls were young and luscious, the music loud, and Topper was a loud, hearty-laughing extrovert who kept things lively. There had already been a couple of busts, and there were a number of pending cases that promised large bounty for the agency.

For the past six months Jack and Calvin Jefferson had used Topper's as a cover job, monitoring dope buys and meeting prospective perps at the bar.

This afternoon, as they waited for Topper to come back from testifying at a trial, Jack smiled at one of the young strippers, Angel Morrison, who was walking across the stage, half-naked. Angel herself had been popped only three months ago and was now acting as a snitch for the Agency. She had a great body, but Jack didn't have any fantasies about her. When she wasn't taking off her clothes or lap dancing in front of stoned, screeching bikers or out-of-town conventioneers, she was bust-pumping iron at the Hollywood YMCA. Her arms and legs were seriously muscled in a way that Jack could find attractive only after he'd had one too many drinks.

She smiled at him now and turned on the stereo. Bob Seger came pouring from the speakers—"Against the Wind"—and Angel began to sing in her little-girl monotone.

"Shit, turn that down, babe," Calvin Jefferson said, as he read the L.A. *Times*.

"Oh, whatsa matter, man, chu don't like it?" Angel said. "I played it 'cause it is all bout your generation of old fucks."

Jack laughed, but C.J. just grunted.

"I gave up on Bob Seger when he started making them tire commercials," C.J. said. " 'Like a rock,' my ass."

Angel shrugged and licked her lips.

"Chu don't like that?" she said. "That's my favorite commercial of all time."

She did a little sexy spin, leapt up on the circular bar, slid down the golden pole in the center, and sang in a voice filled with sex:

"Like a roooooock. *Ooooooh,* baby. You are likkkke a roooock."

Jack smiled and thought, maybe he could get into women bodybuilders after all. Then he remembered Charlotte Rae Wingate and he began to feel something happening to him. Something that cut right through his attitude.

He went back into the kitchen, grabbed the pizza paddle, and opened the red-hot oven. He grimaced and pulled out C.J.'s lunch, a pizza covered with pineapple, pine nuts, and Smithfield ham.

"Jesus," Jack said, as he carried in the pizza to his partner. "This is the most revolting pizza I've ever seen."

"So what?" Calvin said, grabbing a piece while looking at the real estate section of the paper. "You ain't gotta eat it. Now, this is where I want to be. Down here in Laguna Beach.

Get me a place near the sand, go home at night, walk out and feed the gulls."

"Yeah," Jack said, going back behind the bar. "It sounds charming until you start thinking about the beachheads. I had a girlfriend from down there at one time, and we had to go to parties with these stoners from the area. Everything was *rad* and *bitchin'* and *gnarly dude*. Sorry, but I can't see you in that scene."

Calvin looked up, and Jack was a little surprised to see the degree of annoyance on his face.

"Not everybody down there is like that," he said.

"No," Jack said, laughing. "Those are the nice people. The rest of them are like Orange County Ku Klux Klaners and skinheads. Not to mention the Vietnamese gang scene. You can go to human barbecues with those guys. Yeah, you're gonna love it there, C.J."

C.J. removed his glasses and looked up. There was a stricken quality to his mouth.

"Hey, fuck you, Jack. That's just a bunch of liberal clichés. You don't really know shit about it."

There was real anger in his voice. Jack knew he should back off, but his own nerves were wired from too much coffee and thoughts of Charlotte Rae Wingate.

"Hey, all I mean is, as a black man, I don't think you'd dig it down there for very long."

Now C.J. got up from his chair and walked toward Jack. He struck out his index finger, punching the air between them.

"Hey, man, we're partners but don't be commenting on race, okay? 'Cause you really don't know shit about it, dig?"

"No?" Jack said. "I haven't been to your house? I haven't hung with you and your family? Come on, C.J.? Gimme a break."

C.J. pushed his glasses back on his head.

"I love it. White boy listens to jazz at the Catalina Bar and Grill a couple times a month and thinks he knows all about what it's like to live like a black man in this world."

"Hey," Jack said, trying to laugh his partner out of it. "I never said that."

"But you think it, man," C.J. said. "Well, jes remember, you don't know and you will never know, so don't be telling me what I'm gonna like and what the fuck I should do. Dig?"

"Geez," Angel said, rubbing her forefinger through her eyebrow. "And I thought you two boys loved each other."

"Fuck you too, Angel," C.J. said.

He went back to his paper and stared at it as if he were trying to start a fire.

Angel pouted and continued her dance even though the music had stopped. Jack shook his head and started to wash some glasses. C.J. was obviously having troubles at home again. He wanted to talk to him about it, but he'd have to wait for him to calm down. Suddenly, someone pushed back the black velvet curtain at the front door and light flooded the dark room.

Jack looked up and saw her there. Charlotte Rae Wingate.

She wore a black T-shirt with thin pink suspenders and tight black Levi's. Her blonde hair seemed to absorb the street light, and her dark sunglasses gave her an extra touch of glamour.

"Hi, Larry," she said to C.J. "This is a charming place."

"Hey, honey, we don't need no dancers," Angel said, doing a split on the platform.

"Relax, sweetie, I've already lived your life," Charlotte Rae said.

Now C.J. looked up and automatically turned on the charm. "Well, well, if we ain't got the Dragon Lady herself. I heard they're looking for you up at Mann's Chinese."

Jack admired his partner for showing no trace of the anger and frustration he had obviously felt.

"Well, they're going to have to keep on looking, honey," Charlotte Rae said, smiling at C.J., "because I avoid that place like the plague now."

Jack smiled and caught his breath. She did something to him, something they didn't talk about at the academy.

What was it about her? Sex, obviously, but something else too. Maybe it was the charming and witty spin she put on her own desperation.

"Hi, Jack," she said, walking toward him.

"Hi, yourself. What you doing around here?"

"Well," she said, rubbing her finger up and down the bar. "I was going to call you, but then I sort of became nervous that you wouldn't invite me over here. So I invited myself. Hope that's okay."

"I'd say it's very okay," Jack said. There were times when he was amazed at his ability to sound like someone else, literally be someone else. But this wasn't one of them. She shook him up too much.

C.J. got up and joined them at the bar.

"We are always delighted to see human beings in this bar, though we don't recommend they stay very long."

Angel walked by them now, back toward her dressing room.

"I got to work on my routines, okay?"

She smiled at Charlotte Rae.

"I do a whole new lap thing to Snoop Doggy. It would blow a round hole in your mind."

"Well, I can hardly wait," Charlotte Rae said.

"I think she likes you," Jack said, when Angel had gone behind the stage.

"No, I think she likes *you,*" Charlotte Rae said. "But then why shouldn't she?"

"I can think of about fifty reasons," Calvin said.

"But fathers are always toughest on their sons," Charlotte said.

Calvin laughed as if he was surprised.

"I think you might have a bright as well as beautiful woman here, Jack. That's a very scary prospect for an old guy like me."

"Listen to that," Charlotte said. "I bet you drive all the women crazy." She smiled and Jack watched C.J. light up.

"I got to get in there and make pizza. Nice seeing you, kid," C.J. said. "And go easy on Jackie. He's just a poor hip white boy."

He walked back into the kitchen, and Jack sensed a little more spring in his step. That's what she did for you.

"Want a drink?" Jack said.

"No thanks. I'm on my way to the gym. I did have an ulterior motive for coming by, though. I'm here to offer you to come away with me and Buddy for the weekend. Up to our place in Tahoe. We have a hundred acres, about forty minutes from town. Completely cut off from everything. And on the property is the most beautiful lake you've ever seen. Lake Echo."

"You and Buddy, huh?" Jack said.

She smiled and shook her head.

"Jack, I was afraid you and he had gotten off on the wrong foot. Buddy can be a little overbearing sometimes. Especially when he's nervous. But he really likes you. He wants to show you around, and I want you to see Lake Echo. It's a very special place."

Her voice had grown softer, and she had taken the glasses off now. She looked at Jack in a way that made him feel as though the bar was revolving beneath his feet.

"Tell me the truth," Jack said. "How does Buddy really feel about me?"

"He likes you. I think he wants to help you."

"Yeah?" Jack said. "Is that a good thing?"

"Of course it is," Charlotte Rae said, smiling. "Look, you're making too much out of all this. He's grateful for what you did for me, and he wants to show you a good time. We can go out on the lake in the daytime and hit the casinos at night. Come on, you need a break from this place."

She reached over and touched his wrist. It was clear to him that she had been sent here by her husband. But her hand was warm anyway.

"Okay," he said. "So happens I have the weekend off."

"I know." She smiled.

Jack smiled back. "You know? You already checked my schedule?"

"Uh-huh. Am I a bad girl?"

She pouted, then smiled.

"I promise to make it all up to you," she said. "Really."

She flipped her glasses down over her eyes.

"Almost forgot," she said. "What's your address?"

He wrote it down on a bar business card, and she put it in her leather bag.

"Good. Be ready around seven. I'll have the car pick you up then."

"The car?" Jack said.

"The limo," she said. "I think I see your problem already, Jack. You don't have enough fun. But we're going to fix that. I promise."

She leaned over and kissed him on the cheek, and he felt something inside of him stir, something he hadn't expected. He had wanted her at first sight, no man in his right mind wouldn't, but there was something else here, something both bold and appealingly shy in that kiss, and afterward, when he looked at her face, he saw the fear again—fear, and a sweet vulnerability.

It was almost as though she was begging him to come, that underneath all the actressy bravado and sexual joking she was saying, "You've got to come. I can't stand being alone with him."

And then, as quickly as it had appeared, it was gone, and she was smiling at him brazenly, all fresh confidence.

"See you soon, Jack. You won't be sorry."

She turned and walked out then, and when she was gone, he sat down heavily on a stool behind the bar and felt like all the light had been sucked out of the room.

He should feel great, he knew it. It was working, working beautifully. They had swallowed the bait whole. But he felt something else. Was it something about her? He wasn't sure, but something made him grind his teeth, want to take a drink at lunch—or maybe two.

Chapter 6

Brandau stood on top of a stack of cargo containers a mile away from the San Pedro docks. He looked through his Nikon 10×50 binoculars, at Pier 23, which was over a mile away. This was the latest spot where drug smuggling activity had been spotted, and according to his snitches, it might be the rendezvous point for Wingate's big deal. It was Brandau's job to see if any of Wingate's crew was setting things up.

In truth, though, his mind was elsewhere. Agent Brandau was thinking of lunch. Maybe he'd make it a grilled chicken Caesar at Louise's, or he'd cruise out to the Valley for sushi at Nozawa, which was too damned expensive but the best in the world. What the hell, he was forty-two years old, and he didn't spend his money on anything else. Besides, his new girlfriend, Suzie, wasn't poor. She came from a well-to-do Hong Kong family.

Man, he was hungry right now.

In fact, he was hungry all the time. After a lifetime of starving himself, trying to be fit, running five miles a day, there had been a subtle change in his psyche, which he didn't fully understand, though he thought that maybe it had something to do with going to the shrink after his marriage had broken up.

Thank God, he had gone to Dr. Terri Bascomb. It wasn't his idea really, but Suzie Chow's. Actually he had fought tooth and nail against going to any "goddamned shrink." The truth was that if Suzie hadn't threatened to leave him, he might not have ever made the move.

He might have gone right on drinking and staying up late and making weird calls to his ex-wife, calls from pay phones where he just held the receiver in his hand like a ghoul from a horror movie. Held it and listened to her voice, saying:

"Hello, hello. Who is this? Hello. Is this you, Richard, you total asshole? Well, I'll be calling my lawyer tomorrow, Richard. I'll be calling the goddamned bureau tomorrow and talking to Zampas, I'll be talking to a lot of people, but I won't be talking to you, shithead!"

And then she would slam down the phone, and Brandau would start giggling, like some kind of fucking weirdo . . . and he realized fairly soon that if he didn't get help, he would blow his brains out. It was that simple.

Which was where his shrink came in—black-haired, thick-lipped, sexy, charismatic Dr. Terri Bascomb, who taught him a whole other way to be, for godsake.

Brandau had been floored by his therapist. He was such an old-school guy that he'd been afraid that she'd come down on him, like some Sunday school teacher, showing him what a jerk he'd been in his marriage.

But she'd been beautiful. She'd given him a completely new perspective on his life. It was really wonderful, amazing. For the first time he realized he hadn't taken care of himself, that he'd spent too much time trying to please others. It had started with his own parents, who were always at each other's throats, forcing him to play referee, and it had gone on in his relationships with guys at the frat house at UCLA and right on up into the Agency and his marriage.

Brandau had always hated it when celebrities got on some talk show and practically foamed at the mouth as they told how therapy had saved their lives, but now he understood their almost religious enthusiasm.

Because Dr. Terri had made him understand everything in a whole new way, she made him feel happy about who he was, about his potential. Let the other cops laugh when he waxed a little New Age at the Agency gym. To hell with them, they didn't understand; they were all mired in the old cop "drink and hate the citizens" death trip.

The bottom line was, he was entitled to good things and to happiness, and now he had things going his way.

He had Suzie and he had power in the Agency and a good future, and he was really stopping to smell the roses. He even let himself get a few pounds on him, eating out occasionally.

Of course, he didn't want to become a fat slob, but why become a nut about that? To hell with the chicken Caesar, what he really wanted today was a fat steak.

After he got done with his surveillance, he'd head for the Palm, eat a steak and onion rings, have a cold brew. Maybe he'd even run into Parker Morton, the movie director whom he'd recently met through Suzie at Babe N Rickey's blues club. Parker said he ate lunch there and he might want Brandau to "consult" on a movie. Beautiful. One more example of good things happening once you empower yourself.

He put the binoculars away and laughed to himself.

Nothing happening here, time for lunch.

He climbed down the side of the cargo containers, walked across the macadam to his car. He felt the salt air from the ocean and took a deep breath.

Life was beautiful. Really.

Brandau got in, dropped his binocs on the seat, and drove away.

A half mile away from him, a man dressed as a dock worker, in overalls and a baggy old brown sweater, put away his binoculars and got into his car as well. Agent Brandau had headed toward the 405, and in a second the man would be right behind.

Chapter 7

Jack Walker lived in the Chateau des Roses, in the 1920s a fantastic hotel, but now a crumbling California Gothic in the violent crime and smack-dealing district at Franklin and Cherokee, just up the hill from Musso and Frank's Restaurant on the tawdriest stretch of Hollywood Boulevard. Jack had lived in the hulking Chateau for ten months now, and each time he paid his rent check to his astrologer landlord, a black Jamaican named Dorian "Toots" Riley, he swore that this would be the last month he would spend there. But the rail-thin Rastaman would only run his long, elegant fingers through his matted dreadlocks and then his little goatee.

"I see you here, mon. I see you here for a long, long time."

"How long?" Jack had said one time, smiling but feeling a small panic inside.

Riley had turned and shuffled across the bright blue terrazzo tile in the Chateau's grand old lobby, saying nothing more but laughing to himself.

"Very long, mon."

"Come on, Mr. Fortune," Jack said, trying for a light tone. "Tell me how long."

"Until the emperor himself comes back to retake the throne," Riley said, smiling as he shut the big wooden door to his apartment. "Until the Lion of Judah roars again!"

"But the emperor is dead," Jack said.

"Don't sweat the small stuff, mon," Riley said. Then with a

whiff of sinsemilla smoke and the craggy, visionary sounds of Bob Marley, Toots was gone.

After that exchange, Jack didn't ask him anymore. Riley was a little mad, though he had a steady clientele who came either to have their charts read or to buy dope, probably both. The truth was that Jack should have busted him, but he didn't bother with small stuff. Besides, he liked Riley, liked knowing that there was a party going on in his landlord's apartment, anytime, night or day. It was good that someone on the screwed-up planet was still having fun.

Still, he knew that there were guys at the Agency who thought it was highly questionable that he lived where he did, in bad old Hollywood, among the very perps and weirdos that he was sworn to bust. Most of the guys in the DEA lived in the Valley or Pasadena; a few of the Latin guys, in Silverlake; but nobody else lived in Hollyweird. Jack knew that it made him a little suspect among the others and a lot suspect to Michaels, who thought he was some kind of wild man.

Which was the way Jack liked to be seen. Everyone cuts a wild man more slack.

Besides, before he had moved to the Chateau, Jack had tried the straight life. For two years he had lived with a makeup artist named Elaine Swanson, a beautiful, classic blue-eyed blonde from Iowa. During the first six months of their relationship, Jack had marveled at Elaine's stability, enjoyed meeting her showbiz friends, actors, directors, and writers.

But he'd grown tired of both Elaine and her scene within a year. He became bored with all the hysteria her friends felt about their movie and television projects, their endless nattering about who made what deal, who was lying to whom, eating with whom, sleeping with whom, as if all of it was of earthshaking importance. For Elaine, the show business world had endless fascination. She saw herself as someone who had transcended her Midwestern roots and who was on her way to the top. To Jack, show business was playacting. He found it especially irritating when Elaine talked about how he would be sure to like a certain movie because the writing or acting was "on the edge." Inevitably, this would be some cop drama or action-adventure movie that was witless idiocy from start to finish. When he'd told her that, she'd accused him of having contempt for anything that wasn't in his world. Then she'd nailed him with her best shot.

She said, "To you, Jack, humanity is broken down into two classes, cops and germs, which makes you and your holy brethren on the force more narrow, vain, and self-involved than anybody in show business could ever be."

Jack said nothing to that. Why talk about it, when mostly it was the truth? He had his ego, and he loved-hated his own world, and there wasn't much room for anything else.

Still, it wasn't the way he wanted to be.

Some nights, as he lay in his bed, looking at the hallucinatory lights of Hollywood below him, he thought of his mother, Ruth Ann, of her slim California-girl figure, her love of dancing, her piano playing, her ability to make anything grow (ice plants and bougainvillea and birds-of-paradise) in their back garden in Laurel Canyon. Jack could remember nights, sitting on the high steps that led down to the balloon-and-lantern-strung deck, watching his dad and mom cha-cha as Bobby Darin wailed "Mack the Knife" through the towering eucalyptus trees—his mother gracefully making the steps, his dad lumbering happily after her; the other cops and their wives laughing, joining in.

He had watched them and listened and felt that the world was a good place.

Then his mother got sick. Cancer, the doctors whispered. Don't tell the boy, his relatives said, as if he couldn't hear them, as if he didn't know they were lying when he asked them how she was. How he hated them all, his father, his uncles, even Zampas, as they all furtively looked away and said she was doing much much better. Not to worry, son. She'll be fine.

Six months later it was over. Jack was fifteen, and when they laid her in the ground, he expected to feel crushed. Instead, he felt nothing at all. That year he became a star halfback on the school football team, was popular with girls, and a good student. Sometimes in his room at night he would put on the old Sinatra records his mother had loved and talk to her. He'd say, "I'm handling it really well, Mom. See that? I'm fine. Don't worry, Mom. Okay?"

The funny thing was, he thought now, he had actually believed it for a while. But there was something else too, something deeper than grief. It was a realization that true goodness and real happiness had the duration of a cha-cha record or the brief bloom of a plant.

And these were feelings, he knew now, that he never got over. Certainly becoming a cop did nothing to dispel them.

But even if it was true, he didn't want to be a cynic. He was tired of being tough, being the fastest, the hippest, the wildest. Deep down he hated his own act. It was killing him, he sometimes thought, faster than the job ever could.

The problem was he had gotten too good at the act. What could he replace it with?

Was he supposed to get married and go live in the Valley? Hang out at barbecues? Little League games? That didn't make it for him, no matter how appealing it might seem at midnight, alone in the Chateau.

Or should he be like C.J., invent a mythical good place (Orange County, for Chrissakes?) where he'd feel like a normal citizen. No, he hadn't found it yet, hadn't found who he might be when he wasn't being a cop. So for now, maybe it was better to live here at the Chateau with the other shadow people. Live here in his third-floor one-bedroom apartment with latticed windows that gave the place the strange feeling of a boardinghouse in a movie about the Alps—a little like *Heidi Becomes a Junkie*.

Still, it was almost like home, and a residual benefit of the place was that the other residents were so far-out, they made Jack feel mainstream. Besides Riley, there were Ona and Rita, two model/actress/hookers who lived on the first floor and were given to walking naked in the hotel's little walled-in bonsai garden. And there was Katsu, a Japanese performance artist, who drained himself of blood by using leeches on his wrists now and then in order to rid himself of poisonous toxins. He urged Jack to do likewise and even offered to take Jack to meet his "dear friend and mentor, the Leech Man." Jack graciously declined. Up on the fifth floor was Jack's favorite citizen in the hotel, Anton LeRoy, who introduced himself as "once a great Hollywood director, now forced by fortune to ply the skin-flick trade." This was one show business person Jack could warm to. Just looking at his list of hit films made Jack smile with affection: *Star Whores, Thelma Eats Louise,* and his latest low-rent masterpiece, *Forest Hump.*

But even as funky and congenial as the place was, there were still nights when he missed having someone to care for, nights when he walked the floors staring down at the tortured palms on Hollywood Boulevard. Then there were the nights he did fall into a restless sleep but suffered cold blue nightmares of Jose Benvenides, nights he dreamed of the bust that went wrong last year in the Trail's End Motel in Tucson, a bust that ended with Jose Benvenides pulling a .44 magnum from under his black Armani sport coat, pointing its barrel (magnified a thousand times in the dream until it seemed as big as a nineteenth-century cannon) at Jack's head, laughing as he squeezed the trigger, and Jack felt his soul already floating from his bullet-ridden corpse.

And then came the real shock—the gun had misfired. And without quite knowing how he did it, Jack was on him, clawing at Jose's face, rolling over the linoleum floor, smashing into the end table with the fake Frederic Remington cowboy lamps and into the cockroach-infested bed, knocking down the painting of the lonely pastel Apache at his sacred burial ground.

Then, there was a flash of light, a blurt of sound, and Jose Benvenides's left jaw flew away from his shattered, bloody nose. Improbably, it was Jack who was alive. Alive and haunted—he dreamed about it three nights a week for the first six months. He would wake up screaming, covered with cold, clammy sweat. Jose Benvenides was dead . . . not him. He was alive, so why was he still shaking, waking up in the middle of the night, certain that he'd seen somebody flashing by his bedroom door?

Welcome to life on the edge, Elaine. Do you want it? Can you dig it?

Still, for all their problems, on nights like these, he wished he had her to hold again—her or somebody, anybody. He would fantasize about his imaginary lover, somebody hip and funny who would understand his hang-ups and who would make him laugh.

Somebody like Charlotte Rae Wingate.

He'd been thinking of her constantly since their wild meeting in front of Mann's Chinese, thinking of not only her skin and her breasts, her hair and her eyes, but the way she turned a phrase, the way he didn't have to finish a sentence because he knew she had already gotten it. Throw in the danger of being attracted to what he could never have and she became irresistible.

The night before the trip up to Tahoe from Burbank, Jack dreamed that Charlotte Rae and he were having sex in the men's room of the plane. The dream was so vivid that he could nearly taste her, and when he awoke, he felt an aching in his loins. God, he wanted her, more than he'd wanted anyone else in years. As it turned out, the flight to Tahoe *was* intense, but not because of sex. Rather, L.A. had one of its infrequent summer downpours. Booming thunder and streaks of cancerous yellow lightning crashed around the plane. Charlotte Rae sat next to Wingate, nestled her head in his shoulder, and barely looked up once during the entire flight. Jack sat across the aisle from them, alone with his *Sports Illustrated*. Sweat dripped down his arms, and he felt like bailing. It was funny. Put him in a room with five gun-and-knife-toting dope dealers who would cut his heart out for a laugh and he was fine, but cram him into an airplane and toss in a few doses of thunder and lightning and he felt like a panicky kid. To keep sane, Jack read an article by a sports psychiatrist named Dr. Arnie Mazur, who explained in excruciating detail why greater numbers of professional athletes were suffering from clinical depression. ("They often feel unworthy of the great sums of money they earn," the good doctor wrote.)

Jack shook his head and wondered what it would be like to have a shot at that kind of depression. He thought of what

C.J. had told him just two days ago. He couldn't afford to send his son to a decent private school and the one in his neighborhood had recently become a target for drug dealers. Only two days earlier a twelve-year-old had asked Calvin's boy, Demetrius, if he'd like to make a little extra comic-book money by dealing speed. Calvin had sent two local cops over, who busted the kid and scared him into giving up his dealer—a twenty-year-old, out-of-work house painter, who cooked up crank at his "vacation trailer" in Palmdale. When the cops busted the trailer, they found something else out there too, bones, the bones of a thirteen-year-old runaway kid.

"That coulda been my kid," C.J. had said.

That was the world cops lived in; they couldn't afford the gated neighborhoods like Bel Air, but they were expected to lay down their lives for people who wouldn't dream of "lunching" with them. Yeah, Jack thought he could handle quite a few unworthy feelings to make the kind of money Shaquille O'Neal was pulling down.

He lurched in his seat as the plane rocked and felt his stomach heave again. Let the drug dealers come in droves, just get him off this fucking model airplane.

Jack stood in the light rain, watching a skycap throw his bag into the back of Wingate's trendy silver-gray off-road vehicle. He started to get into the backseat, but Charlotte Rae beat him to the door and quickly climbed inside.

"I have a headache, cowboy," she said, trying for a light witty tone. But Jack heard something else in it. The fear again. On the plane he had chalked up her depressed mood to flight anxiety, but this was something else, and he felt troubled by it.

"You ride up here with me," Wingate said, smiling.

Jack shrugged and climbed in.

"Fasten that seat belt, son, 'cause you're in for a ride."

Jack looked at him curiously, but Wingate only smiled and sat silently behind the wheel.

"Just waiting for traffic to thin out," he said.

Buddy adjusted the seat and gripped the wheel.

"I know what you are thinking," he said. "You're thinking,

that ole Buddy's one of them typical businessman assholes got himself an off-road vehicle when the only place he ever visits is the fucking Seven-Eleven."

Jack gave a noncommittal smile but said nothing.

"Well, I got me a little surprise for you. This here vehicle is called a Typhoon, and it's altogether another breed of monster. She only looks like the other suburbo wagons, which is the whole beauty of it. You check this out. First, I place my left foot down on the brake real hard. Now I push my right foot down on the gas, crush that baby down like so, see what I mean?"

Jack nodded. And reflexively gripped the armrest hard with his right hand.

"Very impressive," he said.

"Yeah? Well, impress this!" Wingate said.

He suddenly lifted his left foot off the brake, simultaneously leaving his right foot tromped full bore down on the accelerator, and the Typhoon tore out of the parking lot as though it had been slung from some cosmic slingshot. Wingate could barely control the vehicle as it skidded, slid, and rocketed past the two other cars in the right lane.

"Son of a bitch," Jack said, his stomach churning.

"Buddy, watch out!" Charlotte Rae screamed.

Just a few feet ahead of them were two wealthy Indian women dressed in saris, purple snow parkas, and bright red snow boots. Jack watched in horror as they screamed and threw up their hands, paralyzed with fear. By sheer luck, the Typhoon passed a half inch to the right of them. Buddy gave a wild cowboy yell, as the Typhoon skidded madly up on a grass plot and then snaked back off of it, nearly colliding with a Shell gas tanker. From behind him, Jack heard Charlotte Rae scream again, "Buddy, you goddamned maniac! Stop this car, now!"

That was all; Jack had had enough. He reached over and grabbed the wheel from Wingate.

" 'Sum bitch, what you doing, boy?"

"You crazy bastard," Jack said. "Hit the fucking brakes, now!"

He was yelling now, furious, yet at the same time he was trying to stay in character. Wingate was obviously testing him to see how much he'd put up with.

"Listen to me, Buddy," Jack said, after he had successfully steered the car to the side of the road. "I don't care how you treat the guys who work for you, but you don't fuck with me like that. You hear me, partner? Thanks for the trip, but I'm outta here."

He opened the door, slid off his seat belt, and stepped onto the curb.

"Hey, now wait a second," Wingate gasped. "I was just having a little fun."

"Yeah, I know," Jack said. "*You* were having fun, but I wasn't. Flip open the trunk, and I'll get my bags."

"No, Jack, don't . . ." Charlotte Rae said.

But Jack didn't meet her eyes.

"Give me my bags, Wingate, before I pull you out of the car and stuff you up your own asshole. *Comprende,* Buddy?"

Wingate's little mouth fell open, like a trapdoor with a broken hinge.

"Boy, you got a hard bark on you, talking to me like that."

"Open the back, Buddy," Jack said. "Don't make me start counting."

"Hey, hey, hey," Buddy Wingate said, opening his palms. "What do you want me to do, give you a hump job or something? Look, I'm sorry, okay. It was a dumb move, and I can see how you maybe wouldn't dig it. Come on, pal, you get back in here. I'm real sorry. I mean it now."

Jack felt a silent thrill pass through him like a shadow. His little gamble had paid off. Wingate had tried to intimidate him, but Jack turned it around on him. For now, he had the upper hand.

Silently, as though he was still mightily pissed, he climbed up the step and got back inside.

He'd let Wingate thaw him out, but slowly, by degrees.

They climbed into the mountains, and Jack looked out the windows at the great Douglas firs, the drooping pine trees, and the massive black rocks that lay by the side of the curving road. Up here the sky itself was bluer, the air crisp and clear, and Jack felt himself relax a little.

Wingate turned the car into a dirt road, and they began to climb through the trees and over washed-out potholes two feet wide.

Then they came to a gate, and Wingate got out and unlocked it.

"Welcome to my hideaway," he said, as he got back in the Typhoon.

Though Jack was probably overwhelmed by the natural beauty of Buddy Wingate's luxurious Tahoe retreat, he didn't have a chance to say so. Wingate used up all the available oxygen having the reaction for both of them.

"You ever see such a place?" Buddy said. "Bet you thought this old country boy was gonna have one of them glass-and-beam deals. But I wanted something that felt like early Americana. Same as with my commercials. Got to be vintage or I jest can't handle it. We're talking natural beauty, wraparound front porch for jest sitting and thinking, movie-set floaty clouds, and piss-yourself-you're-so-happy fucking trees. You hear what I'm saying, Jack?"

"I just bet Jack got it," Charlotte Rae said.

Buddy shot her a look, but Jack quietly intervened.

"The place is Fantasy Island, Buddy. Really."

Wingate gave him a forty-karat smile, and they drove up the gravel road to the house.

Inside, the cabin was surprisingly tastefully decorated in a rustic style, complete with rocking chairs and a straight-back oak dining room set. There were braided circular rugs and a magnificent stone fireplace.

"See all this?" Buddy said. "This here is real American, which is why I like it."

"The truth is," Charlotte Rae said, smiling with affection, "that I had to practically kill him to get him to keep it like this. Buddy wanted to put razorback hogs all over the walls."

"That's 'cause I'm an ole razorback from Arkansas," Buddy said. "You ever hear 'em call the hogs, Jack?"

"No," Jack said. "I must have missed it."

"Buddy," Charlotte Rae said with a grimace.

"Shush, now," Wingate said. "If calling the hogs is good enough for Bubba Bill, it's good enough for you, baby. Here we go!"

He got into a quaint little stoop, thrust his belly out, and cupped his hands to his mouth. Charlotte Rae put her hands over her ears.

"Oooooooooh Peeeeeg!" he screamed at a decibel level designed to smash china. *"Sooooooooooieeeeeeeeee!!"*

Jack stood in stunned disbelief. Wingate finished and smiled happily.

"Damn, does a man good to get it out. Down in Little Rock, they say ole Bubba did that every time him and one his concubabes met at the No-Tell Motel."

"Classy people that they are," Charlotte Rae said. "Let's all get changed and take Jack for a hike up to Echo Lake. That's how I relax."

"Nah. You two go ahead," Buddy said, walking toward the antique telephone that hung from the dining room wall. "I got a little business I got to take care of. Just get back before dark, 'cause I got reservations for us down at Harrah's."

"Oh, Buddy, do we have to on the first night?" Charlotte Rae said.

"Hell, yes. I come up here to unwind. It's going to be fun. You gamble much, Jack?"

"Not for me," Jack said. "I leave it to the pros."

"Good," Buddy said. "Shows you're a smart man. Gambling's for suckers, I know it. But hell, a man has to have some vices."

Wingate winked at Jack, and Jack felt a kind of twisting in his stomach. It suddenly occurred to him that this was going to be harder undercover than he had anticipated, not because of any great immediate danger to himself, but because he had a desire to stick Wingate's oversized head into a trash can. If you could like a guy at least on some level, it made it easier to play.

"Come on," Charlotte Rae said. "Grab your bag, and I'll show you up to your room."

Wingate winked at him, and Jack picked up his bag and followed her, trying not to look too hard at her body as she moved like a dancer in front of him up the steps.

They walked above crystal blue Echo Lake among a field of wild blue and red flowers. The sun was sinking fast, and Charlotte Rae had bundled up in a brilliantly colored Indian sweater. They maneuvered their way up a rocky ledge, and she climbed ahead of him in long, confident strides. Jack found it difficult to keep up the pace.

"What's the matter, Jack, you out of shape?"

"How high up are we?"

"Just ten thousand feet. By tonight you'll be like a mountain goat. Come on."

They came to a switchback, and she seemed to float up it. Jack attempted to stay with her and lost his footing. He felt a moment of terror as he slid backward, but she was above him then, offering a hand. He took it and she pulled him up. She was remarkably strong.

"Thanks," he said, looking at the sharp rocks below. "I don't have my aviator's license."

She smiled, and they let their fingers stay together longer than was necessary. She turned and went up a little higher and found a great slab of white rock, which overlooked the west end of the lake. She sat down and opened the picnic basket, and Jack joined her, out of breath, glad for a chance to rest.

Inside the basket was a bottle of Pinot Grigio, some French bread, cheese, a Comice pear, and a paring knife.

"I love it here," she said, fixing Jack's food as he uncorked the wine. "It's like the rest of the world doesn't exist."

"Yeah," Jack said. "This is stone perfect."

She looked at him and smiled.

"Do you really like it?"

"Sure, why?"

"You seem like such a city boy. I bet if you were up here for more than a day, you'd go nuts, like Buddy. I took him up here once last year, and he looked down and said, 'Now we could build us a nice little dock here, maybe get a helio pad over there, and maybe we could build us a restaurant, Buddy's Lakefront.' "

"Buddy, Buddy," Jack said.

She looked at him and shook her head.

"It's okay," she said. "You can ask. Eventually everybody does."

"What you're doing with him? It's not my business."

"But aren't you a little curious? We don't seem like oil and water to you?"

"No," Jack said. "I wouldn't say so. Not at all. I know he's a smart cookie underneath all that redneck jive."

She raised an eyebrow, licked her forefinger, and painted an imaginary one on an invisible blackboard.

"Score one for you. Most people see only the smoke screen, and that's when Buddy nails them. Let me tell you about me and him. I grew up in a place in Texas called the Army and Navy Home for Orphans. It wasn't exactly *The Bells of St. Mary's*, though the nun who ran it, Sister Jane, liked to show that picture to us every Christmas. She had a thing for Ingrid Bergman."

She looked down at the lake below, picked up a stone, and threw it down to the crystal blue water.

"While I was in there, I began to develop physically faster than the other girls. I saw the way the nuns looked at me, but they didn't win the derby. No, I was raped three times by the parish priest. He said if I told anybody, Satan would force him to cut my tongue out of my head."

"Jesus," Jack said.

She smiled sadly and sipped the wine.

"At fourteen I decided I'd had enough of life in the kindly orphanage, so I escaped. I knew I had one relative in Houston, my aunt Clara, so I headed there. Figured I might be able to find my mother. I did. My aunt finally introduced me to my dear, kind sweet junked-out mom, the lady who gave me away. She was a woman who worked at a truck stop waitressing, except she spent most of her time in the cabs of trucks. It paid a lot better than serving chicken-fried steak ever did.

My old man was one of maybe fifty truckers who came through there. I've always had a soft spot for tanker trucks though."

She stopped talking, collecting herself. Then she took another sip of wine, broke off a piece of bread, and smeared it with rich goat cheese.

"French wine and this delicious food," she said. "Who would have thought I would have ever been living like this?"

"What happened when you met your mother?"

"She was about half dead from rotgut. They didn't want her at the restaurant anymore, and they didn't want her in the parking lot either. Three months after I found her, her liver gave out."

"Did you ever talk with her?"

"You mean, did we have one of those magical moments, like in the television movies, where she held me and said, 'I always loved you, I just didn't feel worthy to have a baby?' No, I'm afraid not. She did give me two bits of advice. A man will do anything for you if he thinks you'll give him head, and always drink bourbon with ice and you'll never get the spins."

She sighed deeply and looked out over the clear blue water.

"Yeah, I showed up just in time to bury her. All those truckers, all those men she gave pleasure to. None of 'em came to the funeral. My aunt and I were the only ones at the grave."

"I'm sorry . . ."

Charlotte Rae stopped talking now, and the tears rolled down her cheeks. She reached over and took Jack's hand. There was nothing sexual in it; rather, she seemed to him like a needy child.

"Hey, it's all right if you don't want to talk about it," he said, squeezing her hand.

"No," she said. "It helps. After that I took a bus to Dallas and started dancing in bars. I drank, did enough cocaine to send the *Apollo* to the moon. Saw guys. Lots of guys."

She hesitated and looked at Jack briefly, as if she was waiting for him to scold her, but he met her gaze without flinching.

"There was one guy there, Billy Tatum. He decided I was going to be his girl, though I told him to get his ass away from me. That pissed him off, so one night after everybody was wasted, and we were having a private employees' party, he took me off into a back room and beat the shit out of me."

"Son of a bitch," Jack said, quietly.

"Two nights later I was coming out of the club . . . the back alley exit, and he was there waiting for me. Said he was going to give me one more chance."

She sighed and looked down at the lake. A couple of tears rolled down her cheeks. Jack reached over and wiped them off, and she burrowed into his side. Now he could smell her skin, as intoxicating as the clear water below.

"I don't know what got into me, but I told him to go fuck himself. Then I saw the look on his mean little face. There was no doubt about it. He was going to take me out on the road somewhere and kill me. He was moving toward me, when this little fat guy showed up . . . like outta nowhere . . . I mean *poof* . . . this fat little prince . . . and he was standing there between me and Billy, and he said to Tatum, 'Get the fuck outta here, Billy, or I will stick you in that Dumpster with your short little dick in your mouth.' Hey, it wasn't poetry, but to me it sounded like Sir Lancelot. Tatum was not used to being told what to do. He looked shocked. He reached into his pocket and he pulled out a knife, a push-button . . . it had a six-inch blade. God, I was shaking . . . but he never got a chance to use it. Buddy hit him in the throat with a karate blow . . . and he fell on the ground gagging and holding his Adam's apple. Then Buddy kicked him in the ribs three times. The son of a bitch Tatum was in the hospital for three months and still talks like he's got throat cancer. That's how I met Buddy Wingate, and I've been with him ever since."

"That's quite a story," Jack said. "And does *he* treat you right?"

She squeezed Jack's hand.

"Yeah," she said. "He treats me fine."

She was lying. Jack could hear it plainly in her voice. But now was not the time to push it.

"Then, here's to white knights and complicated relationships," Jack said.

Charlotte Rae looked up at him shyly and smiled softly at that. They clicked glasses as the sun began its final descent over the green hills.

Chapter 8

The gaudy lights of Tahoe were a jarring contrast to the serenity of Lake Echo. As Wingate drove Jack and Charlotte Rae down the crowded highway outside of town, it seemed to Jack that there was a special perversity in placing Tahoe in the middle of one of God's most perfect natural creations.

He looked out the window and saw the gaudy red and blue lights that spelled out Harrah's, the wasted-looking patrons, coming from their old cars, many of their faces lined from years of hard work. They came for excitement, the chance for the big score. They went home full of cheap booze and with nothing but lint in their pockets. He sighed. Gamblers were the twin brothers of junkies, and equally pathetic.

Jack shook his head. He had to get that kind of morose compassion out of his brain. He was, after all, supposed to be having fun, with his good buddy, Buddy-boy himself. Buddy-boy, who was dressed to kill tonight, with a black linen banker's cowboy suit, a handsome mother-of-pearl bolo, and a jet-black ten-gallon hat. On his feet were cowboy boots made of rattlesnake hide; the toes of each boot featured the actual head of a rattlesnake. By contrast, Charlotte Rae looked elegantly understated. She had on a black Dior gown, a simple strand of white pearls, and black Manolo Blahnik high heels. Beauty and the Beast.

Buddy took her arm as the parking lot attendant took their keys. In Buddy's left hand was an expensive leather briefcase, which was filled with hundred dollar bills and a plastic gray Glock ten-millimeter handgun. As they came within twenty yards of the main door to Harrah's, Buddy veered off and went around a stand of evergreens to a stairway that lead to a red basement doorway. A uniformed doorman led them directly in; he nodded to Wingate and Charlotte Rae:

"Nice to see you, Mr. and Mrs. Wingate."

"Good to see you, Don," Wingate said. "This is a good friend of ours."

Jack followed Wingate and Charlotte Rae down a short hallway and through a double-glass door into the main gaming room. Jack noticed that the last door was conveniently located equidistant from a small bar and the blackjack tables.

"You ever play any blackjack?" Wingate asked.

"Badly," Jack said. "Cards aren't my thing."

"They aren't Buddy's either," Charlotte Rae said, "but that doesn't stop him."

Buddy turned and looked at her with his little razorback squint, then caught himself again and turned his fury into comedy.

"The truth is I am one hell of a blackjack player," he said, walking up to the table. "Just that I have been on a bad run of luck lately. Happens to the best of them."

Charlotte Rae rolled her eyes at Jack, then turned her attention to a stunning blonde waitress who appeared to take their drink order. Jack ordered vodka straight up, Charlotte Rae had champagne, and Wingate, a double Jack Daniel's.

"Loosens me up. Get the blood flowing to my cerebellum."

"Buddy?" came a happy cry.

The pit boss was a gray-haired man of about fifty-five,

dressed in a tux. His thinning hair was combed straight back, so that he had a rooster crest on his forehead.

"Enzio," Wingate said, hugging the man.

"Your usual place at the table, Buddy," he said.

"Let's hope it brings me a little luck tonight," Wingate said, as he smiled at the sexy blonde dealer.

"The dealers get younger every time we get in here," Charlotte Rae said. "Eventually they're gonna attract Woody Allen to this game."

Jack laughed.

"You don't think they do that to distract the players, do you?" he said.

"Maybe," Charlotte Rae said. "Which is bad news for Buddy. 'Cause he needs to pay all the attention he can."

Jack watched as Wingate snapped opened the briefcase and took out pile after pile of wrapped one-hundred-dollar bills.

"The man comes to play."

"Doesn't he though," Charlotte Rae said. She sipped her champagne and let out a great sigh.

When Wingate had taken all the money out of the case, he shoved it across the table toward the blonde dealer.

"Here you go, darlin'," he said. "One hundred thousand large. I'd like my chips now, if you please. By the way, what'd your mama name you, honey?"

"Lu Anne Philips, Mr. Wingate," the dealer said, smiling in a way that seemed to promise more than cards.

"How many hands will you be playing, sir?"

"Start with one," Wingate said. " 'Cause I got a feeling this is gonna be my night."

The dealer took the pile of cash and placed it in a mail chute that was attached under her side of the table. She had no sooner gotten it inside when an armed uniformed guard came to take the money away.

"Efficient, aren't they?" Charlotte Rae said.

Buddy turned around quickly.

"I could use a little support here," he said.

Charlotte Rae said nothing to that but put her right hand on Wingate's shoulder.

Jack turned and looked at the little string of hangers-on who had left the surrounding tables and were watching Wingate play his big hand. There was a fat woman with a red Saran Wrap dress that revealed all her unsightly bulges. Next to her was her husband, a man not more than five foot three without his elevator shoes. He wore a short-sleeved shirt that was made out of a crude oil product, and Jack wondered how fast he would go up if someone lit him. Next to him was a short man with his hair conked up so high that it looked like a plate of black spaghetti. He had a smile that looked more like a cry of pain. These were Wingate's people, his gallery of the grotesque, their faces leering, the smell of sweat and envy and raw need coming off of them as strongly as musk reeked from an ox. They offered little cries of support for Buddy Wingate, but it was obvious to Jack that they didn't care whether he won or not. They were there because they needed action, any kind of action. They needed the cards to fly, the money to change hands, the tension of the game. Jack looked at them all, hunched behind Wingate, and he felt his emotions run the gamut, from an almost physical revulsion, to something else—terror. For, as grotesque as they were, how different were they from him? They were night people like him; they probably went through their day lives as he went through his paperwork, in a half trance. They waited for the heat of the blackjack table, the roulette table, the same way he waited for the smell of the kill. They had to be here to stay alive and so did he. They were all of them junkies of the night.

The first bet was five thousand dollars.

Jack watched as Lu Anne dealt herself a hole card down, and Buddy's first two, straight up. This hand was over before it began. Buddy hit for an ace and a queen, and the dealer's second card was merely a six, her hole card a ten. Buddy won easily, 20–16 and quickly pocketed seventy-five hundred bucks. The table was buzzing, and Buddy lit a Cuban cigar.

"It's flowing, baby. It's all flowing. Right through these fat little digits," Buddy said, turning and smiling at Jack and Charlotte Rae. There was a kind of goofy haze on his eyes, as though he was stoned. Stoned on risks, Jack thought as he looked at Charlotte Rae, her eyes and skin translucent, as though someone had lit a candle inside her.

The tension began to build as Jack watched the second hand unfold. Buddy's first card was a king, and he wasted no time signaling for a hit by scratching the table with his fingers.

The second card came: a nine. Nineteen.

Buddy turned and looked at Charlotte Rae.

"I believe I'll stand pat," he said.

Lu Anne smiled. And took a hit. A four. Now Buddy's chances seemed better than ever. The dealer shrugged, as if all was lost, so why not take a spin. She gave herself another hit and drew a jack. With consummate professional understatement she turned over her hole card.

"Sorry, Mr. Wingate. Your bad luck."

"Twenty," Buddy said. "Damn. What was the odds of you pulling that card?"

"About three to one," she said, smiling.

From being twenty-five hundred dollars up, Buddy Wingate was now down twelve thousand five hundred.

Charlotte Rae signaled for the waitress to come over.

"As they say at the table, hit me. Champagne, please."

Jack declined to have another drink. He watched as more people drifted over to the table and found himself caught up in the action of the game. He had been to a couple of high-stakes poker games in the Valley on his last assignment, and he recalled a player named Hector Cortez who always seemed to win. A huge man with a violent nature, Cortez was coolness personified at the tables. When Jack had asked him one night what he attributed his winning ways to, he had simply said, "Memory and instinct, in that order. I remember every card played. I know the probabilities of each card showing up. The instinct comes in when you know the person you are playing, but in blackjack it's mainly memory. That and don't split your cards. That's for suckers."

Jack thought of that advice now, for Buddy Wingate had drawn a pair of eights and chose to split them. His bet this time was a mere five thousand, but he took a sip of his drink, flashed his brown eyes at the dealer, who flirted back at him.

"Let the five ride for ten, sweetheart," Buddy said.

Two for one. Jack watched with fascination and, in spite of himself, began to root for Buddy against the house.

On the first hand Buddy drew a ten.

Ordinarily, though, an eighteen stood a good chance to be a winner.

But once again luck was with Lu Anne. She drew a ten and had a nine in the hole. Nineteen, and Buddy had blown the double.

He sighed deeply, and Jack saw him slump forward in his chair, as though someone had kicked him in the ribs.

"Buddy," Charlotte Rae said, as he ordered another whiskey. "You're already down twenty thousand. Don't you think we ought to quit. Or at least change tables."

"Bullshit," Buddy said. "What we wanta do here is peel the deck. You hear me, lady?"

He stared at Lu Anne with animal ferocity.

The dealer looked over at the floor manager, Enzio, who had already overheard Buddy's request. He smiled and gave a world-weary nod of his head.

"I'm betting fifty large on this hand," Buddy said.

"Buddy," Charlotte Rae said. "For godsake. You're in a death spiral."

Buddy turned with surprising speed and grabbed Charlotte Rae by the wrist.

"You know better than to ever say anything like that. Now, shut up, darling!"

He squeezed her wrist until she gave out a small cry of pain, then he turned and pushed a huge pile of chips toward the center of the table. Jack had to restrain an urge to grab him by the throat.

Jack watched the hand unfold with the curiosity of a mourner looking at a well-preserved corpse.

Buddy drew a queen, and the dealer's face card was a seven. Then Buddy drew a nine and stayed pat at nineteen. Jack could see the sweat break out on his upper lip and watched Buddy's whole body sag forward in the chair as Lu Anne took another card . . . a seven, giving her fourteen.

"Doesn't look promising," she said. "Guess I have to take another hit."

The dealer flipped the final card. A six, which gave her twenty. And made Buddy Wingate a loser again.

"Son of a bitch," he said, reaching for his drink.

"I'm sorry, sir," she said, raking in the chips. "May you have better luck next time."

Jack watched as Buddy pushed away from the table. He was down seventy-five thousand dollars—perhaps he could still walk away with his final twenty-five grand.

"Come on, Buddy," Charlotte Rae said. "Let's go see a show. Merle Haggard is in the main room."

"Fuck Merle Haggard and the horse he rode in on," Buddy said. "Gimme another drink."

His words were slurred, and his eyes were glassy. It didn't make sense. He'd had maybe three drinks. Then Jack understood. Buddy was wasted on something besides booze. He had the glazed-over look of a man who was on downers.

"Twenty-five on the last hand, and I bet I make the greatest comeback since the fucking Buffalo Bills," he said.

Jack watched him push the money forward. There was no cockiness in the action now. It was as though he was giving the money away, the game a mere formality.

The hand was over before it began. Buddy had seventeen showing, and against the advice of almost everyone at the table, he took a hit and busted out at twenty-five. The dealer won, and Buddy demanded to see her hole card. She had a four, which went nicely with her ten. She had won on a pat hand of fourteen.

Buddy staggered to his feet and took a long sip of whiskey.

"Some fun, hey, Jackie?" he said.

"Yeah, a million laughs," Jack said. "You always this lucky?"

"Usually. But, hey, there's always more green, Jackie. Always more green."

He gave a wild little laugh, took a step forward, and nearly fell on the floor. Jack caught him and threw an arm around his back.

"Come on," Buddy said. "At least we got comps to the shows and all the drinks we want. I aim to get hammered."

He headed for the bar, one arm over Jack's shoulder. When Jack looked at Charlotte Rae, he saw that her face was a mask of humiliation and pain.

By the time they left Harrah's, Buddy Wingate was walking like a broken-field runner through the tables. He staggered over a craps table, knocking aside a small dark-faced man with a deep scar on his cheek. The man, like everyone else in Harrah's, seemed to know Buddy. But his tone wasn't friendly.

"You wanta watch running into people, Buddy," he said, straightening his tie. "That gets old real quick."

Jack waited for Buddy to go for the guy, but Buddy was strangely passive.

"Sorry," he said. "I'm heading home."

"Good idea," the guy said.

Jack stared at the man. He had mob written all over him. Even Buddy couldn't afford to offend them.

"Come on, pal," Jack said, getting his arm around Buddy's back.

"Hey, a free ride. I like that," Buddy said, and giggled a bit as Jack got him out of the door and dragged him to the car.

With a mighty effort Jack placed Buddy into the car's backseat and took the wheel.

Charlotte Rae got into the passenger side and smiled at Jack.

"You're kind of handy to have around," she said.

"Damn right he is," Buddy said, from the backseat. "Now, you get this chariot home, while I take me a little snooze."

"Sweet dreams," Jack said, as he turned the key and heard the roaring raw power of the Typhoon.

Jack stared at the mountain highway, which was brightly illuminated by the Typhoon's powerful headlight beams. From the backseat, Buddy Wingate's snores echoed throughout the cabin.

"He's going to have one hell of a hangover tomorrow," Jack said.

"No, he won't," Charlotte Rae said, smiling. "Buddy doesn't' have hangovers. He says it's because he's always got something working for him—booze, pot, pills, sometimes a little something else."

There. She had said it. Jack smiled a little, as if he had suspected as much.

"That right?" Jack said. "What's his drug of choice? No, let me guess. Downers."

"You win the Amana freezer," Charlotte Rae said, sounding a little surprised. "How'd you know?"

"'Cause he's wired all the time. Guys like that don't need coke or crank."

"God, he used to do coke," she said, a shudder in her voice. "You should have seen him behind that stuff. He'd turn into a wolverine."

"As opposed to the gentle little lamb he is now. So what's he like, Tuinals, Secs?"

"Sometimes. He used to get bootleg Quaaludes, but they're harder to come by now. Besides, he got tired of feeling like a balloon. No, these days he uses a little smack now and again."

Jack liked the "now and again" part. Made it sound like it was a weekend hobby, gardening.

"He does like to live dangerously. You into it too?"

"I've chipped a few items. But that was a long time ago."

"Is Buddy hooked?"

"No. He's wild, but he's also very smart. There's plenty of people who get down once in a while who aren't hooked."

"Yeah," Jack said. "That's right."

He gunned the powerful engine, and the car shot up a straightaway, like a sled rocket on the Bonneville Salt Flats. The dark, drooping branches of the trees made a black canopy, and Jack felt her powerful sexual presence, could smell her soft perfume.

"You say it, but you don't mean it," she said.

"You're wrong," Jack said. "What people do is their business. I don't put drugs into my body outside of a little alcohol, but I got no problem with it."

"No?" she said. "You wouldn't worry a little if you saw me shooting drugs?"

He gave a short snort of a laugh. Buddy snored like a happy hog in the backseat, but there was real danger here.

"I don't tell people what to do with their lives," Jack said. "That's for ministers, and I haven't been to church in a long time."

"That's a cute answer," she said in a voice that was practically a whisper, "but it's not the answer to the question I asked you, Jack."

"I know what you asked me," Jack said. "It might bother me a little bit. But only because I get sick seeing needles stuck into people."

"Oh," she said. "That's all, is it?"

"Yeah," Jack said. "That's all. We turn here?"

"Uh-huh," Charlotte Rae said. "I just think it's kind of sad."

"What is?"

"That I thought I'd found my white knight and it turns out he doesn't give a damn whether I live or die."

"You're right," Jack said. "That's maybe the saddest story in the world."

But he smiled at her when he said it.

He made the turn, then went up the steep, dark dirt road toward Wingate's property. But he hadn't gone twenty feet across the bumpy road when he sensed something was wrong. There was a flash off to the left of the car, something metallic illuminated by moonlight.

"Get down!" Jack said.

He reached over and, with his right hand, pushed Charlotte Rae's head down.

"What are you doing?"

"On the floor! Now!"

Jack gunned the Typhoon's engine and ducked as low as he could.

Suddenly, shots rang out from the darkness, exploding the windshield. A shower of glass cascaded in on Jack, cutting his face and hands. There was another burst, and Jack heard the back side window blow. He had already gunned the Typhoon straight ahead, trying to clear the cross fire, but he now realized he would never be able to outrun the snipers on the road. The car careened crazily forward, lurching to the left. Jack was barely able to keep it under control. More shots rang out, from behind them, and the rear windshield was smashed into a thousand shards of glass.

"It's Salazar, Buddy," Charlotte Rae whispered. She was crouched down in the seat, her eyes wide open with fear.

Jack made a mental note of her slip. . . . It was just as he had thought. Salazar's crew was taking a shot at Wingate. Good information. Now all he had to do was survive long enough to use it.

From the backseat, Jack heard a groan, and Buddy Wingate's big, whiskey-smelling face was suddenly thrust over the backseat, near Jack's.

"Son of a bitch," he said.

"Are you hit?" Jack said.

"Not yet."

"Then get the fuck down or you're gonna be," Jack said.

There was more rifle fire, and Jack saw a pair of headlights in the rearview mirror. To his left, Jack spied an opening between two huge fir trees.

"What's down there?"

"The creek, and across it, the cliff trail that goes over to Echo Lake," Charlotte Rae said.

"Hang on," Jack said.

He jerked the wheel in a hard left and sent the vehicle crashing through the underbrush.

"Holy shit," Wingate said.

"They said this son of a bitch is an off-road vehicle," Jack said. "So we're putting our faith in American advertising."

They flew downhill over jagged rocks, the car leaning wildly. Tree limbs smashed into the shattered window. Jack saw a log lying in their path, but he was hemmed in; there was no escaping it. The Typhoon's tires crashed into it and all three of its occupants were thrown upward from their seats. They smashed their heads on the roof. Jack felt blood trickling down his face, but kept his foot on the accelerator as they raced downhill. When they hit an open space on the forest floor, he straightened the rearview mirror and looked into the now-cracked glass. For a brief second he felt relieved. There was nothing behind him but fractured trees and a cloud of dust.

Then he heard an engine and saw two powerful headlights.

"Bastards . . ."

Jack tromped down on the Typhoon's powerful brake, then hit the accelerator hard. The engine made a wild whirring sound as the turbocharger kicked in. He held the steering wheel bone-tight with both hands, then let up on the brake. The engine gave a roar, and the car shot forward rapidly, the two front tires actually lifting off the ground. In seconds they were across the clearing and headed directly between two huge fir trees. There was barely enough room for them to pass through, and the tree limbs scraped like bones on the window. Jack felt his heart pumping wildly through his chest. But it had worked for now. The turbo had gotten them clear of their pursuers. The headlights had disappeared on the hill above them.

"Made it," Jack said.

"Yeah, but we're still fucked," Wingate said. "The stream's straight ahead."

"How close?" Jack said.

"About a hundred yards. And then another fifty yards down, through the trees. No way we can take a car down there."

"What happens if we turn, run parallel to the stream? Any way to find a road, go back up, and connect to the highway?"

"No way. You turn left you end up in a thicket. You turn right, you end up in more trees, too dense to drive through. The only way's across the stream, up to the north, then back across on the rope bridge."

Jack hesitated for a split second, then turned right.

"What the hell?" Wingate said.

"Hang on," Jack said.

He smashed his foot on the accelerator, turned the wheel radically to the right, running parallel to the stream below, and soon saw in front of him a thick grove of trees. There was a narrow opening between the trees. A perfect place to park the Typhoon. Jack turned the wheel violently to the left, and Charlotte Rae was thrust over into his lap, as they squealed on the hard ground. Jack hit the brakes in time to avoid a collision with a huge Douglas fir that towered over them like a silent ghost.

"Give me the pistol," Jack said.

Charlotte Rae popped open the now-empty briefcase and handed the Glock to Jack.

"Out," he said.

Charlotte Rae was out of the door instantly, and Buddy tumbled out behind her.

"Can you walk, Buddy?"

"Fuck'n A. Nothing like cold fear to sober a man up."

"Then move. Down toward the stream."

"We going fishing? 'Cause I left my tackle home."

"No," Jack said. "We're going across the stream . . . right there."

He pointed to what he hoped was a shallows.

"Then we're going up the other side."

"They could pick us off as we climb," Buddy said.

"Yeah," Jack said. "But they have to see us first. We make it up there, we can stand them off. Come on."

They scrambled madly down the bank, the three of them grabbing roots, limbs, anything that would support them. They were halfway down the hill when they heard the sound of the truck engine up above the hill, on the tree line.

"Keep down, and keep moving," Jack whispered.

Charlotte Rae stumbled over a stone and fell into Wingate, who grabbed her with one meat-hook hand.

They were at the foot of the hill now. The cool stream flowed rapidly in front of them.

"Get in the water and keep low. If they start to fire, go under and swim for the other side. See those logs on the other shore? Try and come up under them for cover. "Go!"

Jack took a step in, but Charlotte Rae and Wingate stood as still as trees.

"What the hell you waiting for, Mario Cuomo?"

"Got a little problem here, son. I don't swim."

"No?" Jack said, coming back out of the water.

He walked up next to Wingate. Up above him he could hear

doors slamming, the sound of men talking to one another in rapid Spanish.

"Time to learn, friend."

Jack shoved Wingate hard toward the stream. He fell in face-first, then came up fast. . . .

"You daddy-jacking lame son of a bitch," he coughed.

"Thank me later. Go!" Jack said.

Charlotte Rae cast a look toward the voices at the top of the hill and leapt into the water herself. She grabbed Wingate's hand and began pulling him toward the middle of the stream. Jack joined them seconds later, the coldness of the water surprising him, taking his breath away.

The moonlight shone on them like a searchlight. Jack wished he could fire at it and put out the soft yellow light. They advanced cross-stream maddeningly slowly, the current knocking Wingate down. But they were making progress, when suddenly they heard cries from above them on the shore:

"Down here. *Abajo. En la agua.*"

"*Andale. Andale.*"

Jack saw them then, coming down the hill. Two men with rifles. A third seemed to be holding a pistol in one hand, something else in the other. What was it?

Then there was a round beam of light that powerfully illuminated the water. Christ, they had a flashlight. The bastards had thought of everything.

Without a word, Jack pushed Wingate underwater.

"Swim," he commanded.

As he grabbed Wingate's arm and pulled him toward the other shore, he heard the bullets popping only a few feet away. It was an odd sensation: as they harmlessly hit the water, they seemed like children's toy bullets. He could only move slowly under water, looking back at Wingate, whose eyes bulged in panic. To his right, Charlotte Rae had already reached the logs and was surfacing between two of them, under the cover of brush. Jack felt the pocket of his coat. The Glock was supposed to be waterproof. God help him if it wasn't true.

Jack headed for the logs, which he could see dimly in front of him. He came up quickly and gasped for breath. Wingate came up a half second later. He was rasping badly; it sounded as though his lungs were bursting.

Jack looked at the other side of the stream. No sign of the assassins yet. Jack knew the men were scrambling down the same hill they'd just come from, which left them only a few precious minutes before the men would be on the opposite shore with their high-powered rifles. This was the only chance they would have to climb.

"Come on," Jack said. "We've got to make that bluff."

"No way," Wingate said, gasping. "I can't."

"Bullshit," Jack said. "Get out of the water, now!"

"I'm telling you son. I ain't got the wind."

Jack tried to keep the chilling hand of panic off his throat. He looked around. Downstream.

"All right," he said. "You two stay here. Under this brush. Don't move."

"But they'll be coming," Charlotte Rae said.

"That's right," Jack said.

He scrambled up onto the muddy bank, looked ten yards downstream, and saw a log floating by the river's edge, caught on some roots or a rock.

Jack checked the load in his pistol.

"Stay down," he said.

The two of them hid their heads, and Jack tossed a couple more branches over them.

Then he ran ten yards downstream and got back into the water. He was right. The log was caught up on a jagged boulder. It was anybody's guess how long it would stay that way, but he had to take the chance. If he hid farther up the hill, he would be out of reliable pistol range.

He cocked the hammer and sat there waiting, his feet getting numb. He looked at the alien moon and suddenly felt an overwhelming desire for a blanket and a drink. It wasn't fair. He might die protecting the very people he hoped to bust. Why not let these guys . . . undoubtedly Salazar's men . . . kill the two of them and be done with it? He laughed at the sheer absurdity of it and looked out across the dark, rippling water.

Less than twenty seconds later he saw them, the three men,

on the other side. They came slowly down to the clearing, moving cautiously, not speaking.

Their leader, the one with the pistol and the searchlight, looked up and down the river. Then he turned on his powerful lamp and trained it on the other side of the river, sweeping it up and down the bank. Jack felt panic rising in his stomach.

The light played across the bank, at first landing on the logs under which Wingate and Charlotte Rae were hiding. It stayed there for what seemed like forever, before moving on, sweeping downstream until it landed on Jack's log.

He sucked in his breath deeply and ducked underwater, but the light stayed right over him, like a halo.

Jack waited, his chest burning. It almost seemed amusing to him, that he could be so wet and yet his lungs felt as though they were literally roasting over a bonfire. He would have to come up soon, then it would be all over. They would pick him off with their M-16s.

But at last, the leader moved the searchlight on.

And then Jack heard him grunt to the other two men.

"Go. Over there."

Jack came up, gasping, raising his head just above the level of the log. The two men hesitated for a second, looking at one another. Though he couldn't see their faces, he knew what they were thinking: What if someone was waiting for them?

Suddenly Jack felt clammy with fear again.

What if the killers decided to split up, one of them crossing at another place? That would spoil everything. He was counting on the fact that they wouldn't play it that way. They had to figure that the three people they were chasing were scared shitless, were just trying to put as much distance between them and their pursuers as possible.

Jack waited, cocking the gun.

He watched as the two men came across the stream. They moved awkwardly, their M-16s slung over their backs. He got them in his sights, waited, waited, the smell of his own fear making him gag.

As they moved closer, the leader on the other side started sweeping the light back again. Jack wanted to wait until they were ten yards away, nearly on top of Wingate and Charlotte Rae, but if the light came over him then, he would be blinded. Finished. It was now or never.

He aimed at the first man, a short, black-haired man with a great black beard. Aimed at the center of his chest.

And fired.

There was a flash of light and then a scream in the still night. The man fell heavily backward into the dark water.

The second man panicked for a split second, trying desperately to get his carbine off his shoulder. Jack saw the searchlight beam sweeping toward him and fired again, but missed.

Now the man was no longer coming toward Jack's side of the river. Instead, he fled toward the side from which he came.

The man with the spotlight was still on the shore, taking out his pistol, but he seemed confused, hesitant, and Jack knew that now was his chance. It wasn't enough to scare them back.... They would simply wait in the trees, until Jack, Wingate, and Charlotte Rae came out of their hiding places. He had to take the offensive now, while the element of surprise worked in his favor. He surfaced from his hiding place and began to wade directly toward the fleeing man, screaming wildly as he went.

"Oooooooh pigggggg, Sooooooieeeeeee!!"

The man in the water was panicked now. He half turned and saw a madman with a gun coming toward him, shooting, screaming some mad, savage pig gibberish. He let out a frightened cry and waded furiously toward the shore. Jack fired at his back, and the man toppled into the water and was borne downstream by the current. This left only the man with the light . . . but when he saw what had happened to the second of the two assassins, he dropped the light and ran down the beach, into the trees.

Jack dove back into the water now and headed toward Wingate and Charlotte Rae.

"Come on. Both of you."

"Son of a bitch," Wingate said. "You called the hogs, son. That was fucking amazing."

"Thank Bill Clinton for me," Jack said. "But we still have to get to the rope bridge and then to your house. How far is it?"

"About a hundred yards north," Charlotte Rae said. "But what if that other one . . . ?"

She shuddered and looked suddenly lovely and afraid.

"I don't think he'll bother us," Jack said. "They're finished for tonight. Come on."

Wingate looked at Jack and shook his head.

"You saved my life, son," he said. "You didn't learn all that body guarding for Rizzo, now did you?"

"Not all of it," Jack said. "I did a little tour with the Army . . . Ranger unit."

"Be all you can fucking be." Buddy whistled. "Son of a bitch. Well, I guess I owe you an explanation."

"Save it," Jack said. "We've got a ways to go."

Wingate nodded gravely. There was nothing of the wild redneck yahoo in his face anymore. He looked sober and deadly serious.

"Then let's get to it," he said.

They crawled up the moonlit riverbank then and, crouching low, moved fast toward the bridge.

They arrived back at the house in forty minutes, soaking wet, and freezing cold. Snow had found its ways into Jack's boots and his feet felt numb. When he took off his socks, he saw that his toes were blue.

Charlotte Rae handed Jack a glass of brandy, and the three of them huddled by the fire. She'd taken off her dress and put on a plaid bathrobe and wool slippers. She drank her Courvoisier and nestled in Wingate's big arms, her long right leg protruding from the robe, naked almost to the thigh. Jack had a splitting headache from the tension generated in the chase, but it was nothing compared to the ache he felt in his groin.

"Guess you want to know what the hell that was all about out there tonight," Wingate said.

"Yeah, as a matter of fact," Jack said.

Jack liked the sound of his own voice now. He sounded tough, in control . . . and for now, maybe he was.

"Well, I aim to tell you," Wingate said, getting up and walking with a flourish to the corner bar.

"You see, when I started Discount Rodeo, I had a partner named Salazar. Latino boy . . . smart, good with the women. Him and me had us some real good times . . . gambling and hustling the gals . . . but I found out one day that this ole boy has some serious problems with drugs. . . . Turns out he's knocking down on our profits. So I tell him I want to dissolve the partnership. . . . Course he don't want to. . . . It turns out it's all he's got. Well, to make a sad story short, things took a turn toward UGLY, and we had a very unpleasant divorce. He ended up in jail. Day he went to stir, he swore vengeance. Tonight he almost got himself a piece."

Wingate shook his head, as if he were depressed by the vileness of human kind, picked up a shimmering crystal decanter of brandy, and poured Jack and Charlotte Rae generous drinks.

"Son, you handled yourself real good out there tonight. I could use a guy like you. Help me out . . . with this here problem. After all, it wouldn't be the first time you done this line of work."

Jack smiled, shook his head.

'Salazar," he said. "He get sprung out of jail?"

"Two weeks ago," Wingate said. "So what about it? The pay is gonna be top dollar."

"It ought to be," Charlotte Rae said, smiling at Jack.

Jack smiled at her, stayed in character.

"Thanks," he said, "but I don't think so, Buddy."

Wingate looked genuinely surprised and a little hurt.

"Why the hell not?" he said.

"What difference does it make?" Jack said, smiling and taking a sip of the brandy. "I just don't think I want the gig."

"Don't tell me you're afraid," Wingate said. " 'Cause I seen you down at the stream tonight, and you didn't even sweat."

"I don't think Jack's afraid of anything," Charlotte Rae said, staring into his eyes now.

'Well, you're both wrong there," Jack said. "I was plenty scared. But that isn't the reason. It's just that I'm looking for something bigger than 'companion' work these days. That was all fine when I was a kid, but a man's gotta move onward and upward."

Wingate smiled and shook his head.

"You got something better, that it?"

"Nope," Jack said, smiling. "Not a damned thing. But that's the beauty of my situation. Long as I'm not tied up with a job, I can keep on looking."

"Till your money runs out," Wingate said, but there was a kind of admiration in his voice.

"I don't think Jack cares about the money so much," Charlotte Rae said. "It's something else he's looking for. I wonder what it might be?"

She smiled at Jack and sipped her brandy.

"Me too," Wingate said. "I wonder. Well, here's to our new friendship and to wasting our enemies. And if you change your mind, Jack, you come and see me."

Jack clicked his glass with Wingate and his wife. He could have taken the job then and there, but something told him not to. Not just yet. They had to want him more. Both of them. Then he'd suck them both in.

If he didn't get involved with her. If he could keep himself cooled out, everything was going to work out just fine. Right now, he was running the show.

Chapter 9

Two days later, Jack sat in Topper's Bar, recounting his adventures to C.J.

"Man, you are lucky you are here, baby," C.J. said.

"Don't tell me you'd miss me," Jack said.

"No, I wouldn't miss you exactly," C.J. said. "I didn't say

that. But sometimes I think maybe you one of the few white people who got potential."

"Well, I'm deeply flattered," Jack said.

"How did Zampas take it?" C.J. said.

"He asked me why I didn't kill the other guy too," Jack said, smiling.

C.J. laughed as he washed off a pizza serving plate.

"He spoils you. No doubt about it. Well, I'm glad you ain't got any new holes in your head, partner."

C.J. smiled, then looked toward the door, as they both heard a car horn.

"My lunch date," Jack said.

"You be careful what you eat," C.J. said. "Cream puffs can be fatal."

Jack looked out the doorway at Charlotte Rae Wingate in her red vintage '65 T-Bird. She'd called that morning, said she was picking up the car at the shop, and offered to take him for a ride to the beach.

"Don't worry, partner," Jack said. "I'm into health foods this week."

He smiled, put down a glass, and headed to the street.

"I missed you, Jack," she said, sitting across from him in the red bucket seat and downshifting as if she were an old hand at Daytona.

"Really?" Jack said. "How about Buddy, did he miss me too?"

"You're too hard on him," she said. "He's very grateful."

Jack laughed and looked her over. She had on a tight black knit blouse and Levi's that fit her like they'd been molded onto her legs.

"Funny, I would never have taken him for the grateful type."

She laughed, a little nervously Jack thought, as they roared out Sunset toward the beach.

"Did you just think I was going to disappear?" she said. And though she was smiling, there was pain in her voice.

"I guess I thought our business was over," Jack said, coolly.

She smiled and rubbed her right hand sensuously over her right leg.

"I was hoping maybe you'd miss me," she said, downshifting and pulling away from the light at the Beverly Wilshire Hotel.

"Yeah. Maybe I did, a little," Jack said.

She turned and looked at him and wet her lips with her tongue.

"You seem nervous, Jack. Do I make you nervous?"

"Nah," Jack said. "Maybe it's a little bit dangerous hanging out with you, that's all."

"Gee," she said, "I would have thought you'd like a challenge."

"A challenge is one thing," Jack said, dropping the sexual banter. "Hanging around with people who might and up dead is another. Especially when they're not straight with me."

"I don't have any idea what you mean," she said.

"Sure you do," Jack said. "You don't think I really bought that story about your competitors trying to gun you down because of some cooked books?"

She looked at him and shook her head.

"I don't know why not," she said. "Discount's a ruthless business."

"So's summer camp," Jack said. "Tell me another story."

She smiled and patted his thigh.

"Don't be mad. Look, I never discuss my husband's business. It must be awful to be so suspicious of everybody."

"I'm not . . . of everybody," Jack said.

Charlotte Rae hit the accelerator, and the T-Bird screamed around the banked curves in front of UCLA.

"You look so serious," Charlotte Rae said. She trod the accelerator and sent the T-Bird speeding through the light at the Bel Air gate.

"Why don't you reach back there into the boot. I've got something to lighten your mood."

Jack reached behind him and felt something cold. He pulled out a bottle of freezing Cristal. She smiled at him. . . . There was a sudden sweetness in that smile, as if she enjoyed giving him pleasure. He twisted off the gold wrapping and popped the cap. The champagne came spilling out fast and stained the front of his shirt.

"What a waste," Charlotte Rae said, staring across at him. "There's glasses back there too."

Jack reached back again, found an ice bucket and two glasses. Delicately, he poured the champagne and handed Charlotte Rae a glass.

She smiled and held up her glass, and the sun glistened off the crystal.

"To new friendships," she said.

"To surviving long enough to make them," Jack said.

"Now, there's a romantic toast," she said, pouting.

"It's against the rules to be romantic with a married woman," Jack said, staring at her.

"I guess so," she said.

"On the other hand," Jack said, "maybe I want to forget some of the rules."

She looked nervous at that. Jack poured her another glass of champagne. She drank it and shook her head.

"Sometimes I think that it was listening to the rules that got me here in the first place."

Jack poured the last two glasses of champagne into her glass. They were moving fast downhill past the entrance to Will Rogers State Park.

"I don't know," he said. "I've seen worse jails."

"What do you know about it, tough guy?" she said.

He wanted to reach over, grab her wrist. But he couldn't let that go down—not now, not anytime.

"Driver, where you taking me?" he said, laughing.

"Fantasyland," she said.

"Buddy going to be there dressed like the March Hare?" Jack said.

"No," she said. "Buddy's out of town. I thought you might like to see our place at the beach."

"Sounds nice," Jack said. "My only question is, does Buddy know where you are?"

"Of course," she said. "He sent me."

That set him back again. He knew it was true, but he hadn't expected her to cop to it so quickly.

"He sent me because he wants me to convince you to come see him again. He wants you to work for him."

"Then we're both wasting time," Jack said.

"I told him that it was useless," Charlotte Rae said, shrugging and smiling at him.

"Then why are you here?" Jack said.

"I'm not sure," she said. She looked away quickly from him.

He felt his heart quicken.

"Maybe it's because of the way you listen," she said. "I have a weakness for men who like to hear my story."

"Yeah, but you got a lot of weaknesses," he said.

She sighed and reached over and rubbed his cheek.

"Buddy says it gives me texture."

He started to say only assholes use words like "texture," but her hand was too hot on his skin, and suddenly he was short of breath.

The house was seventy-five feet from the ocean. It was made of redwood and glass, and just sitting on the beachfront porch made Jack feel as though he had entered a miniseries.

"I used to dream of having a place like this," Jack said. "A place where you could hear the surf all night. It's fantastic."

Charlotte Rae walked to the steps. She kicked off her sandals and ran down to the ocean.

"What changed your mind?"

"I don't know exactly," Jack said. "Could be that after a certain amount of time, you don't want to dream of things you can never have. It makes you bitter, and only losers are bitter."

"I think there's nothing sadder than seeing people give up their dreams," Charlotte Rae said. "Come on. Let's walk."

He left the champagne bottle on the porch and joined her by the sea. They walked close to the water, so that a fine mist covered both of them.

"You're wrong about dreams," Jack said. "There's something sadder than giving them up."

"What, Mr. Philosopher?" she said, turning and looking at him with a sincerity that belied her flip tone.

"When you have to pay too high a price for them," Jack said.

"Do you think I have?" she said.

"Only you would know that," Jack said.

They came to an inlet, and Jack found a large smooth rock. She sat down on it and looked at the sun sinking over the Pacific.

"I know what you think," she said, "but I still believe you have to be willing to take a risk to get what you want. You think Buddy's a crude asshole . . . but he's brave, and I love him for that."

Jack nodded and took her hand.

"You're going to have to give a better reading than that," he said.

"What do you mean?"

"I mean, when you got to the part where you had to say 'love,' you looked at the ground."

He pulled her to him then, half expecting her to resist, but she let him do it and threw her arms around his neck. Her mouth was moist, and she smelled like the sea.

"You think you can do whatever you want with me, don't you, Jack," she said.

He felt the heat coming off her, passion rising in him in waves. He could hear Zampas's words, "never, ever fuck somebody you're working," . . . but the voice seemed remote, like a commercial you've heard so many times that it becomes syllables mumbled by an idiot.

All he knew was that he wanted her, had wanted her from the first moment in front of Mann's Chinese, and now they were somehow walking back to the house, arm in arm, and the heat coming off both of their bodies was almost comical in its intensity. Only Jack wasn't laughing. This was dead wrong; he knew it . . . and he had to find a way to stop and intended to, even as they went back into the house and didn't make it into the bedroom, but instead, sank down on the blue rug. Then she was burying herself on top of him, saying his name again and again . . . and he was starting to take off her blouse, when she stopped him, pushed him away.

"What's wrong?" he said.

She said nothing but seemed suddenly shy, and Jack understood her reluctance to get naked in front of him. There were bruises on her left breast and a larger purplish one just below it, which ran all the way around her side.

"Buddy do this?" Jack said.

She bit her lower lip and shook her head.

"No," she said, but she shut her eyes as she spoke.

"Then how?"

"It happened the other night, when we were trying to get away from those guys up at Tahoe. Falling down the hill . . . I guess."

"Sell me something else," Jack said.

She looked at him fiercely, eyes wide open now.

"That's what happened. I'm telling you. Come here. I don't want to waste time talking."

She reached up and pulled him down on her and kissed him hard, and Jack felt the heat rising from her again, felt as though they were melting into one another. Then he had her pants off, and he was entering her, and he was riding above and she was so tight, yet incredibly soft inside, like wet satin, and she was saying, "Jack, Jack . . . Jesus, Jack," and he watched her face, straining with pleasure, and gave everything he had to her, freely, and he didn't care anymore what anyone said, or how many codes he was breaking, fuck the codes, he wanted her. Wanted all of her. Now.

Afterward she fell into his arms, and they lay still, hearing the crashing of the sea.

They slept for a while, in the middle of the floor. Somehow she ended up curled in his arm, and when he finally awoke, it was with a shudder. There were those thirty seconds of sheer terror . . . he had no idea where he was. Then he heard the roar of the surf again and saw the sliver of moon over Malibu and looked at her face, tanned and sweet and childlike. He brushed her blonde hair away from her cheek, and he felt something overtaking him, some tenderness that he hadn't expected, but now that he recognized it, there was no escaping or denying it.

His mouth was dry, and he disengaged himself from her,

felt a little chill coming in through the screen windows, and walked to the couch to get a quilt for her. He picked it up, started to spread it over her sleeping body . . . and saw the bruises again. Gently, Jack turned her over on her stomach and saw older, yellowish-green bruises on her back. There was no way they could have come from their scramble in the brush.

No, she had been beaten, with fists or perhaps with a blunt instrument.

He sat down, cross-legged, next to her and stared down at the bruises, then noticed more on the back of her calves. Someone had kicked her there. He remembered the story she had told him about Buddy Wingate saving her from the slob in Texas and the look she had given him when he had asked her, "And how does he treat you?" Now he had his answer. Jack thought of the way Buddy had talked to Jules Furthman, of Zampas's warnings. He had heard it all, but somehow he hadn't really been listening. Because right up to this very second, Jack had still taken Buddy for some kind of goof.

Now he knew that Buddy Wingate was something else entirely. He beat her, beat her badly. Jack ran his palm across her cheek and thought of Buddy Wingate's huge, calloused hands. She was Buddy's property. He felt he could beat her anytime he wanted . . . because she lived in fear—fear that she would lose the houses at Tahoe and Malibu and the candy-apple red T-Bird. Jack thought of her smile, her quick wit and of her sweetness that had taken him by surprise, and it occurred to him that he was lost, because now he knew for certain what he'd only suspected before. Buddy-boy was a particular kind of monster, and there couldn't really be an adequate jail term for him—not even if he drew seventy-five years.

Jack looked at the bruises on Charlotte Rae's body, and knew that he would have to make Buddy pay, personally. He would have to take it out in flesh. Nothing else would do.

He laid the quilt over her bare, tanned shoulders, kissed her lightly on the cheek and walked out to the porch to stare at the moonlit beach. He had to get himself under control, but even the calming, rhythmical surf couldn't push her bruises from his mind.

Chapter 10

Bob Valle wondered if he was being followed.

He'd gotten on the Hollywood Freeway at Sunset and noticed a blue Trans Am not far behind him. It might be paranoia, he thought, especially given the meeting he was going to. Just because the guy was out there on the road at quarter to midnight, just because the guy had been a couple of carlengths behind him at Highland and Sunset and had then gotten on the Hollywood Freeway when he did, didn't mean a thing.

Still, you couldn't be too careful.

Valle crossed lanes, headed to the Pasadena Freeway, then looked into his rearview mirror.

The blue Trans Am was still behind him, lying back there, two cars between them. It still didn't prove anything, of course.

Valle saw his next exit come up quickly, Hill Street. He turned right, went around the cloverleaf, and downshifted as he came to Chinatown.

He looked behind him. The blue Trans Am was still there, fifty feet back.

A little sweat broke out on Valle's face. The guy might be a tail, a tail who'd gotten wind of what Valle was up to, prying into locked files . . . asking questions of the wrong people.

Now to his left Valle saw a sign for the Ozawa bakery, famous for its elaborately decorated cakes. Inside, he could see a young man and woman standing next to a five-foot high wedding cake. The girl was giggling and the man held her close, while a baker squirted icing curlicues on top of the cake. Watching this little tableau, Valle felt a surge of anger and envy.

He imagined the lovers were innocents, young and hot for each other and for the life they were to lead together He envied them for it. Though he was only forty-one, Valle had long ago lost any remnant of his own innocence.

The innocent were slaughtered in this world. That was one thing he knew for sure.

He turned the corner sharply and quickly pulled his '89 Subaru into an available parking space.

If the Trans Am turned the corner as well, Valle would pull out and be behind it. He didn't want to play games, however, just lose the tail.

Now he waited, looking tensely into the rearview mirror.

A car was coming around the corner, but it wasn't the Trans Am. It drove by him without incident. Valle waited, looked. The Trans Am was gone. Must have turned off another street.

It was okay. He was pretty sure now the guy wasn't following him after all.

He turned the key and pulled out of the parking space. He thought of the kids in the bakery again. They'd learn . . . he thought bitterly. Eventually, everyone learns about betrayal.

And once that happened, Valle thought, you didn't care about joy anymore—didn't care about laughter or, God help you, friendship or honor or any of the other bullshit ideals you used to live by.

What you really wanted was knowledge, knowledge about your enemies, knowledge that you would use to destroy the cocksuckers.

Valle turned into the underground parking lot for the Empress Pavilion Restaurant. That was fitting, given his black mood, for it was the restaurant where he and Walker and some of the other agents used to come in the old days, when they had just begun their careers. As he took his parking ticket from the automatic teller, he thought of the fun they used to have drinking Chinese beer and eating the terrific seafood dishes in the Empress. They were like a gang of college kids. The Four Musketeers. And wasn't that two lifetimes ago?

Valle drove up to the third floor and parked in space 23, as he had arranged. He sat and waited for his man to show—and felt envious of the whole fucking world, which was in bed, happily asleep.

Poindexter showed twenty minutes later. He was a round little man who wore old, battered safari jackets and Eddie Bauer flannel shirts that he never bothered to press; he had a dirty little professorial mustache and drove a dirty little rented Honda. He reminded Valle of a once-promising English teacher who'd gone to seed at some small-cow college. Poindexter parked four spaces away and blinked his lights twice. Valle was intensely irritated by this. There was nobody around in this godforsaken place, so why bother with all the spy-craft? But that was Poindexter. He went by the book, and he loved any chance to make things dramatic.

Valle blinked his own lights twice, then both men got out and walked toward each other.

"Hello, Bob," Poindexter said. His breath smelled of gin.

"How's your health?" Valle said, feeling an even greater irritation. He wanted to drop the code, but he knew that Poindexter would walk if he did. Poindexter was terrified of being overheard and even more so of being recorded.

"My health is not as good as I would like," Poindexter said.

"No?"

"No. I saw my doctor and he told me that I should take his advice and stay where it's sunny."

"He sounds like a very cautious man," Valle said.

"He is a very sensible man," Poindexter said. He took out a gold toothpick and worked on the yellow teeth below the nicotine-stained mustache. "And quite successful. His motto is, let the others become specialists. He's happy right where he is, as a good old-fashioned internist. At which he's doing very well."

"That's fine for him," Valle said. "But I want to know his diagnoses just the same."

Poindexter rubbed his bottom lip. He put the toothpick back

into his shirt pocket. When he spoke again, his eyes pinched together.

"He said that the situation is critical. That the best course of action is to let the game run its course."

Suddenly, Bob Valle's patience ran out. He reached over and grabbed the startled Poindexter.

"Cut the shit. We're talking a major betrayal here. You owe me, and I want to hear a name."

Poindexter may have looked like a rat, but he had survived a long time. He coolly grabbed Valle's hand and pulled it from his throat.

"You're a fool," he said. "What's done is done."

"Tell me. You owe me," Valle said.

"The disease is in the family, just as you thought," Poindexter said. "And nothing can be done. You understand?"

"Yeah," Valle said. "I understand. But it stinks."

Poindexter rubbed his hand over his shirt, straightening out what Valle had roughed up.

"You used to be a good agent, Bob," he said. "And as such, you must remember that in many cases the wisest thing to do is to do nothing. Let the disease run its course. Good night. And be well."

Poindexter turned and walked to his car. Valle watched him slide his big, satisfied belly under the steering wheel, slam the door, and drive away down the ramp. . . .

And envied Poindexter his calmness. . . .

But not his attitude. There were serious things going down here: betrayal, pure and simple. He'd already lost out once; how many more times would he have to lose before he did something about it?

Well, at least he knew what he had come to find out. Now he would have to decide what course of action to take. He knew Poindexter was right about one thing. Any course was dangerous.

He went back to his own car and pulled away. When he was safely down the ramp, a black man of about fifty stepped out from behind the concrete pillar to his right. He was dressed as a workman, but in his hand was a mini–tape recorder with a powerful, ambient microphone. He clicked it off, stuck it in his pocket, and walked back up the ramp to an exit on the fourth floor. He had to hurry. His contact man in the blue Trans Am was due to pick him up outside at 12:15, and he couldn't afford to be late.

Chapter 11

Jack drove his black Mustang down a dirt road deep in the deep heart of the Valley. His head was throbbing, and he felt a violent pressure in his temples. Outside on the sunbaked, dusty road, it was 110 degrees, and his air conditioner was barely working. The combination of the heat, which crept through the windows like some insidious gas, his memories of Charlotte Rae's beautiful but bruised body rising to meet his own, and the voice of Assistant Director Ted Michaels made him feel as though he was drowning in a whirlpool of slime.

He had wakened this morning at Buddy's beach house and told himself that he wasn't going to make love to her again, that this was only a one-time thing, something he had to get out of his soul, that he was blowing it big-time . . . and he felt now that he might have resisted, but she had done something he had found irresistible. Half awake, she had put her head on his chest and begun to cry softly. Against his will he found himself softening and stroking her hair, more like her father or big brother than a lover. It was the same feeling he'd experienced the night before, a species of tenderness that surprised, even shocked him.

Before he had wanted her, dreamed of her. Now there was something else going on, something far more dangerous. He was beginning, he knew, to care for her . . . because beneath the wisecracks and the blonde hair was somebody who needed and responded to his own throttled tenderness, and when they made love this morning, there was a sweetness that engulfed them both and that, he now knew, was undeniable.

He needed her. Not only that, he wanted to save her . . . though he almost laughed at the sheer hopelessness of the idea. When the time came, he was going to have to take her down. But maybe, maybe if she helped him, if she flipped on Buddy, he could get her reduced time. He laughed bitterly. Yeah, he could get her five to ten, and he could get conjugal visiting rights.

Christ, it was like a fucking *True Detective* headline: "Our Love Survived the Big House." Who the fuck was he kidding?

He slammed on the air conditioner again, felt the heat strangling him, and thought of Michaels. What if Michaels learned that he was sleeping with Charlotte Rae? Michaels was already pissed at him anyway. In the debriefing this morning, Michaels had taken him apart. According to Michaels, Jack had acted irresponsibly and foolishly in shooting back at his pursuers at Echo Lake. What Jack should have done was simply outrun them. Jack had pointed out that it was extremely tough to outrun bullets, but Michaels still insisted that he'd compromised the undercover. Michaels had been more intractable than ever, which made Jack think that he had some other agenda, that he wanted to put the screws to the whole operation. Which he very well might pull off, if he knew about Jack and Charlotte Rae.

Jack drove on, trying to put her out of his mind. Why had Wingate asked him to come out here into the deep Valley anyway? This wasn't the Valley that East Coasters he'd met liked to make fun of—the home of goofy Valley Girls who actually squealed, "Fer sher" and "Oh, ma gosh!"—nor the Valley of endless glittering shopping malls, swimming pools, and expensive German cars. This wasn't white-people-Encino-and-Woodland-Hills-land but farther out, past all that, Sunland, a place where rednecks lived in little adobe houses, with maybe a horse trailer hitched to the side of the carport.

Looking at the directions he had scrawled on a Publishers Clearing House envelope (CONGRATULATIONS JACK WALKER, YOU'VE QUALIFIED TO WIN 5 MILLION DOLLARS ! ! !), Jack turned left on a dirt road and saw cows grazing. What was Wingate doing out here anyway?

Jack turned left down another dirt road and within forty feet saw a wooden house, a kind of cowboy bunkhouse, with logs and a cedar-shingle roof. Suddenly Jack heard the sound of gunfire. He felt his pulse race, and he pulled the car into a parking space, snapped open his glove compartment, and got out his nine-millimeter handgun.

He opened the door, crouched down, and heard five more shots go off. The sound came from maybe twenty feet away, in a clearing. Then Jack heard laughter, the unmistakable high-pitched cackle of his host, Buddy Wingate.

"Son of a bitch," Buddy said. "You are fucking amazing, Canyon."

Canyon? Had Jack heard the name right?

He walked from the car now, around a stand of sweet-smelling eucalyptus trees, and found himself at a firing range. There in front of him under a shingled gazebo was Buddy Wingate, dressed in Western garb—white ten-gallon cowboy hat, plaid cowboy shirt with pearl buttons, ridiculously tight Levi's, which accentuated his sagging gut. The topper was a handsome beaded-leather belt and holster, which held a still-smoking six-gun. Standing a few feet away from Wingate was a grizzled, wasted-looking old man, replete with sagging jowls, a T-shirt that said Springdale, Arkansas, Rodeo, Southwestern Champ 1978. Unlike Wingate, the old-timer looked to be the real McCoy. The face was drawn and wasted, but there was life and sprightliness and a light that sparkled emerald green in the eyes. Suddenly, Jack felt that he had known this man before, in some past life. Even his gun seemed familiar, a pearl-handled Colt .45 six-shooter.

"Well, well. Look who has graced us with his presence," Buddy Wingate said. "Young Jack McKenna. And holding a nasty-looking pistol, nonetheless. Well, you can't use that here, *hombre*. This here is the Wild fucking West. We don't even acknowledge such weapons, ain't that right, Canyon?"

"You got it, hoss," the other man said.

"You wouldn't happen to know who this cowpuncher is, would you, Jackie?"

"Canyon Caine," Jack said. "My daddy used to see all your pictures. I just saw one last week myself on cable."

"Som of a bitch, you are all right, hoss. How 'bout that, Mr. Wingate? This young fellah remembers ole Canyon."

"On account of you are totally unforgettable," Buddy Wingate said.

Wingate took out his six-shooter now and turned and aimed it at the target ten feet to his left. It was a great hulking black shadow with a big six-gun. There were a couple of holes in the sinister target's head and a few dead center in his heart, and about twenty-five that came close to him but hit the white border around him instead.

Buddy turned quickly and fired at the target, six quick shots. They hit the target in a sporadic manner, some nailing the head, some landing in the arms and legs, and one or two lodging in the chest.

"Your turn, cowpoke," Wingate said.

Canyon smiled, aimed his gun, and fired off six quick rounds. Every shot hit the target dead-on, right between the eyes.

He smiled and, turning toward Jack, gave a hint of a grin, and for a second Jack could see the Canyon Caine of old, the chaps-wearing bronco rider, who was the idol of every kid in America in the 1940s.

"Waal," Buddy Wingate said, ambling over to the target, "looks as though you nailed this *hombre* a few times, Canyon."

"Just a couple of lucky shots," Canyon said. "I used to be quite the shooter, son, but nowadays Buddy usually outguns me."

Buddy laughed and blew smoke from his own gun.

"You really seen my pictures, son?"

"Yeah," Jack said. "My dad got them all on tape. You were his favorite cowboy. He told me all about these fan clubs you used to have. . . ."

"Ah, the Little Pards," Canyon said, a sudden happiness in

his voice. "They was all my children, yessir. Well, that's right kind of you to remember. There's some who forgot ole Canyon. But I can tell you this, I'm about to make a comeback with the help of ole Buddy Wingate here. We might get the Pards riding down the trail again yet."

"That's certainly true, Canyon," Wingate said, looking at the target with distaste.

Canyon's green eyes shimmered a little, but this time with fear, and Jack watched him reach down to the ground, behind a hitching post, and pick up a bottle of Kentucky Gentleman. He took a long pull, and then he seemed to sag back upon himself. Wingate regarded him with a sneer. If contempt and jealousy had been bullets, Jack thought, the old cowboy star would be lying on the streets of Laredo wrapped in white linen.

"I was darn lucky to meet you, Buddy," Canyon added, which made Jack feel embarrassment and pain for the old cowboy star.

"Damn right you are there, *hombre*," Buddy Wingate said. "See, I recalled ole Canyon in his heyday there for Republic Pictures. Them B-movies, Saturday afternoon, serial watching, jujube-eating classics. But with the advent of television, 'ole Canyon here ended up going on the rodeo circuit. From whence he came."

"It weren't all that bad, Mr. Wingate" Canyon said, his voice trembling, as he took another drink of whiskey. "Folks liked us real well."

"Yeah, I'm certain they did," Buddy Wingate said. "I'm sure you liked playing Fort Smith and Pine Bluff after being a movie star. How come you never made it on the TV?"

"Fucking TV," Canyon said, more than a hint of roughness and anger in his voice. "It's what killed the Bs. . . . Little buckaroos didn't wanta go to the picture show no more when they could watch Rogers and Autry free on the idiot box."

"*Whoaa*, my, my, ain't we the bitter soul," Wingate said. "My guess is you had a little bottle problem, son."

The old cowboy looked at Wingate in a steely way, and for a second Jack thought that Canyon Caine would go for Buddy's throat. But Buddy smiled and opened his arms in mock surrender.

"Just joshing, Canyon. You're a great star, and we're gonna see to it that you ride the celluloid range again. Hey, ain't we already going great guns with our new commercial?"

"That we are, Mr. Wingate," Canyon said.

"See, Canyon and me are doing a Discount Rodeo shoot-out. . . . Course I plug him dead," Buddy said. "It's real funny, plays off his image, and it'll reintroduce him to the fickle American public. Someday, who knows, we might get him a picture again."

Canyon managed a smile at that.

Wingate smiled back. Jack expected it to be a triumphant smirk, as though he had put Canyon in his place and now could afford largesse, but he was surprised to see real respect and even affection in Buddy Wingate's face.

"Listen," Buddy said, in a suddenly emotional voice, "this fella gave me the happiest moments of my life in the theater. I mean it, man. I would go into the theater and I would forget my old man, who was never home except when he was so fucking loaded all he wanted to do was whip up on somebody, namely me, and I would see ole Canyon gunning down the baddies, and I would say to myself, that is what I am gonna do someday, blast all the assholes and all the jerks who don't take care of their kids."

Buddy Wingate then walked over to Canyon Caine and hugged him in a deep, sentimental gesture, and Jack understood that Buddy meant it—maybe not all of it, but some of it—and in his own twisted and demented way, he was going to try to both ruin and help Canyon Caine. God Bless America.

"Gotta run some errands. Nice meeting you, *amigo.*"

"Same here," Jack said.

Canyon smiled and managed a two-fingered ear-to-eye salute, his classic trademark in the old days, when he stood high atop a purple mountain with his big sorrel, Smokey, and the picture faded to black. Then he shuffled off toward the bunkhouse.

"I love that ole boy," Buddy said.

"I can tell," Jack said, aiming his pistol at the target's heart and squeezing off three fast rounds.

Buddy Wingate looked up and saw the holes clustered dead center in the left ventricle and gave out a little sigh-yodel.

"Now, ain't that something?" he said. "You just plugged ole Black Bart dead. Amazing. A man with that kinda shooting ability could stand to make a lot of money in certain professions."

"That right?" Jack said. "Which ones would we be talking about?"

Wingate smiled and aimed his pistol. He hit the target in the middle of its forehead and smiled.

Jack nodded.

"Nice shooting, but frankly I got things to do, so why don't you tell me what you had me come out here for, Buddy?"

"Okay. It's time to play truth or dare," Buddy said. "I understand from my wife that you thought I wasn't being completely forthcoming about that little incident up at Tahoe."

"I wouldn't call it 'little,' " Jack said. "You and me and your charming wife were practically dog meat."

"Okay, I admit it. I wasn't being entirely straight with you, but I couldn't be until I checked you out. Which I now have done. You got a great record back East. Only one thing I can see wrong with it."

"What's that?" Jack said.

"You took all the risks, and yet you didn't make any of the bread."

"I knew the terms when I took the work. I didn't complain."

"No, sir, you did not," Buddy said, smiling and winking at Jack. "And that is undyingly to your credit in this world of cheapies and hustlers and wanna-bes, all trying to come down on other people's action. Which brings us to my little problem, one which I think you are uniquely equipped to handle."

"Which is?" Jack said.

"Well, sir, you were right in your suspicion that I work in . . . how best to put this . . . fields other than discount furniture. Hell, in the kind of economy we got today a man would be a fool to put all his hookers inna same hen house, if you know what I mean?"

"I'm waiting," Jack said.

Buddy wet his lips with his lizard tongue and pushed his cowboy hat back on his bald head. "Okay. I got me a line to something new in the world of pharmaceuticals. Colombian white heroin."

"Heroin?" Jack said, "—from where?"

He'd hoped he had put the right spin on his "astonishment." And apparently he had, because Buddy smiled in a pleased way and paused dramatically before he spoke.

"Bet you thought the Colombian lads were only into coke. Well, that's all changing. They realize there's money to be made in smack, and they got the newest and the highest grade. Fine stuff. In the future the South Americans are gonna put the fucking slopes outta business. This great ole country of ours will be inundated by Colombian white. It's the drug of the future. Believe me, son."

"Sounds interesting," Jack said, squeezing off another shot. "But I thought the Colombians only dealt with their own people."

"Usually that's true. But not always. So happens I got a fantastic relationship with certain very influential people in the great country South of de border. See, a long time ago I did a very big favor for one of them Colombians, and so they made me like one of their family. Result is I got access to major players and unlimited access to high-quality skag."

"So what do you need me for?"

Buddy put his arm through Jack's and began walking with him toward the house.

"My problem is that there is a rival organization, headed by the guy I mentioned to you, Pedro Salazar. Pedro is all muscle and very little brains, but he has a way of getting on my nerves. Like the other night."

"I see," Jack said. "Well, if you are asking me to take him out, that's not my line of work."

"No, not at all," Buddy said. "You see very soon . . . in a week actually, I have a serious shipment coming through. Word I got from my boys is that Pedro wants to hit me . . . maybe down on the Mexican border. What I am doing is hiring some muscle and some brains to make certain that he doesn't give it a shot. I've already rounded up some good boys, but they lack a leader, somebody who can mold them into a unit, somebody who Pedro will respect. I know what you can do if the shit goes down, and by now, so does Pedro. He's gonna think twice about hitting us if you're on my side. So there it is. Sound good?"

"Sounds like Christmas," Jack said. "But there's a few problems. I don't know Mexico, and there's no way I could guarantee you security down there."

Wingate smiled and spun his six-gun on his forefinger.

"Appreciate your candor, son, but who said anything about you working in Mexico? No sir, you see we got us a pretty unique way of getting the stuff into the United States. And I got people on my side—people I pay serious money to to make damn well sure they *are* on my side—in this country and in Mexico. Salazar is less than zip down there . . . and he knows it. The place he'll hit us is on this side of the border, after we bring it across. All I'll want you to do is be there with some of my boys and make damned certain nothing goes wrong."

"So I don't even go into Mexico?" Jack said.

"Don't see any reason you would have to, 'less it's just to have a look-see around to make sure you understand how the whole deal's set up. Beyond that, you go back and wait in a nice hotel, treat yourself to margaritas, swimming pools, and more eighteen-year-old pussy than Jon Bon Jovi. Sound good?"

"Yeah, but aren't you leaving out one detail?" Jack said, as they came to the bunkhouse.

"Ohhh, dear me," Buddy said, laughing. "I knew you wouldn't let me forget. Well, let me put it to you this way. You meet the guys . . . you take who you want, fire who you don't like. And get them to man their stations right. We head south next week. You basically hang out and keep things moving along, and three days later you collect two hundred thousand dollars. How's that sound?"

"Sounds about a hundred thousand short," Jack said, staring coldly into Wingate's eyes.

"Damn, is there anybody in this world who isn't greedy anymore? I'm offering you more money than you ever made in your pissant life, and you wanta hit me up for another hundred?"

"Chalk it up to a character flaw."

"Two fifty," Buddy said. "That's two percent of the deal. And if this works out, it'll be the first of many. Thing is, I like you, son, though I am not sure why."

"It's 'cause you know I can cut it," Jack said.

"Yeah, that's part of it," Buddy said. He squeezed Jack's arm. "The rest, who knows? It's a mystery about human beings, wouldn't you say so? Some you like, and some you would just as soon see die at your feet. All comes down to molecules, genes, and the sense of smell. Okay, I'll give you the three, 'cause I'm betting that you'll want to reinvest it in one of my other projects. Maybe my movie. I plan on making my directorial debut with money we make from these scams, and I see a good-sized part in the film for a stud like you."

"This is a weird kinda casting couch, Buddy," Jack said.

"Oh, ye of little faith," Buddy said. "Lemme explain something to you. The difference between me and Salazar, hell, between me and all the other hard-ons who wanta be in the glamorous business of smuggling, is I only do it with family. I take care of all my people, and they take care of me."

"The Brady Bunch," Jack said.

Buddy patted Jack on the cheek.

"You're a hard guy, Jackie," Buddy said. "But I'm gonna soften you up. You'll see. You can't resist ole Buddy, 'cause in the end, he'll do you right. Now, you run along. I gotta go into the ole bunkhouse here and send a few faxes. We leave soon. I got your number, and I'll be calling you tomorrow. I want you to meet your brothers. Hell, it's gonna be one big barbecue. Take care, son. Good to have you riding the stage with me."

He winked at Jack and walked into the bunkhouse, his spurs jangling in the hot Valley air.

Jack looked after him and felt things creeping over his arms, chest, feet—scaly things with darting tongues. Buddy Wingate was a reptile; Jack could barely wait to take him down.

Chapter 12

"I would like to say for the record that I find this mission completely wrongheaded." Ted Michaels shook his head violently, but Jack thought he still looked and sounded like some kind of prep school headmaster.

Jack looked at C.J., who gave out a sigh and a frustrated whistle and sucked on his gold toothpick. Jack had been sitting here in the DEA strategy room for two hours, listening to Michaels drone on, and now he could stand no more of it.

"Michaels, what is your problem?"

Michaels looked down at Jack as though he were a bug.

"I believe I've enumerated the problems. What if you end up in Mexico . . . in trouble of some kind? There's no way we can protect you. Unless you're talking about wearing a ten-pound SAT track . . . but I don't think that's at all practical, do you, Walker?"

"No one suggested that I was going to do that," Jack said, "and I don't appreciate your patronizing tone."

The usually placid, pipe-smoking Brandau, squinted and looked hard at Michaels.

"Ted, I think Jack's done an excellent job. Buddy Wingate has handed us this thing on a platter, for godsake. . . . He's even said he doesn't want Jack in Mexico. Jack doesn't do him any good there."

"I know what he said, Richard," Michaels said. "I also know how these drug deals can go wrong. We can't ensure Walker's safety . . . even in this country."

"Why not?" Brandau said. He reached down and picked up a Twinkie, which was sitting next to his notebook.

"First of all, we don't know where the deal is going to go down. Is it San Diego, Arizona, or El Paso? Wingate has only told him it's going to be on the border. And we can't track him."

"I could wear an Agent Alert button," Jack said. "I can place the trigger in my pocket and run the wire down my pants leg."

"No, you can't." Michaels said. "This action could take days. You're going to walk around with that in your pocket for a week, or more? I don't think so."

Zampas ran his fingers through his thick hair.

"I agree with Ted on that, Jack. The alert is all right if it goes down in a day or so, but we don't want you out there for a week with that thing in your pocket."

Valle popped his fingers, got up, and walked around the room. He looked, Jack thought, as if he were going to jump out of his skin. Whatever it was that had been bothering him earlier was obviously still eating him.

"The Agent Alert button idea sucks," he said, sticking a fresh piece of gum in his mouth.

There was a lull in the conversation, and Jack felt a fury building inside of him.

"Look," Jack said. "Here's the way it's going down. I'll be somewhere on this side of the border. I don't know exactly where, but so what? He's got to tell me at least two days before the shipment comes, so we can secure the area."

"Wrong," Michaels said. "He's worried about Salazar, so why tell anybody anything right up until the day before it goes down? Lessen the risk, in case he's got a mole in his group. Once he's told you, he'll be watching you. Which means you're going to have to lose a tail in order to make a phone call to us, and that's dangerous as hell."

"I can do it," Jack said. "Remember I saved the guy's life. He trusts me."

"Listen, Walker," Michaels said. "We can't risk exposing the Agency . . ."

Now Brandau got up and looked at Michaels.

"Ted, let's be honest. Jack has brought us this far; he's our best shot."

"Fuck'n A," Valle said. He was leaning against the window, popping his gum. He glowered at Michaels, then shook his head.

"You have something to say to me, Bob, just say it, but don't give me the high school stare."

"High school? You arrogant . . ."

Valle was moving toward Michaels now, but Zampas leapt between them.

"Hey!" Zampas said. "Both of you cut the shit."

Michaels looked angrily at Zampas now.

Jack looked around the room. It was time for him to make his final pitch.

"Look," he said. "I know you think this is a little crazy, Ted, and maybe it is. But I really want to reassure you and everybody else in this room that I know what the fuck I'm doing. I've got it under control. I won't do anything risky or out of line. I'll call the minute I find out the details, and I'll do everything I can to find them out early."

The room became quiet, and Jack heard Brandau blow out his breath in relief. Jack's speech had been a good one, mature, confident.

C.J. winked and kicked Jack's shin.

Brandau nodded his big head and wiped a smudge of Twinkie off his lip.

"I say we go ahead and give them a good old-fashioned ass whipping."

Valle nodded. "Fucking right," he said.

"Okay. We're going to do it," Zampas said softly.

Michaels said nothing but sat silently, with his head down.

Jack smiled and nodded as the men adjourned. But as Michaels left the room, he looked at Jack with a strange expression on his face. Jack expected anger or jealousy, but Michaels looked as if he pitied him. Then he disappeared into the hall.

C.J. joined Jack as they left the room.

"What the fuck is with Ted Michaels?" Jack said. "It's weird. Like he doesn't want to make the bust."

"Tricky Ted," Calvin said. "He's always got his own little games. Important thing is you won the fight."

"I suppose," Jack said. But he thought of Michaels's expression as he left the room, and he felt a chill.

"Hey, fuck Ted Michaels," C.J. said. "Listen, man, why don't you come over tonight. Have some barbecue. Lucille and Demetrius are out of town, and I hate eating alone."

"Like to, partner," Jack said. "But I gotta wait by the phone. My man is supposed to call."

Calvin said nothing but nodded slowly. Jack suddenly realized that C.J. looked exhausted.

"Hey, what's going on with you, bro?" Jack said.

"I told a little white lie," C.J. said. "Lucille ain't just out of town. She took Little D. and went back to Detroit. For good."

"Shit," Jack said. "Man, I'm sorry. But she'll come back."

C.J. looked at Jack with a certain disbelief, rolling his eyes.

"You know, Jackie, sometimes I forget jest how young you are."

"What do you mean?"

"It ain't your fault. You still at the age it's easy to be romantic. . . . Ole C.J. and Lucille, together through thick and thin. Stuff like that."

"So?" Jack said. "That's the way it's always been."

"The operative word is 'been,' " C.J. said, shaking his head. "As in 'has been.' "

"Don't run that stuff on me."

C.J. gripped Jack's arm.

"No offense, Jack, but you ain't there yet. I'm talking about how a woman sees you when you're young—you know, full of promise, hope . . . gonna kick butt, take names. Then one day they wake up and smell the barbecue. They see a house that's falling down and a kid who can't make it to school without getting hit-on by crack dealers, and now they say, 'I backed the wrong horse, baby,' and they want to get theirselves out of there, grab some life, man, before some gang banger shows up on the front porch with a MAC-10."

"Bullshit," Jack said. "I know Lucille. She's just emotional.

She'll wake up in Detroit and wonder where your scraggly ass is, and she'll be begging you to send her a bus ticket."

C.J. shook his head wearily.

"Wrong," he said. "I'll tell you how serious it is. You know what a screamer Lucille is, man? Well, she didn't yell at me once this time. She just said she was taking D. for a little trip to her mother's—so I wouldn't have the chance to stop her—then she called me once she got there and told me real calmly that she was staying. Permanently. Said a lawyer would be getting in touch with me."

C.J.'s voice had sunk to a growl. For a second Jack thought that C.J. might burst into tears. The idea filled Jack with dread and an intense embarrassment. He found himself unable to speak.

Finally, C.J. broke the awkward silence between them.

"Look, man, it's okay. I know you got to wait for Wingate to call you. That's fine. I guess I just told you this as a way of apologizing for ragging your ass the past few weeks."

"Hey," Jack said. "That's nothing. Man, listen when I get back, we'll take some time. Go fishing down in Baja. Make a long weekend of it."

"You got it, partner," C.J. said.

He managed a smile, and Jack put his arm around his partner's broad shoulders and squeezed in an awkward half hug. It wasn't nearly enough, but it was all he could do for now.

Chapter 13

In the dark woody atmosphere of the Union Pacific Railroad Car restaurant, a slender black man of about thirty-five sat across the room from West Coast Agency Director George Zampas and his wife, Ronni. The black man was not a businessman stopping in for a drink before he went home, however. His business was to observe the Agency director and his wife, who sat drinking in a dark leather booth diagonally behind him. The black man watched them in the mirror on the opposite wall. When they left, he would follow Ronni Zampas. Meanwhile, he glanced at a copy of *The Wall Street Journal* and attempted to look interested in the stock quotations.

On the other side of the room, Agency Director George Zampas downed his third Jack Daniel's. Across the dark oak table from him, his wife of ten years, Ronni, shook her head. She was in a foul mood.

"How many drinks is that, George?" she said.

"Two," Zampas lied. He'd had the first one at the bar before she came.

"Right," she said. "You've become such a liar, George. I know it works for you at the office, but why not tell me the truth once in a while?"

The big Greek looked at her through a whiskey haze.

"What makes you think I'm lying, Ronni?"

She laughed and shook her head.

"How long have we been married?" she said.

"Twenty-four years," Zampas said.

She picked up her gin and tonic and sighed.

"Let me ask you something, George. When did you stop loving me?"

"Jesus, Ronni," he said.

"I don't mean to be maudlin," she said. "I just want to know. Was it last year? That's what I thought for a while. I even thought I knew the exact date . . . December twenty third, when we had our big Christmas fight. For a long time I thought that was it . . . the George Zampas fuck-you cutoff date."

"Ronni, don't do this." It occurred to him that maybe she'd had a couple of her own drinks before she left the house.

She waved to the young waiter, who came promptly.

"Another gin . . . make it a double," she said.

"Ronni, I don't think you want . . ."

"You don't know what I want," she said, then looked at the waiter. "Bring it. Okay?"

"Yes, ma'am."

A couple of tears rolled down her face and Zampas felt his guts being pulled out.

"So tell me, George," she said. "Tell me the truth. You're fucking Jane Hawkins, aren't you?"

"Jesus, Ronni, no," he said. "Come on. I'm sorry if I've ignored you lately, but there's a lot of pressure at work. Which doesn't make it right. I know I've been distant."

"Distant?" She laughed bitterly. "How about on Mars? And if it's so damned important, why can't you tell me about it. You used to."

"I just can't. It's classified."

"I bet you tell her about it," she said. "And I bet you tell her all about your cold-bitch wife who doesn't understand you. Isn't that how you guys always cast it . . . the dragon lady at home who spends all her time shopping and playing tennis. Or are you the more subtle type, George? Maybe you tell her that your wife is still a lovely person, it's just that there's no passion in the relationship anymore. Yes, now that I think about it, that would be more your style . . . the phony compassion number, while you stroke her nice, tight, twenty-five-year-old thighs."

His wife's voice had risen now. Zampas looked around the restaurant and found that several people were staring at him.

"Embarrassed, George?"

"Yeah, I'm embarrassed," he said. "Feel better?"

"The thing is," she said. "I still love you. Isn't that the greatest joke of all? I should go out and get the heaviest-hitting attorney I can find, but I don't want to, even now. I guess that makes me some kind of codependent enabler or whatever they call it nowadays."

"Ronni," he said, "stop. Please."

"I guess this is the spot where I'm supposed to throw the drink in your face," she said. Instead she pushed it toward his side of the table.

"Have another one, George. Or better yet, you can save the drink for Jane. Though I imagine she doesn't drink. None of the perfect young people do anymore. They don't smoke; they don't drink; they don't eat red meat. What do you do after you've gone to the motel, George? Eat tofu together? Well, fuck her, and fuck you, love."

She got up and walked out. And as she did the black man, folded his *Wall Street Journal* under his arm, and walked out a few feet behind her.

As Zampas watched his wife leave, a pain began throbbing in his forehead. He was losing it, he thought. It was as though someone had a spade and was shoving it into his guts. He shut his eyes and thought of a beach somewhere, maybe on Kauai—a sparking white beach that fronted a crystal blue lagoon.

He sipped his drink and ached for it. The place no honest cop could ever afford.

Chapter 14

Jack rode shotgun alongside Wingate in his black Mercedes 350 SL. They drove down Victory Boulevard past abandoned factories and a couple of overweight hookers, then turned right and stopped at a guard shack. A huge black man in what looked like a black storm-trooper's uniform stuck his large head in the car window.

"How you doing, Mr. Wingate?"

"Fine, Billy," Wingate said. "You looking good, son. The boys arrive yet?"

"Believe they are all inside, sir."

"Good deal," Wingate said. He winked as if they were fishing buddies and drove on.

"Boy oughta get himself some Sen-Sen, son, his breath smells like warmed-over shit," he said.

They drove through a narrow alley and came to what looked like an abandoned airplane hangar. Wingate parked with an adolescent squeal of brakes.

Jack stepped down and looked at the five men coming from the hangar. He felt a chill run down his left arm. The first was Tommy "Chuey" Escondero, a Colombian hit man who was known for his psychotic temper and unlimited sadism. Jack remembered the case of a confidential informant named Paco Lewis, whose cover had been blown in Bogota three years ago. Word came down from a peasant who claimed to have been there that Chuey had tied Lewis to a tree and sawed through his limbs, as slowly as possible, all the while mimicking and mocking the snitch's death screams. The case had been thrown out, though, because the witness had disappeared from protective custody three days before the trial.

Behind Escondero was another figure Jack recognized from DEA files. This was Loco Larry Altierez, a short, thick man with a long forlorn mustache. Loco Larry was often partnered with Escondero and was an excellent man with a knife. His speciality was slitting throats.

The other three men were strangers to Jack.

"Well, boys," Wingate said, "as I promised you, we got a new leader. No reflection on any of you . . . it's just that this job is what we call stress-intensive, and the way I see it . . . we need new blood at the top to keep everybody piss-ready. Jack McKenna is an old friend of mine from back East, and I know what he can do with a gun . . . so I want you all to listen up when he talks. Course, I don't expect any real problems with this little op, but then again, in the wonderful world of addictive chemicals, a boy never can tell. Especially where our old friend Pedro Salazar is concerned."

The men said nothing but looked at Jack, as if they were waiting for him to address the troops. Instead, Jack remained silent, putting the ball back in Wingate's court.

"Well, let me introduce you to the boys. This here is Cutty Marbella, Cutty is an expert with the AK-47 assault rifle . . . done some very nice work in the Mideast."

Marbella, a thin, gaunt-faced man, with a scar two inches long above his right eye, looked at Jack and nodded slightly. There was something utterly silent and still about him. He looked like a hunter, the kind of man who could sit motionless for three hours in a duck blind or on a road, waiting for birds or politicians to fall into his sights.

"And this kind gentleman is Joe Cerrado, a man of many and varied talents."

Jack started to give Cerrado the same silent treatment, but the big man stepped forward. He had an agitated look on his thick brown face.

"Buddy," he said, in a deceptively soft voice, "we have no need for a new . . . leader."

"Jose, ole buddy," Buddy said, "I explained this to you on the telephone just this morning, and I thought we had it all straightened away, pard. This ain't in any way a reflection on you, it's just that I . . ."

"Excuse me, Buddy," Cerrado said. "It is a matter of pride, my friend. I have done everything you asked. . . ."

"Except provide me with the safety that I require to live my life, pal," Wingate said. "Remember when I asked you about going away to Tahoe for the weekend. You told me I didn't need no backup. Well, it's a damned good thing I happened to invite Jack along, or my ass would be bear shit on the trail right now."

"I'm not accepting demotion, Buddy," Cerrado said. "Besides, I don't think this gringo is man enough to take my job."

He reached into his leather jacket and pulled out a pearl-handled knife. With one click of the button, a six-inch gleaming blade appeared.

"Cool it," Buddy said.

"Hey, man, watch that thing," Jack said, backing away.

Wingate looked shocked as Jack backpedaled.

"You see what I mean, Buddy," Cerrado said, moving toward Jack. "He's a fucking *maricón*. Come here, *amigo* . . . I got something for you."

Jack backed up another step, then turned his back to Cerrado.

"Look at him," Cerrado said, in disbelief. "A woman. Next he will be begging."

Staring at Jack, Wingate's eyes were wide open in disbelief. "Son of a bitch," he said.

The other four men began to laugh nervously, and Escondero said, "You might want to cut him, heh, Joe?"

"I'm coming for you now, chickie," Cerrado said. He moved forward, faster.

But Jack now turned, suddenly, and threw something toward Cerrado. It happened so quickly that it was impossible for anyone to make out what the object was.

"Catch," Jack said.

Cerrado reflexively reached out for the object, and when it

hit his hand, he let out a yell and dropped it on the ground. He looked down to see what had burned him. In an instant, it was obvious he'd been tricked. The object was only a steel cigarette lighter, the flame still glowing.

Now the cowardly gringo would pay.

But these were the last thoughts Cerrado had. In one swift motion, Jack moved forward and kneed him hard in the groin. Cerrado groaned and dropped the knife. He fell forward, holding his gut as Jack's knee came up again, into his face, splitting his nose.

Cerrado fell heavily on the ground, and Jack coolly reached down and picked up both his lighter and the knife. He flicked the button, retracting the knife, and then snapped his lighter shut.

"Nice knife," he said. "I'll add it to my collection."

He looked at the others.

"Take our friend here outside and dump him somewhere. Tell him if I see him again, I'm going to cut his heart out with his own knife and feed it to my dog. *Comprende?"*

Escondero and Altierez nodded silently and moved forward.

"Jesus, son," Wingate said. "You are just chock-full of surprises. But now I'll have to hire me another man."

"Not necessary," Jack said. "We'll be fine with the happy little band you got here. Now, why don't we finish the introductions and get down to work. I hate wasting a fine morning dealing with assholes."

Jack smiled as he drove around a hairpin curve in the Hollywood Hills. Dona Rosa, Dona Pegita . . . from the street names you would think that you were living in some kind of Spanish fantasyland, but in reality many of the million-plus houses looked like real estate offices or overly elaborate Wendy's.

But just as he was expecting Buddy Wingate to live in some tacky Valley box, Jack took a last turn up Rosa Flora Road and faced a setting and home that was as stunning as anything he'd ever seen in Los Angeles. There in front of him was a golden hillside covered with cacti. Jack felt his nerves twitch. Though he had grown up in California, he had never gotten over the alien quality of the land itself. Los Angeles was not really meant for human beings, he thought, as he pulled into Buddy Wingate's circular driveway. It was a goddamned desert, and if Mulholland hadn't stolen the water from the Sacramento Valley, the place would still belong to the coyotes.

"Hey, partner. Glad you could make it for dinner."

Jack looked up, startled. Buddy Wingate walked from the giant wooden Spanish door, replete with massive dead bolt. He walked by a water fountain, a sculpture of a young boy whose lower body was a blue dolphin. Buddy wore a blue track suit, and on his feet were a pair of new three-hundred-dollar track shoes.

"Like my hill? But that's only the overture. I got me the complete symphony down in back of the house. You an admirer of cactus?"

"It does cast a spell," Jack said.

They walked through the big Spanish door, and Jack saw oversized Mexican couches, all leather and dark wood, and a leather-topped coffee table. But the pièce de résistance was a huge eucalyptus tree growing in the middle of the living room. It soared through the roof, which was clear glass and through which Jack could see the newly risen moon.

"You like my friend there?" Wingate said, sniffing the air. "I call him Freddie. He keeps the air smelling California-sweet night and day."

"Remarkable," Jack said.

It was true, he did like it. He liked its pure ostentation, and he was going to like it even more when he put Buddy in a five-by-ten cell where the air smelled of piss and shit all day and night.

They walked through a huge dining room, with a stuffed bear in a tuxedo sitting at the forty-foot dining table. "That's my touch too," Buddy said. "I hate to come into an empty room, you know what I mean?"

Then they were going through another pair of oversized doors and were on a long deck that felt as though it were suspended in midair. Buddy hit a switch and powerful floodlights came on, illuminating the garden. There, below Jack, were hundreds of cacti of every variety and phantasmagoric shape. Taken together they looked like a thousand pin-faced creatures of the night.

Buddy was already walking down the spiral wooden steps.

"Come on, son," he said. "You don't get the full effect, 'less you walk amongst them."

Then he was following his host along a narrow pathway, brushing against the cactus flowers, seeing the small spiky plants at his feet and the huge, monster cereus hovering above his head, and he heard Wingate's voice, like a wigged-out announcer's on some PBS nature special for the criminally insane.

"This one here is one of my favorites," Buddy said, pointing at a plant that looked as though it belonged on Venus. "It's called the black aeonium. It's wild and wonderful. Look at the way that sucker just shoots out at you. It's arrogant, got these wonderful spines all over it. It's a mutating muther. Like a cancer, know what I mean? Some of these plants mutate according to the weather, some according to damage. Some son of a bitch animal eats on it, it'll grow all new spines and impale the bastard. Some of 'em even give off boiling cabbage smells to ward off the little predatory fuckers."

They walked farther down into the yard. Jack felt something tickle his back and looked up and saw a huge hanging cactus, which looked as though it had a wide-open mouth.

Wingate stopped and smiled at him.

"Great, huh?"

"Looks like the surface of Venus," Jack said.

"Right. That's it. They ain't like nothing else. Cactus are tough-assed, surviving, originals, know what I mean?"

"It's a poor host that invites a man out to his house and doesn't give him a drink," said a voice from behind them.

Jack turned and saw Charlotte Rae standing in the path, a ceramic tray of margaritas in her hand. She wore a tight-fitting pair of Levi's and a purple T-shirt that fit tighter than a body stocking. On her feet were three-inch-high platform heels, and her blonde hair was combed like Veronica Lake's, a lock of it falling over her left eye.

She walked toward them, and they each took one of the drinks.

"Welcome to the garden of horrors," she said, smiling.

"Hell, darling, Jack is like me. He appreciates cactus," Wingate said. "You see flowers are safe, predictable ... they bloom, they look pretty, they fucking die. Cactus is big and bad. It's the NFL of plant life."

"Which is certainly another thing to recommend it," Charlotte Rae said, putting down the tray on the edge of a huge urn, which housed a cactus with seven-inch needles. Suddenly, she sniffed the air.

"I think I smell burning meat," she said.

"Aw, hell," Buddy said. "Be right back. Take care of him, will you, sweetheart?"

Buddy hustled back up the cobblestones, and as soon as he was out of sight, Charlotte Rae took Jack's hand and led him farther down the twisting path.

At the bottom of the garden they came to another stone fountain, this one made out of brightly colored tiles.

"Nice," Jack said, but he wasn't looking at the water.

She reached over and touched his hand. Jack felt the electricity striking him again.

"Jack, I want to say something. What happened the other night. I know it can't happen again. But I'm not sorry."

"Me either," Jack said.

He reached for her, but she pushed his hand away.

"Don't, we can't. You don't know how Buddy can be."

"I got a pretty good idea."

"The thing is," she said, sitting on the edge of the fountain, "he really does like you. Which is rare. If he ever found out that you betrayed him ... that we did ..."

"What would he do?" Jack said. "Beat you maybe? Put bruises all over your body?"

"Maybe I deserved them," she said, dropping her eyes.

Jack moved toward her and gently lifted up her chin with his right hand.

"That's the orphan talking," he said. " 'Whatever I get I deserve, 'cause I'm nothing anyway.' "

"No, that's realistic. I can be a bitch, Jack. Maybe I made him do it. I don't deserve all this."

She had suddenly started to cry.

"Or maybe it's because you deserve better."

Then she put her arms around him, and he could feel her breasts pushing into his chest, smell her.

"God, I loved it with you," she whispered. "It's been so long since I felt anything . . . Jack."

Then she was kissing him, and Jack kissed her back and felt the softness of her lips, her tongue inside his mouth.

She took his hand and brought it up under her blouse and bra. He felt her nipples, already hard.

"Stop, Jack," she said. "This is no good." She pushed him away then, and though he ached for her, he was glad, because he wasn't sure he would have stopped.

"Let's go up to the house," she said, regaining her composure.

"Sure," Jack said, as they walked beneath the phantom cactus. "Dinner for three."

She stopped and looked at him.

"I try, but I can't stop thinking about you. God help me."

"I know," Jack said—and no longer knew if he was acting or not.

He took her hand as they walked up toward the great house, through the wild cactus garden. Jack felt her pulse beating in her palm, saw the needles glistening on the alien-looking plants, and pushed down the panic in his heart.

Chapter 15

Jack parked the Mustang in the underground garage two blocks down from the Chateau des Roses. Now he got out of his car, locked the door, and started the walk back to the street. There was an elevator, but it had been broken for two weeks. He walked back through the gloomy structure, listening to water dripping from some leaking pipe. He thought of Buddy Wingate and his garden, and it occurred to him that the whole damned city was really a cactus garden. Someday the big earthquake would come and waste everyone, and cacti would reclaim the desert. Jack could picture it, the huge spikes jutting defiantly out of the remnants of the burned out office buildings . . . the hustling Gucci-clad citizens lying dead in the streets, while the first buds of the spiky, unkillable plants peeked through the huge rents in the rat-gray concrete of Hollywood Boulevard.

Jack shook his head, tried switching the pictures inside. He told himself to blow through it; it was just preop anxiety. Because now he knew . . . Buddy had finally sprung it on him just as Jack was leaving the little dinner party. The deal was going down tomorrow morning—though Buddy still wouldn't say exactly where they were headed. Jack had tried to push him on it, but not too hard. All Buddy would tell him was that it was south . . . "down the way where the nights were gay," which could mean anywhere.

Jack hunched his shoulders and headed up the bombed-out street. He was about a block away from the Chateau, which rose like a dusty, smog-covered castle in front of him, when he realized that there was a car moving behind him, slowly, inexorably, coming closer. He reached into his jacket, wrapped his fingers around the Glock, and kept walking. There was nowhere to run to. He was trapped here on the goddamned street. But by whom? Salazar's men? Getting their revenge for Tahoe?

Now the car moved faster. It was still fifteen feet behind him but closing. Jack felt a jolt of adrenaline zap through his veins and pulled out the gun, but kept it close to his chest, out of sight. If it was Salazar, in one second he would see the barrel of an Uzi.

To hell with it, turn, face them, shoot first, then run like hell for the Chateau.

Jack turned, aimed the gun at the advancing headlights.

The car blinked its lights twice . . . stopped . . . and someone began to frantically honk the horn.

Jack lowered the sight of his pistol and watched as agent Ted Michaels stepped out.

A black Lincoln Town Car. Of course, it was Michaels. Jack laughed with relief.

Standing on the driver's side, Michaels waved awkwardly to him to get inside.

Jack slid his gun back into the holster and walked to the car.

Once inside, he slammed the door and looked over at Michaels, who gave him a sheepish grin.

"Michaels," Jack said, "what the hell was that about?"

"Sorry. I've been waiting for you for some time. I knew you parked here. Found out from your landlord, the Rastaman, but I dozed off about an hour ago. Must have anyway, because I missed you coming in."

Jack squinted in disbelief. First off, Michaels was telling only a partial truth. He hadn't dozed off from the tedium of surveillance but from drinking scotch and, judging from his breath, quite a bit of it.

Someone blew their horn behind them, and Michaels trod down on the accelerator, a little too hard. They shot forward, bouncing on the potholes that scoured Franklin. Jack bounced on the seat, hit his skull on the low roof.

"What's with all the mysterioso stuff?" Jack said. His own heart rate was almost back to normal now, and he had to admit Michaels's visiting him was intriguing. Nothing could have been farther from his expectations.

Michaels drove across Franklin, through the Armenian neighborhoods, and toward Vermont.

"I know you don't like me, Walker."

"So what?" Jack said. "You don't love me either. I can't believe you hung around all night to tell me that."

Michaels looked nervously in the mirror. It was as though he was afraid they were being tailed.

"The problem is," Michaels said, his speech thick from alcohol, "that because you and I have this hostility toward one another, I doubt if you'll take what I'm about to tell you seriously."

"Try me," Jack said.

"Well, to start, I know that you think that my opposition to this operation is due to politics. You feel that I've got a stake in bringing down Wingate and that I don't want you screwing it up and snatching my glory. . . . Isn't that true?" Michaels said.

"Yeah, it's true," Jack said. "That's exactly what I think. So, you're here to tell me it's not so, is that it?"

"That is precisely why I am here," Michaels said.

"So why didn't you just phone me and tell me?"

Michaels suddenly became quiet again. Then, after a long wait, he shook his head.

"Listen, Walker, I can't tell you any more than this . . . that there is something going down, something bad, very bad . . . If I'm right, and I think I am . . . we'll have to watch out for our asses, all of us."

Michaels shook his head and reached down to a compartment in the armrest between them, opened it, and pulled out a pint bottle of Glenlivet scotch.

He took a pull and handed it to Jack.

"No thanks," Jack said.

"It's a hard time, Jack," he said. "Very hard. I'm here as your friend. I'm asking you to wait on this operation. If Wingate calls you and says you've got to go, find a reason to stall him."

"Why should I?"

"Because there's things going on, things you don't know about."

Jack looked at him hard.

"You setting me up?" he said.

"How could I be?"

"I don't know, Michaels. You're the bright boy with the fancy education."

Michaels shook his head.

"Quite the opposite. I can't tell you any more, but there is more, believe me."

"It's too late," Jack said. "I leave tomorrow. Buddy gave me the word a few hours ago. I haven't even told Zampas yet."

"Jesus," Michaels said.

Jack felt an intense annoyance.

"Listen, Michaels, if you have something to say, you should say it now. Cut the cat and mouse."

Michaels took another hit from the bottle. Some of the booze dripped down his chin. He turned toward Jack, squinted.

"Have you ever heard of Zapata?" he said.

"The Mexican revolutionary?" Jack said. "Yeah, so what?"

Michaels hesitated and shook his head.

"I want to tell you more, Jack, but I can't just yet. Just keep Zapata in the back of your mind. If you need it, you'll know when to use it."

"Oh, great. Come on, cut the bullshit," Jack said.

Michaels took another sip.

"Just promise me this, you won't go into Mexico with them. On whatever pretext."

"I have no intention of going into . . ."

"I'm not talking about intentions, Walker," Michaels said. "Don't go over there, even if it's just for one night to get laid in Juarez."

"Why?" Jack said. "Is my cover blown?"

"I'm not saying that," Michaels said.

"Then what are you saying? Come on!"

But Michaels's head lolled over. It seemed suddenly to Jack that he might be falling asleep at the wheel.

"Michaels, wake up before you kill us both."

Michaels nodded and snapped awake. They turned right at Vermont and Sunset and headed back toward Jack's apartment house. Michaels was silent, seemed to be weighing things, Jack thought. Either that or he was just hustling him, trying to make him fuck up his assignment.

"The important thing is," Michaels said again, as they came up Cherokee, "is that we don't want you down there."

"All right," Jack said. "But this is bullshit. If you have information that pertains to my welfare, I have a right to know what it is."

Michaels looked glassy-eyed out the window.

"Walker, listen. When you get back, if you need to see me and I'm not available, there's a place I can be reached. No one, I mean no one, knows this place even exists. . . . It's my getaway."

He handed Jack a piece of paper with an address written neatly on it: *Michaels—2322 China Island, Boulder Bay, Big Bear.*

"It's just a shack. But I like it. I think you'll like it too."

Jack put the paper in his shirt pocket.

"So now we're going to spend cozy weekends together fly-fishing?" he said.

Michaels laughed a little, and Jack was shocked to see that when he smiled, he looked ten years younger. Michaels craned his neck forward and looked out the window, up at the Chateau.

"You live colorfully, Walker. Take care."

He hit the switch, unlocking Jack's door, and Jack climbed out. Before he shut the door, he leaned in toward Michaels.

"Can you drive?" he said.

"Of course. Good night, Walker." The warmth in his face and tone was gone. His voice was filled with the old imperious arrogance again.

Jack shut the door, and the big Lincoln pulled away up the hill back toward Franklin. What was that about? It made no goddamned sense. And what was all that Zapata crap? Maybe drunken mumblings, jive to convince him to back off.

Yet, there was something about their little drunken drive that made Jack uneasy—that and the ruined look on Michaels's face as he closed the door. Michaels seemed genuinely afraid, haunted.

But it was too late to turn back now. He was deep inside, and he wasn't about to blow it off. Still, as he unlocked the grated door to the Chateau, Jack felt a rumbling inside his stomach. If Michaels had wanted to stir him up, get him worried, he had succeeded only too well.

Chapter 16

Eduardo Morales stared down at the simple wood cross that marked Jose Benvenides's grave. Though Morales had brought a cigar, a Romeo Y Julieta no. 4, he did not light it. Instead, he slowly put it into the pocket of his new Savile Row suit and remembered Jose.

He recalled himself and Jose Benvenides laughing and trading whores in an exclusive bordello just off the Spanish steps in Rome.

He remembered Jose and himself climbing a mountain in Switzerland. They had depended on one another that weekend in a way few men ever do, and they had come away knowing things that few men ever know.

He recalled Jose's laugh, an infectious laugh, a laugh that women and men loved and that Eduardo could hear plainly even now, a year after Jose's death.

The truth was, Eduardo thought now as he shivered in the mountain air, there was no one else like Jose.

It occurred to Eduardo that Jose's death was one of those things—no, the only thing—he would never get over.

It was still inconceivable that Jose was dead. But when it had happened, Eduardo had not felt the full shock. Indeed, he had handled Jose's death with his usual professional manner. First, there was the matter of obtaining the body. Not an easy task, since it was being held in a Tucson, Arizona, morgue. But Eduardo Morales had found long ago that he could reach just about anyone, a lesson he had first learned growing up in the slums of Quito, Ecuador. All he needed was enough patience and enough money. And, perhaps, a few threats.

With the help of two hospital workers, Jose's bullet-ridden body was brought back to Colombia and buried in this beautiful spot high atop the Andes Mountains.

And during the funeral, Eduardo Morales had held up very well. His wife, Sylvia, said so, and his friends and employers all remarked on how tough *el jefe* was.

Yes, during those first few weeks, he had thought that he would survive it better than he had expected. He slept normally; he continued to conduct the business that had made him one of the twenty richest men in the world. He even found time to see his mistress, the actress Sylvia Gennaro, in Rome, and she said he looked remarkably well.

Then, six months after Jose's death, he began to experience strange phenomena. He was driving through Mayfair in London, when he thought he saw Jose standing in the middle of a school crosswalk.

He swerved the car to the left and ran into a parked car, a new Jaguar.

The event, as he came to think of it, badly shook him, and he soon found himself having chills when he slept and dreading the time he would see Jose's ghost again.

For Eduardo Morales was certain that this was what he was seeing, a ghost. The sad, bleeding ghost of Jose Benvenides. And he knew at once what Jose wanted, knew it but tried for a time to put it out of his mind, because he did not believe in vengeance; it wasn't a practical way to conduct his affairs.

For three months, Eduardo Morales sought to forget Jose's bleeding, weeping ghost, until the night Jose came to see him, walked into Eduardo's huge walnut-paneled library at his estate in Colombia (but three miles away from the boy's grave) and said, "Did you not love me?" And Eduardo had cried out, "You know that I did. Why do you torture me?" And Jose had smiled then and put his hand in the bullet hole in his head, and said, "If you love me, why are my murderers still alive?" And then he had sat down on the carpet and wept blood. And Eduardo had wept as well and then said, "I will avenge you. I swear it." And the ghost of Jose Benvenides had looked up and said, "Good, but you must do it soon. You haven't much time," and had disappeared.

Eduardo had been frightened by that, terribly frightened, for he had cancer of the colon. He had been diagnosed a year ago and told that the disease was slowly growing, that "if everything went as expected," he had ten years of life left. But the doctor had warned him no one knew how these things went. Some cancers began as slow-moving as a slug, and others suddenly began to race like cheetahs through the bloodstream.

Then Eduardo Morales began to live in fear. It was such a strange emotion for him. All his life he had been able to battle back against those who tried to smash his empires. He was afraid of no man.

But ghosts and cancer were a different matter. No man could experience these two things and not feel shaken.

If there was a good side to all of this misfortune, it was that Eduardo now knew what he must do—act at once. If he didn't, all his millions, all his power, his life itself, would be nothing.

And now, tonight, it had begun.

He looked down at the grave and said, "I have invited Jaime Martinez to the house tonight, Jose."

He waited, waited for some kind of a sign (he wished the cross would move or that thunder and lightning would roar and flash), but there was none.

Still, he knew that this was the beginning of his elaborate plan for revenge, a plan that would not only avenge Jose's murder, but, in the end, bring down the DEA itself. In a terrible way, he thought as he walked away from the grave back toward his waiting helicopter, he had turned the worst thing that had ever happened in his life to his advantage. For when his plan was realized, he would have consolidated his empire and utterly destroyed his enemies.

He smiled as the chopper whirled into the cold air. This was what Jose would have wanted too. Eduardo was certain of it.

The helicopter sat down in a field behind Eduardo Morales's sixteenth-century mansion. Eduardo was met there by his long-time personal assistant, Vincenzo Juarez. Juarez was a huge man; Morales's nickname for him was "The Bear." He always looked disheveled, especially so when he was dressed formally, as he was tonight.

"The guests have just arrived, *patron*," Vincenzo said.

"Thank you," Eduardo Morales said, ducking under the helicopter blades, and getting into his Land Rover.

Vincenzo Juarez took the wheel.

"Is the dinner prepared?"

"It's magnificent. Everything is perfect."

"Good. This is a very important night for me."

Vincenzo Juarez nodded. There was no need for words. He knew only too well what Jose Benvinedes's death had done to Eduardo.

The first guest tonight was the forty-seven-year-old police chief of Bogota, Herbert Caruso. He had been in Eduardo's pocket for so long, he had lint in his hair. Caruso did whatever Morales wished, whether it be helping to expedite a shipment of drugs by giving the trucks a police escort through the mountains or killing a youthful revolutionary who misguidedly wished to stomp out drug dealers.

The other guest was Jaime Martinez. Martinez, a twenty-seven-year-old, was handsome in a silent-movie-star way. He had jet-black hair, teeth that glimmered so brilliantly that they almost looked false, and a perfect profile, which devastated young women. Ironically, tragically, it was Eduardo himself who introduced Jose to Jaime. Jose had been a brilliant young man, a man with a talent for the business. He rose fast through the ranks and soon became Eduardo Morales's top man in America. But Jose was all business; he rarely had any fun. Eduardo, who had a taste for women and the high life, had asked Jaime to take Jose out on the town, to let him relax and have some fun. Jose had protested he had no real desire to do so, but went in order to please Eduardo. To Eduardo's initial delight, the quiet, studious Jose and the flashy Martinez became fast friends. Jaime soon had Jose dancing and drinking champagne in the clubs and going out with beautiful young women, as he did. And the friendship seemed to be mutually beneficial for Jaime. He became more serious in his work and began to rise through the ranks until he was Jose's second lieutenant. He was good at his job, which was to open new markets for Eduardo's drugs. Jose sang his praises to Eduardo, who smiled and said he was glad Jose was having a good time and that he had found such a close friend. But privately, Eduardo now worried that perhaps Jaime Martinez had a bit too much influence on Jose. Twice Eduardo tried to warn Jose about Jaime, but Jose merely laughed at him. Jose reminded Eduardo that after all he had introduced them and that Jaime was a hard worker. So what if he lived to have a good time. "As you yourself used to say, what's the point of being rich, if you don't live like it?"

Eduardo had acquiesced to Jose's enthusiasm. It was possible, he thought at the time, that he was just getting old, judging Jaime too harshly.

Now, as Eduardo Morales stepped out of the Land Rover and walked up the marble steps to his villa, he was once again struck by a terrible grief and a noxious wave of guilt. If only he had never introduced them at all, none of this would have ever happened.

He stopped, sighed, sucked in some air, then opened the glass and gold-filigree doors to his home. What was past was past. He had business to attend to now.

* * *

Because Jaime Martinez loved Mexican food, Eduardo had had his chef, Raymon Artel, create a masterpiece of a Mexican dinner. There was sangria and gold tequila, hand-painted plates of guacamole and sopas—thick, small tortillas filled with refritos, potatoes, and chorizo—fresh green tomatillo sauce, and flaming red salsa. Then came the soup course, sopa de lima, a lime soup made from the finest homemade tortillas, choice chicken livers, chicken breasts, and bitter limes. After the soup dish came the *entrada,* Pescado a la Veracruzana, red snapper. This was, Morales knew, Jaime Martinez's favorite dish, and he had instructed Artel to make it to perfection.

Which he had. Indeed, the guest of honor could only shake his head in wonderment.

"You have outdone yourself tonight, my *amigo,*" he said, taking another sip of red wine. "The dinner is *fantastico.*"

"I am most gratified that you like it," Morales said. "And you, Chief?"

Caruso grunted and kept chewing.

Martinez smiled and took a generous sip of the Château Petrus, the finest Merlot in the world. It was soft as satin, yet complex, perfect.

"I have had a dinner as good as this one, only once," Martinez said. "It was at a restaurant in Mexico City . . . a place called Veracruz. You really ought to try it someday, Eduardo."

Martinez smiled in a condescending manner and soaked up the last of the sauce on his plate with the torn edge of his tortilla.

"I've been very busy," Eduardo said. "It's not possible for me to travel for pleasure that often. I leave that to my wife and the children."

"And where are they?" the police chief said.

"At the moment they are in Rome," Eduardo Morales said.

"I envy them," Martinez said. "Rome is the perfect city."

"What of Bogota?" Caruso said. "You don't like it here?"

"Of course I do," Martinez said. "This is my home. It is just that as a city . . . well, Rome is magic."

Morales smiled at the police chief. "He's a man of the world now. Our country is too small for him."

Jaime Martinez looked at Morales and blushed slightly. He knew that Morales was baiting him, just as he'd done since the day they met. Morales expected him to play grateful peasant to the *grande patron,* for that was how they'd started out. He would never allow Jaime to grow up, and beyond that he would never admit that in many ways the pupil had outstripped his old master.

Martinez took another sip of his wine. It annoyed him that Eduardo could afford three-hundred-dollar bottles of wine, for he was too uncultured to really appreciate them.

"I am quite serious," Morales said, also sipping the wine. "When you came to this table with Jose nine years ago, who would have thought that the king of the nightclubs would be able to sit at a dinner table such as this one and talk knowledgeably of Rome, Paris, New York, and Los Angeles."

"Los Angeles?" the police chief said. "A puke hole with palm trees."

"You're too harsh," Morales said. "After all, Jaime loves it there."

"Los Angeles is a complex place, like all cities," Martinez said. He sipped the wine again but felt himself withdraw slightly. There was something just beneath the surface of Morales's words, something dangerous. He decided not to give them a lecture on the pleasures of Los Angeles.

Morales smiled. "Can I interest you in some dessert, gentlemen?"

"I am sorry, but no," Martinez said. "I'm trying to keep my weight down."

Morales smiled and shook his head approvingly.

"He has women everywhere," he said to Caruso.

"That's not true," Martinez said warily. "You keep me so busy I have little time for women anymore."

Morales smiled as the waiters brought the steaming, rich coffee.

"Well, we want to keep you even busier, Jaime," Morales said.

Now Martinez relaxed a bit. At last, it was happening. He had suspected as much when they had invited him here. They needed him to front for them in America. He was going to be in the inner circle at last. Then he would get information that he could pawn off to the DEA, but not all of it. He would be able to keep the goddamned police off his back and at the same time amass enough of a fortune to become more powerful than Morales himself—because the information he would get would bring Morales down.

It was a dangerous game, but he had the *cojones* for it. Jaime Martinez relaxed and sipped his coffee.

"I want you to know that I think you have done a great job in Mexico and in California," Morales said.

"Thank you," Martinez said.

"You have made it possible for us to increase our shipments into Mexico, and you have worked well with our friends in America."

"I depend on your guidance, *patron,*" Martinez said.

"Yes," Morales said. "I am aware of that. And you have always been the perfect employee. Or near-perfect, anyway."

"Only near-perfect?" Martinez smiled nervously.

"By that I only mean that you are prone to bragging, Jaime," Morales said.

"I do not understand," Jaime said.

"Oh, it's nothing."

Eduardo Morales looked at Chief Caruso, who was now reaching into the nearby silver humidor for a Romeo Y Julieta.

"He is so sensitive, isn't he, Herbert? I merely mean that I know your weaknesses, *mi amigo.* You brag, you tell people that you have made decisions that you didn't make. But I don't hold it against you. Instead, I see it as a mark of your creativity. To a great extent, creative people are always liars. At least, I think that's true. I'm sure you would know better than me, since you have become friendly with so many people in the arts in Los Angeles."

A small trickle of sweat rolled down Martinez's underarm. Then another and another. He could feel each of them individually, and he knew that if he lifted his arm, he would reveal an ugly patch of sweat.

"I don't know why you keep bringing up Los Angeles," he said. "I haven't spent any time there since . . ."

"Since last year," Morales said.

"Yes, since then," Martinez said.

"I suppose that's true," Eduardo said. "I suppose it only seems like you've spent more time there because you talk about it so much. And now that we have brought the subject up, I would like to know . . . why *do* you talk so much?"

"I don't . . . not really," Jaime said. Now the sweat was starting to run in a steady stream. He dared not move. And there was a pain starting in his stomach. A terrible, burning pain.

"He says he doesn't talk about it so much, Herbert. Do you think he does?" Eduardo said.

"I think he does," the chief said. He turned and smiled at Martinez; there was a piece of red tomato sticking between his front teeth.

"I think you talk about L.A., and I think you talk about Arizona too," the chief said. "Maybe you think you are a cowboy, heh?"

Morales laughed at that, but there was no humor in it.

"What are you two doing?" Martinez said. "Are you putting me on?"

"I don't know," Eduardo said, looking at Caruso, who lit his cigar. "What do you think, Herbert, are we putting him on?"

"No, I don't think we are," the chief said.

Jaime Martinez grasped his stomach. He had thought at first that this pain was merely the product of anxiety, but it seemed much worse than that now.

It was as though someone had lit a match in his bowels.

"What is wrong?" Eduardo Morales said.

"Nothing," Jaime Martinez said. "Nothing at all."

Morales shrugged and looked at the police chief.

"He says nothing is wrong, yet he is holding his stomach. As a trained professional, what do you make of that, Herbert?"

Caruso sighed, sat back, and rubbed his big belly.

"I would be forced to say that he is lying. But that does

not surprise me, because he is always lying about one thing or another."

"Yes," Morales said. "But you have to give Jaime credit where credit is due. For a long time he has been a very good liar."

"I don't know what you mean," Jaime said.

Now there was no longer any use in hiding the sweat or pretending that he was all right because his shirt was suddenly soaked, not just the underarms, but all over the chest as well. And the pain . . . the pain was quickly becoming unbearable. And now, suddenly, he couldn't breathe well either.

"Eduardo," he said in a high-pitched voice, "I don't feel so good."

Eduardo smiled and looked at Caruso.

"He doesn't feel so good," he said in a dead monotone.

The police chief smiled and blew out a smoke ring.

"That doesn't surprise me, because, frankly, he doesn't look so good either."

"This is true," Eduardo said, pouring himself another glass of wine from the decanter.

"What kind of joke are you playing on me, Eduardo?" Jaime said. "Did you put some kind of red peppers in my food?"

"Oh, no," Eduardo Morales said. "I would never do a thing like that. I mean, to waste good food for a joke? I don't think so."

"I'm surprised you would say something like that," Herbert Caruso said, "a sensitive, artistic type like yourself."

"Then why . . . why does my stomach burn so?" Jaime said. There were tears rolling down his face now.

"Because of a drug you have taken," Morales said casually.

"A drug?" There was panic in Jaime Martinez's voice. He tried hard to sit up straight, to rein in the screaming panic he felt.

"You mean poison?"

Eduardo Morales said nothing but simply stared at Jaime Martinez.

"But you couldn't have poisoned me," he said. "Because we all ate off the same plate."

Again, Morales was utterly silent. He simply stared at Martinez.

Martinez felt his heart skip a beat, then another, and a pain shot up his left arm.

"The wine," he said. "But you couldn't have poisoned the wine either, because we all drank from . . ."

Jaime Martinez stopped talking in order to grab his stomach again, which now felt as though it were roasting over an open fire.

Morales smiled slightly and turned to Herbert Caruso.

"He is such a bright boy," he said.

"I agree, Eduardo. They don't come any smarter than him."

"Stop it," Martinez said, suddenly finding his courage. "Stop it. If you have poisoned me, then be man enough to say so . . . but stop this mockery."

Eduardo Morales got up from his seat. He stared at Jaime Martinez as he walked around the table.

"You want the truth. All right. It's true, we all drank from the same wine bottle, but only you drank from that glass."

He pointed to Martinez's drinking glass. Jaime stared at it in horror.

"You see, a few minutes before you arrived, your glass was given a special treatment with a drug called sodium flouroacetate."

"Poison. Eduardo, but why?" Martinez slipped from the chair and fell to his knees on the brightly tiled floor.

"Why? You ask that?" Eduardo said.

He walked away from Martinez now, toward an antique chest, which he had inherited from his grandmother. Eduardo Morales opened the top drawer of the chest and pulled out a small black zippered bag.

"You see this?" Morales said. "In it, I have the antidote to the drug you have taken. You tell me the truth, and I will administer it to you."

Jaime Martinez began to cry.

"The truth about Jose Benvenides, and why you set him up for the DEA."

"Eduardo, please," Jaime said. "Please . . ."

"You will be dead in ten more minutes," Morales said.

He sat down in the chair next to Jaime Martinez and unzipped the black bag. He then pulled out a hypodermic needle and a bottle with a clear liquid in it. He struck the syringe into the bottle and drew up a full measure of the liquid.

"Tell me," he said softly. "They jammed you up and made you do it. That young agent, Jack Walker, isn't that right?"

The tears rolled from Jaime's eyes. His body shook with convulsions.

"All right, yes," he said. "Yes, Walker made me. He told me I would go to prison for life. Unless I led him to Jose. I didn't want to do it. I loved Jose like a brother. You know that, Eduardo . . ."

Eduardo Morales slapped the kneeling Martinez hard in the face.

"Your brother? You led him to Walker, who murdered him. You know what that means? It's as if you killed him yourself."

Jaime Martinez held his stomach and cried.

"No. I didn't know. Please . . . the antidote."

He clutched frantically at Eduardo's knees, and suddenly Eduardo spoke in a kindly, almost fatherly voice.

"Tell me how sorry you are, Jaime."

"As God is my witness, I am sorry," Martinez said. "I have regretted Jose's death since the day he died. I will kill Jack Walker for you. Believe me, *patron*."

The sweat was rolling down Martinez's face now, and he felt a hand squeezing his stomach, tighter and tighter. His heart was beating wildly . . . faster, faster . . . double—and triple—time . . . and he remembered a cloudless night he had run across the desert in Mexico, barely escaping the DEA agent who had busted their operation in Tijuana . . . that day five years ago when the desert sand stretched out before him like a dry, parched tongue.

The end of his sentence was nearly inaudible, for he was choking on black bile that suddenly squirted from his stomach into his mouth.

"Please," he begged. "Please."

Eduardo waited for a long dramatic moment, then took a

white linen napkin and wiped the sweat from Jaime Martinez's brow.

"I believe you," he said. "What the hell, killing you won't bring Jose back. Give me your arm and make a fist."

Jaime Martinez offered his arm and, with all of his fast-sapping strength, made a fist. Then Eduardo Morales was roughly taking his arm, tying his elbow up with a red silk sash and administering the precious antidote to him. Jaime Martinez fell backward onto the floor and felt the terrible pressure in his chest disappear, the horrible convulsions in his face and throat seemed to melt away. He could breathe again. The pain in his stomach was receding, his heart had stopped its terrible crazed arrhythmia, and he knew that he was going to live.

"Do you feel better, my friend?" his host said.

"Yes, yes."

"Good. You see I am not a vengeful man."

"No . . . No . . . thank you," Jaime Martinez said, and his own voice sounded fragile to him like that of a small child who has been scolded by the village priest.

"And because I have spared you, I want you to tell me all about it."

Jaime Martinez shook his head and wept like a schoolchild.

"I never wanted to," he said. "I tried to give them other people, nobodies, but they wanted Jose. But they knew nothing of his relationship to you. They thought he operated alone. So you are safe. Because Jose told them nothing. Nothing at all."

Eduardo Morales turned and looked at the police chief, who was drinking a second cup of coffee. He looked a little bored, as though he had gone to a not very interesting cockfight.

"He still does not understand," Morales said. "Do you think that I brought you here because I was worried that Jose sold me out before they killed him?"

He slapped the kneeling Martinez with the back of his hand.

"But . . ." Martinez blubbered.

"He would never sell me out, even if they cut his heart out. Jose was a man. It takes a worm like you, Martinez, to forsake the man who has made him."

"I am sorry," Martinez said over and over again.

"Really?" Eduardo Morales said. "You are sorry? And what have you been doing for Jack Walker lately?"

"Nothing. Nothing at all. Believe me."

Morales shook his head, slowly, with finality.

"No," he said, "I don't think so, *pendejo*."

Martinez looked up, confused. It made no sense. He had been forgiven, yet the look on Morales's face said something else.

Then, suddenly, the pain in his stomach returned, like a lightning bolt, and he felt as though he were going to pass out.

"What is it, *amigo?*" Morales said.

"You gave me the antidote?" Jaime Martinez said. "But the pain is beginning again, Eduardo, and my heart . . . Oh, God. I must need more of the antidote . . . Please. Again."

Morales opened his sleepy eyes in mock surprise and looked over at Caruso, who seemed vaguely interested now.

"Do you think another shot of the antidote would do him any good?" Morales said.

"No, I don't think so," Caruso said. "Not a bit of good."

"But it stopped it before," Jaime Martinez said, his voice shaking with fear.

"Yes, it did, you little scum . . . you shit-eating little Judas," Morales said. "But I am afraid it was only a temporary antidote. It gives you a five-minute respite. So if you want to make peace with your maker, now is the time, Jaime."

He stared down at Jaime Martinez coldly, as though he were examining a cockroach.

Jaime Martinez could not believe this. The impossible cruelty of it. It was worse to think he had been saved, only to suffer again. Far worse.

"Please . . . please . . . You must save me, Eduardo. I have been good to you . . . Please."

He could talk no longer, for he was holding his burning throat. He looked up again, but he saw five sets of eyes on Eduardo Morales, and he fell backward, screaming. Seconds later, he was squirming like a crushed insect on the red tile floor, while above him the cool eyes of Eduardo Morales observed his final death spasms.

"A shame," Morales said, afterward. He reached for a pearl button under the table and pushed it. Three Indian servants, dressed immaculately in white linen, came silently into the room.

"Get rid of him," he said. "And be discreet about it."

They nodded and picked up the limp, twisted body of Jaime Martinez.

Eduardo Morales turned to the police chief.

"Number one," he said.

Herbert Caruso nodded his head and smoked his cigar. He thought of a plan he had once had to displace Eduardo. Fortunately, he had never told it to anyone and had abandoned the notion due to lack of courage. He now thanked Jesus for his cowardice.

"I am glad you came, Herbert," Eduardo said. "But I think we have all had enough. I am very tired. Good night, and stay in touch."

"I will, *patron*," Herbert Caruso said. He thought about taking a cigar for the road, then dropped the idea. No need to get Eduardo riled up again. Slowly he walked to the massive oak doors.

Eduardo sat at the great table alone. He waited for some sense of satisfaction to overtake him, some relief, but there was precious little. He would never feel any real satisfaction until his entire plan had worked. No, this was only the prelude, the warm-up.

From another room he heard the telephone ring. A few seconds later Vincenzo walked into the room.

"It is the American. Wingate."

There was a slight tone of distaste in Vincenzo's voice. Eduardo knew that Vincenzo found Wingate uncultured and insufferable. Of course, this was true, but Eduardo didn't allow himself to have any personal feelings toward the loud, brash American. All that mattered was that Wingate did what he was told, played his part in the drama. And so far he had done so perfectly.

"Thank you. I'll be right there."

Vincenzo nodded and exited silently from the room.

Eduardo Morales picked up the glass he had just used to

kill Martinez and spoke to the ghost of Jose Benvenides, which stood silently in the corner, blood dripping down its cheeks.

"For you, Jose," he said.

Then he threw the poisoned glass into the great fireplace, shattering it into a hundred fragments, and went to talk to the American on the phone.

Chapter 17

They flew from Burbank through a cloud bank that was so dark that Jack felt as though they were heading straight down the funnel of a volcano. Charlotte Rae caught his eye twice as they found their seats. She was dressed in a white muslin summer dress on top of black leotards, and her hair was tied up on her head in a tight bun. The look accentuated her perfect cheekbones and green eyes, and Jack felt himself turned on by her from five feet away. It was her perfume too, he thought . . . he would know it anywhere. Wingate shook Jack's hand and smiled widely.

"Son, I am glad you are one of us now. You're in for some real fun."

Jack nodded and sat down next to Tommy Escondero, who waited until Charlotte Rae and Wingate were seated, then let out a little stream of breath and sighed.

"That is some woman *el jefe* has, hey, Jackie?"

"You know it," Jack said.

"No, but I would like to."

"I wouldn't suggest trying it," Jack said. "It would probably shorten your life."

"Yeah, you are right," Escondero said. "If *el jefe* caught me, he would hire someone to cut off my nuts, and if he didn't, she would fuck me to death."

He gave a laugh that sounded more like a cough and then picked up the newspaper.

"Look at this," he said. "Dennis Barrientez just got his two hundredth win."

He smiled with a kind of childish delight.

"You into baseball?" Jack said.

"Oh, yeah, man. Especially Dennis. You know, I played with him in the Mexican League for a time."

"Come on, man," Jack said.

"*Es verdad.* I swear to you on my mother's grave," Escondero said. "Okay, you don't believe me, you look at this."

He reached into his back pocket and pulled out an old wallet. It was stuffed with money, but tucked away in one corner was a yellowish newspaper clipping. Escondero unfolded it slowly, solemnly, as if he were handling a rare parchment. Then he spread it out in front of Jack, half of it on his lap and half on Jack's. It was a curiously intimate thing to do; it reminded Jack of his aunt reading him a comic book when he was a child.

Jack looked at the sports page of the Mexican tabloid *El Nacional.* Escondero pointed to the date, June 12, 1970. He pointed to the headlines. Jack read in Spanish, *Barrientez wins 22 games; winning single by Escondero in the tenth inning.*

"Son of a bitch," Jack said. "You did play with him."

"You know it, man," Escondero said. "Not only that, I was drafted too."

"By who?"

"The Dodgers, man. I hit three-forty in spring training."

"So?"

"I had an accident, man. Turned my car over on one of those streets up in Laurel Canyon. I was in a deep sleep for three days, *ese.* Then when I woke up, I found out I had broken my wrist and right shoulder. The doctor, he put a pin in it, but I could never turn on the ball again. That was it for me."

Jack shook his head. The story reminded him of Charles Manson. There was a school of thought that argued that if

Manson had become the rock star he wanted to be, he would have never killed anyone. Hell, today he might have been featured on *Unplugged* on MTV.

"That's heavy, man. So how'd you break into this business?"

"My uncle, *ese*. He lived down in Mexico City, and he took care of me when the Dodgers shipped me home."

Escondero smiled again; there was something sweet and sad in there, Jack thought, and the thought chilled him a little. It was weird about his job. It wasn't when guys like Escondero talked about killing people or hacking families into little pieces that he got frightened. He had steeled himself to that stuff long ago. It was when he saw glimpses of the child that had been there before they made the turn that scared him.

"Hey, man, when we going to find out where we are going?" someone said.

Jack turned and looked behind him. Loco Larry Altierez was hanging over the seat. His large sad eyes looked red and bleary.

"Guess we'll all find out at once," Jack said.

"You mean the man hasn't told you yet?" Larry said.

"Nope," Jack said. "Hasn't said a word."

"Fucking strange man. Making me and Cutty here a little uptight."

Jack looked up and saw Wingate climb from his seat and walk back toward them. Behind them was a young Mexican girl, with a tray of drinks in her hand.

"Well, boys," he said, "we are in the air, so I guess it won't hurt none to tell you our destination."

The four hired men said nothing but looked at him dead-on.

"We are heading first down to a little town called Villa Ahumada. I believe some of you boys know it."

"Hey, *ese*, that's beautiful country," Altierez said.

"Yeah, man, nice farms and good hunting up in the Sierra Madres."

Wingate smiled at Jack.

"We're gonna have a little wait for our product . . . not long, mind you . . . jest a few days," Wingate said, taking off his cowboy hat and scratching his head. "So I thought . . . now, would we rather wait on some crummy border joint or would we rather go on down to the farm, have us some fun? And believe me, friends, Buddy has taken care of your every need. There's swimming pools and tequila, a world-class chef, and I even imagine there'll be a few pretty señoritas there for you. Sound good?"

"I think I can handle it, *jefe*," Escondero said.

The others laughed. All except Jack.

Wingate looked at him and smiled.

"I see you a minute, Jackie?"

Jack slid out past Escondero, and the two men moved toward the back of the plane.

Once they were out of earshot, Wingate put his arm around Jack's shoulder.

"Now, don't get all riled up," he said. "I know I told you we wouldn't go into Mexico, but this is purely for rest and relaxation. Besides, I want to show you how the deal's going down."

"I told you I don't work in Mexico," Jack said, furious. "Things go wrong down there . . . you're fucked."

"Don't I know it, son," Wingate said. "Which is why I spend so much money . . . making sure things *don't* go wrong. Don't worry, this place is safer than a nun's pussy."

Jack stared at Buddy in a way that finally made the shorter man look away.

"What the hell, Jack. You're gonna love this. Trust me."

"You lied to me," Jack said. "Nobody fucks with me like that."

"Not a lie. Look, you spend a day or so there, you don't like it . . . we'll go back to El Paso. Deal?"

Jack hesitated for a long second.

"This is bullshit, Buddy," he said, as he nodded.

"Good," Buddy said. "Now, why don't you come on up front with me and Charlotte Rae. We're going to drink us a couple champagne cocktails. This is going to be some great holiday. Thing to do now is enjoy ourselves for the next few days. Relax, son, you are only a few days away from becoming a real player."

He put his big hand on Jack's shoulder and guided him back up the aisle, past the other men, who were already bragging about how many women they would have at the ranch.

Chapter 18

The Cessna landed at a private airstrip just south of the small village of Villa Ahumada and was met by three silent mestizos. Quick and efficient, they picked up all the bags, piled them in a jet-black Jeep Cherokee, and took off with Escondero, Altierez, and Marbella. A second off-road vehicle—another Typhoon, this one silver gray—was waiting for Wingate, who sat up front with Charlotte Rae. Looking at the winding, hilly road, Jack was grateful he was seated in the rear.

They drove on through a barren landscape without speaking, a desert dotted with huge cacti, and Jack got the creeps in his stomach again. He thought of Michaels's warning, and felt trapped.

To hell with Michaels, to hell with the cacti. . . . Wingate had no idea who he really was, and the only way he could blow it was to let them see him sweat. In an undercover, a man's own nerves were as much his enemy as the perps he was trying to bring down.

"I love this country, don't you, Jack?" Wingate said, looking over his shoulder. "Got your big sky and the Sierra Madres over there. It's wide open down here, *amigo,* wide open."

"Buddy Wingate, the hardy pioneer," Charlotte Rae said, filing her nails. "All he needs is a coonskin cap."

"Hey, don't laugh, sweetheart. I come from good pioneer stock. My great grandfather went to Arkansas in a mule wagon from Texas, where he'd been railroaded for a crime he didn't commit."

Charlotte Rae turned and smiled sexily at Jack.

"All the Wingates were forced into lives of crime," she said, "by unscrupulous cops who misunderstood their good intentions."

"Not far from the truth," Wingate said. "The rich boys with their Harvard educations got ways of robbing you with a fountain pen. My people had to be a little less subtle. All amounts to the same thing. Check out the Kennedys, the Rockefellers, you think they got where they did by running orphanages?"

He smiled at her in a way that made Jack want to break his face, but Charlotte Rae only snorted at him, seemingly unfazed by the cheap shot.

They turned up a dirt road and drove up into the foothills, then Jack saw the coyote fence and a house made of flagstone, glass, and steel that made the one in the Hollywood Hills look like a shack. There was a huge waterfall pouring off a second-story deck, and a stream that ran off into a grove of cottonwood trees.

"Here's our little ranch," Wingate said.

He pulled around to the side of the place, and Jack saw two large adobe guest houses. Between the magnificent home and the ranch houses was a giant swimming pool, complete with a second, smaller waterfall and a series of rock and tree grottos.

"Welcome to Casa Wingate," Buddy said. "You sleep in the guest house. Why don't you get unpacked and then come on around to the pool, and we'll have us a few drinks and get ready for the celebration tonight."

"Celebration?" Jack said.

"Guess I forgot to tell you. Jest thought you knew. Tonight is a very special occasion in Mexico. It's the Day of the Dead."

Jack managed to look faintly interested, but the words sent a warning through him.

"We have a few people from the community over," Charlotte Rae said. "Friends. It's interesting, Jack."

" 'Specially this year," Wingate said. "Father Herrera's gonna be here."

"He's an amazing man," Charlotte Rae said.

Jack looked doubtful and Wingate laughed.

"I know, I know . . . you think it sounds like hocus-pocus. Well, maybe it is. But I think after you meet him you're gonna be impressed. I ain't never met anybody who wasn't. Man leaves his mark on you. Trust me on that. He's a real *brujo*."

Jack looked confused.

"That's a witch, a magician," Charlotte Rae said.

"Abracadabra," Jack said back, but this time neither Wingate nor Charlotte Rae laughed.

The guest house was furnished pure Santa Fe, with colorful Indian tapestries on the walls, a little Indian kiva in the corner of the living room, charming exposed *vigas* with their crossed *latillas* on the ceiling, and lamps that were made to look like Aztec gods. The couches were covered with red and blue Navajo blankets, and there was a forty-five-inch television set in the living room.

Larry Altierez was fixing himself a large scotch and soda from the wet bar.

"All the comforts of home," he said. "The other boys are upstairs. You want a drink?"

"Not right now," Jack said.

Altierez shrugged his shoulders and sipped his drink. Then he smiled and fell back onto the couch.

"I miss something?" Jack said.

"No, I guess not. But ever since I saw you that first day, seems like I know you from somewhere else, *ese*."

"Sure," Jack said. "I felt the same way."

"Really?" Altierez said. "Where would that magic place be, I wonder?"

"The track," Jack said. "Hollywood Park. You used to go out there with Freddy Calabasas."

Altierez smiled with a curled upper lip, a bad Elvis impression.

"Freddy," he said. "You know the Dude?"

"Knew him a little before he ended up in that lime pit outside of Palmdale. That was real sad."

"Yeah," Altierez said. "That was major sad 'cause the Dude had a way with the nags. He could pick winners just about every time out. Inside info, I think he had. But you didn't go out with him. Least ways, not when I was there."

Jack picked up his grip, headed up the steps. He walked slowly, so it wouldn't appear he was trying to escape the conversation.

"No, I used to make the track scene when I was working for Jerry Wallenstein."

"The Jewish Prince," Altierez said. "Man owned Head For Trouble. Too bad she had that fall."

"Sadder than Freddy Calabasas," Jack said. "I met you a couple times when I was out with Wallenstein."

"Where'd Wally ever get to?" Altierez said.

"Disappeared one afternoon," Jack said.

"Hey, maybe he's living with Jimmy Hoffa?" Altierez said, lifting his lip again.

He took out his knife, hit the switchblade, and picked his fingers.

"Or Judge Crater," Jack said.

"Yeah, him too," Altierez said. "I guess we did meet when you were with the Jew. You remember it that way?"

"Sure," Jack said. "Why wouldn't I? Everybody remembers Loco Larry."

Larry managed to give almost a full smile. He liked the star treatment. Jack smiled back at him and went on up the steps.

At the top he let out a long sigh. It was possible that Larry had seen him on another caper, working under another name. And if that other name suddenly came to him. . . .

No use thinking about it. He was all right for now. He turned, walked down the hall, found an empty bedroom, went inside, and shut the door.

He quickly unpacked his bag. He wanted to get to the pool as soon as possible. The faster they were all drunk and lying around in the sun with the whores Wingate had provided for them, the better off he'd be.

At the pool that afternoon, Jack had yet another surprise. Wingate introduced him to one of his business associates, a German doctor named Gunther Baumgartner. He was in his mid-fifties and balding, but in excellent shape. There was something that troubled Jack about his face though. It was as though he could be any age at all, his skin was stretched so tightly over his bones. From one vantage point he looked young, no more than thirty-five, but from another he looked sixty. Jack decided that he'd had plastic surgery, perhaps out of vanity, but perhaps to conceal his identity. There was something terribly familiar about the man—not his face, but his walk, his stooped-over posture, the sound of his voice. For a second Jack thought he might be able to recall whom Baumgartner reminded him of, but then he lost it.

But whoever he was, it was obvious that the doctor had the hots for Charlotte Rae. He strutted and preened around the swimming pool, flashing his smile as he drank his glass of sparkling water.

"It is very good to see you and Mrs. Wingate, Buddy," he said. "And a real pleasure to meet you, McKenna."

"Likewise," Jack said.

"I hear from Mrs. Wingate that you are just the man they have been looking for."

It was impossible to ignore the sexual edge of what the German said, but Wingate laughed and made a joke out of it.

"Yeah, he's the man of our dreams. We seen him do his stuff, Gunther, and I wouldn't advise you to mess with him."

"Impressive," Baumgartner said. "I have spent much time with Buddy and his wife, and I have never heard them so impressed with anyone. You must be a dangerous man, Mr. McKenna."

"Only to my enemies," Jack said.

"And witty as well," the German said. He walked to the diving board then, climbed the steps and walked to the edge, then walked back and began his preparation for the dive.

A few seconds later he sprang into the air and did a perfect half gainer, barely rippling the surface.

"Hooray for Tarzan," Charlotte Rae said. "All he needs is a chimp."

"That's not funny," Wingate said. "You oughta watch your mouth. Dr. Gunther is a very good friend of ours."

"You mean good customer, don't you?" Charlotte Rae said.

Wingate turned to Charlotte Rae as the German climbed out of the pool. He looked at her with narrow eyes, the eyes of a razorback hog, Jack thought.

"You talk too much, darlin'. Dr. G. has very good friends all over Europe. People I want to be our friends. So treat him nice, you hear me?"

She smiled pleasantly as the doctor approached them. Jack squinted, trying to imagine what the doctor looked like before his surgery. He had seen him before, or someone who looked a lot like him. But no name came to mind.

"Bravo, Doctor. That was an excellent dive," Wingate said, handing the German a towel.

"Thank you. Do you do any diving, Mr. McKenna?"

"Only for cover," Jack said.

Charlotte Rae smiled and brushed her leg against Jack's ankle.

"Amusing," the German said. "I like amusing people. I hope you will come to Germany sometime so that I might show you some of our amusements."

"I'll bet you know just where they are too," Charlotte Rae said.

"Yes, I do," Baumgartner said. "I've spent a lifetime cultivating them. There are even some interesting amusements in Juarez. Perhaps, if we have time, I will show them to you, McKenna."

Jack decided not to answer the German. Instead, he put on his wire sunglasses and looked across the grotto, where there was now a squealing sound.

A young whore of about fifteen came swimming naked from behind the rocks, but she was quickly overtaken by Loco Larry, who playfully dragged her back behind the rocks and vegetation.

"Children," Baumgartner said. "For them pleasure is a simple thing."

He shook his head and sipped his mineral water.

"Well, I think you're gonna like our little ceremony tonight, Gunther," Wingate said, walking over to the grill. "You've never met anyone like Father Herrera."

"So I've been told," Baumgartner said. "I hear he has mystical powers."

"Which you think is all bullshit," Charlotte Rae said.

"No, you are wrong," the German said. "My country has always believed in a certain amount of mysticism. I've known men who could look at someone deeply and know who they are, what they desired, what they feared. Fortune, destiny . . . I believe in these things."

"That's right," Charlotte Rae said. "I forgot. You were the people who started the mystical empire that was going to last ten thousand years."

The German said nothing but set his mineral water down heavily on the poolside table. Jack wanted to lean over and give her a kiss.

The Mexican sun beat down on them as if it had a score to settle, so that by five o'clock Jack and the others retired to their rooms—his men with their teenage whores, Jack alone. He fell into a restless sleep and woke up twice, disoriented, holding his breath through twenty seconds of terror as he looked around the strange and completely unfamiliar room. But gradually it came back to him. He was in Mexico, completely surrounded by his enemies. With no chance for outside help if anything went sour. Maybe it was better not to remember after all.

He looked out at the heavens. It was beautiful here. The sky took on a density and quality that was so unlike its appearance in Los Angeles. In Mexico you could actually see the stars twinkle, and he reminded himself that after the case was over, he might come back to this country, perhaps go down the coast to Zihuatanejo, maybe with C.J. He wondered how his partner was doing, if Lucille and Demetrius had come home.

Then, from outside his window, Jack heard the beating of drums. They were soft, hypnotic. He got up from the bed and looked down out of the window. There in front of him in the dark, two ghosts floated by, followed by a man dressed in a devil's costume, complete with barbed tail and pitchfork. There was some other music as well, several pan pipes, like the kind he'd heard among the natives of Colombia. Everybody seemed to be heading up the desert trail toward a large fire that burned at the top of the mesa.

"You ready to go, man?"

Jack turned and saw Cutty Marbella standing in his doorway. The eerie light of the moon accentuated the scar on his right cheek. Marbella didn't need a costume, Jack thought. He looked like a ghoul without one.

"Sure," Jack said. "I wouldn't want to miss Father Herrera."

"It's no joke, man," Marbella said. "He's a man of power."

Jack started to make another crack, but Marbella's look made him keep silent.

They walked up the winding hill to the tabletop mesa, about two hundred yards from the house. Ghosts, devils, and skeletons danced among the huge cacti, and Jack felt his head swim with a sense of unreality. As they neared the circle of people, Jack realized that Wingate had invited many of their neighbors in the town to the party.

Who were they under the costumes, Jack thought?

Probably dopers themselves, living the outlaw life in Mexico, where they couldn't be touched.

Jack saw Marbella go over and join Altierez and felt icy fingers on his neck. He turned quickly and saw a ghoulish-looking Charlotte Rae smiling at him with a double row of teeth. Besides the perfect white teeth in her mouth, there was another set around the outside of her lips that she had painted on. Her cheeks were bloodred, and there were deep black charcoaled bags under her eyes. She was wearing a bright-red leather mini-dress, which had to have been plastered onto her body, and black mesh hose, which revealed her long, hard legs.

"You're not in costume," she said.

"Sorry."

"No problem."

She pulled a black Magic Marker from her pocket and pulled Jack close to her.

"Hold still, cowboy," she said, pressing her breasts to his chest as she drew something on his forehead. She did it swiftly, deftly, then playfully pushed him away, and held up a hand mirror.

"A spider," he said. "Thank you. I've always wanted a black widow on my head. Does he sting?"

"Only his friends," she said.

"I'll feed mine flies," Jack said. "When's the fun begin?"

"It's begun. Come on."

She grabbed his hand and led him toward the fire. They were a few feet away when Jack saw the man in the mask. The mask was so strange, so otherworldly that it took Jack's breath away. It was painted a copper color, and it had blue spokes that ran from the center, just above and on the side of the nose, out toward the ears and up to the hairline. There were three eyes painted on the mask's face, the third one dead in the middle of the head, and the mouth was full lipped and open to reveal three stubby, thick teeth. They weren't human teeth at all, Jack thought, but the teeth of a wild animal, some kind of pig or bush hog.

"That's Father Miguel," Charlotte Rae said. "We have to wait our turn."

Jack became aware of the flute music again, the beating of the drums, and for the first time he realized he and Charlotte Rae were waiting in a line, a snake line, which coiled up the hill, through the cacti, and finally led to the masked, blue-robed Father Herrera.

"What do we do when we get there," Jack said, "kiss his ring?"

"No genuflecting is necessary," Charlotte said.

A waiter suddenly came by, a short fat man who was dressed like a vampire. He carried a silver tray with flutes of champagne.

"Thanks," Jack said, taking one for himself and one for Charlotte Rae.

She took it and sipped it.

"Cold, just right for a ghoul," she said.

Jack sipped his own glass. In the dry desert heat it tasted like ambrosia. He turned and looked out at the three tall cacti that surrounded him. They appeared to be three crucifixes, and Jack waited for them to start a little spontaneous bleeding. He turned once more and saw a great rock cactus, with its warty tubercles. It looked as though it belonged under the sea, and suddenly Jack felt that way . . . as though he had been submerged and was drowning.

He felt dizzy, prayed he wouldn't fall.

And if he did, would Charlotte Rae pick him up again or would she turn like the rest of the pack of predators and devour his flesh with her double row of meat-eating teeth?

They were closer now, and Jack looked as Father Herrera gave Altierez something to eat. The big man took it but didn't put it in his mouth.

"Are we taking sacrament?" Jack asked.

"No, that's *pan de muerte,*" Charlotte Rae said. "Bread of the dead. We don't eat it."

They walked on, and then Jack was standing in front of Father Miguel Herrera. The man stared at him through the eye holes in his mask and spoke in a deep, resonant voice.

"We are here to honor Death," the voice said. He handed Jack a golden tray, on which were pieces of the bread.

"This is the flesh of those who came before you, your grandmother, your aunt, your father."

Jack felt a creeping fear in the pit of his stomach.

"Take the *pan de muerte,* young man," the priest said.

"Wait, father," Jack said.

But before Jack could finish speaking, the priest reached out and touched Jack's shoulder. He squeezed, and Jack was aware of the tremendous strength in his hands.

Suddenly, someone behind Jack banged a gong, and the crowd of ghosts and goblins became silent. Jack felt overwhelmed by a strange sensation, as though the man were looking clear through him. He wanted to go on, but Father Herrera moved away from him and stood at the top of the hill, in front of the roaring fire, which cast shadows over his mask.

Jack felt a great urgency building in him. He drank the rest of the champagne and listened as the priest began speaking in a deep, sonorous voice.

"Friends," he began, "we are here tonight to honor our dead, our ancestors, those who made us, nourished us, gave us life. We are here not only to honor but to speak to them, for we know that they are still with us, even though they have shed their physical bodies. We gave them *pan de muerte,* the bread of the dead, which has been distributed to you and which you will leave for the dead. For this, some people call us primitive, our beliefs are laughed at as mere 'superstition,' but I say to you, that it is mere superstition to think that the dead do not hear. That is dangerous foolishness, for any man of even elemental wisdom knows that they move restlessly in the wind, among the cactus that surround us. I say to you they are with us now, all of the dead. The ones we loved are watching us, waiting for what we will do, how we will honor them. They judge us. They know us, and they remember everything that was done to them." His voice had grown low, rumbling, and he seemed to be staring in Jack's direction.

Jack wanted to think of a wisecrack to ward him off, but language was beyond him now.

"Think of each plant that surrounds us as the spirit of someone you have lost . . . a grandmother, an uncle or an aunt . . . a dearly loved mother, or . . . a friend."

Jack felt a cold wind blow through him. On the word "friend" the priest stared straight at him—or was it his imagination? No . . . he *was* looking at him.

What the hell did that mean?

"Now I will ask you to walk with us in the procession and remember a departed loved one who has already left this troubled world. Take the *pan de muerte.* Place it at the altar at the west wall of Senor Wingate's estate. Come with us, and know that we do not fear death, but celebrate it, for the living and the dead are all one."

From the rear of the crowd someone started beating a drum, and Jack turned and saw three fiercely painted Mexican Indians, naked except for loincloths, their copper-colored bodies shimmering with oil. They were beating hand-painted bass drums and chanting.

Charlotte Rae leaned against Jack's shoulder.

"What did you think of the father's speech?"

"Impressive," Jack said.

"You felt something," she said.

Jack pushed down an incipient panic.

"Yeah, but I'm not sure I liked it."

Now the drum beat quickened, and at the bottom of the hill they weaved their way through the fantastically shaped cacti that hovered over them, like shapes in an elegant nightmare.

Jack felt his heart beat faster as they walked on behind the throng, then suddenly, there in front of them was a stone wall, the Altar of the Dead. The installation was a twelve-foot-high sculpture of the Virgin Mary with many little brightly colored boxes contained in a great square case at the Virgin's feet. Each of the compartments held some new bit of playfulness or remembrance, a lock of human hair, a candied sugar skull, a comb, a set of keys, a book of Garcia Lorca's poetry, a knife on which was painted a dancing skeleton. . . .

Jack knelt down next to Charlotte Rae and watched as she put her *pan de muerte* in one of the empty boxes at the Altar of the Dead.

Then it was Jack's turn. He suddenly felt paralyzed. There was something wrong, very wrong . . .

Softly, he lay the bread on the Altar of the Dead and half expected to hear a screaming in his soul, like in some old vampire movie. But there was nothing, only the sound of the wind as it whipped across the night plains.

"How'd you like it, son?"

Jack turned and saw Buddy Wingate standing there in a comical Zorro costume, complete with mask. He looked so foolish that he broke the spell, and Jack was able to give a real laugh of relief.

"Very interesting, Don Delorro."

"Yeah, ole Father's one intense dude," Buddy said. "Seen him look at people and have them faint dead away. Not that I expected you to. Hell of a security man if that happened, huh?"

"Don't worry," Jack said. "If I felt lightheaded at all, I'd just shoot him and worry about my soul later."

Buddy howled at that.

"You're a pisser, Jack. That's no shit. Well, honey, you and me got to get some sleep. Tomorrow, we are going to show Jackie here some of the real magic."

"That'd be nice," Jack said.

Buddy put one arm around Charlotte Rae, who couldn't help but wince. Jack watched them as they wandered off toward the main house. Then he turned and saw the townspeople headed for their village. He scanned the horizon for Father Herrera, but he was nowhere to be seen.

Jack still felt the creeps, but told himself to have a drink and cool out. Tomorrow Buddy was going to lay the news on him, and then he'd take them all down. And get the hell out of this spook world.

Chapter 19

Valle stopped at the light at La Brea and Santa Monica and stared at the black-haired, teenage boy who primped and winked at him from the bus stop. Wonderful. The kid was no more than sixteen and probably had every communicable disease known to man.

Valle gunned the motor when the light changed and thought of Colombia; thought of the Casa del Sol, the fabulous place he'd lived five years ago when he was stationed there; thought of the rose trellis that wound up a beautiful garden path to his house; thought of his servant, Sylvia, and of the cut flowers she left on his oak breakfast table every morning; thought of the parties he attended and the beauty of the mountains.

He could be there. He should be there. Instead, he was here, here in this pit, this human sewer, watching children peddle their ass and die, watching kids gunning down each other at graduation parties in San Marino. Just today he had heard about a drug-related murder in Los Feliz—a choirmaster had been shot down while buying a bottle of milk at a convenience store.

Oh, man, he wanted out. He wanted out, he wanted the kind of lifestyle he deserved. Now, up ahead, Valle saw the shabby red paint of the old Formosa Cafe and turned right into the parking lot.

As Valle looked toward the bar's side entrance, he saw an old man staggering from it, probably a grip from the movie business. The guy was tanked, could barely walk. Valle looked at his ruined face, his half-closed eyes, and shuddered.

Think about that, getting old in the land of eternal youth. There was nothing he wouldn't do to avoid that. No fucking way, baby. He waited in the parking lot for a couple of seconds, then got out and went inside.

The side hallway was dark, and Valle blinked. When his eyes adjusted, he saw on the wall in front of him a picture of Clark Gable, looking young and fit. Next to Gable was a smiling picture of Marilyn Monroe, looking as if she had just had a sexy assignation with Kennedy. And a little farther away was a picture of Elvis, in his cowboy costume, from *Love Me Tender*. Great, Valle thought, all the dead gods and goddesses. No one seemed to mind that they were all dead about fifty years too soon. They'd made it! They'd become legends in Tinseltown. The thought chilled him again.

He had to get back to Colombia, that was all there was to it.

He walked past the dark booths where kids with shaved heads, ripped jeans, and Dr. Martens sat with predictable scowls on their faces.

At the end of the bar, he saw Julio, but he didn't sit down next to him. Instead, he signaled to him to come to the back part of the Formosa, the dining car where there were small red leatherette booths that accommodated only two people.

"Hey, *ese,* what's going on?" Julio Blanco said, as they slid into their seats.

He was a wiry Colombian agent and had proved invaluable to Valle in the past. But he was a pain in the ass.

"Same old, same old," Valle said. "Did you talk to the people in Bogota?"

"Hey, man, you look tense. Ain't we gonna have a little drink first?"

The waitress, Margie, came toward them. She was heavyset and wore more makeup than Joan Crawford did in her last horror movie, *Trog*.

"Gimme a Jack Daniel's," Valle said.

"Perrier for me," Julio said.

She made a face at him and left.

"You getting too old to drink, Bobby," Julio said.

"Let me worry about that," Valle said. "I want to know what you got, but first I want to ask you very up front: You aren't wearing a wire, are you?"

"Please," Julio said. "That's a huge insult."

"So I apologize. I'm not going to pat you down, because you know what will happen if you play those games with me. So tell me. What's going down?"

"Ahhh, the lack of trust in this world of ours. It is sad," Julio said. He rubbed his thumb and forefinger over his mustache.

"Come on, Julio. I don't got all night."

"*Hmmmm,* well, how's this? I found out all about a certain young man. *Ooooh,* he is a very nasty boy. It was as you expected; he was Wilson's and he's not clean."

Valle made a fist and then slowly opened his hand.

"As I thought," he said. "Where is he?"

"They took him from Colombia to a private place. All done hush-hush, used military transport."

"You got pictures?"

"Not yet."

"Get them," Valle said. "I want the pictures. I want the bank statements."

"That's hard," Julio said. "That's gonna cost. It's going down in Switzerland."

Valle shook his head and stared hard at Blanco. "Listen, man, I don't give a fuck what it costs, and I don't care if he's protected by heat-seeking Dobermans, asshole. I want the goods. Get em. 'Cause time is running out. You hear me?"

"You're over the line, Valle," Julio said, as Valle shoved him back in his seat and stood up. "You're going to piss some people off, very big people who could squash you like a bug, man."

"We'll see about that," Valle said.

Behind him Margie came with the drink tray.

"Sorry, I'm late," she said.

"Why should you be on time?" Valle said. "Nobody else is."

He pointed menacingly at Julio, then turned and walked toward the door.

"You're very unsociable, Bob. That's too bad," Julio called after him.

Julio smiled and tossed back the Jack Daniel's. Then, he reached into his pocket, found a quarter, and walked toward the back of the restaurant to make a call. He'd been following Valle for two weeks now, and he knew somebody who was going to be very interested in what had just passed between them.

Chapter 20

The next morning, after breakfast around the pool, Wingate was in an expansive mood.

"This afternoon I want to show you my operation, Jack. You about ready?"

"You know it," Jack said. He was thankful it was finally happening. Waiting spooked him, not to mention Herrera, who gave him dreams of masked dancers with sharp knives. And then there was still the matter of Dr. Gunther Baumgartner. There was something familiar about that man . . . and not being able to nail it down was driving Jack crazy. Where had he seen him before? And why was he here? He obviously knew of Wingate's plans, but what part did he play in it all? Jack pondered these questions as he drank his orange juice and watched Marbella toss one of his whores into the swimming pool.

"I got a few things I got to take care of first," Wingate said, rubbing his big belly and sipping a Bloody Mary. "You take a swim, Jackie, and I'll see you round two."

"Sounds good," Jack said, though the prospect of swimming with Marbella and the others didn't thrill him.

But Charlotte Rae came to his rescue.

"Tell you the truth," she said, "I'd like to go into town."

Dr. Baumgartner practically leapt from his pool chair.

"I'll be happy to take you," he said. "I want to go into town myself."

"Well, aren't you thoughtful, Doctor," Charlotte Rae said, though her tone said the exact opposite.

"No, no," Wingate said. "Jack's the professional. I want him with her. I don't anticipate any of Salazar's boys making a move here in town, but you never know."

"You don't think I could take care of her?" The doctor said, and there was a trace of anger in his voice.

"Of course you could, Doc," Charlotte Rae said. "You're a regular superman."

The doctor winced at her words.

"Jackie will take her in," Wingate said. "After all, what am I paying him for?"

"Of course, that is best," Gunther said, but the words came out of his mouth with a squawk.

"Ready if you are, Jack," Charlotte Rae said.

She turned and did her best slinky walk for Gunther, who stared openmouthed at her back. Jack turned and followed her, feeling the German's eyes boring in on his neck, and he couldn't repress a small smile.

* * *

As they drove through the desert heat in the black Jeep Cherokee, Jack became intensely aware of her physical presence. She wore tight-fitting jeans and a blue chamois-cloth work shirt, and her blonde hair was tied up on top of her head with a bright red bandana with monkeys on it.

"Guess what," she said.

"What?" He stared dead ahead at the road and watched as a five-inch lizard darted in front of them and disappeared down a hole.

She put her long fingers on his thigh.

"I don't really need to do any shopping."

"Really?"

"That's right," she said.

She leaned across the seat and kissed him on the neck.

"I like that," he said.

"So do I," she said, suddenly pulling away.

"What is it?"

She gave no answer.

Jack turned and looked at her, and she smiled at him, but there was sadness in her eyes.

"I'm sorry," she said. "I was going to be fun. I was going to charm you and make you care about me. Instead, I seem to have fallen into a funk."

"That's all right," Jack said. "I like funky ladies."

She laughed a little and reached over to him again, but this time there was something tentative and sweet about her touch. She held three fingers of his right hand, like a child hanging on to her father.

Jack was stunned by the shifts in her moods.

"I've been thinking about you, Jack."

"Yeah?"

"Yes. I have. I confess."

She looked at him and smiled.

"I'm starting to have a problem thinking about anything else," she said.

"Yeah," Jack said. "I know what you mean."

"Do you?"

Her words thrilled him. The inflection was both sexy and childlike.

He pulled the Jeep to the side of the road. In front of them there was a six-foot cactus, which looked to Jack like the singing, dancing, sombrero-wearing cacti in Walt Disney movies. They were supposed to look funny, charming, but they had scared Jack badly as a child.

He turned to her, and she fell into his arms. He kissed her long and hard and felt the richness and fullness of her.

"You're such a surprise," he said.

"I am? Tell me. How?"

"Kiss me first."

"No, tell me first."

She looked up at him, and there was a naked need in her face, which made him breathless and his heart race triple time.

"Tell me, Jack. I want to hear the words."

"They matter more than the kisses?"

"Yes. Everyone wants to kiss me. So what?"

Jack sighed, shook his head.

"That's it," he said. "You just said it. Of course I want to make love to you . . . for godsake . . . but I just didn't expect you to be who you are."

"You're stumbling, Jack."

"You make me stumble."

"Maybe that's the nicest thing you've ever said to me. Because I know how quick you are."

"It's more than that," Jack said. "You fill me up."

He hadn't expected to say anything like that. Now he felt blinded and confused by the seriousness of his own words.

She put her hand tenderly on his cheek.

"Jack, I love you," she said.

"I love you," he said, but there was misery in his voice, as though he had just confessed to a crime.

Why was he saying this? Was it possible that between the shadow and the act, he might actually mean it?

He patted her hair and felt a wave of sweetness overtake him.

"Jack, I'm afraid. I didn't want this. . . . You have to believe me."

"Me, either," Jack said. And that admission was another nail in his coffin.

"You don't know him. . . . This kind of thing doesn't happen to him. If he finds out . . ."

She began to shake, and Jack held her close to him.

"He's not going to find out," he said.

"He will, Jack. He could have someone watching us right now."

Jack looked out the Jeep window.

"Unless he's disguised as a saguaro cactus, we don't have to worry."

She laughed a little.

"Isn't this the part where you tell me you're going to take me away from all this?"

"Yeah, but I'm not sure you want to leave," he said. "You got a life with Buddy. Isn't that what you told me once?"

"I know. I know what I said. Because I was scared. I'm still scared. But I don't want it anymore. It used to be enough to laugh at him, but that's no good anymore. That only works when there's nothing else, no one else to compare him to. Now there's you."

Jack looked down at the steering wheel.

He had to stop this, now. He couldn't let her put all her hope in him. But then again, why not? He had found his own hope in her, the girl he had to bust.

"We don't have to do anything yet," he said. "We have time."

She shook her head.

"I don't know, Jack."

She unbuttoned her blouse and pulled down the left sleeve. There was a black-and-blue mark.

"He beat me last night," she said.

"Son of a bitch."

"He's not always that way. It comes over him, like some kind of madness. It's like he's possessed."

The last words were delivered in a monotone, as though she

were the weather girl on television reporting on some light storm warnings.

"I'm going to get him," Jack said.

She looked at him, blinked.

"You're going to do him? No, Jack, I don't want you to go against him."

"What, then?" Jack said, and he no longer knew if he was acting at all. It occurred to him that he did want to kill Buddy.

"Jack, I think we should go right now."

"Now? You mean just drive out of here? Catch a plane?"

"Yes, why not? I've put away some money."

"We're about to make a huge score. I can't walk out on that, Charlotte."

"But . . ."

"Come on. Let's get real. I've got nothing earning six percent in a bank account. You're used to the high life. What would we do? Have a kid and go to the PTA? Eat Hamburger Helper?"

"Why not, Jack? It would be better than this. You . . . you're too much."

"What? Me? I'm not the one whacking you around."

She turned on him then and looked him straight in the eye.

"No, but you're the one who made me think about things. You made me feel like I could maybe be somebody, but now you just want your piece of ass like all the rest. You're a little more low-key about it, that's all. How about that? I fell for a modulated voice."

Jack turned from her and looked out the window. No, he thought, it isn't that. It's worse than that. It's not just a piece of ass. I want to set you up and arrest you and your husband. And the best I can do is maybe make you a deal that'll get you a short jail stay. As for love, whatever love I feel I've got to crush and toss away like old parking tickets.

"Jack, I mean it," she said. "If you really care about me, we should leave now. I've got some money. We could go to another country, take our chances. Buddy wouldn't waste time coming after us. Eventually he'd forget."

Jack turned back to her and shook his head.

"You don't really believe that. Buddy's too small to forget."

She threw her arms around him and pressed her head against his chest.

"You said you loved me. Do you mean it, even a little, Jack?"

"Yeah," Jack said. "I mean it. But it's a hard world, and we're not ever gonna make it like the Brady Bunch."

"Then you won't go with me now."

"I can't. We can't. But, if it means anything, I wish we could."

She nodded her head.

"All right, Jack," she said. "I don't know why, but I believe you. Maybe I'm crazy."

"Yeah," Jack said. "But keep it up. I like it."

He kissed her on the forehead, then turned the Jeep around in the desert and headed back to the compound. It was time to play Buddy's game.

"A lot of people think Juarez is a puke hole," Wingate said, pushing his black Stetson back on his head as Jack drove the Mercedes through the trash-covered streets of the city. "But me, I see it as the gateway to the land o' opportunity. Kinda like America was the majors and Juarez was good ole triple-A ball. Everybody wants to play under the hot lights of Hollywood, but you can't pull it off without having the right kinda minor league organization. That's what this town, hell, what this country is to us. It's like our Toledo Mud Hens supplying us with their best assets. Know what I mean, Jack?"

"Yeah, know exactly what you mean," Jack said.

Charlotte Rae leaned over the front seat.

"Well, I'm sure that the Mexicans would be delighted to know that you consider them minor leaguers."

That made Buddy laugh.

"You are jest too sensitive, sweetness," he said. "I mean, it's only natural that we should use them for our own benefit. Does the shark take any shit from the minnows? No, sir. That's like natural law."

"You mean the law of the jungle," Charlotte Rae said.

"Same damned thing." Buddy smiled. "Look at that."

He pointed to a whole family of Mexican Indians, father, mother, young daughter, and baby boy. They were standing out in the street with pink plastic-covered boxes of Chiclets in their hands.

"Now, take that, for example. That seriously amazes me," he said. "I mean, in the last twenty years Americans have undergone a chewing gum revolution. We got sugarless, like Care Free, and Plent-T-Pak and Bubblicious, not to mention Big fucking Red, and these people exist on selling Chiclets. I mean, Chiclets is like post-World War II, GI-Joe-comes-back-to-tract-home-paradise kinda shit, and you tell me the Mexes aren't triple A?"

He shook his head and indicated with a silent wave of his pudgy fingers that Jack should turn right.

Jack did and drove by a disco called Happy World. Though it looked new, the paint was already peeling off of it. The actual club was inside a huge globe that was suspended on a platform and revolved in the sickening dusty heat. Jack looked at the gunmetal gray spiral staircase, which led up into a battered doorway. The outside walls of the globe were painted with the continents, and the oceans were a garish bright blue.

Buddy saw Jack staring at the place and smacked his own knee.

"That's what passes for a high-class disco here. Pure imitation L.A. They got Mexican hookers in there all dressed up like Jean Harlow and Marilyn Monroe. The dealers all sit around with their beepers on. I been in there when DEA boys drop by and try staring everyone down. Don't stop nobody's action one bit, though, and they got a nice Mexican pizza in there."

"What's a Mexican pizza?" Jack said.

"One made with dog 'n' toe cheese," Wingate said. "Hey, now, don't go too fast and lose our friends."

Jack looked in the rearview and saw Altierez driving the Jeep. Escondero was leaning insolently in the passenger seat.

"Now, right here," Wingate said, indicating that they had to turn down an alley.

"And right again, through these gates."

Jack turned and saw a guard shack. The guard looked into the window and smiled. He had no teeth and blue gums.

"Señor!" he said to Wingate.

"Hildalgo," Wingate said, as though he were a long lost relative.

They passed through, and Jack made note of the sign: Tampico Furniture.

"Welcome to my little warehouse," Wingate said.

"A furniture store," Jack said. "Why the name Tampico?"

"A movie name," Buddy said. "Seen it years and years ago. I don't remember the plot anymore, jest that it was about spies and smugglers, and girls, and double crosses. I think the moral was 'Crime doesn't pay,' but that ain't the message I got. Crime looked like a hell of a lot of fun. Sure beat working in a body shop, which is what my old man did, right up till he died of paint fumes, age fifty-six. Park over there, son."

Jack pulled the car into a parking space marked "Reserve," turned off the key, and got out. The Jeep pulled in just behind him, and Jack could see Escondero's eyes staring bullets at him, even from behind the dark glasses.

They walked through the factory, and Wingate was expansive on how successful his latest line of furniture was.

"It's all made outta bamboo. I hired me a designer, and I told him I wanted it to be jest like one of them old movie sets. But I didn't want hippie bamboo. Had to be, you know, bamboo chic."

"Buddy knows what he wants when it comes to bamboo," Charlotte Rae said, but this time Buddy gave her a killing look, and she broke off her wisecrack. Jack looked at her and thought about the bruises. Was this the little deal they'd struck a long time ago? She got to puncture his balloon daily, and once or twice a week he made her pay for it by beating her senseless?

Jack looked down at the bamboo furniture. It did look like movie set furniture—junky, cheap, exotic—if you were slightly campy or very young.

"Bamboo has another nice feature," Buddy said.

He picked up a chair, pulled off the end of an arm, and let Jack look inside.

"Hollow. Ain't that nice?"

"Yeah, very," Jack said. "But I would think that the customs guys would realize that too."

"They do," Buddy said, walking by several workers who were working at a lathe. "They look at every single piece of bamboo furniture which comes through the big gate."

He smiled and went through a door, leading Jack and the others down some chartreuse cement steps.

"The thing is, though," he said, slipping his key into a locked door at the bottom of the building, "they are always disappointed. All they ever find is furniture."

He took them into a new room, and Jack was surprised to find three pool tables, a Ping-Pong table, and a Coke machine. The cement floor was painted chartreuse, and the walls lime green. A pool room disguised as a fun house.

"This here is the employees' rec room," Wingate said, as Jack and the others stood up against the wall. "State of the art, hey?"

Marbella looked over at Jack and rolled his eyes.

"It's aces," Jack said.

"Knew you'd like it. You play any pool, Jack?" Wingate said.

"A little."

"How about right now?"

Jack looked at Charlotte Rae, who smiled at him with a certain measured encouragement.

"Why not?"

Jack walked to the wall rack and picked out a cue. He chalked it up and walked to the nearest table.

Wingate stood across the room at the other table.

"I'd rather play on this one," he said.

He reached into his pocket and pulled out a remote control device, no bigger than an ordinary television channel changer.

He aimed it at the pool table, pressed a button, and the table began at once to lift off of the floor.

The table rose two feet off the ground, then Wingate hit

another button on his little black box, and it moved to the left, clearing the space on the floor it had occupied.

Next, Wingate aimed the remote control at the floor and an electronic door slid open. Jack and the others hurried to the spot and looked down. There was an escalator built into the five-foot-high tunnel. It went straight down into the earth for about forty feet, then gradually leveled off into the tunnel. At the bottom Jack saw several furniture boxes. Wingate hit a third button and lights came on inside the passage. He hit another button, and the escalator started to gradually descend underground.

"Best ride since Disneyland," Wingate said. "Hop on, boys. You are gonna see an engineering marvel."

Jack moved forward, and felt Charlotte Rae press up against him. Escondero, Altierez, and Marbella were chattering in amazement, but Jack remained quiet. Inside though, his excitement was so great that he could barely restrain himself. He felt as though his hands were shaking, and he worried that someone might notice, but when he looked down at them, they were still.

He was here, he thought, as he got on and ducked low. He was here, one step away from nailing Wingate and shutting down the whole operation. The bust of a lifetime. . . .

"I gotta hand it to you, Buddy, this is amazing," Jack said, trying to funnel his nervous energy into his performance.

"Course it is," Wingate said, staring at him as they went deeper into the earth. "What did you think I was anyway, some ole country boy?"

They traveled on, going deeper and deeper into the earth. The way was lit by naked bulbs placed every three feet, and Jack marveled at the cement lagging in the ceiling, the hardwood joists. The tunnel was built to last.

"Jesus, this is creepy," Marbella said.

"Yeah, like in a sci-fi movie, man. I seen it once long time ago. *Attack of the Mole People.*"

"Yeah, but you can breathe really well."

"That's because we're fully air-conditioned," Wingate said.

"The generator is in a wall unit behind the Coke machine in the office upstairs. Now we're going to level off a bit."

A few feet more and they came to a stop.

Wingate pointed to the tunnel, which now flattened out and headed straight across the border.

"This tunnel was dug by our people upstairs in three months. Used pneumatic drills and five-pound buckets to lug out the dirt and rocks with. We had a couple of cave-ins . . . and lost three boys, but they got the job done, by God."

"How long this thing been here?" Escondero said.

"Don't suppose there's any harm in you knowing," Wingate said. "This little baby has been used for five sweet years. During that time we've maybe made us a buck or two."

Jack let out an inaudible sigh. He thought of Koch, a DEA agent he'd once met at an Agency retreat in Montana. Jack had been only a rookie and had asked him how effective the Agency really was, since no one had ever actually given him their success rate. Koch had looked at him and said, "The truth is we only catch the dumb ones, Jack. Or the ones that get too damned brazen about it." At first Jack had thought Koch was joking, but one look at his severe blue eyes let him know that it was the sad truth.

Five years. The amount of drugs that had passed through here must have been staggering. The lives wasted . . . mothers selling their children for crack, babies born with what they call euphemistically "learning disabilities" in the prevention pamphlets. Kids who can't read a sentence, can't sit still, are driven mad by the rerouting of their own barely formed nervous systems, condemned to walk feverishly around the city streets mumbling to themselves, like ancient senile beggars in some third-world country, kids trying to scratch some invisible psychic itch that can never be reached. Yes, crack drove them mad, and now Buddy Wingate and his friends were moving heroin, Colombian white, which would soothe the savage beasts, turn them into Play-Doh, at the cost of their will, their creativity, and in many cases, their lives. That was the choice drugs gave you in the end. You can have madness and then you can have death. Have another taste.

Five years. Jack was staggered by a sense of futility. And how many more of these underground railways existed?

He took a breath and shut the thought out of his mind. He was going to bring them down—that was the important thing.

"No need to go all the way through on the tunnel. All you got to know is this: We come up inside our own furniture warehouse just outside the third checkpoint on the good ole Texas highway. The trucks that roll through customs are, of course, clean. They get their certificate of inspection from the border officials, then they drive to the warehouse, where we take off certain boxes of furniture and put on these boxes. Inside these is the coke, the heroin, whatever we're moving this week. There's one more checkpoint they got to cross, but the guards are overwhelmed there, and besides we've already got our inspection certificate nice and stamped by U.S. Customs, so they don't ever bother us. Once we're past there, it's all she wrote, clear sailing to Arizona, California, and points west. Your jobs, *mi amigos,* is to make sure no one bothers us on the American side. We're going to go over there after lunch and visit our warehouse. Hey, you're gonna love it. It's right up the road from Rose's Cantina, the cafe Marty Robbins made famous in that ole El Paso song. They got one hell of a green chili tortilla there."

He turned to Jack.

"Well, son, how do you like it?"

"Damned impressive, Buddy. First-rate deal."

He kept his tone respectful, no hint of wiseass, which was easy, because the truth was, he was impressed—sickened but impressed.

"Knew you would be, son. Now, let's get back. I got a few things to take care of with the landing. The plane from Colombia is coming in tomorrow night at midnight. And I want to make sure our cover is good on this side."

"We can work that too," Jack said. "If you want?"

"Well, I hadn't intended you to," Buddy said. "We're usually okay here. The Mexicans know to look out for us, but this is an especially rich shipment. Colombian white heroin. Worth about ten million bucks. And believe me, son, I need my cut of it."

Wingate smiled and put his arm around Jack's shoulders. "When we get upstairs, you take it easy. You boys can go to a club or two and get yourself some sweet pussy, you want to. Just be back by four."

Jack nodded and stretched his neck, as Wingate hit his remote control and the escalator started back toward the top.

Though Jack had underplayed his concern in the DEA briefings, the truth was he had always been worried about how he would get away to make the phone call to his partner. Michaels had gotten on his nerves when he brought it up, precisely because underneath all the bravado, Jack knew he was right. It wasn't going to be easy. He was sure of that.

If there was ever a time his cover could be blown, it was now. But this opportunity seemed to be tailor-made. Escondero, Altierez, Marbella, and he were sitting in the third-world splendor of Happy World. The floor was covered with a bright maroon shag rug, and the circular bar in front of him featured teenage Mexican hookers dressed like Hollywood movie stars, just as Wingate had advertised.

Right now "Marilyn Monroe" was dancing in a lesbian embrace with "Madonna," both of them too dark-skinned, thin, and youthful-looking underneath their platinum wigs to be convincing. Their awkward embraces and clumsy, amateurish dancing wouldn't have made it in places like the Body Shop in Los Angeles, but Jack's crew wasn't particular. They drank their cuba libres and sat two feet away from the girls, sticking fifty-dollar bills in their G-strings, spurring them on. Jack tossed them a couple of hundreds and pounded Marbella on the back.

"Do it girls."

"Let us see you do the trick, mama."

"Oh, yes, lick good now, baby . . ."

Jack looked down the row, watched the hot, blinking pink and purple lights play over their faces, which were twisted grotesquely with desire. One of the girls looked as if she was about thirteen, and Jack felt a sickness in the pit of his stomach.

He leaned over to Marbella.

"Be right back man. I got something I need to take care of."

Marbella smiled dreamily.

"Good, man. Do her one time for me."

Jack nodded to the others and left smiling. They were too far gone into their fantasy world to really give a shit where he went.

Outside, Jack turned out on Hidalgo Street into a marketplace, where a great fat woman sold rugs.

"You like one of these, señor?" she said.

"Sorry. I need a phone," he said.

She smiled.

"Telephone," he said, gesturing as though he was making a phone call.

"Ahhh," she said. "Over there."

She pointed down the street, but Jack saw nothing.

"Where?"

She smiled and kept pointing.

Suddenly, a city bus pulled away from the corner, and Jack saw the telephone stand.

"*Gracias,*" he said, handing her a five-dollar bill.

She smiled and stuck it into her skirt as Jack ran down the street.

He dialed the operator, gave her the number, and stood waiting nervously. All his life he'd heard comics doing jokes about the telephone service in Mexico, and now his life might depend on their promptness.

His luck held. Within seconds the phone began to ring, and miraculously on the third ring he was listening to C.J.'s smoky voice:

"Cal's Pizza."

"You got goat cheese and pancetta, *amigo?*"

C.J. let out a long sigh of relief.

"Baby, where the hell are you?"

"Juarez."

"Oh, man, I was afraid of that. Everybody here has been

going apeshit. They thought you were planted out there under the cactus."

"Not a chance," Jack said. "Listen, I don't have much time, man. So listen up. The deal is going down in a tunnel. . . . You wouldn't believe this place—I mean it's got air-conditioning and moving sidewalks, everything but a fucking sushi bar. The smack is inside bamboo furniture. Wingate's cover company is called Tampico, and he's got an office here in Juarez, and the tunnel comes up in his El Paso warehouse, which is out Route Twenty-five, just past the second checkpoint. The shit's being flown in from Colombia. Man, this could net us some heavies, who just might want to help bring down Morales."

"Fantastic," Jefferson said.

"Can't talk much longer. The deal is going down between midnight and dawn tomorrow night. You got it?"

"Got it. You all right, man?"

"I'm fine. How's Zampas holding up?"

"He's okay. Michaels is pissed, though. He wants your ass."

"Yeah, well, he'll be a lot more pissed when we bring these fuckers down and his little plan, whatever it is, is dead in the water."

"Good work, baby."

"Okay. I gotta go man."

Jack hung up and looked around nervously. There were five hookers on the street in front of him. They wore pastel jump-suits, mini-skirts with white plastic go-go boots, and looked like they were competing in a Charo look-alike contest. They were laughing at some sailors who were yelling at them from a battered white Cadillac.

He gave out a long sigh of relief. He'd done it. The worst was over. . . .

But his satisfaction was short-lived. On the opposite corner, the sailors and the hookers had moved on. His view of the bar was no longer obstructed, and now he could see them coming toward him. Escondero, Altierez, Marbella, and Wingate.

Jack moved away from the phone. It took all his discipline not to cut and run. What was Wingate doing here? Had he simply finished his work early and stopped by to join the boys for a little drink?

Silently, Jack prayed that this last explanation was the truth, but as the four men came closer, he could see on their faces that it wasn't so.

"Making a little phone call, son?" Wingate said.

"That's right," Jack said. "Calling my father. He's got a problem with his heart and I wanted to make sure he's all right."

"And how is he?" Wingate said.

"He's fine," Jack said.

"I find that hard to believe," Wingate said. "Since we know your dad has been dead for quite a few years now, Agent Walker."

Marbella's smile was like a knife blade, glinting, as Escondero moved in. Jack kicked him in the groin, spun quickly, and bashed the onrushing Marbella in the nose with his elbow, then turned and ran.

He fled across the traffic-filled street, narrowly avoiding getting run down by a tourist bus, then turned and ran up the street. The others took up the chase, Wingate and Altierez coming directly behind him, not fifteen feet away. Jack ran by a boot-maker's and a butcher shop. A man was walking into the store with cages of birds—chickens, turkeys—and Jack ran into him, sending the squawking birds flying.

Jack turned, looked. Altierez was gaining on him. Jack picked up a cage with a rooster in it and threw it in his path. A perfect shot. Altierez tripped over it and fell into the street. Jack turned and started to run back across the street, but Escondero and Marbella were waiting on the other side. He had no choice but to keep going straight ahead. In front of him was some kind of tour group. Maybe if he could mix in with them for a second, he could lose his pursuers. He ran toward the group . . . mostly middle-age people with guide books in their hands. They stood in front of a small chapel and stared at a stained-glass window. Jack heard a teenage kid say to his mother, "Oh, man, virgins and bullfighters. I wanta go watch TV."

Jack tried to enter the little band of travelers, but suddenly a knife flashed from the crowd. Jack saw it coming, almost as though it were in slow motion, but he found himself unable to dodge, and the blade sliced into his right shoulder. The pain was intense. The tourists screamed as Jack headed down a back alley, tripping over trash cans, nearly falling, then righting himself, turning, and looking back at them as they piled in on top of him, all arms, legs, and he thought that Wingate had a baseball bat . . . and as he fell onto the trash-littered street, he wondered how he'd gotten hold of it. Son of a bitch is no country boy, Jack thought, as he fell on the ground and the blows rained down on him until he passed into darkness.

Chapter 21

Brandau stood at the podium and looked out at the auditorium of Gardena High School. Every seat was filled, the students were sitting quietly, and for the first ten minutes of his antidrug speech, he began to have the faint hope that this time was going to be different. This time maybe they were going to listen.

He started to tell the story of Paco Huerta, a former football star at Crenshaw High who had died the previous year at the team homecoming party when he freebased cocaine right in his parent's backyard . . . died in hideous spasms while all his teammates and school pals stood helplessly by. Brandau had gotten to Paco's funeral in the rain when the first shout came from the audience.

"Fuck Paco Huerta, homes, he was a fucking *maricón*."

There was nervous laughter from a couple of other students. A teacher ran toward the voice.

"You shut right up, mister," the teacher said, pointing at a bandana-wearing student in the fifth or sixth row.

Brandau felt the sweat break out on his upper lip. Shit, he hated this. He had to keep control, show them that they were not going to get to him.

He started in again:

"Then there was the case of the famous Hollywood actor Terry Darnay. You all remember him?"

"Yeah, and he was a faggot too," someone else yelled.

That got a much bigger and much longer laugh.

Brandau tried for an I'm-with-it-you-guys grin, but it didn't turn out that way. No, instead, he realized instantly that he looked like a big square, a goof, up there. To these kids, many of whom had automatic weapons in their knapsacks, he was just a white fucking stooge.

"Hey, Mr. Brandau," said a voice in the back now, "You know why people take drugs man? Let me tell you, Mr. D-E-Fucking-A, asshole. They take drugs 'cause they feel fucking good, you see, man? And there ain't nothing else in their whole fucking life, Mr. White Narco Man, that makes them feel good. So why don't you go back to Hancock Park or wherever it is you hang, faggot?"

That was all they needed. Many of the students were screaming now, screaming obscenities and throwing things. Suddenly a projectile hit Brandau in the head, and he felt a wave of nausea sweep through him. Shit, maybe it was a knife. He looked down at the floor and, in shock, picked it up.

But, it wasn't a knife at all. No, it was a banana. In front of him there were ten girls sitting together in the front row, screaming with laughter. Here was the big DEA guy, the guy who was supposed to set them all straight, standing there looking as if he'd just crapped in his pants, holding a banana in his hand.

The auditorium was bedlam. Brandau dropped the banana, turned, and walked slowly toward the exit door.

He sat in his car, his hands shaking, his head throbbing. A couple of the teachers and the principal herself had come out to assure him it wasn't his fault, to thank him for coming, and to beg him to reschedule. Fat fucking chance.

* * *

Now he took deep breaths, practiced his new Zazen breathing techniques that Suzie Chow had taught him. They helped a little, but he still felt furious.

He looked down at his watch. It was twelve-thirty. Christ, he was almost late for his lunch with Suzie at Citrus. He started his car, then noticed the black Mazda parked on the other side of the street. He thought he'd seen it two days ago. Was it possible he was being followed?

If so, by whom?

He took off, keeping the guy in his rearview, but as he turned at the light, the Mazda turned left.

So far so good, but still he wondered. Was somebody watching him? And if so why?

He'd have to keep watch, be careful. Maybe something hinky was going down.

"I love it here," Suzie Chow said, as she and Brandau took seats under one of the chic brown canvas awnings at Citrus. "They have such great food. And it's not that expensive."

Brandau managed a pained smile, but couldn't resist speaking out.

"The hell, it's not," he said. "I should be eating a chili dog down at Pink's, saving some money."

Suzie smiled and looked at the colorful bistro paintings on the wall.

"We've been through all this before, Richard. I'm making good money now. I'm going to get that TV-movie deal soon, and we're going to be fine. You'll pick up a lot of extra money by consulting when you retire. But to do that, you need to be seen in places like this. This is where you meet the right people."

Suzie put her slender hand on Brandau's, and he felt a surge of lust. God, she was one exciting woman. Then he looked across the room at the back table.

"Well," he said, "looks like there are at least three people here you definitely don't want to meet."

"What are you talking about" Suzie said.

"Back there in the corner," Brandau said. "See the tan, slick-looking guy with the black ponytail? Sitting with two other guys?"

"Yes," Suzie said. "I noticed him when I came in. He's an actor, I think, but I can't place his name."

"He's a bad actor, is what he is," Brandau said. "That's Pedro Salazar. Major dope dealer. That's the asshole who came after Jack Walker up in Tahoe. Nearly killed him. I've had a couple of run-ins with him myself."

Brandau's voice was rising now, and several people at nearby tables had turned to look at him.

"I hate eating at the same place with a germ like that."

"Calm down, Richard," Suzie said, "You're drawing attention to yourself."

She reached out to take his sleeve, but Brandau pulled away.

"I just had a rotten experience talking to high school students. And it's flashy assholes like him that are the cause of it. The kids worship scum like Salazar."

Perspiration broke out on Brandau's forehead.

And now, from the corner of the room, Salazar pushed away his chair and started walking toward Brandau.

"He's coming over here," Brandau said.

"Richard," Suzie Chow said. "He's only going to the bathroom. Don't make a scene."

Brandau said nothing but stared holes at the tall, muscular Salazar, who walked with an arrogant, theatrical sway of his shoulders and hips.

As he came near Brandau's table, Salazar turned and smiled at Suzie Chow. It was a lewd and leering smile, filled with mockery and, by implication, contempt for her lunch partner.

"What the fuck are you laughing at, asshole?" Brandau said, standing at his table.

"Richard!" Suzie Chow said. "It's nothing. Let it go."

She blushed and rubbed her forehead as if she were trying to erase herself.

"I don't think so," Brandau said. "I don't think they should let known drug dealers eat at a decent place like this. They oughta' slide their food in to them under the bars of their cages!"

The surrounding tables suddenly became deathly quiet. Brandau moved toward Salazar, who stood stock-still and looked him straight in the eye.

"I don't know what you are talking about, my friend," Salazar said, flashing his capped teeth. "I am a legitimate businessman. In the import and exporting business."

"Bullshit," Brandau said, moving his head so close to Salazar that he could smell the garlic on his breath. "You sell dope to kids. That's what you do, *maricón*."

Salazar smiled, as if this insult meant less than nothing to him.

"It's true, I do work with kids," he said. "I recently opened a mission in my home state of Texas. We've taken in a lot of homeless kids, give them food, shelter, keep them out of trouble. Fact is, they are giving me a humanitarian award down there soon. They ever give you any awards, Agent Brandau?"

Brandau grabbed Salazar by his collar and pulled it tight around his neck.

"Fuck you, you slimebag."

Suddenly from behind Brandau, one of Salazar's two bodyguards grabbed the agent from behind and quickly and expertly bent his left arm behind him. Brandau groaned.

"Let him go," Salazar said. "He's just another frustrated little cop."

The short powerful man let go of Brandau's arm. Salazar laughed.

"We'll get you yet, asshole," Brandau said, but his voice was weak.

Suzie Chow was on her feet, her bag in hand.

"I think we should go at once, Richard," she said.

"Bullshit," Brandau said. "He should go. Not us!"

But she was furious, clutching her bag and heading for the front door. Brandau quickly followed her, Salazar and his men's laughter ringing in his ears.

Chapter 22

In stark contrast to everyone else in the room, Michaels paced the floor in Zampas's comfortable office, perspiration dripping off his face, even though the room was maximally air-conditioned. When he talked, he nearly spat out the words.

"I can't believe he went to Mexico against orders. I want to recommend that upon his return, *if* he makes it back, Agent Walker be put on probation and formal charges be brought against him."

Sitting with his feet up on the couch, Calvin Jefferson laughed.

"Hey, man, way I see it, the day Jack Walker gets back, he's probably going to get a medal of valor."

"Or maybe a fucking presidential citation," Valle kicked in.

Brandau sucked on his pipe and tried not to join in the others' derisive tone. But he nodded his head in agreement.

"Look, Ted, I understand your concern," Brandau said. "Jack . . . has gone against regulations. And I don't think it should be encouraged. But just the same, it sounds as though he's about to succeed, and, frankly, we could use a little success. Appropriations in Congress are coming up, and it's going to look very nice to see our director here, standing in a drug tunnel which we just busted."

"We've made plenty of arrests in the past year," Michaels said.

"That's true," Brandau said. "But this is a timely arrest. And though I don't always agree with you about publicity, I think this one's big. If Bob's information is right, it could lead us directly back to Eduardo Morales."

Valle cracked his knuckles. "Hey, my information is right, count on it. So why don't you just give us a break, Michaels?"

Michaels stopped pacing and looked through Valle.

"Here's the truth: Everybody in this room knows that Eduardo Morales isn't going to be anywhere near this shipment of drugs."

"Hey, nobody said he was gonna pop up and ask us to snap the cuffs on him," Calvin Jefferson said. "But we get some of his men, we are gonna be able to do some righteous infiltration of his little empire down there. And ain't that what's it's all about?"

Michaels said nothing. He was aware that he looked and sounded ridiculous.

Zampas sipped a Diet Coke and took a large bite off his three-pound deli sandwich.

"Ted, we have no choice but to play this out and give Jack every bit of backup he needs. We'll see about disciplining him later. But so far this looks clean."

Michaels said nothing else. He sat through the rest of the meeting in a kind of fog. The DEA was ready for the biggest catch of the last five years and the dramatic capture of a tunnel that would garner them praise from Washington. There was nothing else he could say—not yet anyway.

But if the information he was seeking came through from his snitch, there would be plenty to say, and then they would all have to listen.

He nodded and shook his head as the others cheerfully planned the bust, but in his own mind, he saw something else happening, a side benefit that he hadn't really hoped for.

The truth was, if he got the right information, if he got it in time . . . he might just end up inheriting Zampas's job. To hell with them all . . . that was the way to look at it. He'd tried to warn them, now he had to look out for himself.

At ten o'clock that same night an exhausted Michaels sat staring at his fax machine. Where was the goddamned stuff he'd sent for from his snitch in Mexico City, Vargas? Vargas had assured him he could get what Michaels needed, but snitches, even the best of them, were often unreliable. Still, this wasn't some ordinary bust. Michaels shook his head. No use going into that again. The stuff probably wasn't coming tonight.

He stared moodily out the window at the twinkling lights of downtown Los Angeles. The place looked magical, inviting, from up here. Nearby was a newly built hotel where wealthy Japanese businessmen drank sake, danced to jazz with hookers, and dialed a special number to get heroin sent to their rooms. And a few blocks down the street was some kind of artists' loft scene. Probably every person in there was high on some kind of illegal drug.

Ted Michaels sighed and felt intensely lonely.

What none of them knew about him, what he couldn't get across because of his stiff-assed, pain-in-the-neck personality, was that he actually gave a shit. His problem was he didn't sound as though he did. He sounded, he knew, like an ambitious prig, but that wasn't really who he was. Not at all.

He cared about the integrity of the Agency, cared deeply.

And he feared for their safety.

Yes, he was ambitious, but so were they all. He just couldn't disguise it as well with congenial patter. Small talk didn't come easily to him.

The truth was, he thought, that no one really liked him. It had been true all of his life. If someone else, someone like Walker, were in his position, he would be able to make people listen, simply because they all liked him. But Michaels would have to lay it all out on a platter before anyone would take notice.

Well, by God, he would have it all laid out soon. If he was right, then they would have to listen to him. And maybe they wouldn't like him any better, but they'd respect him.

Where the hell was Vargas? Out getting high himself or getting laid? Did he have the stuff or didn't he? Did he even give a shit? Or was it going to be *mañana?*

Time was running out.

He thought of Walker then. Walker was a lousy cop, by his lights, but in a weird way, he was the only one Michaels trusted. He was too impulsive, too immature, too hung up on himself and his own youthful rebellion, but he was kind, smart, and insanely brave.

But was he honest? Michaels was almost certain he was, but he wasn't a hundred percent sure. With someone as impulsive as Jack, there was always the chance he could be bought, swayed by money or a pretty girl—a girl who looked like Charlotte Rae Wingate.

He'd bet money that Jack was screwing her and justifying it to himself by saying he was getting information. Michaels sighed. Maybe Jack was right. But Jack didn't know the whole story. That was the problem.

Suddenly, Michaels heard the door to the hallway open behind him. He opened the desk drawer, picked up his Glock, and turned.

There at the door was a large black woman with a trash can and broom.

"Lutitia," Michaels said, "you startled me."

"Startled *you?*" the big friendly cleaning woman said, smiling. "Man, I thought you was Carlos Guzman the Drug King in here."

They both laughed.

"What chu doing here so late all by yourself?"

"Just waiting for some information from Mexico. But I think it's going to come tomorrow," he said.

"Mexico," she said. "While you sitting here waiting, you know they drinking tequila and eating tacos."

"I'm afraid you're right. I might as well close up shop tonight," Michaels said.

They both laughed. She smiled at him and dumped a trash can into the larger one. He picked up his holster and laid it over his shoulder, then backed up his work and locked the floppy disc in his desk.

Walker, he thought. Walker is all right. He suddenly wished he'd shared what he knew with Jack.

What if something happened to him?

Nonsense. No one knew anything.

But what if they did? They knew so much. He was almost sure that, at certain times, lately, someone was following him—not every minute and not with the same car. But last night at dinner and the night he had talked to Walker at his apartment, there had been somebody there. He was almost certain of it.

Whom could he trust?

He looked across the room at Walker's office. He didn't dare leave anything in there. He wished he could leave it on Walker's computer at home. Now, that wasn't a bad idea. He could break into Walker's place, leave the stuff there.

But what if Walker didn't make it back? Jesus, he was getting spooked.

Suddenly the phone rang; both he and Lutitia jumped.

"DEA, Michaels."

"I love it when you sound so official."

Michaels sat down on the edge of the desk. Lutitia waved to him and left the room, wheeling her trash can with a grace Michaels knew he would never have.

"Where are you and what are you doing?" Michaels said.

"I'm sitting in my apartment watching an ancient Dick Van Dyke show. Ask me what I'm wearing."

Michaels felt the beginnings of a blush come over him.

"Go ahead. Are you afraid . . . Agent Michaels?"

"I, ah . . . well." Christ, Michaels thought, this is perfect.

"You're just playing me, aren't you, Ted? Come on, admit it. I like it when a man uses a little misdirection."

"What *are* you wearing?" Michaels said, and blushed.

"My little green bathing suit," the voice said. "The same little suit I was wearing the night I met you by the pool. I was under the impression you liked it."

"You were right," Michaels said. "I liked it very much."

"I thought you did."

Michaels felt his pulse racing. It had started six months ago, at a party given by a real estate friend, Tod, in the Hollywood Hills. Michaels had seen the boy standing on the high dive, a glass of champagne in his hand. He had been wearing a green racing Speedo bikini suit. He had a perfectly flat stomach and long handsome legs, and he smiled, tossed the drained glass down to a surprised Michaels, who caught it and watched the boy make a perfect half gainer, creasing the water with no splash. When he came to the surface, Michaels stared at him and felt his stomach flip. The boy pulled himself out of the pool, and Michaels handed him the glass.

Their fingers touched, and there was electricity between them. "Let me get you some champagne," the boy said. Michaels had watched him walk away, the curve of his ass, the soft blond hairs on his leg.

Still, Michaels had tried to avoid what he knew could be a collision course. He'd turned and walked out of the party, without even getting the boy's number.

But it was too late. The next day he had called Tod at his office and asked for the number. Tod had told him the boy's name, Jeffrey, and said he'd just broken up with an older man, that he was sweet, sexy, an Olympic swimmer.

Michaels had waited for two weeks, during which time he couldn't sleep or eat. He found himself obsessed with memories of the boy on the board, of the graceful arc he made in the air. Finally he could stand it no longer. He called Jeffrey and asked him to a private after-hours club called Rey's on La Cienega.

It was a very posh, very private place, with an excellent wine list. But neither of them had been able to eat. It was an effort even to get through the appetizers, and suddenly, shy, cautious Michaels had found himself putting his arm around Jeffrey as they left the club (having left their dinners practically untouched) and running his hands through his hair as they walked around the corner.

Two minutes later they were in the front seat of Michaels's car, Jeffrey's head bobbing in his lap.

In spite of this wild beginning, they had been discreet, though Michaels often felt out of control just thinking of him.

He had become so worried about his own obsession with Jeffrey that he had tried to cut off their relationship. With his other worries about the Agency, with his dark suspicions, he couldn't afford to lose his concentration.

But he had missed Jeffrey, terribly.

He had called him again two nights ago, but only talked to his machine.

Now Jeffrey was calling him back. Playing games with him right here at the office. It was risky, insane. In the past phones had been tapped. God, if anyone found out? But it made Michaels's pulse race, his lips wet.

He was so tired, so very tired of being secret, circumspect Ted Michaels. This risk made him feel alive. Jeffrey made him feel alive.

"Going to take a dip?" Michaels said, scarcely aware of what he was saying, his heart was beating so fast.

"No, I just came back from swimming," the boy said. "Now I'm going to put on my . . . new Levi's and take a little car trip."

"Where?"

"To Mulholland Drive. I'm going to stand up on Mulholland Drive and watch the stars come out. And I'm going to drink champagne. That's still legal, isn't it, Officer?"

"You're crazy," Michaels said. "Completely crazy."

"Sounds like fun. Why don't you come up and apprehend me, Officer? You could snap the cuffs on me."

Then Jeffrey's voice lost its playful edge.

"I've missed you, Teddy," he said. "I can't sleep without you around."

"Me too," Michaels said.

"Can't you come meet me?" Jeffrey said, and there was a deep yearning in his voice. "I want you to."

"Stay where you are. I'll be there in thirty minutes, and we can ride up together," Michaels said.

"That would be nice," the boy said.

Michaels hung up the phone, smiling. Mulholland Drive, champagne, the stars. This wasn't him. This wasn't him at all. Or rather, it was him, it was the him that he had always known existed under the fastidious little bureaucrat.

It had taken this boy . . . this twenty-three-year-old boy to bring him out.

He strapped his shoulder holster tightly, picked up a copy of the disc.

This was crazy. Only minutes before he had been obsessed with his work, and now he was heading out of the office to a romantic rendezvous with his boy lover.

It was mad, but it brought a smile to his face because it occurred to him that it was real life—sloppy, wild, two impossible situations overlapping one another. Life was accidental in the end, Michaels thought. He had dedicated his whole life to minimizing the risks and heading off the accidents, but when it came to passion, it was no use.

Jesus, what was happening to him? Maybe it was the pressure.

He hurried from the office, thinking of the boy, in his Levi's, under the stars on Mulholland Drive. He wished, God how he wished, that that was all he had to think about. But there was Walker down there in Mexico. He had to somehow try and keep his mind on Walker as well. He stopped, remembered the information he had, his idea of leaving it in Walker's house. It still seemed a sensible plan. He picked up the packet marked "Cactus" and put it in his briefcase.

He'd go see Jeffrey, then he'd make a late-night trip to Walker's little apartment on Cherokee.

Michaels smiled in spite of himself. Maybe this was more than just one aberrant evening. Maybe this was the start of a new person, a looser, friendlier Ted Michaels. Why not?

"Would you like another drink?"

"No. . . . Okay. One more."

Ted Michaels sat on a rock at the highest perch of the Fryman Canyon overlook and stared down at the twinkling lights of the San Fernando Valley below.

"Clear tonight," he said.

He could feel Jeffrey's presence next to him, smell his aftershave lotion.

The boy put his head against Michaels's shoulder.

"You look tired tonight," he said.

"I am tired," Michaels said.

"I'm sorry," Jeffrey said. "Your work. It must be exhausting."

"It is," Michaels said. "Especially right now."

"I won't ask why," the boy said.

"Good. You know I couldn't tell you anyway."

"Yes. But I know you're doing something dangerous."

"I've already told you too much," Michaels said. "Believe me, you don't want to know any more about this."

Michaels handed him the champagne, and the boy laid his hand over the agent's fingers.

Michaels turned and looked at him, and the boy smiled.

"Like they say in the soap operas, 'this is madness,'" Michaels said.

"So what?" the boy said. "I like soap operas."

He smiled innocently and took Michaels's face in his hands and kissed him on the lips.

Michaels kissed him back and felt an intense rush of happiness. It was an emotion he was so unaccustomed to that it made him laugh.

"God," he said, "we've drunk a whole magnum of champagne."

"Yes we have," the boy said. "But fortunately the Perrier-Jouet people have been kind enough to make a never-ending supply of it. And I have another bottle in the car."

"No, no," Michaels said. "No more for me. You go get it if you want. I'm just going to sit here and look at the lights of the city."

"I bet I can change your mind," the boy said.

He squeezed Michaels's thigh as he got up. Michaels turned and watched as Jeffrey headed back to the parking lot, watched his trim body, his slightly pigeon-toed athletic stride.

Then he remembered Walker, realized that he'd better not get much drunker or he wouldn't be able to break into his apartment.

Then he laughed again. Of course he would be able to break into Walker's apartment. He was very good at breaking into places—something else most of the guys at the office didn't know about him. He'd served his time in the field, and he was as capable as any of them. So fuck them, fuck them all. . . .

He stared down at the Valley, saw the lights of Laurel Canyon Boulevard stretching out into the Valley, the rows of cars crawling along. It was quite beautiful, he thought, just being here, sitting in the nice cool evening breeze, his feet hanging over. It was really lovely. He wanted to have more moments like this one. Christ, he didn't want to let it all pass him by without feeling anything.

Where was Jeffrey? Where was the boy who brought a smile to his face? Where the hell? . . .

He had begun to feel tired. This wasn't good, not at all. . . . He still had to get to Walker's somehow. So he had to stay awake. Only he felt as though he had a weight on him, crushing him. . . .

When Michaels had fallen on his side, the boy came back and gently picked him up. He carried the agent to Michaels's car. Michaels was light, the boy thought, very light in his arms.

The door was already open, so he wouldn't have to go through that hassle.

He quickly put him in the passenger's side of the car and shut the door. He fished into Michaels's pocket, took out the key, then walked around to the other side and got in the driver's side. He turned on the ignition and drove the car out of the parking lot.

The boy took a right on Mulholland and drove Michaels up to another overlook, about a mile higher than Fryman Canyon. It was nothing more than a small pull-off, surrounded by high scorched brown brush this time of the year. A person could drive right past it and never even see a car off the side of the road. He had chosen this spot for its privacy and for the convenient fact that there was no guardrail.

From the bushes, the boy picked up the can of gasoline and brought it around to the driver's side.

Then he put on the emergency brake, shoved the car into neutral, and dragged the sleeping Michaels behind the wheel.

He quickly dowsed Michaels with gasoline.

This was going to be very simple, he thought. He thought so right up until Michaels's hand reached out and scratched his face.

The boy jumped back and smashed Michaels's head with the can. Michaels groaned and his eyes opened slightly.

"Jeff," he said softly. "What?" There was tenderness in his voice, tenderness and startled disbelief.

"Fuck you," the boy said. "My name's not Jeff."

He smashed Michaels's head again, and the agent fell back inside the car.

The boy waited for a minute, his nerves singing. If anyone came. . . .

He had to fight back the urge to run.

He reached inside and grabbed Michaels's briefcase. Oh, he was going to get a nice fat bonus for this, no doubt about it.

He reached in again and took off the emergency brake and pushed the gear into drive.

Then he dropped a lit match on the floor next to the unconscious Michaels. The gasoline caught at once, and he stepped outside and gave the car a little push. The hill was only six inches away, but it was still difficult to get the car rolling. He looked inside and saw the flames spreading into Michaels's sleeve. God, he had to hurry. He didn't want him to wake up.

But he was too late. It happened. Michaels awoke and saw the flames just as they engulfed his suit.

He turned and looked out the window directly at the boy. His eyes were wide open, and there seemed to be tears coming from them, his mouth wide open in a horrifying scream.

Christ, let the car start rolling, the boy thought. He pushed, and he saw Michaels's hand come up and smash against the window.

"Jeff!" he was screaming. "Jeff!"

The boy saw Michaels's skin start to melt.

Then the car was going, rolling down the hill, with a horrible sound.

The boy watched it go and heard the explosion.

Then he walked a few feet to the grass, where the Harley was hidden. He pulled it upright, put on his helmet, pulled down his visor, and kick-started it. The engine roared, and he stuffed Michaels's briefcase into his knapsack. Without looking at the flames below, he sped east on Mulholland, then turned right and headed down the winding canyon road, driving fast, leaning into all the curves, trying not to see Ted Michaels's burning face in his mind.

Chapter 23

Jack felt himself slowly blurring into consciousness. There was something wrong with his right eye; it was as though someone had stitched the lids together. He tried desperately to open it more than a crack, but felt an intense searing pain, which radiated up into his temples. There was something clinging to his right cheek, a bug with suction cups. It was as though an insect were sucking the flesh away from his cheekbone. He wanted to reach up and swat it away, but when he tried, he realized his hands were tied at his sides. He clenched his teeth and sucked in the fetid air, tried to focus his thoughts. It was no good to give in to fantasy here; the reality was bad enough. There was no insect, he told himself. The trouble was, he had a problem believing it. He tried to work his jaw, and again there was pain on both sides, and he slowly realized that when he had fallen, they had probably kicked him in the head a few times before getting him out of the street.

"Well, well, Sleeping Beauty awakens," Wingate's voice said.

Jack tried turning his head, but the pain in his neck stopped him cold. There was nothing to see anyway. He seemed to be in a pitch-black room.

Then, suddenly, an intensely painful narrow shaft of light poured into his eyes.

He shut his eyes tight, but suddenly someone was behind him, and rough hands pried his eyelids open, as a tight steel band was clasped around his forehead. Now he could no longer shut his eyes at all, nor could he turn away. The light was unbearable; it felt like liquid acid, poured into raw nerves.

"Let there be fucking light," Wingate said.

"Fuck you, fat man," Jack said.

"*Oooooh,* meaner than an ole razorback hog," Wingate said. "Well, that's part of good agent training, I hear tell. Always resist when being tortured. Keeps the will up and the spirit strong. Keeps a man from identifying with his oppressors. Ain't that right, Jackie?"

Jack said nothing. It was also part of training to never agree with them on anything. Never.

"Well, Jack," Wingate said. "You sure almost made me look bad. See, the Mexicans and the Colombians, they don't hardly ever deal with Americans. You got to have earned their trust, baby, and that's hard to do. Taken me a lifetime of goodwill to pull it off, and you come in and just trick the hell out of me. I mean, I am in danger of losing all credibility with these lads. Now, tell me the truth, Jackie, just between you and me . . . was that car-jacking in front of Mann's Chinese Theater . . . was that a setup or did you jest get lucky and decide to try and ride it out?"

Jack tried to laugh at him but choked instead.

"You'll go to your grave not knowing, Buddy."

"*Oooooh.* Can't he talk nasty?" Wingate said. "You know I feel for you, I really do. 'Cause you double-cross a guy like me, I got a certain sense of humor about it . . . a sense of sportsmanship. I mean, I got to give it to you. . . . The whole setup was brilliant. *Oooooh,* and the guys at Tahoe, the guys who 'came after us' . . . the guys you pretended to shoot to win me over . . . I guess that was all part of the setup too, right? Goddamn, that was fucking brilliant. And I jest bet it was you who thought of it all, 'cause I know most of the agents in the DEA, and let's face it, them boys don't have no more imagination than a pimple on a fly's ass. No, sir . . . I'm sure you musta set that up. Come on now, Jack, why don't you tell me the truth?"

"Turn out that light, and I'll tell you anything you want to know," Jack said.

But Wingate's mocking words sent a shock through Jack's system. As he looked up into Buddy Wingate's little eyes, sitting there like two frozen black-eyed peas, it occurred to Jack that the setup had been Wingate's. That had to be it. Wingate was merely playing with him. Was it possible that he had been suckered all along? That Wingate and whoever was behind him had set *him* up . . . the guys at Tahoe for example . . . could they have worked for Wingate? It seemed incredible. Jack's mind reeled. They had actually shot bullets through the windows. Yes, but they didn't hit anybody. With their high-powered infrared scopes such accuracy was entirely possible. And if he had been set up, what of Charlotte Rae? Had she known from the beginning too? The thought of that was more unbearable than his physical agonies.

"How did you find out who I was?" Jack said.

Wingate smiled at him. His teeth looked green.

"Sorry, ole dawg. That's the one you'll take to *your* grave. Nice to see you thinking about it, Jackie. You really don't know what's happening, do you?"

Jack felt the panic rise in his stomach. How *had* they found out?

"There's something I want to know, Jackie. Did you get your call through?"

Jack said nothing.

"Well, it don't matter what you say 'cause we're going to have to assume you did. Guess the boys will be waiting to nail us tomorrow night, but by then we will be long gone. And you, you'll be stone dead."

"Turn the fucking lights out," Jack said, desperately stalling for time. He had to think through this, but he was so tired, in such pain.

"Oh, you want the lights out, do you, Jackie? Well, I'd like to accommodate you, I really would. Like I said, if it was up to me, we'd just stand outside of some old saloon and settle this thing with six-guns at dawn, like real Americanos, but I'm not the only one involved, and you have had the extraordinary bad luck to be caught in a foreign country. And not in jest any foreign country, but in one where certain traditions of violent and antisocial behavior are prescribed for the likes of you, if you get what I mean? And none of them are real humorous, least ways, they won't be to you, hoss. No, sir."

Jack said nothing. The light felt as though it were slicing his eyeballs in half.

"But I did try and reason with these boys a little. Told 'em you was formerly a family friend, so if you tell them what they want to know, they might be encouraged to take it easy on you. I mean you are already a mess, son. Check it out."

Suddenly the lights dimmed enough so that Jack could see his reflection in the mirror that was thrust inches from his face—or rather, some horrible parody of his face. His nose was pushed over to one side, and his right eye was completely closed and encrusted with blood. His top lip was split open, and when he opened his mouth, he saw two teeth were missing.

It took all his discipline not to scream. Instead, he sucked in his breath and retreated to that dark safe place that was still left inviolate inside of him.

Then the mirror was taken away, and the light was slicing his eyes again.

"See what I mean, son," Wingate said. "You look like home-made shit. But I have prevailed upon our hosts in this fine country to take it a little easy on you if you tell us certain things we want to know, meaning the names of all the snitches, excuse me, I mean confidential informants, in this country and in Los Angeles right now."

"Funny, I forget all their names," Jack said.

"Wrong answer, Jackie." Wingate punched him in the right jaw. and Jack felt a flash of pain crunch all the way into his temples.

"Always negotiate from a position of strength, Jackster.

Now, let me ask you that question again," Wingate said. "Who are the informants? What are their names?"

"Go fuck yourself."

"Now, that's funny," Buddy said. "Very clever."

He poked his finger in Jack's right eye, hard, and Jack screamed.

Jack felt as though his eye was falling out of his head. And worse, he now understood. He *had* been set up, set up all along, which meant Charlotte Rae was in on it from the beginning. He thought of their nights together at Malibu, of the bruises she'd shown him. They'd been real, for godsake. Or had they? Could they have been mere makeup? No . . . his mind was playing tricks on him. They were real, all right. But so what? Maybe they were the result of some sick little game between Buddy and her. Maybe she liked it when Buddy used his fists on her. Maybe they laughed wildly as he pummeled her, both of them thinking how easy it would be to suck in one dumb cop who was led around by his prick. The thought of that hurt him more deeply than the pains in his eyes, jaws, or temple. She had gotten inside of him and played him for a sucker. And he remembered his dead father's words now about the fatal Walker family weakness, the love of being the hero, the penchant for playing the big scene.

He'd thought he had them all along. He'd thought he had her too. But he had nothing. It was all blue sky, smoke and mirrors. And now they owned him.

Wingate laughed and shook his head.

"Yep, you been played for a prime sucker, Jackie. Course we made a few mistakes. You was never supposed to make that phone call to your friends back home. The phone in the bar didn't work, but we neglected to look at the pay phone in the street. And it looks like you got to tell your boys quite a bit. So why don't you jest tell us a complete list of your snitches here in Mexico, and in Los Angeles, and maybe you'll come out of this all right."

Now it was Jack's turn to laugh.

"Sell it somewhere else, Buddy," he said. "You wouldn't go to all this trouble to get me in here just to let me go."

"Suit yourself, Jack."

Jack steeled himself for the next punch, but there was none. Instead, he felt himself falling backward, a terrifying sensation, as though the ground were being pulled out from under him. Then he realized he was on a reclinable table. He was flat on his back, his hands, feet, and head tightly manacled.

Wingate stood above him now.

At least Jack thought it was Wingate. The lights were still intense in his eyes, and it was hard to make out a face—just nameless, terrifying shapes above him.

Then he saw one of the shapes raising its arms. It was holding something in its hands, and Jack steeled himself for a beating with a club. But again no blows came. Instead, he observed that this man was shaking something, up and down, like a bartender mixing a martini.

"What the hell?" he said.

Then there was someone else, no, two more of them coming toward him. Escondero? Marbella? He couldn't tell. They had something in their hands too, something that looked like a long, fat sausage, and they were lowering it toward his nose.

Now he could see what it was, not a sausage, but a tightly rolled steaming towel.

And the other thing, the martini shaker . . . it was being lowered near him as well. Only, now that he could see it, it was clear that it wasn't a martini shaker at all. And this sure as hell wasn't Happy Hour.

Finally he could catch a glimpse of it, and his heart sank. The object was a thirty-two-ounce-bottle of good old-fashioned classic Coca-Cola. And Wingate was shaking it up, shaking it hard, with his thumb over the top of it, and Jack now knew exactly what was going to happen.

"*Ahhh,*" Wingate said. "There it is. I see it in your handsome face, Jackie. You just got the message. Yessir. That's always an interesting moment in times like these, when the victim, that would be you, gets the message from the boys who are going to apply the technique, that would be us. Some say that the moment of truth, the apprehension of waiting for what is inevitable, is even worse than the actual torture itself. Course these are your deep thinkers. As for me, well, this ole boy would rather face mental torture any day. Know what I mean? Now you gonna tell us the names? Or are we gonna find out if things really do go better with Coke?"

"Fuck you, you fat piece of shit," Jack said, pressing his head as far back as he could.

"Wrong answer, Jackie."

The steel bands around Jack's head tightened, and he could no longer offer even token resistance. He tried to fight back the panic by telling himself they wouldn't kill him—not until he talked.

Then Jack stopped having thoughts.

He felt the Coke bottle splitting his right nostril, and then the soda was sprayed into his sinus cavity with the force of a fire hose.

Jack heard someone screaming then, and he knew it must be himself, as his legs and arms jerked spasmodically in the tight stirrups. His nasal passage was flooded with an agonizing burning, and Jack knew at once that something was mixed into the bottle as well, probably two or three heaping spoonfuls of scorchingly hot cayenne pepper. Desperately, he attempted to keep his mouth open, spit the stuff out as it came pouring into his throat and lungs. But within seconds that was no longer an option, for rough hands applied the burning hot rolled towel over his nose and mouth. There was no way to emit the scorching soda as it flooded his nose, then quickly began filling up his lungs.

Now Wingate moved the Coke bottle from the right to the left nostril and the sticky spray erupted into his nostril once again. The hands kept the pressure up on the towel, and Jack saw a white stallion bucking wildly as someone lowered him with blinders on into a tank of bubbling, scalding water.

He felt his heart rate reach some ridiculous level. And there was no holding back the panic. . . . He was drowning, drowning . . . in this godforsaken room in Juarez. Oh, Christ, Christ. . . .

As he felt the liquid flooding into his lungs, he tried to cough it out, but the towel kept it all down, and then he threw up breakfast, and he choked on that as well . . . and he felt a wild animal terror, like nothing he could ever have anticipated, and then he was gone . . . gone . . . and he couldn't hear or see anything at all.

But at precisely the moment he was grateful for death, they pulled the towel from his mouth, and Jack began to violently throw up the Coke and his breakfast.

In between heaves, he gasped wildly for air.

And someone, it wasn't Wingate, he was certain, was gently wiping a towel over him, cleaning up the mess. Then they put something else over his face, and though he at first tried to fight against it, he realized that it was an oxygen mask, with pure, clear, cool air in it; he gasped it down like a beached fish.

"There, my son. Isn't that better?"

It wasn't Wingate's voice anymore.

But a kinder, wiser, infinitely benevolent voice, the voice he had known deep inside that he would hear again—the voice of Father Miguel Herrera.

"Do you know who I am, my son?"

Father Herrera touched him gently on the cheek. Jack jerked his head away and found that the bonds on his forehead had been loosened. He felt such a huge wave of gratitude that it nearly sickened him. He was like a starving man being given a great, pink, disgusting marzipan candy, which he gobbles down in one bite. He wanted badly to resist such slavish gratitude. But the caress, so tender and caring that it seemed like that of a mature and understanding father, was followed by a few gentle drops of water, which were sprinkled lightly on Jack's face.

"Is that better, son?" the voice said.

Jack was unable to make words; it felt as though someone had severed his tongue.

"You did well, my friend," the smooth, unflappable voice said. "You're remarkably resilient. Most people scream much louder than that."

Jack found that he was able to swallow. He moved his tongue around in his mouth.

"Where's Wingate?" he said, choking.

"Señor Wingate has to tend to some other details, Jack. I

will be talking with you now. I find it disturbing to see you this way."

"Do you? Really. That's touching."

Jack coughed up some more of the vile fluid and gasped for air.

Father Herrera said nothing, but reached over and applied a wet towel to Jack's cheek. Jack squinted but could not make out his face.

"How does that feel?"

Jack answered in as hard and angry a voice as he could muster.

"You want me to talk," said Jack, gagging again. His throat felt like raw meat.

"Yes. That's right. I won't lie to you."

"Then why don't you turn the light out?"

"I don't think so, Jack. I wouldn't want you to become too comfortable. You might go to sleep."

Jack felt a glass of water being pressed near his burned lips.

Jack looked down into it. A clear liquid.

"It's only mineral water, Jack," the priest said. "It's good for you."

Jack's throat was raw from vomiting and gagging. But he knew that he had to resist it. He turned his head as far as the steel bands allowed.

"If you are worried about poison, Jack, don't be. I would never do such a thing to you."

"I know that, Father. Because you like me so much."

As he finished speaking, Jack heard a cough from his right and craned his head that way. He was able to see just a flash of someone's shoe, a pointy-toed brown loafer with a tassel, but then two hands grabbed his head from behind.

"Too late, Doc," Jack said. "I saw your neat little Nazi shoes. Standing there with your little harpoon?"

"Impressive," Father Herrera said. "Your recovery time is very impressive. But you surprise me, Jack, you really do. I have heard from everyone that you are a highly intelligent man, yet you seem to think that this is only about information.

But it's not, Jack. No, it is much more than that. Let me ask you a question. Do you understand what it is to love someone?"

"You tell me, Father," Jack said, his voice sounding like sandpaper.

Suddenly Father Herrera smacked Jack hard in the face with the back of his hand, and Jack felt a sharp sting and then his own blood running down his chin.

"You would do well to take this seriously, Jack. I am not talking about sexual love. I am talking about a love between two men, a friendship if you will. A friendship—I am not ashamed to say it—that was deeper than any man-woman relationship can ever be. Do you know the meaning of such friendships, Jack?"

This time Jack said nothing. Father Herrera rubbed his hand over Jack's cheek in a gesture that was almost a caress.

"I am talking to you, Jack. I expect an answer."

"Yes," Jack said. It was as though someone had attached red hot electrodes to his retina.

" 'Yes,' because I want to hear yes?" Father Herrera said. "Or yes because you have such friendships yourself? And don't lie to me, Jack. I always know when someone is lying."

"Yes, yes. I've had friendships like that."

"I wonder?" Herrera said. "Truly. I doubt it, Jack. I think people in your country, the wonderful land of freedom and dignity for all, I think they have no understanding of such love. I think they measure everything in terms of money, of power, of status. To Americans, love is like buying a car. You trade in your old love every two or three years for a nice new shiny one. I think you are a pathetic people, really."

"And you prove your moral superiority by selling us drugs, is that it?" Jack said.

"Why shouldn't we?" Father Herrera said, his voice rising now. "Your CIA encourages it. Your government has, for years, taken my money. It's business as usual, my friend. Some of your own people are on the take, Jack. Oh, you would be quite surprised if I told you their names. Granted, the DEA is mostly clean. So what? Your Agency is nothing more than a pathetic contemporary version of the Peace Corps. Remember those high-minded children of the sixties who came to the unfortunate downtrodden third world and built bridges and dams, while Kennedy and the American CIA undercut the very reforms they advocated? That is exactly the position of the DEA, my friend. You catch a few of the dumber dealers, while your government and your businessmen make billions of dollars in the drug trade. So why shouldn't we sell your people drugs? In our own way, we are liberating our world by infecting and enslaving yours. You see?"

"I see," Jack said, hoarsely. "You're not drug dealers. You're emancipators."

"Exactly," Herrera said. "Like Bolivar, or Zapata."

For a second Father Herrera sounded as though he wanted to go on, but then there was an ever-so-slight pause, and Jack knew that he had gotten Herrera to say more than he wanted to. Zapata? Michaels had said something about that. But what could it mean? What was this tirade really about? If the Agency was so pathetic, why was Herrera so furious? Father Herrera cleared his throat, sucked in air. It seemed to Jack that he was trying to get a handle on his own emotions.

"We were speaking of love, Jack. I loved someone. More than I have ever loved anyone."

The father stopped again. Jack heard him wheezing and was astonished. It seemed he was almost crying.

"But because of you, he is dead," Herrera finally said.

"Who was he?"

There was a silence between the two men, and suddenly both Jack and Father Herrera were aware of a strange intimacy that passed between them, an intimacy that shared death bestows, no matter what the circumstances.

"His name was Jose Benvenides. You shot him to death last year in Tucson."

And now Jack knew, knew for certain what he had felt uneasy about since he first laid eyes on the "priest." Father Herrera was Eduardo Morales, himself. Jack couldn't prove it, but he knew in a way that was beyond logic. After all, who else could have planned so elaborate a revenge and had the resources to carry it out?

"Do you remember him, Jack?"

Morales's voice was very quiet and reverential, as if he were saying a prayer.

"Yeah, I do."

In his mind Jack could again see Benvenides's revolver aimed at his head. He recalled his own absolute certainty that he would soon be dead. He could hear the click of the gun, as it jammed. And he could see the flash of fire from his Glock as he shot Benvenides in the head.

"It might matter to you to know that I didn't want to kill him, father," Jack said, putting an ironic spin on the last word. "Jose shot at me first, but his gun jammed. I had no choice."

"Is that true?"

"Yes," Jack said.

"Do you think that matters?"

"Yes. I do."

Morales nodded.

"Yes, I can see you would. I can see you are a brave and honorable man. But it does not matter to me, Jack. What matters to me is that you and your clever little boss, what's his name, Zampas? You two set your little trap, and you lured Jose in. Fooled and then killed him. And for that you must die."

Morales stopped talking now, and Jack heard him breathing hard, the breath of a rage and loss that could never be quenched until his revenge was carried out.

And upon hearing that breath, Jack realized that his case was hopeless. He was finished, because this wasn't about drugs at all. No, it was about obsession. It was deeply personal, which left him no room to negotiate.

"You are going to die, Jack. But because I like you a little, I am going to give you a choice. You can tell us everything we ask you and die like Jose died, from a bullet to the head. Or you can stonewall and die like a snitch dies."

The sound of Morales's voice cut into Jack's soul.

"No door number three?" Jack said, but the words sounded hollow, even to himself.

"I admire your sense of humor, Jack. I really do. I wonder

how long you can keep it. Perhaps you need another drink of Coke."

"You son of a bitch," Jack said.

Then they were descending on him again. And he felt the bottle jam into his broken nose. His screams became obscene gags, and just before he passed out, he wondered if Charlotte Rae was out there somewhere in the dark, watching it all go down.

When he awakened, he was no longer in the room, but in a cactus garden. All around him there were terrifying shapes, huge cacti that looked like skeletons and crucifixes and hanged men with melting faces. The sky above him was black and blue, as though God had beaten it with his bare fists.

There was a high corrugated tin fence, and mariachi music blared from speakers that hung overhead. He was manacled in a chair, and then, suddenly, Wingate was above him.

"Hey, welcome to my world, Jackie," Wingate said. "Long as I've got my little garden, any place can be real homey."

Jack felt a searing pain in his neck and sucked in a lung full of air.

Wingate walked toward him. He leaned to one side a bit, and Jack thought that he looked drunk.

"You are so fucking dumb, Walker. You and the whole DEA are so dumb, so hopeless, so pathetic. The elephant and the ant, Walker. We're the elephant, and you're the little fucking ant."

Wingate's face loomed like an insect's above him.

"Go ahead and scream, Jackie. No one can hear above the music."

Jack said nothing. But stared at him through bloodied, half-closed eyes.

"Scream into the night, Jack. It's good for the soul. I love it out here. Don't you love it, Jackie?"

Jack looked around, felt the fear flood through him.

"Wouldn't you love to get away, Jackie? Wouldn't you love to escape? Think of what you could do to us, Jackie? Think of how you could bring us down."

"Fuck you, Wingate. And Morales too."

"Morales?"

"Yeah. I know it's him. Where is that cowardly piece of shit?"

"He's busy, Jackie. Busy making other plans for our little dope shipment. Just think of it, Jack. One thousand kilos of white heroin at a hundred grand a key. That's a hundred million bucks, you might have brought in. And that's only the beginning. What we're talking about here, my friend, is a whole new market. We're cutting out the Chinese, all them slope-eyed Asians. We can deliver a better product for one-third what them Chinks get. They're gonna be dead meat. And you mighta stopped us. *Whew,* a bust like that, and maybe you would have replaced Zampas."

Jack blinked.

"Zampas one of your heroes, Jackie? That little shit-heel bureaucrat."

"Fuck you, Buddy. He's worth more than twenty of you."

"*Ohhh,* still got a little fight in you. That's good. You know your problem, Jackie? You're arrogant, pushy. You think you can fly by on a song. I bet you think my old lady has the hots for you too. Or, no . . . I guess not. Even a young hotshot like you doesn't think that anymore. Not after the way she set you up."

Wingate began to laugh, and Jack strained against his bonds.

"See, Jackie, you think 'cause you're young and thin that you can charm us to death. But you been raised on the MTV, son, and charm don't cut it. Truth is, Jackie, you're too fucking dumb to bring anybody down, least of all anybody in this organization. Hey, I know what you're thinking, 'If I could only get out of here . . .' Well, you ain't gonna, you are heading for the Big D, son. But, jest for fun, let's talk about what might happen if you did get away. Yeah, let's play it out. You could go to your boys and say that you had us dead on dealing drugs. But would it hold up in court, Jackie? I don't think so. Why? 'Cause you never ever saw any drugs. All you saw was a tunnel and a pool table, Jackie boy. And Father Herrera, well, he wore a mask in the ceremony. As did all the others. And you couldn't see him when he was here. But let's just pretend, Jackie, that you were successful in getting us arrested and in court . . . let's imagine my defense."

Wingate laughed and showed Jack some Polaroids.

"*Hmmm,* what's this?"

Jack felt a new shock enter his system.

He looked at a picture of him and Charlotte Rae, making love at Malibu. Jack felt sickened, crushed, and ashamed. The thought had crossed his mind that the house in Malibu wasn't safe, but he had not listened to his inner voice. He had wanted her too badly, been too convinced of her need for him. He had rushed in to play hero and ended up being the court jester instead.

"See . . . see what we have here, Jackie. If you did get away, look what I have. I can say that you framed me because you wanted my wife. Oh, and there's always the matter of the guys you killed at Tahoe. See, my people and Salazar's people have come to an understanding. He's no longer my competitor, so he'd be happy to get on the stand and say that you killed two of his people, just to get in with me. Yeah, he'd say it was a DEA setup. Why, we might even be able to get you indicted for murder. Imagine how effective those poor widows are gonna be on the stand, Jackie, talking about how you killed the fathers of their babies just to entrap me. Sad, Jackie, real sad."

Jack's head dropped. He'd fucked it all up. And they had him. There was nothing more to say.

"I bring this up just for the hell of it, Jackie, 'cause you ain't ever gonna leave this place. I think we're gonna bury you right under ole monstera deliciosa, my favorite cactus. You have been dumb, Jackie. Real, real dumb. We had your ass from day numero uno, hoss. See, I wasn't born with no good luck, so I jest naturally had to be smarter than the next guy. Truth is, Jack, I am gonna miss you, though. I liked seeing you do your little swashbuckling undercover number. It was real amusing. For a while."

"Yeah, Buddy, well I guess I'll see you in hell."

"I reckon so," Wingate said. "Meanwhile, Father Herrera has made you a generous offer. The bullet to the head or something much worse. Might give you a Cartagena necktie. You know, cut out your tongue and hang it down your chest. They even give you a little anaesthetic so you don't pass out from the pain right away. Wonder what Charlotte Rae will think of you when she sees you like that?"

Wingate took a Romeo Y Julieta cigar from his pocket, lit it, then turned and blew the smoke in Jack's face.

"You are a sorry motherfucker," he said, looking away.

Wingate turned back and put out the tip of his cigar on Jack's cheek.

"You're gonna talk, asshole," he said. "In the end everybody talks. So you sit here for a while, Jackie. Sit here and think about how you want it to be. Shithead."

Then there was something being stuck in Jack's arm, and though he fought it, he found himself falling down a blue drain into the phantom blackness below.

Chapter 24

There were monsters roaring in his head; he saw himself standing amidst an entire city that was ashen, demolished, the buildings black from soot, their windows broken like a face with its eyes put out. All along the city streets were golden electric snakes attacking children, who screamed and ran frantically for the illusory safety of brightly painted doorways. But Jack knew, knew as one can know only in a dream, that there was no safety behind those doorways, for the blackened, crooked houses had their own demons inside, demons far worse than the bright, yellow snakes that slithered on the city's bombed-out streets. Inside the houses were the greatest monsters of all, men: white, black, Latino, Chinese, all the masses of men in the world, all of them huddled together on the oily floors with their syringes and their cacti and their great vats filled with money and their lying tongues.

He awoke with a start, then opened one bloody eye and looked around at the room, at the mirrors that reflected his battered, swollen face.

He groaned. That couldn't be him: chained, back in the standing position again, his face pummeled, his lips purple and swollen, his right eye completely closed and bloated with fluid, so that it looked like some grotesque, overripe fruit.

He was dead on his feet, he knew it. And in the end he would tell them the names of every snitch he could recall, because under torture everybody cracked—which Wingate and Father Herrera knew. No, they had pumped him full of drugs to soften up what was left of his will and left him here simply to make him suffer more, to think about how he had been suckered, how they had played him—putting the girl out as bait, knowing that he would try to stop the car-jacking, and then letting him get close to her, letting her tell him the story of her past at Tahoe. Her story about her sad life as an orphan—Christ, an orphan, for godsake—it was like something out of a fairy tale, and he had bought it because of her tits and her ass and the pain in her voice, but most of all because of his own preening ego, his need to play hero.

They had been so far ahead of him that he hadn't even been in the game. They must have waited and watched and figured him out ever since the day he pulled the trigger on Jose Benvenides.

But how had they known he'd shot Jose? That was the question that had no answer.

Not that it mattered anymore. Because now he was finished—done in by his own lack of judgment.

His head fell upon his chest. He sucked in air. Then he looked around. His hands and feet were manacled to the tilting table.

There was no way he was going to get out of here—unless somehow he could get a key. There must be a guard outside.

He had to get him in here, try something, anything, before they came back with their knives and syringes.

He thought for a second, then began to scream.

Loud, piercing screams that cut through the darkness. Maybe the guard would come in just to shut him up . . . that would give him a chance.

But there was only the buzzing of the flies in the room. No one came.

He waited, tried it again, knowing that this game could backfire. His screams might irritate them so badly that they simply would kill him right now. But he had to take that chance.

And then, astonishingly enough, this much of his plan seemed to work. From the right side of the room, a door opened quickly, sending in dim yellow light from a hallway. The door shut rapidly, but someone had come into the room and was walking quickly toward him.

"Shut up," a flat, cool voice said.

Jack squinted through his swollen bloody eye.

He couldn't believe who was standing in front of him—Charlotte Rae Wingate.

She smiled mockingly, shook her head. "Why are you screaming?" she said.

"Just trying to get in touch with my inner child," Jack said through swollen, thick lips, amazed that he could still make a joke.

"Something I haven't figured out about you," she said. "For a guy who always has a good line, you do a lot of really dumb things."

"Yeah," Jack said. "And of all the dumb things I ever did, you were the dumbest."

She came closer to him and touched his lip lightly, and he jerked away in pain. "You look like hell, Jack."

"Compared to how I feel, I look great," Jack said. "Funny, I was just thinking about you . . . about how good an actress you are. I mean, to sell a story about your lonely life as an orphan . . . you got to be very good."

She smiled at him. Patted his head.

"Trick is to use as much of the real back story as possible. In my case all of that was true. All I had to do was tap into it and feel a little sorry for myself. Acting one-o-one."

"*Ahhh,* I see," Jack said. "And the bruises. Get those from the makeup truck?"

"Those are my business," she said. She snorted and shook her head. "You know, you're really funny."

"How's that?"

"We played a game, you and I, and you lost, but now I hear self-righteousness in your voice. Like I sold you out or something."

"Well, didn't you?" Jack said, staring directly into her eyes.

"I suppose, but what were you going to do to me as soon as the bust went down, Agent Walker?"

Jack managed a shrug.

"All's fair in love and war," she said.

Jack said nothing, but kept his gaze steady into her face. She broke off from his gaze, stared at the floor as if she was considering something, then quickly met his eyes again.

"Was any of it real, Jack?"

"Truth?"

She nodded.

"Yeah, it was. I didn't let myself go all the way, but I thought about it. I thought about you all the time."

She smiled at him.

"Then it was the same for both of us."

"How's that?"

"I didn't let myself think what might happen to you, and you tried to forget that you were setting me up to bust me. In the end that makes us even—a couple of liars."

"I don't think so," Jack said. "I'm not selling heroin. I'm not killing kids. Destroying families. Call me old-fashioned, but I think that's a difference worth noting."

She stood looking at him for what seemed like the longest time, then reached up softly and touched his battered, bruised cheek.

"You surprised me with your tenderness, Jack. I knew it was an Academy Award–winning performance, but part of me still bought it. I even tried to warn you out there in the desert. If you had listened to me then, I'd have come with you."

Jack nodded.

"It's not to late, Charlotte."

She shook her head.

"Oh, yeah, it is. Way too late. But that's okay. I'm a specialist in 'too late,' and 'big regrets.' "

Jack laughed a little.

"Me, I'm a specialist in last-minute heroics. Maybe that's why we're meant for each other. Get me out of here, Charlotte."

She looked at him noncommittally, sudden blankness in her eyes, as though she had turned him out forever, and that look frightened Jack more than anything he had yet seen.

"Charlotte, I need you to do the right thing. Now."

She smiled slightly.

"We'll never get out. And if they catch us, then I get the same treatment you do."

Jack stared into her eyes.

"You did care, didn't you?" she said.

"I do care, and if we get out of here, I can help you."

She reached beneath her black cloak and took out a long, serrated knife, with a fancy carving of a black ivory bull on its handle.

"I brought this for you," she said, her voice resonating an ethereal emptiness.

"And this."

She reached into her pocket and pulled out a key.

"I decided to talk to you and see if any of it was real. Or if I'd just fallen in love with an illusion. Funny thing was, I was sure that after we talked, I'd know whether to use the knife or help you escape."

"And which way is it going to be?"

She shrugged and laughed in an ironic way.

"The test was a failure, Jack. I talked to you, and you sound sincere. I might even buy it, but I still don't know if anything you said is really true."

"You don't believe me when I say I care about you?"

"I'd believe you more if you said you had a hard-on for me."

"You already know that. I'm telling you the truth. You make me laugh. I don't know anybody else who does that."

"Yeah," she said. "There is that."

"And there's something else too."

"What's that?"

"I think you're better than these assholes. It's not only that they're going down in the end, and that you'll end up in jail for the next forty years, but that you have a choice right here to be yourself or be Buddy's whore. Which is it going to be?"

Her eyes flashed at Jack, anger that was like heat lightning.

"That's not really the choice you're offering me, Jack. It's more like 'Will I be Buddy's whore or your whore.' "

Jack looked directly into her eyes.

"I don't think so," he said. "I don't think they're the same, and I don't really believe you do either."

She moved the knife closer to his throat. Jack felt his head pressing back against the steel table.

"I think I've decided something, Jack."

"Yeah?"

"Yeah. I've decided that the test doesn't matter?"

"No?"

"No. I don't think I'll ever know if you mean what you're saying to me or not. I don't even think you know. Maybe you're just so used to lying that you think you care."

She knelt down in front of him and put the key into the lock on the manacle clamped on his right foot.

"You're a bastard, Jack, and you probably don't deserve my help," she said.

"So why then?" Jack said, as he heard the lock click open.

" 'Cause none of us are angels, Jack, and if I waited to help somebody who deserved it, I'd end up being as big a shit-heel as Buddy. And I can't live with that."

Jack didn't say anything but heard the lock on his other foot click open and felt something click open in his heart as well.

Charlotte opened the door slowly and peered down the dimly lit hallway.

"It's all right," she said.

"The guard?"

She opened the door a crack wider, and Jack saw Cutty Marbella sitting in a chair next to the door. His head rested sleepily on his chest. He made a slight snoring sound. Quickly, she shut the door again.

"What did you do to him?"

"He said he was thirsty, so I fixed him a cuba libre. Five ounces of one-fifty-one dark rum, one ounce Coke, and nine Tuinals. I think he's gonna have a bad headache."

Jack managed a laugh and felt as if his face had cracked.

"Jesus, I'm glad you're on my side."

He groaned and felt a sharp pain in his right ribs.

"Can you make it?" she said.

"I'm fine. We need to get a car. You could drive, and I'll roll up in the trunk."

"Forget it," she whispered. "The parking lot is all the way across the compound, and they've got guards every ten feet. There's only one way outta here, and I'm not sure I can carry you."

"I'd bet on you," Jack said. "But we don't have to find out, 'cause I can make it."

"I hope so," she said. " 'Cause our only shot is the tunnel. The entrance is in a building just to the east of us. There's an alley, and usually there's two big and very ugly guards stationed there."

"Only two," Jack said. "Against you and me? That's not even fair." But he coughed, and an electric pain shot through his chest and back.

"What I'm worried about is who's waiting for us on the other end," she said.

"I know what you mean. I'd give my pension for a gun," Jack said.

"After they review this case, you aren't going to have a pension," she said. "But take this one anyway."

She reached into her coat and pulled out Jack's Glock. He smiled in astonishment, as he felt the cool grip in his palm.

"I owe you one."

"You owe me a hell of a lot more than one," she said.

Jack sucked in his breath and shuffled forward into the hallway. It wasn't going to be easy. Somewhere between the Coke party and the cigar Wingate had put out on his cheek, he had also put a few dents in his right kneecap. In fact, he doubted if he had a right kneecap.

"You keep up that pace, and we're both gonna look uglier than you do now," Charlotte Rae said.

Jack wanted to say something sharp back to her, but all the funny stuff had drained out of him a few seconds ago, and suddenly he felt as if he were carrying a safe. She helped support him as they worked their way down the gray hallway, toward a black iron door that seemed to recede with every step. He felt his lungs screaming from the effects of the cayenne pepper, and he was afraid he'd black out.

When they finally came to the door, he leaned on it and gasped for air.

"Hang in, baby," she said.

"Lead me to the next event," Jack coughed, sagging on the wall.

Suddenly, from behind them they heard a scraping sound. Both of them jumped, and Jack turned and saw Marbella fall off his chair and sprawl on the floor.

"At least he won't hurt himself by falling on his gun," Charlotte Rae said.

She reached into her coat and took out Marbella's Walther PPK.

"I knew you had a maternal side," Jack said.

Outside was chocolate dark, the moon receding behind some huge cotton clouds. They shuffled along, hugging an adobe wall, until they came to an alley twenty feet away.

"Our handy little pool table's maybe fifty yards down. The guards have the key. But I don't think they're going to let us use it."

She looked at Jack expectantly.

"So what do we do now?"

Jack leaned on the wall, panting. "Hell if I know," he said.

"Great," she said. "The man with all the ideas."

"All right. All right. I just got an idea, you're gonna love it."

"What is it?"

"Here's what you do. You walk down there by the doorway like a lap dancer in a Motley Crue video, and when the guards come out to try and fuck you, you kill 'em."

She shook her head.

"Maybe I should have left you tied up. Look, Jack, I can't just kill 'em."

"Why not? Don't tell me you've developed a sudden aversion to violence?"

"No, Jack. It's the noise. I shoot 'em, we bring down the whole camp on us."

Jack managed a smile.

"You didn't even bring a silencer with you?" he said. "What kinda rescue is this anyway?"

"You could always go back, love."

"No, this will have to do," Jack said. "Okay, see if you can divert their attention, while I come in from the rear."

"Try not to collapse," she said. "'Cause I've seen both of the guys, and they aren't my type."

Then she patted his cheek and started forward.

Jack felt another wave of dizziness come over him and sucked in his breath.

Painfully, he moved along. He sent up a silent prayer that he wouldn't pass out. His hand coiled around the pistol grip.

Charlotte slinked past the door, using a walk that would have charmed a cobra out of a basket.

Nothing happened.

From his vantage point, Jack watched Charlotte Rae look into the door. She gave a sexy little cough—*"a-ha-hem"*—and stood there in the squalid yellow light, looking wanton and sex starved.

Still nothing happened. Jack swallowed. What was happening here? Gay Latino guards?

Then, in a lightning move, two figures tumbled out of the doorway, flashing claws, fists. They were all over her knocking her to the ground, screaming, pulling her hair, ripping her clothes.

Behind them came the two guards, smoking, drinking shots of tequila, laughing wildly.

Charlotte Rae tried to get up, but the two women beat her down again and screamed in Spanish:

"You *puta!* You have come on the wrong ground, *gringa* bitch!"

"We will teach you to try and take our men!"

Jack's mouth dropped in disbelief. It seemed that the two guards were already engaged with two hookers. Now the guards slammed each other on the back, watching their crazy, drunken concubines rip the rival "hooker" to shreds.

"Don't kill her," the fat guard with the sleepy eyes said. "She looks pretty good."

"She won't in a minute, Luis, you pig," the big red-haired hooker said.

She raised her hand in the air to strike Charlotte Rae, when Jack raised the pistol.

"Playtime's over, ladies."

The fatter of the guards went for his gun, and Jack hit him across the back of the head. He fell with a thud.

He aimed the pistol at the second guard.

"Hand over the gun, friend."

The two whores climbed off Charlotte Rae. Now they were docile, their eyes terrified.

"All three of you, inside," Jack said.

The three of them backed into the door, with perplexed looks on their faces.

Jack pulled Charlotte Rae to her feet. She had a few scrapes on her face, and her blouse was torn, but other than that she seemed fine.

"Great little idea you had," she said.

"Well, I was right about one thing," he said. "You sure caused a sensation. Here, take the gun and hold it on these three, while I drag *el gordo* inside."

She took the gun a little too quickly.

"No shooting," Jack said, as he grabbed the guard's chubby wrists.

Inside the guard shack, Jack handcuffed all four of them to

the door, bound their feet with telephone wire, and gagged them with their own stockings.

"We have to find the key to the goddamn pool table," he said.

But Charlotte was already ahead of him. She held it up, smiling.

"It's here, right in the desk. I've seen Buddy put it in here before."

"Beautiful. Let's go."

They started through the warehouse toward the back cellar steps, hurrying by boxes and boxes of crates marked Tampico Furniture.

Then they found the steps and descended to the false recreation room.

A few minutes later, they stood in front of the pool table, and Charlotte Rae stuck the key into the switch and turned it to the right. The pool table immediately rose on its hydraulic lifters nearly to the ceiling, then docked off to the right, two feet off of the floor.

"Right outta the movies," Jack said, in admiration.

"Yeah, the B-movies," Charlotte Rae said. "Buddy's favorite old TV series was *Time Tunnel*. Tell you the truth, there's a lotta ways you can smuggle drugs that aren't as mysterioso as this, but I think Buddy just likes the sci-fi quality of it all."

"I can understand that," Jack said. "I kind of like it myself."

"I'll like it when we get out of it. Let's go."

"How do we turn on the escalator?" Jack said.

"We don't," she said. "It broke yesterday, and they're not finished fixing it yet. We're walking."

Though the tunnel was four feet wide it was only five-feet high, causing Jack and Charlotte Rae to scurry hunched like dwarfs through the dark passage.

Jack went first and held tight to her hand.

"Christ, if we could only turn the lights on. Or even light a match."

"We can't risk it," Jack said. "They might see them at the other end. How far is it?"

"About a mile. Christ, I hate the dark. When I was a kid, if you acted human, laughed, had to pee in church, the priests would lock you in the cellar, all night, with the goddamn rats and the bugs."

"This was in the famous orphanage?" Jack said, cryptically.

"Yes, it was," Charlotte Rae said. "That part happens to be the truth."

"Oh," Jack said. "Well, when we get out of here, maybe you can draw me a picture of your life, and highlight the nonfictional details."

"You first," Charlotte Rae said. Then she stopped and squeezed his hand.

"What are you doing?"

"I want you to know something."

"All right."

"A lot of what I told you . . . the stuff about my mother and how I met Buddy . . . that was all true. Something else too. The bruises I showed you. They weren't makeup. Buddy's got a bad temper when he loses at gambling. And he always loses. Morales owns the casinos at Tahoe where Buddy gambles. Buddy owes millions of dollars, Jack. Then he started stealing a little of the coke and the heroin and selling it on his own to pay Morales off. Morales found out, and he was going to kill Buddy . . . and me too."

"Why you?"

"Because that's the kind of animal he is. I was with Buddy, so I had to go. He had the guns to our heads more than once, Jack. Then, he suggested this scheme, a way we could pay up our debts and get clean."

"Trick and then kill the DEA agent who killed his friend?"

She stopped walking, and Jack heard her lean against the wall and sigh.

"Jack, I swear I didn't know anything about what they were going to do with you. Besides, they told me stories about you. You and Zampas."

"Like what?"

"That you were both dirty. That you were intent on destroying us only because you had cut your own deal with the Asians."

"Your competitors in the heroin trade. You believed that?"

Suddenly, she began to cry, and Jack held on to her in the dark.

"I don't know, Jack. I was so scared I didn't know what to believe. I knew about the kind of things they did to people who stole. I didn't sleep for weeks. I got most of these bruises from Buddy then. He was terrified of them, and he took it out on me."

She sobbed deeply, and Jack stroked her hair.

"It's all right," he said. "But we've got to keep moving."

Slowly, she straightened up, and they began to trudge again through the damp darkness.

"Where will Buddy go now?" Jack said.

"I don't know. You were never supposed to survive, so he could just go back to his old life. Now I guess he'll split the country."

"If Morales doesn't kill him first."

"Yeah," she said. "He might. Buddy's no use to him anymore, and he could hurt him if he makes a deal with the government."

They moved on through the gloom. She held on to his hand tightly, and Jack felt that although he was pulling her along, it was she who was giving him the strength to deny his own pain.

"The thing I still don't understand is how they knew who I was," he said. "Did they ever tell you that?"

"No. You think they tell me those kind of things? I could get whacked out just for asking. The only thing I know about this whole deal is that it became more urgent for Morales to get his revenge right away because he got sick."

"How sick?"

"Cancer. It was bad last year, though they've got it in remission now. Buddy was praying he'd die so we wouldn't have to go through with this whole scam."

"That does explain a few things," Jack said. "A man gets sick like that, he'll take more chances. But that still doesn't explain how he knew who I was."

"Pardon me, Jack, but why is that such a mystery? Look, you killed that guy Benvenides in Arizona, I know that much."

"Yeah, so?"

"So that's how they must have found out. I mean wasn't it on TV or in the papers?"

"That's just the point," Jack said, feeling his way along the tunnel wall. "It wasn't reported by the press. We managed to keep my cover clean. All anyone said on either the television or in the newspapers was that a Colombian was found shot dead in a motel and that it was suspected that he had been involved in a drug dispute. End of story."

They kept walking silently, then Jack turned to her.

"Jesus, have I been looking in the wrong place. It's Michaels. It's got to be."

"Michaels? Who's that?"

"My fellow agent," Jack said in a voice thick with bitterness. "He's an assistant director. He warned me about coming down here before I left. He could be on Morales's payroll and had an attack of conscience. Yeah, that fits because he was drunk and maudlin the night he warned me."

Jack felt his hatred of Michaels reach a new level. Of course, it made perfect sense. Michaels must have known what would happen to Jack once he got to Mexico. He even mentioned Zapata, which must have been some oblique reference to Morales. But if that was the case, why did he warn him? Jack really didn't believe it was because Michaels had a conscience attack. No, he thought, as his hand raked over some slime on the tunnel wall, it was more likely that Michaels warned him because he was afraid that something like this might happen. Rather than die in Mexico, Jack would survive and come back and tear his face off.

Which, if Jack had anything to say about it, was precisely what was going to happen.

"There it is, Jack. Just up there."

Jack looked up and saw the light in the distance.

"What are we going to find?"

"A ladder. It comes up in the back part of the warehouse."

"Why no escalator?"

"They haven't put it in yet."

"What about workers, guards?"

"No workers at this hour of the night. Guards, probably. There could be a lot of them."

"You got a clip in your gun?"

"I'm like a Girl Scout. I come prepared."

"I remember."

"I hope you do. Jack?"

"Yeah."

"If I don't make it, it's been nice."

"Forget that kind of talk. We're gonna make it. You ready?"

"Uh-huh."

"We get up, we get out, we get a car, and we cruise. Pretty soon we're in Los Angeles drinking a margarita, watching a sunset."

"Sounds nice."

"It is. Come on, I'm thirsty."

It was the tallest ladder Jack had ever seen, at least seventy-five feet straight up. At the top there was a cast-iron trapdoor, and as he climbed, the Glock in his right hand, it occurred to him that the door could be locked.

And if it was, they were finished. It was that simple. They had no way to blow the door open, and there was no going back to the Mexican side.

Below him, Charlotte Rae had the same idea.

"If it's locked, Jack, we could always knock and tell them we're Jehovah's Witnesses."

Jack climbed higher, looked down once, and felt a dizziness overtake him so quickly that he had to grasp the handrail.

Finally he came to the top, only inches away from freedom.

He reached up and touched the door, lightly, and gave a silent prayer that it would be unlocked and that the guards wouldn't be nearby.

Slowly, trying to be quiet, he pushed. The door opened easily into blessed darkness, and Jack quickly pulled himself up and out.

He looked around the darkened warehouse, his eyes slowly adjusting to the level of light. He half expected to see a great number of trucks ready to move out, but they hadn't arrived yet.

And where were the guards? Perhaps outside, which gave them half a chance.

He reached down and pulled Charlotte Rae through the trapdoor.

"The outside door's over there," she whispered, pointing across the huge, dark room.

"Get down low and move like a snake," Jack said.

"That comes natural, honey," she said.

They started across the floor, Jack holding the Glock in front of him.

Light filtered in from outside, illuminating the walls of boxes that towered over them. Jack looked around and saw crates marked "Rattan Chairs." Was this the real stuff or the hollowed-out furniture filled with the new Colombian white heroin? No way to stop and find out now.

Keeping low, they had made it halfway across the room, when they came to a great empty space in the center.

"We've got to go across there," Charlotte Rae said. "Then down the center aisle and we hit the door. The guards are outside. But they come in sometimes too. There's a fridge in the room above us. They have drinks in there. A real little party scene."

Jack looked up and saw two flights of steel steps leading up to an office. The windows emitted a dull orange glow.

"Could be somebody up there now. You know how many of them there are?"

"Two usually, but the night before a shipment, there could be four or five."

"Great. And I suppose they all love machine guns?"

"Each and every man," she said.

"Can't let that stop us. You go first. I'll cover you."

"Me? Why me? You go first. I'll cover you."

"I don't think so," Jack whispered.

"I can outshoot you. Believe it. Remember, I just acted helpless."

Jack was stunned.

"Well, you go first, because if you run into the guards, you can say Buddy sent you over to look up some manifests."

"Yeah, like they're gonna believe that."

"Come on. They aren't gonna shoot the boss's wife."

"Girlfriend."

"Girlfriend? Come on. You said you were his wife."

"That was just part of the setup. We knew you would want to fuck his wife more than his girlfriend."

Jack was flabbergasted.

"Jesus. And I liked you," he said. "Look, you get out there. As soon as you make it to the corridor, give me a sign and I'll come."

"All right, but if I run into the guards, try not to shoot me in the butt. Okay?"

"Don't worry. I like your butt just the way it is," Jack said.

"Pig," she said. She leaned down, waiting, then quickly darted across the open space.

Jack glanced at her in amazement and wondered about what she had just said.

Was it true that he'd rather fuck Wingate's wife? The greater the taboo the greater the temptation? He'd never done it before. He'd always hated guys who would do it to other guys. But then Buddy wasn't so much a guy as a lizard with human skin. Maybe, in her case, it was true. Maybe he admired her all the more for telling him. He looked across the room.

She'd made it and was now signaling to him from behind the pile of crates.

He looked up at the office, which was still emitting an orange glow of Happy Hour bonhomie. The guards were probably inside drinking blood cocktails, he thought.

He was moving then, moving slowly, painfully, but crossing. Fifty feet, and it seemed like a hundred yards.

Then he was there by her side, panting for breath. Every bone in his body felt as if it had been ripped out and reassembled by an amateur.

"The door is right down there," she said.

"But it's locked, señorita," a voice said behind her.

Jack turned and looked down the barrel of an AK-47 assault rifle.

The beady eyes and the mustache at the other end of the rifle looked coolly at Jack.

"What the hell's wrong with you, Pancho?" Charlotte Rae said. "Mr. Wingate sent us over here to look at these Barca-Loungers. He wants one for his own private study."

"How did you get in?" Pancho said. "And who is this?"

"I walked in, with this key, while you were upstairs in Mr. Wingate's private office having some of his Herradura tequila," she said. "And this is . . . my assistant."

"And who is going to assist him?" Pancho laughed.

"I had a little accident," Jack said. "Got hit with a few dozen margaritas. You know how that can be?"

"Pancho knows all about it," Charlotte Rae said.

Pancho dropped the barrel of the gun a quarter-inch.

"You need help with this? Where's your car?"

"Outside. But no, we can handle it ourselves."

Pancho lowered the gun barrel toward the floor, but as he did, the outer door opened and another guard entered.

"Pancho, I just had a call from the compound. The American . . ."

He looked up, saw Jack, aimed his rifle and fired. Jack heard the bullet tear into the boxes behind him.

Jack pulled out the Glock, aimed, and shot the guard in the head, then wheeled and shot Pancho, point-blank, in the neck.

"Not bad," Charlotte Rae said.

"We've overstayed our welcome," Jack said.

He grabbed her hand, and they ran down the corridor, stepping over the dead guard's body as they reached the door. Jack peered cautiously out of the door to the parking lot illuminated by sodium lights.

There in front of him was a pickup truck. He turned and looked at Charlotte Rae, who reached down to the guard's pocket and pulled out his truck keys.

"I love your mind," Jack said.

"What do we do now, Agent Walker?"

"I'm out of clever ideas. Now we run."

She nodded, squeezed his hand once, and they took off across the macadam.

They were within five yards of the truck when the firing began, and the first bullet hit Charlotte Rae. Jack heard her moan, saw her left side sag. He wanted to turn and fire back, but it was no good. He had to get her to the safety of the truck.

He reached for her, as she fell toward him, barely able to keep her feet.

"Go ahead," she said. "Leave me."

"Wrong, orphan," he said.

He pulled her along, then turned and saw two guards running from the east end of the warehouse. They had automatic weapons and were firing again.

He pushed her to the safe side of the truck, then crouched by the fender and returned their fire.

He hit the first man in the kneecap and saw his leg explode with a bright cherry-red burst. The man screamed and went down, and the second guard dodged behind a dumpster.

That gave Jack the time he needed.

He climbed into the truck from the passenger's side and pulled Charlotte Rae in behind him.

Her eyes were milky and stared straight ahead. She was still moving, but Jack worried that she was badly hit and might pass out on him.

"The keys."

She handed them to him, and he put them in the ignition and turned them, flooring the truck's gas pedal from the passenger's side.

The engine roared to life, and Jack slid over behind the wheel, only to be met with a bullet in his right shoulder. The pain was searing, and for a second he lost control of the truck, narrowly missing smashing into one of the sodium lights.

He saw three more guards rushing toward them now, and he shook his head fighting his own blackout and turned the truck away from them toward the highway.

"Keep down," he said, reflexively, but it was wasted advice. Charlotte Rae was already down, down and out. Her beautiful mouth lay open in a grotesque manner, and Jack thought, "She's gone," and felt his heart break.

He heard the bullets slamming into the back of the truck,

felt one whistle right through the cabin and smash into the windshield, making a spider's web of cracked glass.

He had no choice but to go on, the pain in his shoulder searing up into his temples.

He was on the highway now, and he knew that they would be getting into their own cars to come after them. He had to turn off, find a hiding place.

Ahead in the dark, was a small road, which ran downhill toward some adobe homes.

Maybe here there would be a garage, a place to park, so he could see the extent of her wounds.

He made the turn and roared over the deeply rutted path, but the headlights seemed dim to him, and he suddenly knew that he had lost his way. There was something up ahead there in the dark, something he could almost see. What the hell was wrong with his sight?

He never woke up, even as the truck rolled off the road, down an embankment, and smashed through the high weeds on the beaches of the Rio Grande, bursting into flames as it smashed into a grove of elegant, lonely cottonwood trees.

Chapter 25

It was very pleasant lying in the mountain cave. Even though he knew he was freezing to death, Jack didn't really mind at all. The stalactites hanging down over him were spectacular, and the ice beneath him was somehow reassuring, even though he might freeze to death.

Maybe that was it, he thought. Maybe cold death itself was

reassuring. No double-crosses in the land of the big freeze. No tunnels, no ghost cactus, just good solid reliable cold . . . cold that could freeze away all the pain and all the loss and all the blown chances.

So go with it. Shut the eyes and let the cold take you away.

Only there was something irritating going on, something that probed and twisted the body, something that took away all the snow and the ice, something warm and relentless, and he wanted to strike out at it, tell it (whatever the hell it was) to get the fuck away from him.

He was doing just fine freezing here.

And most of all, he didn't want to hear any goddamned voices. Didn't want to be drawn back into the world. Didn't want to think of the girl, what was her name? No, don't remember, don't think of it. And isn't that the ugliest little trick that memory plays, you can't will yourself *not* to remember.

No, no, don't think of that one; let the ice come and freeze everything out, baby, freeze out all the names and all the faces . . .

And let the voices stop:

"Jack, Jack, Jack . . . wake up, babe."

"Fuck you."

"Ah, that's better. That's the Jack we know and love."

"Get away. Get away. . . . Come on."

Lights, lights, lights, who put the strobe lights in the cave? Hot stage lights (this is a set, isn't it?) burning away all the cool, crystal, embalming snow.

Turn away from them, get the head back into the white cave. But there's no escaping them, no escaping the lights.

"Come on, Jack. Open those blue eyes and make our day."

"C.J.?"

"*Whoa!* Listen to the man!"

The comforting snow melting away, and now Jack became acutely aware of a terrible pain in his right shoulder, as if somebody had shot a harpoon inside his skin and forgotten to pull it out. He opened his eyes slowly, painfully, and saw Calvin Jefferson beaming down at him.

"C.J. Where the fuck am I?"

"Believe the kind sisters call this place Angel of Mercy Hospital. It's in El Paso."

"I don't want to die in fucking Texas," Jack said.

"Don't believe you're gonna die at all, Jackie. Can you move?"

"I don't know."

"Well, you are one tough Mick, Jackie. All you got out of the deal was a bad concussion, a neat hole in your arm, and a couple broken ribs. I wouldn't try playing any one-on-one for a while, but you should be okay in a week or two. How do you feel?"

"Wasted. Can't keep awake. Like somebody grew cotton in my mouth."

"That's probably from the lovely narcotics they've been pumping into you."

"How ironic. How's Charlotte Rae?"

"You were alone, Jack. Some local guys found you, took you to this hospital. You saying you were with the girl?"

"Yeah. . . . She got me out of there."

Jack fought to stay awake, but the cold was coming back now in waves, clear, crystal ice . . . and he was slipping away, back to his mountain cave. He could hear singing, and some kind of chanting, and he half expected to see adorable ice dwarfs. He was almost gone, out there on the big glacier, when he felt a wave of adrenaline panic. With all his remaining strength, he reached up and clutched C.J.

"C.J.? You gotta find her. If Wingate or Morales get to her, they'll kill her."

"Don't worry, man. I'll take care of it," C.J. said.

"And, C.J., there's something else."

He was slipping away again.

"You rest, man. Whatever it is, it can wait."

"No, the tunnel. Morales. . . ."

"Don't worry about the tunnel, Jackie. We hit it two days ago. They were all cleared out, but they left about a hundred pounds of Colombian white."

"They were gone?" Jack said. He could barely hear C.J. now. . . . His head was pounding, and the drugs were shutting him down as if someone were drawing a big zipper over his head.

"Yeah . . . but it's okay. It's a partial victory. We get the drugs, shut down one of their best routes, and our bosses get their pictures in the paper. So don't worry, man. You just rest. I'm really glad you made it back, Jack."

"But there's something else," Jack said. "I can't think . . . something . . . Michaels . . . Where's Michaels?"

"Will you stop it?" C.J. said. "For godsake. Let it go."

"No," Jack said. "Listen to me . . . Michaels . . ."

"—is dead," C.J. said.

"Dead?"

"As in, stone cold. He was speeding up on Mulholland, blind drunk, and he went right over at Fryman Canyon. Man, he had enough booze in his system to open a bar."

"Dead?" Jack said.

That was impossible. Why would he be dead? Michaels was the cartel's agent in place. It made no sense . . . made none at all. . . . He fought to stay awake, to think it through, but it was too much for him. . . .

And he fell back into the comforting, freezing snow.

Jack awoke, chills running through his body. Still half-asleep, he looked up and realized that the air-conditioner vent was directly above him. It was pouring sheets of freezing air down on him. Great, between the painkillers that had pushed his circulation down to zero and the subarctic blasts sweeping down on him, he was practically a Popsicle.

His shoulder burned, and he had a splitting headache.

Mercifully, the nurse had come in at one point during his big sleep, awakened him, and shot him full of Demerol again, so his true misery was still hidden by the gauzy tissue of narcotics. It occurred to him now just why people would do anything, sell their children, murder their parents, to get this stuff. You were absolved of pain, of all effort, of even the idea that struggle or family meant anything. All that mattered was that the cool dream and the body rushes never end.

God, how he wanted to simply lie here and dream. But he

knew he had to resist that. He had to think, however difficult it was.

But lying here, thinking was impossible. He was already half falling asleep again. No, he had to force himself out of the bed.

Slowly he made it to a sitting position and flung his legs over the bedside. Then he managed to slide into his slippers, put on his bathrobe, and shuffle out toward the hall. He felt dizzy, and the antiseptic smells of the hospital corridor turned his stomach.

Then he thought of C.J. hovering over his bed, telling him something. What was it? Michaels. Yes, Michaels was dead.

Gingerly, he made his way down the hall and found the water fountain. His mouth was as dry as the desert they had almost buried him in, and the first mouthful of cold water was a shock to his system. The water wakened him, and he leaned against the wall.

Now it came back to him. Charlotte Rae was gone. The tunnel had been hit, but Morales and Wingate had gotten away.

He got another drink, then headed back to his room, his head spinning . . .

"Mr. Walker, what are you doing out of bed?"

The nurse was a friendly-looking Mexican woman about fifty years old. Jack walked past her, opened the closet door. There were new clothes hanging neatly there. A T-shirt, jeans, and his own boots. C.J.'s work. Jack smiled. He reached for the Levi's.

"Mr. Walker, you aren't thinking about checking out are you?"

"Not really," Jack said. "I don't have time for the paperwork. If there are charges, send them to my work address. DEA Headquarters, Los Angeles, California."

He took off the hospital gown and started to put on his pants.

"Mr. Walker, you've been shot, you've suffered trauma to your head. You cannot just walk out of here. You could suffer a severe relapse, even a blackout. What if you were driving a car?"

"It's okay," Jack said. "I always buckle up."

"I'm getting your doctor right this minute."

She turned, and Jack hurried to pull on his T-shirt and boots. Now that the Demerol was wearing off, his body had become a map of pain. He had to keep moving.

He headed toward the elevator, then realized he would have to go by the nurse's station. No good.

Jack went back down the hall, found the fire stairs, pushed open the exit door, and began to descend.

He felt dizzy, weak, and realized that the nurse was right. He could pass out any second.

He held on to the round steel railing and took the steps three at a time, half falling at the first landing.

He had to think. Michaels was involved. That much he knew. Or was he? For the first time another thought formed in his mind. Maybe Michaels wasn't involved but had known who was.

Maybe Michaels had been working on finding out. That was possible. Maybe he had been working on it and had actually found out, and they'd killed him.

Jack stopped, caught his breath.

He was at the second floor now. He panted, felt clammy sweat rolling down his head.

Something Morales had said to him in the torture room was important, but his memory was like a bunch of clouds. Clouds with Doughboy faces, floating by in disarray. . . . If he could just stop them from floating, make them line up in some kind of order. But you couldn't make a line out of clouds.

Still, he had to try. What was it that bothered him so about all of this?

It was this fact—Morales was a businessman. It was obvious he wanted revenge, wanted it badly. His voice had cracked when he spoke of the death of his friend Jose Benvenides. And clearly he wanted to humiliate Jack and the DEA. Perhaps it could all be chalked up to his bout with cancer. Perhaps his mind had become unhinged.

But Jack didn't really think so.

There had to be something more here, something greater than mere personal revenge.

Something else, something bigger was at stake.

Then Jack remembered something else as well—Dr. Baumgartner, in Mexico. He knew that face, goddamn, if he could only think.

And Zapata . . . Michaels had said something about that. But Jack couldn't focus. Just another cloud drifting by.

Jack stepped down to the last floor, opened the door to the lobby. There, directly across the room, was the nurse he'd spoken to and a doctor.

Jack saw them looking around and waited tensely. If they came over, if they grabbed him, he wouldn't have enough strength to stop them from taking him back, shooting him up again.

He waited, saw them go outside, look around, then come back in, shake their heads, and go toward the elevators.

Now was his chance.

He pushed open the door and walked through the lobby, past anxious patients waiting their rides home, past a uniformed security guard who seemed to do a double take as he walked by, and past a small barrel cactus sitting at the door. He looked down at it, thought of the cactus garden in Mexico, and shuddered with revulsion, then pushed himself through the revolving doors and headed outside to the muggy heat of El Paso.

Chapter 26

Jack caught the Delta Airlines midnight flight to LAX. He slept fitfully until fifteen minutes before landing, then quickly drank three cups of coffee, which wired his swollen eyes open. He walked like a zombie through the ugly expanse of the terminal, staggered out into the soft moonlight of Los Angeles, and grabbed a cab to his office. On the way in, he stared at the oil wells on La Cienega, and that barren, strange landscape reminded him of the hellhole in Juarez.

The cab dropped him off at Hill Street. As the Russian driver pulled away, Jack stood shakily on the pavement, staring up at the blank windows of DEA headquarters, as a bank of huge clouds passed theatrically by overhead.

It was a beautiful night, and the silence of downtown Los Angeles was a blessing. He sucked in his breath, cleared his mind. There was something he hadn't seen, something crucial that Michaels knew. He hadn't listened to Michaels, because he didn't want to lose his advantage.

It occurred to him now that he had been terminally stupid with the girl and too smart by half with Michaels. Instead of assuming that Michaels was trying to screw him, maybe he should have made some excuse to Wingate why he couldn't meet with him in the morning and checked out what Michaels had told him.

But that wasn't his way. He had gone to Mexico with them, partially because he was afraid that if he didn't go when they asked, he would draw suspicion to himself. That was a good motive, surely.

But he had also gone, he knew, because he loved the action. He wanted to go where the risk was, get to that spot inside himself where the adrenaline was flowing, where things were cooking. He believed that he could control events best, will them to be what he wanted, when he was in the "zone," that place where he was no longer acting but had become one with the role. Once he was truly there, he radiated a kind of confidence and charisma that criminals, hustlers, and all the bad-acting players in town couldn't resist.

He laughed a little at this.

It was true, he thought. When he was at his best, everything seemed to flow from him. He knew what people were going to say, what they were going to do, before they did.

But Wingate and Morales had turned it around on him. They had used all his cockiness, all his charm, against him. They'd played him, used him, then thrown him away like garbage—but not before letting him know how fucking lame he'd been. That was the part that hurt most of all . . . worse than even the broken ribs, his battered face.

As he let himself into the DEA offices and walked to the elevators, the enormity of their deception hit him full force.

Every single time he had said something hip or clever, or done something designed to win them over, they had known he was acting and used his act against him.

From day one.

Jack walked across the fourth floor and sagged against Michaels's doorway.

Yet something had gotten him out of that hellhole in Juarez, something inside himself. He knew that too. And what it was, he thought now, was the thing he had always resisted in himself.

That was his softness, his kindness, the thing his father had told him he had to burn out of his soul if he wanted to be a good cop.

Because it was the real person inside him who really did care about Charlotte Rae, who really did want to help her. It was that essential decency that she had responded to; that and only that had gotten him out.

She had saved him, he knew now, because she saw through him, beyond all his games, to a place he barely knew existed within himself and had never trusted. She had seen and touched his heart.

And now she had disappeared, might be injured somewhere or not even alive. And there was even a possibility worse than death. Wingate's men might have grabbed her. Jack shuddered to think what Buddy and Morales might do to her for helping Jack escape.

The thought that she might still be alive, that she was at this very moment being tortured preyed on his mind like an electric needle.

It made it all the more urgent that he figure out what was going on.

* * *

Jack stood in front of Michaels's door. It opened via a set of numbers and letters, which you had to punch in on a small computer screen by the doorknob. Each man's was supposed to be a secret, but Jack had long ago found out what Michaels's code was. One drunken night he and C.J. had gotten into the mainframe of the DEA's computer and gotten access to Michaels's code. They had fantasized about using it to find out what skeletons Michaels had in his closet, just in case he tried to set either of them up.

Up until now they had never done it.

He hit the number-letter code and watched the small grid light up, and then heard the click on Michaels's door. Quickly, he let himself inside.

Jack booted up Michaels's computer. The Halloween orange print came on in the dark, a series of random numbers, letters. He felt the tension leaking out of his system.

"Come on," he said. "Tell me something. . . ."

Then the words came on the screen:

Files Erased 11-9. Files in Custody. Impound.

That was what he had feared. When a man died, someone, usually the agent's secretary, wiped his computer clean and took all his floppy discs to Custody.

The problem was there were two places where files were kept—one in the basement of the building, the other in a warehouse on Temple Street. He had an idea and hit the computer again, asking which place he should check. But answer came up *UNKNOWN.*

He was screwed. He didn't have the access to Custody, and James Bond couldn't break into the basement or the warehouse without setting off alarms all the way to Pasadena.

He would have to get hold of Diane, Michaels's secretary, and ask her where the files were stored. Then he would have to call Security, but that was risky, because Security would have to contact Zampas or Brandau to get him clearance. Once either of them got into the act, he would never get the clearance. After all, everyone was already pissed at him for disobeying orders and flying to Mexico. Now if he came back with some wild hunch that one of the assistant directors of the DEA was dirty, they might have him locked up in the paranoid wing at Cedars.

Still, he would have to risk it. Diane must know where they were. Maybe he'd get lucky and find she hadn't stored them yet.

Jack looked at Diane's neatly organized desk just outside of Michaels's office. There was her Rolodex. He walked over, sat in her swivel chair, and turned on the desk lamp. A cone of light shone down on the address file, and he found her last name, Gibson—12855 Moorpark, Studio City—and the number, neatly printed out in block letters with Magic Marker. Her own little address and number in her own little Rolodex. Thank God for anal retentives.

He dialed the number, drumming his fingers on the desk. Christ, she had a musical message on her machine, a snatch of a Barry Manilow tune, "Copacabana," a song that always sent shivers of creepiness up Jack's spine. After the first two insipid bars, Diane's pert, eager voice chippered its way onto the line.

"Hiii, this is Diane."

For a second Jack was certain he was talking to an answering machine.

"Diane, this is Jack Walker. Great song on the machine."

"It's a theme thing, Jack. Pat and I are having a seventies party at our house this weekend. We're going to watch *Saturday Night Fever* and dance to 'Stayin' Alive!' But what am I talking about. Here you are in a hospital in, where is it . . . Texas, and I'm rattling on."

"Texas is history, Diane," Jack said. "I'm in Los Angeles, and I have to see Ted's files. It's extremely urgent."

"Gee, his files. I don't know, Jack. I'm supposed to take them to Custody."

"Supposed to? You mean you haven't yet?"

"Well, no . . . I was going to Friday, but we were trying to get ready for the party, and, well, the leisure suits we ordered came with narrow lapels, can you believe that? And the platform heels weren't right either, so I ended up having to go over to the costume store and personally supervise the whole . . ."

"Listen, Diane, I'd love to reminisce about Barry White with you, but this is urgent. Where are the files?"

"Right where they always were," she said, a little sheepishly. "In his computer."

"I get it," Jack said. "Under a code. What is it?"

"Jack, honey, I am not sure I have the authorization to . . ."

"Give it to me, Diane, and go disco out to Donna Summer."

"All right. I suppose I can trust you. You know, Ted did."

"Right," Jack said. "The code."

"The code is 'Feelings.' "

" 'Feelings'?"

"Well, Ted was dead, rest his soul, and it's my favorite song. I mean it was only temporary. God, don't tell anybody, will you? They'll think I'm unprofessional."

"Don't worry," Jack said. "Your secret's safe with me. Thanks."

Jack hung up and limped back into Michaels's office. He punched up the computer, typed in the code and instantly the files came up.

He looked through the whole list in shocked disbelief—not one mention of Wingate, Morales, Mexico, Colombia. He thought about the informal name he'd given the operation, CACTUS, punched in the letters—nothing.

He then tried ZAPATA, remembering Michaels's strange raving the night before he had gone to Mexico. But that came up empty as well.

For an hour Jack went painstakingly through other cases, thinking that Michaels might have entered his case with some adjoining one. But there was nothing there either.

Jack slammed his hand against the computer, cursed silently.

Then it occurred to him. If Michaels had been bought by the Colombians, he couldn't afford to mention the case in his office computer, because there was too much incriminating evidence.

If he had had information, it would be somewhere else.

In his computer at home in Encino? Not likely. Whoever killed him would probably rob his home computer as well.

Jack sat back in Michaels's chair, stretched his right leg, and felt the pain coil up his spine. His temples and shoulder burned.

Where would it be?

Then he remembered. Michaels's hideaway at Big Bear. What was the address? China Island, Boulder Bay at Big Bear. . . . Yes, if the information existed at all, that would be the place.

He got up and switched off the computer.

Standing there in the darkness, a new question haunted him.

Who knew what Michaels knew? . . . Who could? And then it came to him. The answer was suddenly and stunningly clear: only someone else in the Agency. Jesus, it was possible that Michaels wasn't the mole at all. One of the others was. Either Brandau, Valle, or, God help them, Zampas himself.

Something was going to happen, something bad. And if he couldn't come up with the answers now, he wasn't going to be able to stop it.

Jack turned, took a deep breath, and went to his own office. He punched in the code, heard the door click open. He went inside, turned on the desk lamp, and walked to the mahogany cabinet that sat in the corner. He turned the combination lock to the cabinet, heard the cylinders click, and opened it.

Inside the cabinet was backup pistol, a .38 police revolver sitting in a shoulder holster. He took out the gun, thought of the day his father had given it to him, when he was twenty-one years old. He'd used it only twice before at the firing range. It was a good gun, and now it felt right in his hand.

He put the gun and holster on, tightening the buckles so it fit snugly on his shoulder. Then he grabbed his leather jacket from the hanger on the back of his office door and put it on. He felt the pain in his right arm again, and sagged momentarily by his desk. God, he wanted to sleep. But there was no time. He shut the cabinet, switched off the light, turned, and walked as quickly as he could for the door.

Chapter 27

Jack called a cab from the DEA office, and miraculously the driver showed up within fifteen minutes. Now they headed out on the empty Hollywood Freeway. In the early morning darkness the freeway had a ghostly look, as though someone had dropped a clean bomb on Los Angeles, leaving the strange signs that hovered over the road and vaporizing all the people.

Jack took a deep breath and told himself to keep his mind on the task at hand. Having gone through hell, it was too easy to fall into a kind of psychic creep show. What he had to do was go back to the Chateau, grab a sandwich, ammo, and his car, then head out to Big Bear. The drive took about three hours, so he could be there by five in the morning. That was if he didn't fall asleep at the wheel and end up careening off one of the twisting mountain roads. Maybe he'd have to make one more stop too, at Dupar's coffee shop, where he could buy a thermos full.

The driver, a silent Iranian, pulled up and pointed to the meter. Thirteen dollars and fifty-eight cents. Jack handed him a twenty and gave him a three-dollar tip. He thought it might make the guy cheer up a little, but he only grunted and turned away. Jack got out and felt a morning chill in the air. Then, as the cab driver pulled away, Jack headed up the steps to the Chateau des Roses.

Jack got off the ancient slow-motion elevator and walked

toward his apartment. As he did, he heard the sound of footsteps moving inside.

He reached into his holster, pulled out the pistol. Then, slowly, he reached into his pocket and pulled out his keys. As quietly as possible, he turned the lock, kicked the door open, and entered the room, his gun in the two-handed shooter's position.

"Whoever's in there ought to come out now," he said. "'Cause I'm not in the mood for receiving visitors."

He waited, there was nothing.

"I said, come out, asshole."

"*Oooh,* you sound so tough," a voice said. "But I'm still not convinced. Hey, I got an idea though. Why don't you and I fly down to Mexico for a romantic weekend."

Jack's hands dropped to his side. He shut the door behind him.

"Mexico? Nah, I'll pass," he said, smiling.

Charlotte Rae sat on the old maroon couch, which was Jack's only decent piece of furniture. Her right arm was in a sling, and her right cheek was bruised, but other than that, she looked remarkably well.

"How the hell did you get here?"

"Well, it wasn't easy, I can tell you that. But I remembered you told me this address once a million years ago, and I thought, hey, he's got to show up here sooner or later. I'd get up and kiss you, but then I might bust all my stitches and bleed to death."

"But I thought you . . ."

"Come on," she said. "You think I'm going to let a little bullet wound and truck crash kill me. Remember, I've survived a lot worse than that. I was almost married to Buddy Wingate."

Jack walked over, sat on the couch next to her, and put his arm around her shoulders.

"Goddamn, I'm so glad to see you."

Being careful not to press her back or arm, Jack gently squeezed her and kissed her on the lips.

"Jack," she said. "That was the nicest kiss you ever gave me."

"Think so?"

"Yeah, 'cause it was the first one that came a hundred per cent from you."

He smiled and mussed her hair.

"How the hell did you get in here?"

"The Jamaican, Toots Riley. Oh, mon, he so happy to see Jackie's sister come to stay with him. He worries about you, mon, and he wants you to know that when the emperor comes, he is gonna put in a special word for you, even if you are a white devil."

Jack shook his head and felt his heart fill with happiness.

"You're alive," he said. "Goddamn. I love your ass. And you're alive."

He kissed her again, and a tear came down her face.

"I love you too, you maniac," she said, touching his cheek tenderly. "And I thought you were finished. I came to right after the truck crashed. Well, the crash was probably what woke me. You were out cold, there was a fire somewhere. I pulled you out and ran to get help. I guess I was bleeding and delirious. I found a Mexican family, two teenage brothers, they came and got you. They took you to the hospital. And they wanted to take me there too, but I wouldn't let them. See, Jack, I'm not all that interested in doing jail time. This is something illegal immigrants understand very well. Jesus, those beautiful people. They took me to their own doctor in Juarez. I was scared to death he'd be some butcher, but he was okay. He took out the bullet, stitched me up, and let me lay around a little, until my girlfriend came for me."

"Your girlfriend?"

"Delores Delgado. She was a dancer at Finochio's, one of the few that got what she hoped for out of the life. She married a rich rancher named Clyde Randall and has three kids and a private jet. She owed me from the old days. I called her and she came through. A day later I was in their ranch outside Dallas, staring at a place that looked like the Ponderosa. I kept expecting Hoss Cartwright to show up."

Jack laughed and stroked her hair.

"So why are you here? You could have left the country." She turned to him and smiled.

"I bet even a dummy like you can figure out that one out."

Jack felt a red flush come over his face.

"I believe you're blushing, Jack."

"That's not a blush," she said. "That's pleasure."

Then they were gently in each other's arms. He kissed her twice and imagined what it would be like to simply lock the door and spend the next forty-eight hours in bed with her.

But he had to break away.

"You look like you're in a hurry, Jackie."

"I am."

"This about that guy we talked about in the tunnel? . . . What was his name?"

"Michaels. Yeah, he's involved. Except for one minor detail. Michaels is dead. And he was never the mole."

"Dead? But who then?"

"Whoever wanted to shut him up. And I'm also pretty sure the information will be at his hideaway up at Big Bear Lake. I was just stopping here to get some supplies and my car."

"Great," Charlotte Rae said, smiling. "I'll keep you company."

Jack looked at her and shook his head.

"You're not well enough."

"The hell I'm not. I got here didn't I? Listen, I've got enough codeine in me to float to Big Bear. This is the first time since I met you that we can actually be on the same side, and I'm not about to blow it. So, let's go, huh. We're wasting time."

It was still dark when Jack negotiated the last twisting turn on Highway 18 and the two of them pulled into the mountain resort town of Big Bear.

"Very rustic, but a little over the top with the bear theme, don't you think?" Charlotte Rae said, as they drove down the main drag, Big Bear Boulevard.

In spite of his aching head, Jack managed a laugh. What she said was true. They drove past endless small businesses, most of which were housed in fake rustic log cabins and nearly all of which sported the bear motif. They passed Boo Bears Den, the Teddy Bear Restaurant, the Leisure Bear Motel, the Grizzly

Manor Cafe, the Sugar Bear Smorgasbord, and Bear Necessities Health Food.

"Promise me one thing, Jack," Charlotte Rae said.

"What's that?"

"That we won't die here. My whole life has been one big, tacky strip mall, but at least it wasn't cute. I don't want to die in a place that's cute."

"I promise," Jack said, putting his hand on hers.

He pulled into a gas station, Big Otto's Pooh Bear Exxon, got out, and talked to the station manager, who was wearing a green waistcoat, replete with arched feather, and kelly green lederhosen. The man squinted at Jack, then gave a gap-toothed smile at Charlotte Rae, who flashed him a little thigh as she climbed out of the Mustang.

"*Guten morgen,*" he said.

"Good morning to you, sir," Jack said.

"Name's Otto. You here for our Thanksgiving festival?" the man said, as he stuck a gas hose into Jack's car.

"Not exactly," Jack said. "We're trying to find China Island."

"Out there in Boulder Bay," the man said. "You passed it if you came in on eighteen. About a mile outside of town on your right. But you'll need a boat to get out there . . . unless you can swim."

"You're kidding," Jack said. "There's no ferry or bridge?"

The man laughed.

"'Fraid not," he said. "You a friend of the gentleman who lived there?"

"Yeah," Jack said. "My cousin. Just picking up some family heirlooms."

"Oh," the man said. "I heard he passed on. Too bad."

"Very sad," Jack said. "How did he get out there?"

"Think he had a rowboat. But I don't know if it's still there or not. There's been some looting," the man said, putting the hose back. "That'll be eight dollars and sixty-three cents."

Jack gave a quick look to Charlotte Rae.

"Looting?" he said. "When?"

"Other night. Sheriff got a report from neighbors that there was a light on in the place. Went out there, didn't find nobody, but the place was turned every which way but loose."

"Damn," Jack said.

Somebody had already beaten them there. They had probably found whatever evidence Michaels had had and destroyed it.

"Thanks," Jack said, as the man handed him back the credit card.

"Hell of a world," the man said. "Don't know who to trust these days."

Jack parked his car in a small turnoff at Boulder Bay and unfolded his map.

"According to this, it's on the other side of that boulder."

"Great," Charlotte Rae said. "You realize this is the first healthy thing we've done together since our picnic in Tahoe."

"Don't remind me of that," Jack said.

She laughed and put her head on his shoulder.

"Such a bad sport," she said. But there was sweetness in her tone.

They left the car and walked down a short sandy road to the lake's edge.

"God, it is beautiful here," she said.

The morning sun fell on perfect blue water, which was dotted with impressively huge boulders, survivors of the Ice Age. Jack looked just south of the harbor and saw the little island. Otto had been right. The island was cut off by fifty yards of water from the shoreline. Michaels's getaway home was a rundown but charming redwood cabin of mock Mandarin design. It looked like a Hollywood version of a hooch one might see in 1920s Shanghai. It even had oversized Chinese characters on the front door.

"Charming," Charlotte Rae said. "It makes me nostalgic."

"For what?"

"Well, that's the Mann's Chinese Theater school of architecture, which reminds me of that romantic day you risked your life to save mine."

"You just like it because it reminds you of how clever you were to set me up."

"That could be part of it," she admitted. "So how do we get over there?" She pointed to the left of the island. The rowboat was already on the island.

"Looks like I'm going to get wet. You've got to stay here."

"Why?"

"Because of your bandages."

"Really? What about your bandages? Besides, I bet the water never gets over your head. And you're gonna need me over there."

Jack laughed.

"Now that I'm getting to know the real you," he said, "it occurs to me that you're impossible."

"That's true," she said happily. And stepped into the water.

"Jesus, that is cold and wet. You're right, wading won't work. Help me take off my Levi's."

"I will not," Jack said. "People could come by and see us."

She laughed and kissed him on the cheek.

"Well, I'm not getting my clothes freezing wet," she said. "I could catch my death of cold. And I'd advise you to take off your gun. You'll want to keep your powder dry, won't you cowboy?"

She winked at him as he sighed and helped her take off her Levi's. Jack took off his jacket, then unstrapped his shoulder holster.

He looked at her, smiling, and half-naked on the rocks.

"Last one in's got to star in Buddy's next movie," she said. Then, holding her clothes above her head with her good arm, she walked, trembling, into the water.

Jack smiled and jumped in behind her. The water was freezing cold and cut straight through to the bone, but at least it woke him up.

A few minutes later, their teeth chattering, they reached the island, then walked up the pebbly beach to Michaels's house.

"This is romantic," Charlotte Rae said, reaching for the low branch of a big maple tree. "We dry off with leaves. And do a sun dance to appease the gods."

"Yeah," Jack said, rubbing the leaves over his shoulder and reaching for his clothes. "But the gods didn't do that."

He pointed up at the front door, which was ajar, its lock broken.

Throwing on his clothes over his still wet body, Jack took out the .38, pushed the door open, and stared at a jumble of rustic, cozy furniture, now overturned, the guts ripped out of the oversized pillows.

"Ugly. Very Buddy," Charlotte Rae said, as she came in behind him.

They moved into the living room warily, saw smashed picture frames, crushed crockery, hardcover books with their spines broken, their pages ripped out. There was an expensive rolltop desk in the corner that had been smashed to bits.

Michaels's little fantasy world . . . crushed, totally destroyed.

They moved into the kitchen. More of the same. Every pot and pan was on the floor; the stove had been hastily, clumsily disassembled.

"Let's try upstairs."

They went up the pine steps. In an attic workroom they found Michaels's study. Jack felt a sudden depression. The place had obviously been warm and homey. The Navajo throw rugs that had been on the walls as decorative tapestries were now tossed in a heap on the floor. There were family pictures, now torn from their frames and balled up at his feet. Jack reached down, picked up a picture, and was shocked to see a happier, younger Michaels, a smiling adolescent surrounded by two beaming parents. The three of them were standing in front of the cabin, and a robust Michaels held up an impressive string of bass. He gazed up at the big man behind him, in the glasses and hunting jacket, with a mixture of awe and love.

"Is that him?" Charlotte Rae said, staring over Jack's shoulder.

"Was him," Jack said.

Jack looked around at the devastation in the room, the battered PC on Michaels's work desk.

"Doesn't look promising, does it?" Charlotte Rae said.

"I don't know," Jack said. "You look around this room, what do you see?"

"Well, it's not decorated by Martha Stewart," Charlotte Rae said.

"You see frustration," Jack said. "I don't think they trashed this place just to get kicks. They wasted it because they were pissed off, angry."

She smiled.

"You don't think they found what they were looking for."

"Maybe not. Which doesn't mean we're going to. But we aren't going to leave here until we've given it a serious shot. All right?"

"I'll take downstairs," she said. "By the way, what am I looking for?"

"I don't know. Probably a floppy disc that will fit right into this computer. Maybe a tape recording, maybe even a video tape."

"Got it."

She leaned over and kissed him.

"I love it when you get professional, Jack."

"Uh-huh," Jack said.

She laughed. "You're still smarting that I won the first round? Well, if it makes your punctured male ego feel any better, I think you won in the end."

"Oh, yeah? How's that?"

"I fell in love with you, dope. Just in case you haven't noticed."

Jack smiled and kissed her.

"I noticed," he said.

She smiled at him again, then headed downstairs.

An hour and a half later, Jack slumped in front of the computer, frustrated and furious. Neither he nor Charlotte Rae had found even one scrap of information in the cabin. Nothing. Jack snapped a pencil in half and cursed silently.

"We'll have to start over again," she said.

"I know," Jack said. "I just have this bad feeling that whatever is going to happen is going to happen soon. Where the hell can it be?"

He looked around the room. There seemed to be nothing left to search. He'd ripped all the remaining stuffing from pillows and mattresses, looked inside old bottles, smashed open shaving cream cans, taken the television apart in Michaels's bedroom, looked inside every paperback book in the bookcase, and ripped open all the CDs. He'd gone over all of Charlotte Rae's area as well. She'd done a thorough job and come up with exactly nothing.

Now he sat in Michaels's old rocker and felt the pains starting again, in the ribs and in his jaw.

Nothing. Nothing here at all.

"Goddamn it," Jack said. "I see it now. Morales talked about himself as Zapata the great liberator and rotting us from within. That means there has to be a mole and there had to be a greater plan. But without Michaels's file . . . we'll never figure it out."

Jack took a deep breath, fighting off pain and exhaustion. His neck and temples were pounding now. He put his head back, rotating it slightly, trying to loosen up his tight, throbbing muscles—and looked at a smoke detector on the study ceiling.

"Jesus," he said. "Look at that."

Charlotte Rae looked at the ceiling.

"The smoke detector. So?"

"Did we open it?"

"No, I guess we didn't. But he wouldn't put it in there. Would he?"

"Let's find out."

Jack pulled a chair from across the room, climbed up on it, and undid the spring locks that held the detector together.

"Well?" she said, holding on to his legs to steady him.

He sighed heavily.

"Goddamn it. I was sure that was it. Nothing."

He started to get down, then looked across the room, at the open closet door.

"Jesus," he said.

"What?"

"You see anything funny there. In the closet?"

She looked hard.

"No, just . . . God. Another smoke detector."

"Yeah. . . . Now, that's a very odd feature. A smoke detector for the study and another special one for the closet."

He hopped down and dragged the chair across the room, got back up, and popped open the detector. A three-and-a-half-inch floppy disc fell out into his hands.

Jack and Charlotte Rae sat close together at Michaels's desk. The computer was battered, as if someone had slammed something down on it in frustration, but the screen and hard drive were still intact. He slipped the disc in, switched on the hard drive, and after four lightninglike flashes, the directory came up on the screen.

There it was before him.

Operation Cactus.

The first directory was called Wingate, and there, spelled out, was Wingate's profile, his gambling debts, his connection with Morales, and his relationship to Charlotte Rae.

"Oh, how nice. I rate a whole file. I can't wait to see what he wrote about me."

"Later," Jack said.

The second file was on Morales, and there were endless documentations of Morales's criminal empire. It made for fascinating reading: the drug cartel leader's endless holdings in Germany, Switzerland's sweetheart numbered bank accounts, his recent foray into homegrown heroin. Interesting, but nothing Jack didn't already know.

But the third file was something else again. It was called The Zapata File.

Jack punched it up and felt his heart racing. The file documented the death of every man who had had anything to do with Jose Benvenides's death. There was also a hospital report, apparently stolen from the Santa Maria Hospital in Colombia. Morales's cancer was of the colon and was in temporary remission. The prognosis was that under the best circumstances he might live three to four years more.

Under the hospital report were notes taken by Michaels.

"Given the fact that Morales is under sentence of death, he will try anything, he will be bold. He wants personal revenge, on who? On Walker, if my guess is right, and perhaps on the whole DEA. But more than revenge, he wants to secure the future, he wants his organization to be his own measure of immortality. He wants CONTROL. He wants his enemies eliminated or destroyed from within. The options are terrorism and intelligence . . . a man inside the Agency. This makes sense. In the past year, three of our most promising investigations have gone bad. It's as though the enemy knew we were coming. I'm convinced there is a mole within the DEA. But who is it? Probably not Walker, but you can't rule it out. He's young, brash, wild, but also cunning. He might be bored. Is it possible he could be approached with an offer? Seems unlikely. Then, could the contamination be at the highest level? Brandau, Valle, or Zampas himself? One of them is Morales's man. One of them must be compromised. One of them must be Zapata.

"Question, how does all of this connect with my discovery, that Buddy Wingate met recently with Dr. Hans Becker in Mexico City? Must make connection . . ."

The file ended, and Jack was left breathless.

"Hans Becker? Jesus."

"Who's he?"

"I'm not sure. Let me try something."

Jack escaped from the file, turned on Michaels's modem, and then punched his own private code into the DEA Information mainframe. Seconds later a glossary appeared on his window and Jack hit the letters *N,A,D,D,I,S*—the Narcotic and Dangerous Drug Information System.

The screen scrolled, and Jack was now within the DEA's private information system. He wrote in the words *Dr. Hans Becker–info and photo.*

They waited tensely until the information came up. In front of Jack and Charlotte Rae was a picture of a young German male in his twenties with long hair and intense blue eyes. Jack hit the resolution button on Michaels's computer, and the picture appeared in greater close-up. Then Jack split the window and watched a scroll of Becker's biography.

"Here it is," Jack said. "Becker was born in forty-eight, birth name Joseph Kroeger. Wealthy parents, Kroeger attended the

Sorbonne. This was the late sixties. Dr. K. was an activist but a proponent of democratic reforms. Then his girlfriend, one Olga Kimmel, was beaten senseless by a cop in a peaceful antigovernment protest. Olga Kimmel was beautiful and smart before that beating, afterward she was a vegetable. She lived three years as a brain-stem case before someone mysteriously pulled the plug on her. Most people suspected it was Kroeger himself, though no one could ever prove it. Shortly after her funeral Kroeger disappeared.

"Now, look here," Jack said, pointing at the screen. "About a year later the Bader-Meinhoff Gang began a series of bank robberies and kidnappings. Dr. Joseph K. was spotted along with them. It was said that, using his knowledge of chemistry, he had become an expert in explosives. He was now a full-fledged revolutionary, as dedicated to destruction as he had formerly been to healing."

"Interesting, but I don't see what this has to do with . . ."

"Wait," Jack said. "Later information had him linked to the Red Brigade. Now he's changed his name to Hans Becker. But here . . . the story ends."

Jack read on:

"Becker died along with two other suspected terrorists, August eighteenth, 1985, in an explosion on the West Bank. B.N.R."

"What's that stand for?"

"That's the most important part of this report," Jack said. "Body Never Recovered. Now, let me try something."

He hit Escape and then turned on the laser printer, which sat on a wooden table next to the computer.

Seconds later the photo of Dr. Hans Becker printed out. Jack picked it up and looked at it.

"Hand me that pencil," he said.

Charlotte Rae gave Jack the pencil, and he began to draw lines on Becker's face, then wrinkles around the eyes.

"That's not right," he said. "The eyes go more like this."

Then Charlotte Rae laughed.

"I hope you never have to teach art for a living," she said. "It's like this."

She erased Jack's wrinkles and moved the chin higher and tighter.

"That's it," he said. "How the hell did you know that?"

"You're trying to do aging and plastic surgery, aren't you?" She laughed. "Well, honey, coming from the world I do, everybody knows about that."

"And it looks just like him, doesn't it?"

"It does, Jack."

"Dr. Hans Becker, the mad bomber himself, is Buddy's good and true friend Dr. Gunther Baumgartner. I knew I recognized that asshole. His mug has been on wanted posters for twenty years. Now, the question is what would Buddy and Morales want with a bombing expert?"

She was silent for a second, confused. Then:

"God, they're going to blow your people up."

"You got it. And what better place than the tunnel? That's gotta be it."

"Why the tunnel?"

"'Cause there's going to be a press conference at the tunnel. And if you remember our little escape, there was a certain broken escalator."

"Jesus," she said. "You mean they were wiring it?"

"I'd bet the farm on it. What better time for Morales to get even. He'll kill Zampas and put his own man in power. That's why they killed Michaels. Michaels was getting too close. It's perfect. They'll use a Semtex bomb, and then when Zampas goes into the tunnel in front of all the nation's TV cameras and press, they blow him to hell."

"You're right. Buddy once told me that all drug dealers' routes are mined, so that any rival gangs will think twice about coming to rip you off. It'll look like an accident."

Jack nodded his head.

"I gotta give it to him. It's perfect. Morales is going to try and kill the top man in the DEA, the man he holds responsible for Jose Benvenides's death, and install his own mole. That way he combines his personal revenge with a brilliant business move. I knew this was more than just blood lust. He'll completely control us from within. And we won't even be able to get an indictment against him for it, because I'm the only one who can put either Buddy or Morales in Mexico, and who's going to believe my testimony?"

Charlotte Rae dropped her head.

"I'm sorry, Jack. I never knew what all of this meant. I pretended it was just a game. Me versus you . . . nobody would really get hurt. But I knew all along, it was much more serious. I wish to God I had never taken part in any of it."

She began to cry, and Jack reached over and pulled her close.

"It's all right," he said. "Maybe it's not too late."

Jack reached for his portable phone—then hesitated. He didn't dare call either of his bosses at the Texas office. If there was a Morales man in place, then the phone would be tapped. Better to call C.J., have him run with it.

He felt a surge of relief when his partner's voice answered the call.

"Calvin Jefferson. The man, his own self."

"C.J. It's me."

"Jack! Where the hell are you? They got an APB out on you, my man."

"Never mind. Listen, I need to talk to Zampas."

"Sure, but it'll have to be later. He's over in Juarez. Out of phone reach just now."

"Get him out," Jack said briskly, trying to cover the panic he was feeling.

"Do what?"

"Get him out. Now!"

"Hey, do you know what you're saying? The publicity mill is cranked up, full bore. Man, they got the press down here. Senators coming from Washington. This is big-time. Would take a nuclear explosion to stop it."

"Well, you might be getting just that. I've got proof that Morales is working with Hans Becker, and I'm sure they plan to pull something down there. My guess is, given Morales's love of drama, it will be at the tunnel ceremony itself."

"Becker? The mad bomber? Man, he's dead. Remember?"

"'Fraid not, C.J. I saw him in Mexico. Plastic surgery has

made him a new man. And he's working with Morales. Don't you see what that means? Zampas is going to be hit."

There was a long pause. Jack knew that C.J. was thinking about his retirement.

"Jack, listen to me, man, we've swept the whole damn tunnel three times. Even if what you say is true, there's no way they can get to Zampas or anybody else."

"Bullshit. They can get to anybody. If the tunnel's clean, then they're going to hit a car, or a restaurant. Listen to me. There's more, a lot more. But I'm not talking about it over the phone. I know it'll be an embarrassment to stop the dog-and-pony show, but we've got no choice."

"You going to cost me my pension, man."

"You'll do it then?"

"Yeah. All right."

"Good. Listen, I'm getting an afternoon flight down there. I'll call you later with the time. Can you meet me?"

"Sure. Hell, after I deliver this message to the bosses, I'm probably going to have plenty of time to make runs to the airport. Be driving hack full-time."

Jack laughed.

"More likely, they're gonna give you a medal. See you soon, partner."

"Yeah, that's what I'm afraid of."

Jack hung up the phone.

"You were in time?" Charlotte Rae said.

"Yeah, I think so. The thing is, whoever is the bad apple must have left a trail. Once I get Zampas out of Juarez, I can call on my snitches, find out which one is working with Buddy and Morales."

"We've just got to stop it," she said. Then she began to cry again. "When I think of how I took part in all this . . . Christ."

Jack put his arm around her and held her close.

"You've done fine," he said. "The only question is, what do I do with you now? I've got to go down there."

She wiped her eyes.

"That's no question," she said. "I'm going with you."

"No, I can't let you do that. It could be dangerous."

"Look," she said. "I want to find out who the mole is. Then I'll give myself up. But after all we've been through, you can't deny me that."

Jack looked at her and nodded his head.

"All right, partner," he said. "We're going to Texas."

Chapter 28

C.J. wore a bright blue shirt with red parrots on it. He looked rested and his smile made Jack feel as though he had somehow come home.

"Man, it is good to see you," Jack said, hugging his partner, as they walked across the runway at El Paso Airport.

"Wish I could say the same 'bout you," C.J. said, smiling. "But you look like some kinda zombie outta one of them George Romero flicks. Man, your skin's all gray, like oatmeal and shit. And look who we got here."

He smiled at Charlotte Rae, but warily.

"It's a long story," Jack said. "But if it wasn't for her, I wouldn't be here. That's for certain."

Charlotte Rae smiled silently. Jack noticed she'd been quiet on the plane as well. It was as though the enormity of her part in the conspiracy had finally hit her full force.

Now Jack put his arm around her, and she looked at him with a vulnerable and appealing smile.

They picked up their bags from the carousel and headed out into the parking lot. Jack looked at the desert around them.

"Man, it occurs to me," he said, as they got into C.J.'s rented Nova, "I hate this fucking place. Texas."

"I hear that," C.J. said. "But I'm afraid you ain't going to like where we're going then."

He grabbed Jack's and Charlotte Rae's bags and shoved them into the trunk.

"Where's that?" Jack said.

"About five miles outside town. Zampas wants you to meet him there. Said for me to bring you as soon as you got off the plane. Question is, where are we going to park this lady?"

"She goes with us," Jack said. "She's already under arrest. Besides we don't have time to process her. Now tell me what's going on with this meeting."

"Found a new tunnel out there. Comes out inside an old mission. Turns out this place is honeycombed with tunnels. Did you know about this, Miss Wingate?"

"No, I didn't," she said. "But it doesn't surprise me. Morales always has contingency plans."

"You told Zampas everything, then?" Jack said, as they pulled out of the lot.

"Yeah," C.J. said. "Everything you told me, that is. But I got a feeling there's a lot more to it than what I've heard."

Jack stared out the highway at the brown desert and the lonely cacti. He felt invaded by the serious creeps again.

"I think there's a mole in the Agency, C.J.," Jack said.

"You serious?"

"Yeah, unfortunately, I am. Michaels was hip to it too; I'm convinced that's why he was killed."

"Man, you got to be wrong, Jack. I would swear by any of these guys. Fact, the only one I was never certain about was Michaels himself."

"Yeah, I know, me too. But it wasn't him. He was a jerk sometimes, but he was dead-on about this. . . ."

"You know who it is, partner?"

"No," Jack said. "But it's not gonna be impossible to find out. I'm gonna lay the whole thing out to Zampas tonight."

"Good," C.J. said. "Course he's gonna think you're stone nuts."

"Maybe," Jack said. "But he's gonna listen just the same."

C.J. nodded, stuck a stick of gum in his mouth, and bore down on the accelerator. They shot out into the desert now, and Jack looked at the shadow of the speeding car and the halo of dusty light around the alien moon.

Then the unthinkable occurred to him again. What if it was Zampas himself? What if he had had it all wrong from day one?

As Charlotte Rae squeezed his hand, Jack took a deep breath and shut his eyes.

They turned up a dirt road, called Flores Negras, which coiled behind a large sand dune, and in the distance Jack saw the ruins of an old Spanish mission.

"Strange place."

"Yes. It was the old Mission of Guadalupe," C.J. said. "I read somewhere that people used to come here to see a priest who was said to perform miracles. They'd bring their sick babies, their old parents . . . and the priest would pour holy water on their heads, say rosary over them."

"Yeah," Jack said. "And how many of them were saved?"

"Not enough, I guess. A man brought his two children here with scarlet fever. The priest did his thing, but the children died anyway. Their daddy came back and shot the priest five times, then disappeared into Mexico."

They pulled up ten feet from the half-collapsed entrance to the mission. Jack looked at the bell tower, which was still in pretty good shape.

"Very romantic," Charlotte Rae said.

"Isn't it," Jack said. "Zampas inside?"

"Don't see his car. Guess he's late."

They got out, Jack and Charlotte Rae walking ten feet in front of C.J. Inside, the church had broken pews, a ruined redwood altar on which sat an armless plaster statue of the Crucifixion.

Jack and Charlotte Rae walked toward it, and she touched Jesus' feet.

"It's very powerful," she said, with no hint of irony.

"Yeah, it is," Jack said, looking at the statue. "Where's the tunnel come out, C.J.?"

Behind him, at the mission's entrance, Jack heard the click of a revolver being cocked. He turned quickly, reaching for his own gun.

"Don't try it, Jack," C.J. said. He looked at Jack with dead eyes. Then he waved the gun barrel at Charlotte Rae.

"Move real close to your boyfriend, baby. I like to see the two of you together."

"Jesus. Not you."

C.J.'s eyes dropped and his voice cracked, but the Glock remained steady in his hand.

"Sorry, Jack. I never wanted it to be like this."

"Oh, man," Jack said. He felt as though someone had kicked him in his bruised ribs.

"I don't believe it," Jack said. "You're the best cop I know."

C.J. cleared his throat. Spat on the floor. Jack knew he was trying to pump himself up in order to do what he had to do.

"Was," C.J. said, his voice raspy with emotion. "But what did it get me, man? Do I have a house in fucking Pasadena? Do I drive a decent car? Am I on the fucking studio lists to go see screenings? Where the fuck are my wife and kids? Detroit."

"That's the Agency's fault?" Jack said. He turned his head slightly and looked at the statue.

"Yeah, I would say it is. I would say that I gave the fucking Agency the best years of my life, and they gave me shit. The white boys get promoted, 'cause they're so smart. The niggers get to stay in the streets, 'cause that's where they belong."

"Come on, man," Jack said. "You're the best street cop I know. You never wanted to be a desk jockey."

"Bullshit," C.J. said. "That was a game I had to play 'cause I knew no one was gonna let me get to a desk. You know that your nigger just doesn't have managerial skills."

Jack was near the statue, but he was afraid to move because Charlotte Rae was near him. If C.J. shot wide, he would hit her.

He shook his head, only slightly exaggerating the deep sadness he felt.

"How long they owned you, man?"

"You mean how long has it been since I got smart? 'Bout two years. Now pull out your gun and drop it. Very slowly."

Jack took it out carefully and tossed it aside.

"How come you didn't just shoot us both in the back, partner."

"Don't try that hostage negotiation bullshit on me, Jackie. I took all the same courses you did, remember. Like I said before, I didn't want it to go down this way. You were never supposed to come out of Mexico. But now that you have . . . we can't let you ruin the party, man. As for you, miss, I'm sorry. You shouldn't be here at all."

"Well, you being sorry makes all the difference," Charlotte Rae said.

"Let her go, C.J.," Jack said. "She just wants out of this. She won't say anything to anybody. She'll disappear."

C.J. shook his head.

"Sorry, baby, but you're both gonna disappear."

"You don't really think this is gonna work, do you?" Jack said. "What little fairy tale are you going to tell Zampas, after you finish here?"

He edged toward Charlotte Rae, pressing her body slightly with his hip, hoping she understood what he was trying to tell her. *Get ready.*

"Well, first off, I'm going to be real sad, Jack. Which is gonna be easy, 'cause I feel real sad. I'm gonna tell him you were a mole for Señor Morales. I discovered this sad fact, and confronted you, you went for your gun, and I had no choice."

"You think anybody's going to buy that?"

"Yeah, I think so, Jackie, I really do. Look at the evidence. You went down to Mexico, you say you were captured by the bad guys, but you miraculously escaped, and when we came in to hit the drug dealers, they had all gotten away. Sounds a little hinky to me. Then there's all those photos of you with Lady Godiva here. It's gonna look real bad, Jack. But you brought it on yourself, babe. That's no lie. You think you're a badass, a renegade. What you are, baby, is young. You got a lot of balls, I'll give you that. But that's not enough. Morales and Wingate were always smarter than you. Don't feel bad about it though. They're smarter than the DEA and the FBI combined. That's why they make billions of dollars, and we make dog shit."

Jack edged closer to the altar to his left. The crucifix lay there just out of reach. Jack knew he couldn't reach it without getting hit, but he had no other choice.

"You can't do it, C.J."

"Bullshit," C.J. said. "You think I got here easy, man? Took years. Years of living bad and watching the germs buying the big cars and the condos. Having my boy getting hit on in school. How long's he gonna resist the crack dealers? Years of feeling like shit every time I put some scumbag away, just to watch him drive away in his BMW. Finally, I got the message, man. What we do don't mean shit. To anybody. We're put out there like sacrificial lambs, while businessmen and lawyers and politicians and everybody else is cashing in. See, baby, to do this you got to be either young and full of piss, like you, which I ain't no more, or you got to be some kind of saint, and you know what happens to them. They get burned at the stake. Now we're gonna take us a little hike out into the desert in the moonlight. Move."

"Wrong," Jack said.

With a swift motion he pushed Charlotte Rae out of the way. She fell to the floor as Jack grabbed the crucifix and flung it desperately at C.J. C.J. fired two shots into Jack's chest. Jack fell backward into the altar, screaming in pain.

The crucifix hit C.J. in the forehead, opening a three-inch gash. He staggered but stayed upright, rubbed the wound, felt a little blood on his fingers, then walked down the aisle toward Jack, who lay up against the altar on his back.

Charlotte Rae was up on one knee, facing C.J.'s gun.

C.J. looked down and saw his partner lying dead still. He shook his head, as he turned toward Charlotte Rae, who put her hands over her face.

"Crazy son of a bitch. He always did have more nerve than sense."

C.J. raised his gun for a final shot to the forehead.

Jack's right hand had been tucked up under his side. Now it appeared, wrapped around the handle of his father's .38.

He shot C.J. in the right shoulder with the first bullet, then in the neck with the second.

C.J. cried out, then crumpled to his knees, his own gun falling from his hand. He held his left hand over the neck wound, which bled profusely.

"How?" he murmured.

Jack scrambled to his feet, kicked away C.J.'s gun. Charlotte Rae stood behind Jack, breathing hard.

He opened his leather jacket and showed C.J. his Kevlar protective vest.

"You knew it was me?" C.J. said, his eyes bright with surprise and pain.

"No," Jack said. "Just playing it safe, for a change. I figured some bad shit might go down here. But I never figured on you."

C.J. fell over on his side, his mouth open.

Jack knelt next to him and held C.J.'s large, battered hand tight in his own.

"I just couldn't see any other way, Jack. I just couldn't. I'm sorry, man."

"Yeah, me too," Jack said. He felt his chest crushed, burning, and he wondered if it was from the bullets or his own heart breaking.

"You keep it from my boy?" C.J. said.

"I'll try," Jack said. "C.J., you gotta' tell me, man. Who's the mole?"

C.J. looked up at him. A tear rolled down his cheek.

"There's no use going up against them, Jack. Believe me, man. They're everywhere."

"I know," Jack said. "But I'm still young and dumb enough to try. Who is it? Valle?"

"No," C.J. said. "Brandau. Man, I'm in the tunnel . . . I don't see you anymore."

"Then the press conference is going off tomorrow?"

"No, man. Now . . . at nine o'clock. I can't hear the world anymore, man. Hey, baby, what's happening to me?"

He grasped Jack's arm and squeezed until his fingers had scraped flesh. Then he gasped for air and died.

Jack shut his eyes, as Charlotte Rae lightly touched his shoulder.

"It's eight-thirty," she said.

He grabbed her arm, and together they ran for the car.

Chapter 29

As Jack and Charlotte Rae tore through the cluttered, filthy streets of Juarez, they nearly ran over a man selling garish, purple talking-donkey puppets and almost sideswiped a parked BMW. Taking a curve too fast, Jack ended up on the wrong side of the street, and they faced a bus full of screaming passengers. Jack cut the wheel hard to the right and managed to get back on the right side of the crowded street. He felt a sharp pain in his chest. Though the Kevlar vest had stopped C.J.'s bullets, it hadn't stopped the powder burns, and now his chest felt as though someone had dropped a piano on it. There was an even sharper jolt of pain when he gasped for air. He wondered if a rib was sticking through his right lung.

In the passenger seat Charlotte Rae held on to the armrest, her knuckles ghost white.

"I'm never going to forgive you if, after I risked my life getting you out of here, you kill us trying to get back in," she said.

"Don't worry, I'm totally in control," Jack said.

"I can tell," she said. "That's why you're going to hit that ice-cream truck."

She fell to one side, holding her hands over her eyes.

"Jesus, Jack. . . ."

"How's the time?"

"I'm not telling you," she said. "It'll only make you go faster."

Fighting back panic, Jack turned down Matero Street and looked for the entrance to the alley. It was two blocks ahead, but the alleyway was filled with hookers. They moved toward Jack's car, sticking their red-rouged faces in the window.

"Hi, honey, you two looking for some fun?"

"*Ooooh,* three the sweet way? Kinky!"

Two of them pressed their faces up against the window. Charlotte Rae rolled it down and shook her head.

"Beat it, señorita, this is my john."

Jack gunned the motor and watched them leap out of the way. They screamed curses at him as he shot down the alley and turned into the entrance that said "TAMPICO FURNITURE."

There were camera trucks parked everywhere, representing everything from local stations in Texas to the CBS evening news.

Jack and Charlotte Rae were met by two Marines with carbines in their hands.

"I'm sorry, sir. This area is off limits to the public right now."

Jack flashed his identification card through the driver's side window.

"I'm not the public. I'm DEA and this is a Code Red Emergency. Let me in."

The two Marines looked at each other for a second.

"Sorry, sir. You'll have to wait until we can get authorization."

One Marine walked slowly to the guard shack and took his time picking up the phone.

"Who are you calling?"

"Calling Assistant Director Brandau, sir. Those are our orders."

Jack looked at Charlotte Rae.

"Brandau?"

"Yes, sir."

Jack looked again at his watch. The other Marine looked at him suspiciously, keeping his hand on his gun.

Jack suddenly opened the door of the car and fell to the ground, clutching his stomach.

"Oh, God," Charlotte Rae said. "He's having a grand mal!"

The second Marine reflexively reached over to help him, and Jack hit him in the skull with the butt of the .38, dropping him in a heap.

The Marine in the shack reached for his holster.

Jack held the gun on him.

"Bad idea," he said. "Move your hand away."

The Marine did as he was told.

"Come out here," Jack said.

Fury in his face, the Marine came out of the shack.

"You are going to be in a great deal of trouble, sir," he said.

"Believe me," Charlotte Rae said, "he knows it."

Jack walked into the shack and ripped the phone from the wall.

"Hand me your cell phone," Jack said.

The marine gave him the phone.

"Now pick him up. Fast."

The Marine picked up the still unconscious guard.

"Now walk into the guard shack. And hand me the keys."

Reluctantly, the marine carried his buddy inside, laid him on the floor, and handed Jack the keys. Jack quickly shut the door and locked them both inside.

As they headed into the furniture warehouse, Jack could hear the guard banging and kicking on the Plexiglas.

"Not bad, huh," Jack said, smiling at her a little.

"Yeah, terrific," Charlotte Rae said. "We've already got the Colombian and Mexican mafias after us, and of course we can't trust anybody you work with, so I think it's great that we've now made enemies out of the entire United States Marine Corps too."

The press was lined up in a semicircle around the pool table. The print media had been relegated a spot in the back, and the TV cameras jostled to get the best shot. Word had already gone out to the media, leaked actually by Valle, that the DEA's seizure was not simply another bust but was in this case highly visual and had an element of James Bondian fantasy to it: secret cantilevered pool tables, tunnels full of drugs, in short, perfect for a lead story for the nightly news.

Intelligence Officer Valle was in the back chatting up the press, and Assistant Director Brandau stood next to Zampas near the wall switch.

Brandau was clearly leading the parade.

He smiled and loudly cleared his throat.

"Hello, everyone," he said. "Could I have your attention. The show's about to begin."

Jack and Charlotte Rae ran through the warehouse and its maze of furniture boxes.

As they came to the "rec room" entrance, another muscular Marine walked toward them, carrying a machine gun.

"Thank God we found you," Jack said.

"What is it, sir?"

"Outside, in the guard shack," Jack said coolly. "There's some kind of demonstration, and both the guards are locked inside. My wife and I barely got out of there with our lives. The crowd was pouring kerosene over the shack. And lighting matches!"

"Jesus Christ," the Marine said.

He raced down the aisle toward the entrance.

"*Semper fi*," Charlotte Rae said.

"Hurry," Jack said.

He pulled out the .38 and descended the steel stairs.

"So you can plainly see," Assistant Director Brandau said, smiling and looking down into the hole beneath the pool table, "that this little rec room is all about a game that's a lot more high-stakes than pool."

There was a murmur of astonishment from the media.

"I think," Brandau said, "it's only fitting that the first man down in the tunnel should be our director, the man that came up with Operation Cactus, and that's my boss and mentor, Director George Zampas."

There were more murmurs as a smiling Zampas started to step on the escalator.

But before his foot hit the first step, there was a dissenting voice from the top of the stairs. The voice sounded wasted, exhausted, but rang out clearly enough for everyone to hear.

"I don't think so, Richard."

Brandau looked up, and a second later all the media turned toward Jack, who hung over the steel guardrail, the .38 cocked in his right hand. Behind him stood a panting but very interested Charlotte Rae.

Several of the smarter cameramen trained their cameras and lights at Jack, practically blinding him.

"Walker," Brandau said. He sounded stunned, as though he had suddenly walked from reassuring reality into a bad dream.

"Jack, what are you doing?" Zampas said.

"I just think that we have to be fair here, Director," Jack said. "Assistant Director Brandau is far too modest. But it's time to give him his due. Because, folks, the cold truth is, this entire operation was planned by Assistant Director Brandau. He and a few of his friends in the drug trade designed Operation Cactus as an elaborate trap. Like any first-rate sting, this one was designed to humiliate and embarrass as much as it was to catch its prey. Wouldn't you agree, Rich?"

Brandau's face had gone red. He tried for the old calmness and charm, but he sputtered as he talked.

"Jack, you look awful. We've all been worried about you. You've been under a terrible strain, and you're not making any sense."

He started toward Jack, but Jack aimed the gun at him.

"I think you better stay there, Rich," Jack said.

Brandau turned toward Zampas, who looked at him with suspicion.

"George, he's out of his mind. You see that? I mean, look at him, for Chrissake."

"I wonder," Zampas said. "Go ahead, Jack."

"Nothing more to say," Jack said, his head swimming. Whatever happened, he had to stay on his feet.

He grabbed on to the rail to keep from falling.

"I just think that we owe Assistant Director Brandau the first little trip into the tunnel today. He arranged all this and to him should go the glory. So go ahead, Rich. Start the escalator and go on down."

"This is crazy," Brandau said. "It's crazy."

Jack aimed his pistol.

"Go ahead, Richard! Now!"

Brandau's eyes were swimming with panic.

"He's insane," Brandau said. "You can all see that."

"You're right, Rich," Jack said, with a snarl. "I am fucking insane. Now get your ass down there, before I blow it off. Start the escalator, George."

Zampas looked up at Jack, then walked to the wall panel. He hit the start button, and the escalator began to hum.

"Get going," Jack said.

He aimed the gun at Brandau's right leg. Brandau looked up at him, hyperventilating with anger and fear. Then he looked down at the hole, terror on his face. Slowly, he began to back away.

"What's the matter, Rich," Jack said. "You got some kind of phobia?"

"Turn it off! Turn it off!" Brandau screamed. "Turn it off. I'm not going down there! No!"

Brandau had broken into a flat-out, panic-stricken run toward the stairs. Jack signaled to Zampas, who turned the escalator off.

Brandau ran up the stairs, screaming.

"Get out of my way, Walker. Out of my way or I'll kill you. I swear it."

He clawed up at Jack, who leaned back, and kicked him hard in the chest. Brandau cried out like a hurt child and fell backward, tumbling down the steps. He lay at the bottom, drenched in sweat, unconscious, as the cameras rolled.

Jack caught his breath and nodded his head toward Zampas, who walked toward him through the crowd of astonished reporters.

"Glad you could make it," Zampas said.

"Shut the tunnel," Jack said. "And get everybody out of here now."

"You heard him," Zampas said. "Move it."

He climbed the stairs toward Jack.

"I can't wait to hear the story behind this," he said.

"There wouldn't have been any story, if it hadn't been for her," Jack said, indicating Charlotte Rae with a nod of his head.

Zampas looked at him, confused.

"Who?"

"Her . . . The ex-Mrs. Wingate."

Now Jack turned to acknowledge Charlotte Rae, but found her once again gone.

"Son of a bitch," he said.

"Looks like your snitch split during the excitement," Zampas said. "But don't worry. She can't have gotten far. We'll find her.

"I wouldn't count on that, boss," Jack said. "Now let's get the hell out of colorful Mexico. And I don't ever want to come back."

Chapter 30

Former Assistant Director Richard Brandau sat in a three-by-five foot cell at Latuna Federal Prison, four miles outside of El Paso. God, he hated this place. He had seen it before while working drug cases in Texas and had always felt a sense of fear and foreboding whenever he had reason to visit. The place was more than a hundred and twenty years old and looked like some Gothic castle out of a horror novel. The Feds kept it painted this sickening off-white which was supposed to soften its silhouette for the local citizens, but nothing could erase the reality of the place. It was made of ancient stones and adobe, and to be caged here was to feel that you had been locked away from the twentieth century.

He still couldn't believe he was in here. He kept thinking, "There's been a terrible mistake. They're going to come and let me out, and I'm going to be the head of the DEA."

But if his mind wouldn't accept the truth, his body already had. Brandau's back had seized up on him in the cold dampness of the basement cell; it radiated pain into his neck and temples. His eyes ached from the hideous fluorescent light that shined mercilessly down on him from a wire ceiling cage.

And the food, that is, the slop they called food—strained carrots and turnips and a piece of fat-mottled beef, gray as old soaked cardboard—was far different from the gourmet delicacies Assistant Director Brandau had become used to. For food had been his one little luxury, eating the best food at the classiest restaurants in town. He hadn't succumbed to the temptation to buy a new Jaguar, (though he had intended to get one after Zampas was dead and he had been made director of the West Coast Agency), and he hadn't shopped for a new house and pool (though he would definitely have traded up in a few years), but he had eaten great meals every chance he could get. He ate regularly at Matsuhisa on La Cienega, routinely dropping two hundred dollars for a gourmet sushi dinner for two. He took Suzie Chow to Il Mito in the Valley for their great *penne arrabbiata* and casually dropped eighty-five dollars for a bottle of perfect '83 Medoc. He went to Citrus on Sundays at eight o'clock and became "close friends" with the great chef himself, Michel Richard, who said he was honored to have an "important policeman" in the house. He even ate at Spago once in a while and got to know Wolfgang Puck, who threatened to make a pizza called The Detective Pizza, which would have "mysterious contents." As much as Brandau would have liked this honor, he squelched the idea. Wingate had insisted that whatever he do, he do it "so it don't draw flies," and Brandau was afraid that he was already drawing a few too many.

Indeed, that had become a problem between him and Suzie.

He'd told her that their gastronomical adventures had been financed by an inheritance he'd gotten from a rich uncle who lived in East Hampton. Ambitious, sexy Suzie had never questioned this alibi, and soon she'd gotten used to going to the best places in Los Angeles. For that matter, so had Brandau. Neither one of them wanted to give up Spago and being seen with famous people.

But Brandau knew it was a losing game. He'd have to quit playing the great gourmet, or someone might find out. Unfortunately, when he mentioned the idea to Suzie, she was hugely disappointed and stopped talking to him. "I thought you were breaking out," she said huffishly when he called one night, "but you're headed right back to the police boy's club."

He could hardly blame her. What good was it go get a fat paycheck every month from Wingate if he had to live the same old dull cop's lifestyle?

He had to remind himself why he got into this—to get power, to be able to cash in the real dough, and to retire early in luxury.

The problem was he was forty-two and getting through the next six years pretending to be one of the guys was killing him. He didn't want to be that tweedy, friendly person anymore. He didn't want to be the conciliator; he didn't want to go to any more fucking community centers and talk to black preachers about how to keep their little savages off crack. Fuck them all, he thought. Let them all smoke crack until their brains run out of their heads and let them stab and shoot one another until all of them are dead. He didn't give a shit. He only wanted out; he wanted to have a house in Rome and an Italian mistress who looked like a young Sophia Loren, and what's more, he could have it . . . because as director of the DEA he was going to be making four million dollars a year, paid directly into his numbered Swiss bank account by Eduardo Morales.

He held his hands over his head, felt the chill come through the floor.

It had all been within his grasp, that is, until Michaels came along. Michaels, that little faggot, began to dig, to run background checks on everyone at the top level in the Agency.

Sooner or later, Michaels would have used his connections and his status to look at Brandau's Visa and MasterCard bills.

If he had only paid cash, like he was supposed to, Brandau would never have had to worry. But that problem involved Suzie as well. She kept saying, "Put it on your MasterCard and you can write it off your taxes, Rich!" and he would have to come up with some lame excuse why he always paid cash.

He had tried a lot of them, such as: "I was a poor boy, Suzie, and so I like to have money around," but her response to that was, "That's so neurotic, Richard. You're not poor anymore, you're a successful man, and you should start acting like one instead of like some two-bit gangster who flashes around a lot of green."

Little did she know how close to the truth that assessment was.

So in the end he had used the cards and told himself everything was okay, nobody suspected him anyway. After all, it wasn't as if he ever ran into any of the other agents at these places, and if they had casually suspected anything, he could use the inheritance story.

But Michaels had started to dig, and so they had to do away with him, and then there was the wild plan to kill Jack and blow up Zampas.

It was brilliant, really. The bomb was under the escalator, about thirty feet down in the tunnel. Of course, the DEA would sweep the tunnel the night before. They used trained dogs, two beautiful Labs, to check every inch for explosives. The dogs were real professionals, top of the line, more effective than any minesweeper could be. The only problem was that the dogs couldn't sniff Semtex. The same plastique that had been used to blow up Pan Am 103 was attached to a liquid-crystal-display watch, complete with a countdown timer, underneath the escalator. At exactly 9:00 P.M. Director George Zampas was going to descend into the tunnel and be blown into a thousand pieces, and Richard Brandau was going to succeed him as director of West Coast DEA.

The next day, of course, a shocked and deeply disturbed Brandau would demand that the heat be on until their noble leader's assassins were found. But it would be difficult to prove anything. A bomb had gone off; the dogs had missed it. These things happen. After all, everyone knew that drug dealers laid traps in their tunnels in order to discourage rival drug dealers; unfortunately, the DEA'd missed this one, and that was that . . . a terrible tragedy.

In the end the investigation would come up empty. The United States couldn't afford to push too hard anyway. Every time we sent our FBI or DEA agents into a foreign country, we were accused of police brutality, and the liberals screamed that we were trying to start Vietnam all over again. And with the new NAFTA agreement in such a precarious position, no one wanted to make waves.

No, in the end, Director Zampas's killers would never be caught, and business would resume. But not quite as usual. Director Richard Brandau would help establish Morales's new drug routes. Time to move on. There were many new ideas, the most promising of which was to turn the heroin into a chemical compound that could be applied as paint to cars, and once the vehicles were safely on the U.S. side, they would be chemically treated at a special processing plant, and, presto, the heroin would reemerge. More potent and deadly than ever. And more lucrative.

God, it had all been so beautiful, until fucking Walker had escaped—helped by Wingate's broad. Who would have believed it, after she set him up?

And somehow, crazy, loaded-gun Walker had put it all together and even managed to get past C.J., Brandau's ace in the hole.

It was outrageous really.

Today should have been his coronation, but instead, he was in solitary, unable to breathe and freezing, in September, in Latuna Castle, the coldest hellhole in all of Texas.

Suddenly, Brandau heard the creak of the cell door opening. He turned, half expecting to see his lawyer, but his face froze as he confronted Jack Walker.

"Hi, Rich. Nice place you got here."

"Fuck you, Walker."

Jack walked over slowly, smiling at him.

"Gee, Rich, that doesn't sound like you. You were always such a cozy, pipe-smoking kind of guy."

"I have nothing to say to you, Walker. You want to know anything about me, talk to my lawyer."

"That's a wise man," Jack said. "A very wise man. But you always were smart, a heck of a lot smarter than the rest of us.... God knows, you're a thousand times smarter than me. I mean, you guys almost pulled this thing off. Tell you the truth, I was just lucky to get out of there. I should be pushing up a monstera cactus out in the Mexican desert right now."

Brandau said nothing, but his eyes told Jack that he agreed with him. Jack should be buried under the Mexican sun, in five different locations.

"Thing is, though," Jack said, "what I lack in brains, I am gonna try to make up for with ... what I like to think of as my zest for life and for the job."

"What's that supposed to mean?" Brandau turned from him and stared at the stone cell wall.

"It means that though I'm not as clever as you, I do take the job seriously. I mean, I feel strongly about certain things. I hate cops who go bad. I don't care what their reason is, I hate them. They poison the profession. I believe they should be punished to the max. And I didn't like being tortured much, either. So now I'm going to make you pay for it, Rich. Personally."

Brandau turned, an alarmed look on his face.

"You're crazy. I had nothing whatsoever to do with any of that."

"No? I think so. My guess is you knew all about it and let it happen. And since I don't have the others here, you're going to have to do."

"You're full of shit. What the fuck can you do, Walker?"

Jack walked over and kicked Brandau in the face, splitting his lip.

"That, for starters," Jack said.

Brandau wobbled to his knees, rubbed his mouth. There was

panic in his eyes; he was afraid he was going to urinate into his prison pants.

"You're a fucking maniac, Walker. We'll make mincemeat of you in court for this."

"I don't think so," Jack said. "'Cause nobody knows I'm in here. And if you bring it up, I'm gonna deny it. Get up, now, pal. Let's make this a fair fight."

Brandau crawled away, trying to disappear into the wall.

"I'm not going to fight you."

"No?" Jack said. "That's too bad. 'Cause being kinda dumb, I have to rely on stupid shit like physical violence."

He picked up Brandau and slapped him hard in the face. Three times. Then he threw him on the floor.

"Stop. Stop it, God."

"Ah, okay," Jack said. "You're right. This isn't any fun. I guess I don't want to really beat up someone who can't defend himself."

"Asshole," Brandau said. He wiped his nose with the Kleenex Jack threw to him.

"But that's because I'm really a softhearted jerk," Jack said, leaning in so that his head was only three inches away from his former boss. "But some of the guys you're gonna be rooming with, as of tonight . . . *ooooh,* they aren't very nice. Fact is, I think a lot of them prefer it when a guy like you, a former cop, doesn't fight back. Just makes it easier for them to carve their initials on the guy's arms, chest, wherever."

"What are you talking about?"

Brandau tried to keep his voice level, cool, but it came out high-pitched, with a gasp attached to the words.

Jack stood up and scratched his ear.

"Didn't you hear? Gee, with your connections I would have sworn you already knew. See, there's only so many single cells, and last night the Feds caught a serial killer. Guy's been knocking off prostitutes in El Paso. He's a big catch, and, of course, they are very worried he'll get offed in prison, so they're gonna put him in this cell. You are going to the general population. Course, they aren't gonna tell anybody you're a former cop. They don't want anything to happen to you.

You'll have a cover and all . . . but it's not gonna do you much good."

"Why? What the hell are you talking about?"

"Why?" Jack said, moving in close to the cowering Brandau. "Because unless you tell me exactly where Buddy Wingate is right now, I'm gonna make sure that your cover is blown. Every con in Latuna is gonna know who and what you are. My guess is you're gonna become the cell block punchboard by dinnertime tomorrow. And some of those guys are not very nice in bed. I mean very few of them would qualify as the new sensitive male."

"You're bluffing. They won't take me out of here."

"Thought you'd say that," Jack said. He reached into his back pocket, pulled out some papers and let them float lazily down to the terrified Brandau.

Brandau snatched them from the air and looked at them. His face collapsed in fear.

"What the hell? This is a Federal court order."

"Tell you the truth," Jack said, "I think Zampas might have spoken to the judge. You know how it is with those Greek guys. They're very emotional. I mean, they're primitive throwbacks to another century. Imagine anybody in this world of ours taking loyalty or friendship seriously. George actually thinks that what you did constitutes a personal betrayal. Hey, I tried to tell him it was only a career move on your part, but I might as well be talking to T. Rex. He wants you in there. And all the fancy lawyers in the world aren't gonna keep you out."

"Oh, Jesus Christ," Brandau said, dropping the paper on the floor. "You wouldn't blow my cover, would you, Jack?"

"Watch me." Jack smiled. "Of course, if you happen to remember Buddy Wingate's current address. . . ."

"I don't know. Really."

"Really? That's a shame."

Jack reached down and picked up the court orders and smiled cruelly at Brandau.

"I swear."

"Oh, you swear. Well, that does it. I can't fight that. Good luck in your new home, Rich. I bet you get a whole slew of dates tonight."

Jack turned and headed toward the door.

"Walker, wait . . . wait. . . ."

"Yeah, Rich?"

"Just remembered something. Wingate said he had a place he always gets away to, down in Mexico. Not far from Puerto Vallarta. I don't know if he's there. But I remember part of the address. Coronado Street. On the beach."

"That all you remember, Rich?"

"No. He said he had it painted shocking pink 'cause Hillary Clinton liked pink, and when the President called him to D.C. he was going to invite Bill and Hillary to spend the weekend with him there. Said she'd be thrilled."

Jack laughed, and even Brandau managed a little laugh.

"Thanks, Rich. By the way, relax. You're not going anywhere."

"What? But the court order?"

"I swiped it and filled it out myself. Kind of a dumb trick, huh?"

"You son of a bitch, Walker. You rotten bastard!"

"See you around, boss."

Jack rapped on the door, and the guard came to let him out. He could still hear Brandau cursing and beating on the bars as he walked away from the cell.

Chapter 31

On the dusty road ahead of him, Jack saw a white-bearded old man walking next to a donkey and three children. There, beneath the perfect azure sky and the wavering palm trees, the four people in front of him were a vision from a simpler world, a world that existed in Puerto Vallarta before the Americans started to come—before the big houses on the coast, before the health spas and tennis instructors and Body by Jake muscle freaks, before the private helicopter launching pads on the front lawns for the studio execs to hover in on, before the endless discos filled with long-greasy-hair metallists with their pouty cheekbones and their spandex-wearing, big-haired girlfriends, before the car phones and the posh, overpriced restaurants.

Before guys like Buddy Wingate moved here with his twenty-thousand-square-foot Casa de Pink.

Jack eased his car up behind that of the man ahead of him and watched as the guy took his own sweet time about moving over.

"Good for you," Jack thought, as he drove by.

From his vantage point on the beach Jack could see Wingate's monstrous pink home about fifty yards down the road. Jack got out of the car and shut the door behind him. It was a relief to be out of the death trap. The once-midnight-blue Malibu was battered, dented, and barely ran. He'd picked it up in a used car lot in Long Beach just last night for three hundred bucks. The salesman assured him that the car had only been lovingly driven by a terrific guy named Dwight Jones, a loyal and long-standing member of Robert Schuller's Crystal Cathedral. Dwight, the sales guy said, only used it once a week to drive to Garden Grove to attend services. Jack had his doubts about that, since the Malibu had overheated twice on the trip down the coast; when Jack had taken a close look at the engine, he was less than stunned to see that it was held together with bailing wire and ancient green chewing gum. Care Free, Jack thought.

Jack opened the trunk of the car and took out the four caps of dynamite attached to the infrared timing device. He set the package down gently on the ground next to the half-collapsed back bumper, opened the trunk, and took out a tape recorder and two portable Bose speakers.

He reached into the pocket on his blue nylon Windbreaker and took out his mini cell phone and the two-inch-long activating mechanism.

He looked around and saw nothing but a few seagulls working on a dead crab. They looked like they were having a good time, and he hated to bother them. On the other hand, they were fat birds and could probably use a little exercise.

Jack looked at the Sony digital tape recorder, made sure that the timer was set correctly at 8:00 A.M., then punched *start.* Then he dialed the local police.

"*Policia. Buenos Días.*"

"*Buenos días* to you, lucky *hombre,*" Jack said.

Standing in the five-foot-high whip grass in front of Buddy's fortress, Jack could see that Coronado Street wasn't really a street at all. It was a sandy stretch of road, which reached back into as yet unspoiled dunes. A beautiful spot—you had to hand it to Buddy, Jack thought, as he aimed the infrared device in the direction of the car, pushed the button, and threw himself face-first into the sand. A second later the Malibu exploded in one great ball of hellfire and twisted, overheated wreckage. Five seconds after the explosion, the prerecorded tape kicked in. It featured the sounds of high-decibel rapid fire with light weapons and the voices of men screaming out assault tactics in both Spanish and English. Jack listened for a second and caught the phrases, "Attack to the west," and "If they refuse to surrender, kill all the motherfuckers." Very effective and very loud. It ought to be. He'd made the tape himself, splicing together bits from his favorite war movies, *The Dirty Dozen, The Alamo, Bataan*. He'd worried that you wouldn't be able to hear the words from this far away, above the roaring of the fire and the explosion of the car engine, but it wasn't so. You could hear it all just fine—fire, wreckage, military screams, machine-gun chatter, detonating hand grenades, the cries of the maimed, dying, and delirious.

He vowed to write the Bose people a fan letter—great little assault speaker you have there.

Now Jack looked at his watch, and counted off the seconds. Ten, nine, eight, seven. . . . On six the pink iron gates to Wingate's home opened and two black Mercedes came screaming out of the driveway, toward the fire and the chatter.

There looked to be about three guys in each car. And the expression on the first driver's face said it all. He was scared shitless.

And with good reason, Jack thought.

He looked at the big iron gate. In their hurry, Wingate's bodyguards had left it swinging open. Great. His back and leg still pained him, and he hadn't looked forward to climbing over a ten-foot wall.

The huge house was surrounded by the inevitable cactus garden. As Jack crept by it, he thought of Buddy Wingate's first speech about cacti, that day at his house. Mutations and survivors, Wingate had said. Like himself. And it was true. Wingate was more like a cactus than a man.

But even the toughest cactus dies.

He moved forward, toward the absurdly huge wraparound front porch, as big as one found on a resort hotel. He took out the .38 and climbed the steps.

Jack pushed open the front door to the pink stucco mansion. Inside, the place was all dark wood, Mexican and Indian motifs. There were cowboy paintings on the far wall, with noble sad-eyed horses and pink sunsets—very romantic.

But no sign of Buddy.

Jack started to go into the dining room, when he heard someone walking upstairs.

He changed direction and began slowly creeping up the wide steps, staying hunched next to the wall. His gun was cocked, ready.

He half expected Buddy to come charging down the steps toward him, guns blazing. After all, he'd anticipated everything else Jack was going to do. Why not this as well?

But Buddy didn't appear. Now Jack was at the top of the stairs. He heard something coming from just down the hall; someone was singing, for godsake.

Jack stopped, listened. It was Buddy Wingate, singing in a high, sweet voice. "As I walked out in the streets of Laredo, as I walked out in Laredo one day. I spied a young cowboy, all dressed in white linen, all dressed in white linen and cold as the clay."

Jack felt a chill pass into his stomach. There was something wrong here.

But there was no going back now.

Jack moved quickly down the hall, holding both hands on his pistol grip.

When he got to the door, he flattened himself against the wall, took a deep breath, counted three, and then swerved into the hallway, kicking open the door and quickly moving inside the room.

Buddy Wingate stood in front of a full-length wall mirror. He wore tight Levi's, which accentuated his belly, and he was trying on a black cowboy hat. When he saw Jack, he dropped the hat and turned. Though he'd gotten fatter, Jack could see the muscles in his arms, the strength in his thick fingers and wrists.

"Jack," he said, a startled yodel in his voice. "Well, what brings you here, partner?"

"You, Buddy," Jack said walking into the room, looking left and right. "I thought it was time we get reacquainted."

"Hey, I'm for that," Buddy said. "And this time without that fucking megalomaniac Morales around to screw up our friendship. Mind if I put on a robe?"

He indicated a red silk robe sitting on the king-sized Spanish bed with four-foot-high, hand-carved headboard and footboard, to Jack's left. Jack picked it up, checked the pockets to make certain there wasn't a weapon inside, and tossed it to Buddy. Buddy swirled it over his broad shoulders with a regal flourish and smiled at Jack.

"You think I'm kidding, but I always did like you, Jackie. You got a lot of balls."

"Yeah, but you liked them most of all because you were squeezing them," Jack said.

Wingate laughed appreciatively.

"That's the other thing I like about you. You got a quick mind. Morales always thought you was stupid, but I knew different. Take that diversion you just set up outside. Explosions and all that death chatter. That had me scared shitless, tell you the truth. I was just trying on this here cowboy hat prior to biting the last bullet. No shit, I was thinking, "Well, it's Morales's boys come to get me, and the question is, do I die like Davy Crockett, fighting Santa Anna to the end, or do I pull a Nero and find me an asp."

"Wrong emperor. That was Cleopatra. Nero disemboweled himself."

"*Ooooh,*" Wingate said. "He musta been part gook to do something like that. No, I was leaning toward the old gun-in-the-mouth routine, though I don't know if I coulda done it or not. I was going to wait till I saw a few of 'em pouring into the gate before I made the final decision."

"Don't chicken out until you see the whites of their eyes," Jack said.

"Something like that, yeah. Well, a man can't expect much better working with a maniac like Morales. I told him it was madness all along, but Eduardo cherishes his obsessions. Very self-indulgent that way."

"Yeah," Jack said. "He went to an awful lot of trouble, and gave away his nice little money tunnel."

"Well, that's Eduardo. You know he loves his drama. Anything short of total humiliation wouldn't do. Might seem crazy to you and me, but he had his reasons. You do know who you killed in Tucson, don't you?"

"Jose Benvenides. His friend."

"That's his name, all right," Wingate said. "But he was a lot more than a friend. See, *Benvenides* was Jose's mother's name, which is the only one the boy could take because Eduardo is married to somebody else. Jack, my boy, you had the honor of shooting Eduardo Morales's only son."

Jack gave out a low whistle.

"Now it figures," he said.

"Yessir. And given the fact that Eduardo has the big C, it's likely to be the only kid he ever does have. You know, the old boy don't give two shits about most things, but losing that boy almost killed him. Hey, even I can understand that. A man loses somebody he loves, it can tear the heart right outta his chest."

Jack walked toward Wingate now, keeping the gun leveled at his stomach.

"How would you know?" he said.

Buddy's florid face drained of color.

"Jest a minute. You suggesting I didn't love Charlotte Rae?"

"Loved her enough to beat her."

"Oh, don't gimme that politically correct crapola. This here was a girl who ate her violence with a spoon. If I didn't whack her around occasionally, she would get all pouty, say I didn't care no more."

"Oh," Jack said. "So when you covered her body with bruises and welts, you were doing her a favor. That it?"

"I don't expect somebody like you to understand. We had a lasting bond, and she'd be alive today, if it wasn't for her misguided attempt to help you."

Jack smiled and shook his head.

"What makes you think she isn't?" he said.

Wingate blinked, and his mouth dropped open.

"She was shot when she left the warehouse. My guards told me they saw her drop."

"They lied. She's as alive as me or you."

"Where is she, Jackie? I gotta know."

"Somewhere where you will never find her," Jack said. "Now, I've enjoyed this little chat, but it's time for me and you to get the hell out of here, before your boys come back. Move it, Buddy."

Wingate smiled.

"I don't know. Nah. I jest don't feel like it."

"Move or die here," Jack said, cocking the gun.

Wingate shook his head and smiled cockily.

"You are a smart boy, Jackie. But, you are always jest one beat behind the drummer."

He shifted his gaze and looked behind Jack. Jack half turned and, from the corner of his eye, saw someone standing behind him.

"Put it down, Mr. Walker. Slow and easy, partner."

Jack heard the growling voice behind him and turned to face the old cowboy star, Canyon Caine, holding his cowboy Colt .45 on Jack.

"Don't try anything, boy, or I will drop you like a bad habit."

Jack knew it was true. He dropped the .38 on the floor, and Buddy Wingate smiled as he picked it up.

"Good work, Canyon."

"What's he doing here, Mr. Wingate?" Canyon said.

"Just another disappointed office seeker," Buddy said, sticking the gun into Jack's side. "Why don't we walk out here on the porch now, Walker."

Wingate poked Jack with the gun, and they slowly started out to the deck. Canyon Caine lowered his Colt and trailed on behind them.

As they got outside, Jack noticed the quiet. And so did Wingate.

"Well, well, looks like my men have seen through your little joke. Soon, they'll be back here, and I'll just have to improvise a little. I know, I'll tell 'em that you created a diversion, so you could break in here and rob the place, and I was forced to shoot you off this balcony. I'll kind of shake my head in wonderment and stare down at your lifeless form in the cactus garden. How's that sound?"

"Dumb," Jack said. "I doubt if anyone over five will buy it."

"Now, Jack, I've known you to be devious," Buddy said, pushing him out a little farther, "but I have never heard you out and out desperate before."

Wingate laughed out loud and put the pistol under Jack's chin.

"Look out there, Jack," Buddy said. "See the ocean out there? Ever-changing yet the same, huh? See the beach, the gulls? This here is what is called a vista, asshole. That is the real difference between you and me. I see a vista and you don't. You're smart, you're a plugger, you're ballsy. I'm the first to admit it. But you ain't got no vision, son. You're like the poor redneck assholes I grew up with in Little Rock. They could only see to the next drink, the next dance, but ole Buddy could see the whole damned rodeo, which is why you are gonna die, while I go right on roping steers. And I might add, with you out of the way, I think I can reason with Charlotte Rae and get her to come back home where she belongs."

"Reason, huh?" Jack said. "Does that mean using your fists, or will it be your boots this time?"

Buddy smashed Jack in the mouth with the back of his gun. Jack's head snapped back as his lip split open.

"You stupid asshole," Buddy said. "She will always love me."

"Wrong," Jack said. "She hates you. How do you think I found this place? She told me where you'd be."

Buddy looked shocked. For once he had no answer.

"That's a lie. You found out through somebody else. She'd never give me up. Never! After all I done for her! I was like a . . . father to that girl."

"She couldn't wait to give you up," Jack said. "You little fucking troll."

Buddy's cheeks got red. He began to sputter.

"I'm through talking to you, asshole. Where do you want your bullet. In the temple, under the chin? You tell me, you stupid shit. Tell me where."

"Fuck you, Buddy," Jack said. "It's all over for you."

Buddy laughed wildly and turned to Canyon Caine, who watched with a confused look on his face.

"You hear what old Jack's saying, Canyon? That it's all over for me? You believe this guy?"

Suddenly, from down the beach, there was new shooting, new cries. Wingate's ears pricked up as he looked down the land. But all the action was obscured by the thick grove of palms.

"What's that?"

"The local Federales," Jack said. "I called them and told them that there was a group of asshole Americans who had blown up a car and were stealing their nice Mexican drugs. This makes them very angry. I don't think they're gonna treat your boys with much respect. And after they finish with them, I think they're going to be coming around here. Looking for you."

"Mr. Wingate," Canyon Caine said. "I mean to know what's going on. I don't want to end up in any trouble."

"Shut up, Canyon," Wingate said. "There's not going to be any trouble. We're just going to shoot this intruder and tell the Federales that he was one of the bad guys come to rob me."

"But they won't buy that, Canyon," Jack said. "They'll identify me as DEA, and you'll go away for life for accessory to murder one. Instead of a new film career, you'll spend your golden years eating SpaghettiOs in San Quentin."

"DEA?" Canyon said. "Mr. Wingate, you didn't say nothing 'bout that."

"You don't believe any of that crap, do you, Canyon?" Wingate said. "This man is a drug dealer, pure and simple. Now shoot him off this roof, cause I'm tired of hearing his talk."

"Mr. Wingate, I can't do time. I jest can't."

Wingate turned and glowered at the old man.

"Shut your ignorant mouth," he said, spitting out the words. "Remember this, cowboy. Without me, you're nothing more than a broken-down cough-syrup junkie I found hanging out at the Thrifty ice-cream stand."

Jack saw the flint come back into Canyon's eyes.

"Don't talk to me that way, sir."

"I'll talk to you any way I damned well like, buckaroo," Wingate said. "This isn't any Republic Pictures serial, you hear me? This is the real world, and I fucking run it. Now, get out here and shoot this asshole."

"I will not," Canyon Caine said.

"The hell you won't, you broken-down, pathetic, wino throwback, the hell you won't!"

Jack watched in disbelief as the old cowboy, Canyon Caine raised his Colt .45. He squinted with the easy menace he'd assumed in a thousand cowboy epics and nearly brought it off. But Buddy Wingate was thirty years younger, and already had his gun trained on Canyon's tired old heart. There was a sound like a whip cracking, smoke poured from Wingate's gun, and Canyon Caine went down to his knees, clutching his heart, as so many bad guys had clutched theirs all those thousand kiddie-matinee Saturday afternoons so long ago.

For a brief second Jack was transfixed by the drama unfolding in front of him. But he quickly realized that this was his chance, his last chance.

As Buddy turned to give him a bullet in the head, Jack leapt forward, grabbing for the gun. Wingate fired, the bullet grazing Jack's temple, but instead of slowing Jack down, the powder burn seemed to fill him with adrenalized madness. He punched Wingate in the face, knocking him back against the low adobe balcony wall. Wingate tried to aim the gun, but Jack knocked it from his hands. But the move cost Jack. He left himself open, and Wingate kicked him in the groin, sending shock waves of pain through Jack's stomach and legs. He fell to one knee, and Wingate was on him, raining down blows on him with hammerlike fists. Jack felt himself passing out. Desperately, he shot out the palm of his hand into Wingate's kneecap and felt it buckle, as Wingate fell backward, letting out a scream. Jack staggered to his feet, but Wingate was at him again, his huge hands around Jack's throat, pushing him backward toward the balcony wall. "You're going to die now, Jack. It's time, you cop asswipe!"

Jack felt his head exploding and, with his last energy,

clasped his hands together and brought them up against Wingate's arms, breaking his grasp. Then, with the heel of his hand, Jack punched Wingate in the throat, sending him falling backward, gagging.

Jack wanted to follow up that blow with his own offensive, but he had no energy and no wind left. He stood helpless by the balcony wall, gasping, telling himself to move forward, charge him for Chrissake, but he was unable to move. And so, when Wingate recovered from the blow to his throat and charged screaming at him, it was all Jack could do to duck. He felt Wingate's big body suddenly hanging over him, draped on him like a great side of beef, and with his remaining strength, Jack stood straight up and flipped Buddy Wingate off the balcony.

Jack turned, leaning on the wall, and watched as Buddy Wingate went flying through the perfectly blue Mexican sky, down into the cactus garden below.

Jack turned his head, as he watched Buddy land face-first onto the huge barrel cactus. He saw the great needles puncture Wingate's face, his chest, his stomach. Buddy's short, sturdy legs flopped for a few seconds, and then, for the first time Jack could recall, Buddy Wingate was still.

Chapter 32

Zampas sat in the back booth of the Union Pacific Railroad Car drinking his whiskey. His wife, Ronni, sat across from him. She looked at him and shook her head.

"I know what day this is," she said.

"You do?"

"Yes, I do. There's a kind of seedy compassion on your face. It's the look of someone who has decided to dump his wife and already feels a kind of loving afterglow. You're sitting there thinking, 'She was a decent person. We had some good years together. It wasn't all bad. She'll come to see me in the same light after a while.' Well, I won't, George. I'll hate you from this moment on, you bastard."

She began to cry. Zampas reached over and stroked her hand. She started to pull away, but he held on.

"Let me go," she said.

"No," he said. "No way."

"Cut it out. Don't mock me. At least don't do that."

"Ronni," he said. "I love you. I want things to be right between us again."

He looked at her, at her green eyes, at the worry lines in her face.

"You don't mean it," she said, her voice barely a whisper.

"Yes, I do," Zampas said. "Believe me."

"What about . . . Jane?" Ronni said, her voice barely a whisper. Zampas sipped his drink and shook his head.

"There was never anything between me and Jane," Zampas

said. "The stuff I was going through wasn't about her. It was like I said, it was all about my work. And it was classified. See, after a long time denying it to myself, I had begun to suspect that we had a mole in the Agency. Too many things were getting screwed up, too many ops were blown. So I sent three of my own operatives out to keep tabs on Michaels, Valle, and Brandau. It had to be one of them, but, the truth is, I had my money down on the wrong guy."

His wife leaned forward, chin in her hands, in her direct, interested manner. Zampas felt a terrific surge of affection for her.

"Who did you think it was?"

"Bob Valle. He was furious about getting passed over for a promotion, and what made him even more suspicious was that he wanted to be transferred back to his last post in Colombia. I had a feeling that he was expecting some shit to come down and he wanted to be over there so that he might go for diplomatic immunity when we tried to arrest him. But it turned out that Valle is okay. He'll get to go overseas in a couple of years, and meanwhile, now that Brandau is gone, we're going to expand Bob's duties."

His wife smiled, reached across the table, and held his hand. There was a troubled look on her face.

"Richard Brandau. That's hard to believe. He always seemed so gung ho."

"That's right," Zampas said. "But he was a bad apple. He even got C.J. Jefferson to turn. Then he staged a little scream-out with Pedro Salazar at Citrus to put us off. If it wasn't for Jack Walker, he might be running the show."

Ronni shook her head and laughed for the first time.

"Jack's a maniac. But I love him."

Zampas shook his head.

"Me too, the crazy, twisted bastard. He's gonna give me a heart attack though."

"So you sent a team of spies to watch your own people?" Ronni said.

"Yes," Zampas said. "For all the good it did me."

"But there's something odd here," Ronni said. "Because during the last few weeks, I was sure there was someone following me too."

Zampas laughed and squeezed her hand with his own.

"There was," he said. "I had a tail put on you as well. I was worried that if the mole found out he was about to be arrested, he might try something crazy. Probably unnecessary, but when it comes to you, I don't feel I can be too careful."

His wife smiled at that and squeezed his hand hard.

"And I accused you of . . . Oh, God, I thought it was a typical male midlife crisis. Instead, I think maybe it's my own midlife crisis."

She began to laugh a little.

"It's not so much that I hate getting old, darling," she said. "It's just that I'm afraid you won't find me attractive anymore. I can't bear to think of that."

She sniffled and rubbed her wet cheek.

"Well," Zampas said, smiling, "I don't think you're gonna have to worry about that. Fact is, I'm starting to get turned on right now."

He rubbed his foot on her trim leg under the table, and she blushed a little.

"Let's get out of here," she said.

"Good," Zampas said, smiling. "I'd rather make out in the car anyway."

They both laughed at that, and as she slipped from the booth, Zampas placed his large arms around her slim waist. Then arm in arm, they walked through the dark restaurant to the street.

Chapter 33

Two Months Later

The wind blew the tumbleweeds across Highway 16. Jack, driving his Mustang down the dusty road, stopped at a red light and watched two Mexican women leaning into the wind as they walked.

On the boardwalk he saw a sign—"Las Virgines, New Mexico, Pop. 1493"—and he laughed a little at the irony. It was perfect that Charlotte Rae would want to meet him here.

As the light turned green, an old flyer blew up on his windshield. Jack reached out and pulled it off—an advertisement for a holistic health clinic that was located in town. According to the article, a *curandero*, or witch doctor, was on twenty-four-hour duty for "Spiritual Guidance." Various Miracle Aloe plants were advertised as "Cactus Curatives."

Jack smiled, balled the flyer up, and tossed it out the window into a garbage can.

He'd never heard of this town until Charlotte Rae had called him five days ago. But since he'd agreed to meet her here, high in the San Cristobal Mountains, he'd done a little research and found that Las Virgines was known as the Town of Miracles.

According to a travel guide, the place had a cancer clinic called the Malobar Hostel and a fountain in the center of town in which the local residents regularly saw the reflection of Jesus Christ. There was an artists' colony too, the kind of place for painters and writers who'd fled Los Angeles.

The Town of Miracles, Jack thought, turning the Mustang into an open parking space. Well, there was one miracle he could attest to in the town today; he and Charlotte Rae were both still alive.

He walked up the three short steps to the old-fashioned western boardwalk and through the swinging doors of the Coyote Cafe.

Inside, the place was dark mahogany wood. There was an old bar, with a Navajo bartender who sported a ponytail. Sitting at the bar were two elderly Indian men playing liar's dice. They shook the dice out of a leather cup and grunted at each other to signify the scoring of points.

Jack walked to the back of the restaurant and sat down. A young Indian barmaid walked toward him. Jack ordered a shot of Herradura tequila and sat back and waited for her.

He thought of what Zampas would say if he knew that Jack's vacation days were being spent meeting with Charlotte. The truth was, if anyone found out, he might be brought up on charges. She was, after all, a fugitive.

Then, suddenly, a hand touched his cheek from behind. He turned, startled, almost went for his gun.

But then she was sitting down in the hardwood chair in front of him, and he was shocked by her appearance.

Her blonde hair was gone. Instead, she was a brunette, with a pixie cut. The heavy makeup was gone as well and no lipstick at all.

"Hi, Jack," she said.

"Hi," he said, but he couldn't hide the astonishment in his voice.

"Do I look that bad?"

"No," Jack said. "You look great."

She smiled shyly.

"You sound like you really mean it, but then you always were a good liar."

"I'm not lying. You just surprised me."

"I was in the ladies' room," she said, indicating the little hallway that ran off to the right behind him.

"Were you waiting to see if I would come alone?"

"Yes. I suppose I was."

"I thought we'd gotten beyond all that."

She smiled and put her hand over his.

"I'd like to think so too, Jack, but I know you're still a cop."

He smiled slightly and put his other hand over hers. The Indian girl came again, and Charlotte Rae ordered tequila.

"Where have you been, Charlotte Rae?"

"Moving around. I don't sleep that well, since I left you, Jack. I have these dreams . . . dreams of a girl trapped under the desert. Pushing up through the sand and the cactus . . . but every time she can see the stars and smell the night air, the ground caves in."

Jack felt the hair bristle along his back. He reached across the table and wiped the tear from her cheek.

"It's over, Charlotte Rae. Buddy's dead."

"I heard," she said. "Did you kill him?"

Jack shook his head.

"He died in a fall," Jack said. "But maybe I helped him a little."

She smiled and let out her breath.

"I should feel relieved, I guess," she said. "But I don't. Morales is still out there. As long as he thinks I can testify against him, I won't be safe."

Jack sipped his tequila and squeezed her hand.

"I don't think you have to worry about him. My information tells us he's not even in the country. Split for Europe. And remember, he's got a serious cancer. He'll be spending most of his time dealing with that."

She sighed.

"That's good to hear, but I think I'll keep a low profile anyway. What happened to your esteemed colleague in the Agency?"

"Brandau? *Ahhh,* he's developed an almost operatic singing voice. Thanks to him, we're going to be able to dismantle a lot of Morales's empire."

There was an uncomfortable silence between them then, until Charlotte Rae smiled, knowingly.

"Go ahead, Jack, you can say it. I know you have to."

Walker nodded.

"Okay. I could really use your testimony, Charlotte. There's a lot you could help us with."

"And if I say no?"

"You could be subpoenaed."

"Of course, they'd have to find me first."

"That's right, they would," Jack said.

"But then if I stayed in touch with you, you could tell them where I was."

"Yeah, I could," Jack said. "But then maybe I'd forget your address. I've always been lousy with street names."

She reached over and held his hand.

"You'd do that for me, Jack?"

Jack felt the heat between them.

"Truth is we've got a pretty good case without your testimony." He laughed.

"What is it?" she said.

"I just have a hard time imagining you in the witness protection plan. Living somewhere like Kansas."

She shook her head.

"Shucking corn and going to the Grange meeting? It sounds exciting. Of course, you'd be there with me, Jack. In your overalls, and riding your John Deere tractor."

Jack nodded and took a sip of tequila.

"Some days, it doesn't sound so bad," he said. "Where will you go, Charlotte? How will you live?"

She smiled and touched his cheek.

"Wherever I want. And on my own," she said. "You gave me one thing, Jack. Because of you and me, I won't be able to settle for guys like Buddy Wingate again."

Jack nodded and dropped his money on the table. Then they walked out of the Coyote, hand in hand.

Out on the street, the wind howled and the cafe sign squeaked loudly on its hinges.

"I've been here for a month," she said, as they walked down the boardwalk toward the alley next to the cafe. "It scared me at first, being alone, but then I started to hear something new."

"What's that?"

"Something beyond all the lights and the traffic, something that might even be like a whisper of my own voice."

"What's it say?" he said, pressing her to him.

"I don't know yet," she said. "I've never really listened to it before, so it's in code."

"Well, my money says you can crack it," he said.

"I'll let you know the next time I see you, Jack."

"When will that be?" Jack said.

She smiled at him then, and there was something playful in her eyes.

"I don't know. But soon."

"Soon," Jack said, smiling.

They walked together toward a blue Jaguar parked in the alley beside the bar.

"Gotta go," she said.

"I like your car," he said. "Get it from your girlfriend in Dallas?"

"No. Buddy gave me this one. He wasn't actually aware of it, of course."

Jack laughed.

"Let me guess. You borrowed some of his money while you were living with him?"

She smiled as she opened the door.

"I was a dope to ever be with him, but I wasn't a complete fool. Take care, Jack."

She opened the door to the Jaguar, but Jack stopped her before she could get inside.

"One more thing," he said. "I don't even know your real name."

"Quintana," she said. "Charlotte Rae Quintana."

"Quintana," he said. "I like it."

He shook his head, and there was confusion and longing in his eyes.

"What is it, Jack?"

"Something," he said. "Something we share. I'm not talking about sex. The thing is, I can't put a name on it."

"No?" she said. "Maybe I can. I think it's that we're both orphans."

As she said it, Jack felt something break loose inside of him. He knew at once that in some strange way it was true.

He caught her wrist and pulled her to him. She put her arms around him and he felt her press against him. The kiss took a long time. Finally, they reluctantly pulled apart.

"Good-bye for now, Jack," she said. "I'll call you sometime."

"I'll be counting on it," he said.

He let her go then, and she slipped into the Jaguar, turned on the ignition, and looked out at him. They stayed that way, their eyes locked on each other, until she released the brake and roared away.

Jack walked back toward the Mustang, already keenly aware of the lack of her.

"Charlotte Rae Quintana."

He liked the sound of her real name.

He slid behind the wheel of his car and stared out at the dust-blown street. He knew now that he loved her. She was his match, he thought, his other half. He turned the key in the Mustang and slowly drove down the street.

He suddenly wanted to drive after her, make her come with him. He wanted to protect her. But that was no good for now. Like him, she had to do things her own way. In her own time.

They'd come together again. When they were both ready.

As he drove over the mountain road back toward Santa Fe, Jack could picture both of them walking side by side down a narrow and often blind path, through the sharp, waiting needles of the cactus garden. Walking in fear and excitement, both of them hoping, against the odds, to find a bright cool blue pond at the desert's end.